ON THE MONITOR, LOGAN WAS STILL

The subj... ...or
at his own wrists.

Suddenly, the Professor's ears were battered by
Logan's inhuman howl. Impressed that the anxious technician had managed to restore the sound as well as the visuals, the Professor quickly lowered the volume, then
looked back at the screen.

The image came as a shock. Awestruck, the Professor
cried out.

"Look at that!"

At Logan's wrists, on the backs of his hands, anguished flesh began to bulge and stretch. He doubled
over, the movement tearing out the last remaining medical probes in a fountain of blood. As the subject's cries
intensified, the Professor lowered the volume again—
thankfully not enough to miss the wet, ripping sound of
three razor-sharp points bursting through the epidermis
of the mutant's hand.

Over the auxiliary monitor, the Professor heard the
technician scream like a child.

ON HIS KNEES, HIS FACE BURIED
IN HIS CHEST, FISTS CLENCHING AND
UNCLENCHING SPASMODICALLY.

The subject screamed again and stared in dazed horror

**Don't miss these other original novels
from Pocket Books!**

SPIDER-MAN®
Down These Mean Streets by Keith R.A. DeCandido

FANTASTIC FOUR®
War Zone by Greg Cox

WOLVERINE®
Weapon X® by Marc Cerasini

WOLVERINE®
WEAPON X®

a novel by
Marc Cerasini

based on the
Marvel Comic Book

POCKET STAR BOOKS
NEW YORK   LONDON   TORONTO   SYDNEY

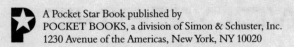

A Pocket Star Book published by
POCKET BOOKS, a division of Simon & Schuster, Inc.
1230 Avenue of the Americas, New York, NY 10020

ISBN-13:   978-1-4165-2164-8
ISBN-10:   1-4165-2164-X

This Pocket Books paperback edition November 2005

10   9   8   7   6   5

POCKET STAR BOOKS and colophon are registered trademarks of Simon & Schuster, Inc.

Cover art by Greg Land and Richard Isanove

Manufactured in the United States of America

For information regarding special discounts for bulk purchases, please contact Simon & Schuster Special Sales at 1-800-456-6798 or business@simonandschuster.com.

Acknowledgments

First off, kudos to Barry Windsor-Smith, who conceived *Wolverine: Weapon X* as a graphic story over a decade ago. His fantastic artwork inspired many of the quirky details of this novel, and his epic story was large enough to invite further exploration.

To Stan Lee, who gave us the X-Men.

To my editor, Ruwan Jayatilleke, who brought lots of great ideas to the table, then stood back and let me digest them, and to Ed Schlesinger, who shepherded this novel from limited release to mass market.

To Dr. Grace Alfonsi, M.D., for helping to make Logan's transformation medically plausible.

To my brother Vance and my niece, Tia.

To my pals Chuck, Bob, CJ, Paul, and Criticus.

Finally and most importantly, to my muse, Alice Alfonsi, who worked as hard and as long on this project as I have.

And to mutants everywhere.

WOLVERINE®

WEAPON X®

1
Prophecy

Rain. Gouging thin canals through soiled windowpanes. Night. Bending from black to phosphorescent green. A sickening hue, like alien pus.

Liquid all around me. But not drowning.

Neon hummed beyond the glass. Twisted tubes. Huge letters spelling out a single word etched in blue-white light: PROPHECY.

The word seemed apocalyptic. No. That isn't right. It was part of the apocalypse. Some drunken bum down the hall had clued him in.

"The apocalypse is coming"—that's what the geezer said. "When all the secrets will be exposed."

No more secrets, no more running.

"Hell is comin' . . ."

That's what he said. He spit when he said it, too. Then the old guy just stopped breathing.

Air. No air here. But breathing still.

It happened a lot at the Prophecy. Old guys. And not so old. Keeling over. Dropping dead.

Trapped inside. Like floating in a coffin. But not dead. Not yet . . .

The water from the sky was as old as the earth. Logan

watched it fall. The same water. Billions of years. Over and over. Fish crawled out of it. Man crawled out of it, too.

Then I crawled out.

Trapped inside. Liquid all aroud. A vile chemical. But not water . . .

Dinosaurs fed on plants, drank from lakes. This rain was part of those lakes. The wells of villages. Warriors, barbarians, samurai. The water they drank went up and came down. The same water. Trapped in a cycle.

Everything, even the earth, has its limits.

A shock of lightning scratched the night. Logan's eyes shined through the glass—feral-sharp, scanning streets lit by shards of bone-white brilliance.

Another strike, a tree split. The energy sundered it. Like a warning of things to come.

"Storm's comin', and it's a big one. *The* big one. The one I've been looking out for."

The road. He remembered the road. The cold steered the wheel. Black woods at night. The far north. Endless wilderness. Soon he'd be back. Soon he'd be home.

Beyond the glass now: wet concrete, rusty Dumpsters, graffiti-scarred alleys, haunting tenements, emptiness. *They haven't found me. Not yet.*

Logan turned from the window, crossed the stained brown carpet. The room was as small as a cage, empty bottles like stalagmites spiking the floor, spiking his brain.

A week-old newspaper ripped under his booted foot, meaningless events. Day after day. He collapsed on a couch, spring-cushioned by a tabloid spread over it. His massive fist tightened, crumpling the newsprint, hurling the ink-black words at the blank TV.

Useless headlines. Day after day after day.

Nearby, a Seagram's bottle, shimmering with many promises. Half-empty. No. Half-full. He poured a healthy swallow into a glass, always grateful.

Ripples of electricity scratched the night.

Searing bolts stab his brain.

Logan winced in shock, retching as a salty trickle rolled down his throat. Then the pain vanished, leaving only the coppery taste of blood—a familiar tang. He touched his throbbing temple, but found no stain. Only beads of salty sweat moistened his fingertips.

He swallowed again, and the metallic sting was gone, too. Were his senses off? Or was the alcohol awakening demons of past mayhem, forgotten violence?

Forgotten . . .

"The apocalypse is here. Time to write home, to make peace with somebody—"

Peace? With whom?

He remembered the saloon, a dozen milling bodies. The usual fog of burning tar. The air had felt frozen. But his muscles, beneath the flannel, had been warm enough. He'd lined up the bottles on the bar in front of him, green pickets. Glass pillars. His fortress.

Time to write home.

"Dear Ma—ya goat-headed, misshapen, walleyed witch. Got some news for ya. The secret is out! Signed: yer son with the hairy paws."

As if he knew who his mother was. Everybody's got one, right? Or two, maybe. Secrets, that is. Logan had a doozy. A serious mother lode. Hard hiding it sometimes. But he got by.

Another shot of whisky straight from the bottle. But no oblivion. Not even a rush, until he noted its absence.

Then the sensation arrived as if he'd conjured it. He sucked his cigar.

Gagging. Tissue rips. A ravaged throat.

Maybe the apocalypse has already begun.

This place where he was hiding, this Prophecy, it was a tenement transformed by the faithful into a refuge for fallen Christians. He'd been a Christian once, a long time ago. He still remembered enough of the lingo to lie his way through the door. It was a dump, of course. But it was free—for the fallen. So he'd qualified.

Warm whisky dribbled past Logan's wiry, raven-black chin stubble, onto his sweat-stained T-shirt.

Choking. Then a voice. But who?

"Enough of the stuff to stun an elephant . . ."

Alcohol alters the flow of electrolyte ions through brain cells. He remembered reading that somewhere— part of his black ops training, maybe. Whisky slows the speed at which neurons fire.

"But I'm not drunk. And I want to be . . . I need to be . . ."

Alcohol suppresses the production of a hormone that keeps the body's fluid reserves in balance. Without that hormone, kidneys begin to steal water from other organs . . .

"Steal water?"

The storm continued to rage, intensifying.

The rain continued to pound on the windows.

Liquid all around. But not drowning.

The brain shrinks as a result.

Logan snatched the bottle again and spilled the dregs into the bottom of his glass. But he paused before shooting it back. Cradling the drink in his heavy fist, Logan slumped into the battered couch.

Violent images flowed over him. A dispute he'd had with a nickel-and-dime crime boss. The idiotic bravado.

"Stupid. He should have known better . . ."

It happened after he'd become an outcast again. This time he'd been booted from a secret branch of the Canadian Intelligence Service. The infraction had been trivial compared to the heinous acts he'd performed in the line of duty. But Logan sensed his peers were happy to rid themselves of the enigma in their midst.

Secrets. I had plenty. More than any man should bear.

Not long after, Logan found work. His reputation became a two-edged sword. An unending line of young punks or fading old-timers always there to challenge him. But that meant jobs were easy to come by.

This time around, it had been Logan's "associates" who'd executed the double cross.

That day, Logan recalled, had gotten off to a bad start. He resented the trip to the gunrunner's garage to collect his cut of the profits. But when he saw the sneer on St. Exeter's face, Logan knew things were about to get much worse.

The gunrunner leaned against a crate of fragmentation grenades, his cashmere sweater, Prada pants, and Gucci loafers incongruous in the junkyard setting.

"I didn't think you'd have the guts to show up here, Logan. Not after your connection failed to deliver the goods."

St. Exeter pushed back his hair with a delicate, manicured hand.

Logan met the man's cool gaze. "You're spewing crap, René. I know for a fact that those air-to-airs are already in the pipeline to your 'clients' in Latin America."

"Perhaps. But the weapons were of . . . inferior quality."

"The Pentagon would be surprised to learn that, considering they were all state-of-the-art Stinger missiles."

As Logan spoke, two of St. Exeter's bodyguards entered the garage behind him. Two more, in greasy coveralls, climbed out of a repair pit to flank him.

Half smile in place, René stared at Logan with eyes like black empty holes.

"You're not gonna pay," said Logan. It was not a question.

Suddenly, the grease monkey on Logan's left pulled a wrench out of his stained coveralls.

Stupid.

Logan hit the man with enough force to drive his jawbone into his brain. A grunt, and the mechanic crumpled. Logan snatched the tool from his dead hand before the man struck the ground.

Dodging a bullet fired at point-blank range, Logan spun and hurled the wrench at the man who'd pulled the trigger.

A crunch of bone, a splash of red, and the shooter's head jerked back. As he fell, his Magnum dropped at Logan's feet.

Logan ducked a wild shot, then snapped up the weapon. He fired without aiming—a lucky shot. The bullet clipped the second bodyguard's throat. Gurgling, he fell to his knees, clutching at his neck in a widening pool on the concrete floor.

Finally, Logan's luck ran out. The last of René's bodyguards charged, in an attempt to push Logan into the repair pit. The pair fell in together.

At the bottom of the deep concrete well, both scrambled to their feet. A shadow fell over them. Logan looked up in time to see St. Exeter toss an object into the hole.

"Catch, *mon ami*."

Logan snatched the grenade out of the air. When the bodyguard saw it, he lunged for the ladder.

"Where you goin'?" Logan grabbed the man by his collar, spun him around, and jammed the grenade into his gut.

Wheezing, the bodyguard folded around the explosive and Logan released it, then dove for the opposite end of the pit. Heat and gore washed over Logan as the muffled blast slammed him against the concrete wall.

Bleeding from a patchwork of wounds, Logan crawled out of the pit that had become the bodyguard's grave, only to discover that René St. Exeter had fled the scene.

Logan caught up with him a few days later, on a public street in the heart of Montreal. The final confrontation occurred amid a dozen gawking witnesses, but Logan didn't care.

Some things, like payback, were too damn important to delay.

Even after the rage had passed, Logan felt no regret—only anger that he was forced to move on. Later that same night, he planned to hop a freight. His destination: the Yukon. As far north as Logan could go, to the very edge of civilization. He'd leave behind everything—a Lotus-Seven, some worthless possesions, his past.

With a bit of luck, Logan could start over.

Start over?

"Good place to start over, eh?"

The voice—familiar—came from years past. Back when Logan was still with the Defense Ministry. Back when he operated out of the Ottawa branch of the CIS.

Logan had been hunched in a corner, honing his

blade, when the stranger approached. He'd looked up long enough to see past the big man's proffered hand, to the name tag tacked onto his broad chest: N. Langram.

The screech of metal on tortured metal resumed as Logan sharpened the edge of his K-bar knife.

The sandy-haired man reluctantly withdrew his hand, then slumped down on a weight bench across from Logan's.

The training area was empty but for them. Minutes before, they'd been told that their training had ended, that their first assignment was at hand.

"I think it's a great place to begin again . . . the CIS, I mean," continued N. Langram. "I've been to a lot of places, done a lot of things, legal and illegal, and I'm happy to forget my past and bury it forever."

Langram slapped his knees. "To my surprise, after all my mischief, the Defense Ministry and the CIS decided to let bygones be bygones and offer me a second chance."

"Good for you," said Logan.

"I figure they've done the same for you, eh?"

Logan fingered the tip of the blade. A drop of blood dewed his fingertip. He tasted it.

"My name's Langram . . . friends call me Neil." This time, the man didn't offer his hand.

"Logan."

"Quiet one, eh?"

Logan spun the knife and plunged it into the scabbard. Then he crossed his arms and stared into the distance.

"I've been wondering why they paired us. You and me. We're strangers and we've never even trained to-gether. So I'm trying to figure out the angles . . ."

"What have you deduced, Langram?"

Missing Logan's sarcasm, Langram tried to answer the question.

"Odd parameters for this mission, don't you think?" he began. "I mean, why not a simple HALO jump? The CDM has hundreds of soldiers who've trained for High Altitude Low Opening insertions, and hundreds more qualified for reconnaissance infiltration of hostile territory. Which means they don't need either of us. We'd be considered overqualified for this mission, except that the men in charge decided to do a few things the hard way."

"Like?"

"You have to admit that there aren't too many operatives in the CIS—or even the CDM—who are proficient in the use of the HAWK harness," said Langram.

The HAWK, or High Altitude Wing Kite, was a specialized piece of "personal aerodynamic hardware" developed for use by the Strategic Hazard Intervention Espionage Logistics Division—and SHIELD didn't give lessons on how to use their high-tech flying suits to just any soldier.

"Maybe the top brass thinks the HAWK is the best means of insertion," said Logan. "With a HAWK we can control our own speed and angle of descent, and when and where we land. And we can fight back—even while we're airborne—if it becomes necessary."

Langram nodded, conceding Logan's points. "I know all that. I've used the HAWK before. And so, apparently, have you, Mr. Logan."

"Your point?"

"Maybe you and I crawled through the same mud," said Langram. "Or maybe we just have some of the same friends . . . and enemies."

Logan sat in silence.

"Secretive one, too, eh?"

Secrets. I've got plenty. Too many for me to handle sometimes.

"That's okay, Logan. I won't pry."

"You already have."

Langram refused to take offense, and they sat in uneasy silence for what seemed like a long time.

"I know the geography pretty well," Langram said at last. "The Korean Peninsula, I mean. And the area where we're going, too."

"Nice place?"

"If North Korea is a prison, then the region around Sook Reservoir is solitary confinement, a cell on death row, and the gallows all rolled up into one ugly bastard of a package."

Logan shrugged. "Sounds delightful."

Langram studied the other man. Logan avoided his gaze.

"So that's my expertise," Langram said. "And since you don't appear to be a nuclear weapons specialist, I figure you know either the local lingo or something about the guys we're chasing."

"Right so far."

"And since you are very skilled with a blade, and you ain't Korean, I have to assume you know plenty about Hideki Musaki and all his Yakuza thugs, and about the weapons-grade plutonium they hijacked on its way to that top secret government laboratory up north—the one processing weapons of terror."

Logan nodded once. "I know Hideki Musaki . . . personally. But we're not tight."

Langram smiled for the first time since their meeting. "So you've wandered the Far East, eh? Somehow I knew it. Seeing you reminded me of a place . . . a dive called Cracklin' Rosa's. And a man, too. A fellow known in those parts as Patch. He had a proclivity for the blade . . . just like you."

Again, Logan did not reply.

Langram glanced at his watch, then stood.

"Got to go, Logan," he said. "But we'll be seeing each other a lot in the coming days. In the meantime, remember what I said about the CIS being a good place to start over. To ditch your past if you want to . . . not many get a second chance."

Langram turned to go.

"Hey, Langram."

This time, Logan was on his feet and facing him.

"I'll watch your back if you'll watch mine. And when this mission's over, if we're both still alive, I'll buy you a drink . . ."

Another drink. And another. But never enough to bring release. Wait. What was I thinking about?

Like wisps of mist, the memories of that first meeting with Neil Langram slipped away.

Reduced by a creeping amnesia to dazedly pondering the drink in his hand, Logan watched as the whisky morphed from clear brown to cloudy green.

Nauseated, he looked away.

On the other side of the window, the word PROPHECY glowed with ghastly phosphorescence. An acrid, chemical stench assailed his nostrils, and battered couch springs dug into his flesh. But despite his physical discomfort, Logan's head lolled and his eyes closed.

Sleep came, but Logan's dreams were no different than his waking life. He longed for escape while he continued to run, his legs pumping on a perpetual incline, stretching farther and farther into the future. At the top was the humming neon of the Prophecy sign, waiting there, waiting for him.

Suddenly awake, Logan bolted upright, crushing the glass in his grip. Thick red blood pooled in his palm, but he felt no pain.

Logan staggered to his feet, impatient now to flee, to escape before the apocalypse swallowed him up.

He tugged the flannel shirt over his wide shoulders. He pondered the predictability of his nightmares. Visions of pain and bones and spikes. Of vile stench and horror. And of dagger hands . . .

Searching for the keys to his car, Logan rummaged through a pile of yellowing newspapers. He noticed a headline on a grease-stained tabloid:

MERCY KILLER "QUACK" ELUDES FBI.

Under the headline, next to the story, a grainy black-and-white image. The photograph of a portly, bearded man with a bland, unremarkable face.

The picture and the headline vaguely troubled Logan, but he didn't know why. When he tried to snatch the memory threads to connect them, they dissolved like streams of vapor in his increasingly clouded mind.

Lightning cracked the sky, split another tree.

Another warning.

Storm's comin', and it's a big one. The *big one. The one I've been looking out for.*

Logan pocketed his money and his keys. He left the Prophecy without a backward glance. His last memory: the neon sign blinking steadily in the rain.

Suddenly, Logan was sitting on a bar stool, hunched over a stained counter of a dingy gin mill. Outside, through filthy plate glass, the rain had stopped. A blanket of dirty snow covered the broken streets and sidewalks.

When did it snow?

Hands shaking, Logan reached for the bottle at his arm. He swallowed, wondering if all the booze had finally caught up with him and induced some kind of mental blackout.

Logan had no memory of the drive, yet through the big window he could see his Lotus-Seven parked in the lot.

Did he drive through rain, then snow? Had hours passed? Or days? Had he missed the freight train . . . and with it his only chance to escape?

For the first time in Logan's memory, panic welled up inside of him. Another swallow of whisky took care of it, but left confusion in its wake.

Logan regained a certain measure of control by observing his surroundings—the bartender calmly washing glasses while watching a muted television tuned to a soccer game. Another man seated at the opposite end of the bar, drinking quietly. Logan sniffed the air, and his nose curled at the smell of rank booze and stale tobacco.

Tubes like worms. Boring their way into his ears, nose, his mouth, his brain.

Outside, a lone traffic signal switched from green to yellow to red and back again. There were no pedestrians on the sidewalks, and the clock on the snow-covered steeple down the block was running backward.

We travel into the future every second we live, but no one can go back in time, according to Einstein. Which proved the old geezer wasn't so smart after all.

In the shadows, under the dartboard, Logan spied three

men with long coats and sunglasses, hats pulled down over their faces, drinks untouched in front of them. They sat at the edge of darkness. Waiting. Watching.

Time to go . . .

Logan rose, tossed a wad of bills on the bar, and headed for the door. The shadow men ignored him . . . or seemed to. Their inaction gave Logan hope, but not much.

Outside, his heavy boots crunched the icy snow.

Boots. Like a soldier's. Like mine. I was a soldier once. No, twice. I fought in two wars. Both of them a long time ago.

Logan looked down to find his boots gone, his feet no longer clad in hard leather, but swathed in soft moccasins. There was still snow. Everywhere. But this covering was pristine and virgin white. The reflective snow of his youth. It coated trees and blanketed rocks. It shimmered with frost under a pale winter sun.

The tavern, the parking lot, the shadow men had disappeared. Logan padded alone through a silent mountain forest.

Home? Could I be home already?

Hoarfrost crunched under the balls of his feet. The chill seeped bone-deep into Logan's wiry, teenaged frame. But despite the frigid air, the darkening sky, the deepening snow, Logan slogged ahead.

It was the burning rage that pushed him, maddened him—an unreasoning need for vengeance that drove Logan farther and farther into the wilderness.

Through calf-deep snow, Logan followed the spoor, moving quickly in a painful effort to catch up to his elusive quarry. Numb fingers clutched his father's long knife, ready to strike, ready to stab, to rend.

Eager to kill.

At a rocky precipice cleared of snow by the relentless wind, the footprints Logan had tracked ended abruptly. Frustrated, Logan scanned the forest, then sniffed the air, hoping to locate his prey by scent alone.

Harsh winds stung Logan's face—a face raw from the bitter cold and bruised from the beating he'd received at the hands of Victor Creed, the bully known to the local settlers of this region by his Blackfoot Indian name, Sabretooth.

I know Creed hates me. But I don't know why. More secrets, deeper and darker than the forest around me.

Sabretooth had turned up at the door of Logan's log cabin hours—or was it days?—before, just as he had every year around this same time. There was neither rhyme nor reason to Creed's visits—only that they always occurred when Logan was alone.

Logan had walked beyond the boundaries of his father's homestead, inside the tree line where he gathered firewood for the cold days and nights ahead. He was alone again. His father had been gone for weeks, fur-trapping up north.

To guard his son, his meager possessions, and the precious furs he'd gathered during trapping season, the elder Logan had left behind his hunting knife and a fierce husky named Razor.

Returning with a heavy bundle of dry timber, Logan had heard Razor's frenzied barks and angry howls, muffled by distance, by snow and by trees. He'd tossed the firewood aside and hurried back to the cabin as fast as he could run.

He found Razor's blood and brains staining the snow, and the Blackfoot helping himself to the pelts Logan's father had left to dry under the winter sun.

Through tears of rage, Logan stared down at the murdered animal while Creed's taunts battered his ears. Then, with the savage cry of an enraged beast, Logan hurled himself at his tormentor, to land on the man's back. Logan clawed at Creed's face and tore at his throat with his teeth.

With a fierce growl of his own, Sabretooth dashed Logan to the frozen ground.

Stunned, he sprawled in the snow next to his dog's stiffening corpse. As he fought for consciousness, Logan saw the Indian loom over him. Heard the man's stinging laughter ringing in his ears. Felt the torrent of kicks and blows that rained down on him.

Finally, the blackness rose and swallowed him up.

Much later, Logan bolted upright, his body numb from the cold. The sun had crossed the sky, the day fading. Logan's memory returned, and with it a murderous rage.

Racing to the cabin, Logan snatched the hunting knife from its place over the mantle. Without regard for the elements or the waning daylight, Logan set off, determined to hunt down Sabretooth and end his enemy's existence once and for all.

Within the first hour, Logan lost Creed's trail, then picked it up again. Now the Blackfoot's spoor was mixed with another's. A bear's. A large one, by the size of the prints. Like Creed, the animal was moving up a crude mountain trail toward higher ground.

Minutes later, as Logan nearly crested a hill, a dark figure rose up from behind a boulder. The grizzly roared a challenge, and Logan reared back in surprise.

Lumbering forward on its short hind legs, the mammoth grizzly towered over him. The animal weighed at least four hundred pounds. When it roared again, hot spittle splashed Logan's cheek. The creature's steaming breath rolled over him.

For a moment, Logan felt paralyzed. Then he raised his knife and let loose with a howl of his own. Moving forward, the blade slashing back and forth, Logan prepared to face the creature's massive onslaught.

The bold, unexpected move startled the bear. The beast halted, eyes wide, ears twitching—just out of the blade's reach.

Legs braced, Logan prepared to charge. His rage clawed his heart and he longed to slash and stab this creature—any creature. Nothing could threaten him.

Time seemed suspended as man and beast eyeballed each other very cautiously and carefully.

Then, from somewhere behind the grizzly, Logan heard a snort, followed by a terrified bleat. In the back of the looming grizzly, Logan spied four black eyes peering at him from under a tangle of low, snow-laden pine branches.

Black fur rippling, brown snouts wet and steaming, the frightened cubs emerged from cover, only to cower behind their mother.

Seeing the helpless pups, Logan lowered his blade. With wary eyes locked on the angry grizzly, he took a single step back, then another.

The bear snorted, her fur bristling, as Logan continued his careful retreat. Even in his harsh world, Logan believed that not everything that was a threat should be destroyed.

"Go in peace. You are not my enemy and I am not yours," Logan whispered softly as he continued to walk backward, down the trail.

The bear sensed Logan's intent. She dropped on all fours, then turned her quivering back on the human.

Slapping the cubs with her front paws to move them along, the grizzly plunged between the snow-covered trees.

Logan watched the creature retreat, her hide dusted with snow, two cubs scurrying at her feet. When the bear had moved out of sight, Logan closed his eyes and leaned against a tree, heart racing from the aftershock of the un-expected encounter.

When he opened them again, Logan found himself outside the tavern, in the middle of the snow-covered parking lot.

The night had grown much colder—unseasonably cold, unless Logan had lost weeks or months since his time at the Prophecy, instead of mere hours.

But he had no time to worry about that now. Not with the shadow men so close . . .

With a stab of relief, Logan spied his Lotus-Seven. The top was down—absurd in this weather, even for someone who did not feel heat or cold like everyone else.

Logan found his keys and slid behind the wheel.

The throbbing roar of the engine reassured him. But before Logan could throw the vehicle into gear, figures emerged from the darkness. Then a man spoke.

"Mr. Logan?"

Logan looked up just as something hard, cold, and sharp struck his shoulder, stabbed through muscle and ribs, and pierced his lung.

A hot gorge closed his throat. Wheezing, Logan strug-gled to rise, as toxins surged through his body, sapping his strength, bringing his mind to a standstill.

Helpless as a dishrag, Logan was dragged from the car.

He lashed out—only to be pummeled to the cold ground by vicious, unseen fists. With the last of his waning strength, Logan fought back. But as the powerful tranquilizer took effect, the dark and the pain devoured him.

Just before consciousness slipped away, Logan felt an odd sense of relief. There was nothing more he could do now. Days of running and nights of hiding were over. Escape was no longer possible.

The apocalypse has begun.

2

The Hive

Behind angular eyeglasses that gleamed in the dim light, the Professor watched the medical team labor over their patient.

A dozen physicians and specialists crowded around a naked figure cocooned behind the thick walls of a translucent tank. Inside the Plexiglas coffin, "Subject X" floated in a greenish chemical soup comprised of interferon-laced plasma, molecular proteins, and cellular nutrients, along with a kind of synthetic embryonic fluid of the Professor's own devise.

A few ounces of that murky liquid were more valuable than those technicians could ever imagine. Worth more than the average North American skyscraper—and far more to the elite few who actually understood its purpose.

The Professor's thought was interrupted by a flashing light on his console. The team leader was informing him that the delicate preparatory process was nearing completion.

Like Subject X's airtight coffin, the Professor's own chamber was hermetically sealed—an electronic realm of steel and glass, fiberglass cables and silicon chips. Inside this chamber, computers purred and processors hummed. Polished adamantium steel walls dully reflected scrolling streams of data on flickering monitors and banks of high-definition TV screens.

The Professor's rail-thin body sat erect and motionless on his ergonomic throne, his pale flesh stretched taut over prominent cheekbones. Coolly, he appraised the medical procedures as they played in real time on a large central monitor.

A rare smile curled his lips as he observed the team's progress. Despite wearing somewhat restrictive environmental hazard suits, cumbersome helmets, and bulky air-scrubbers, the medical staff performed their assigned duties quickly and efficiently—so efficiently that Subject X would be ready for the first experiment tomorrow, well ahead of the original schedule.

The preliminary work had gone splendidly, the Professor decided, and his staff had performed with exemplary efficiency.

And why not? Had he not trained them himself, demanded the highest degree of professionalism, commitment, and self-sacrifice from every last one of them?

The Professor touched a button. On a different level of the compound, a blinking light alerted a second medical team that their skills would soon be needed. He manipulated everything that went on inside the immense research facility from this command-and-control center. Via constant digital recordings, the Professor knew of every action, every sound that transpired within its walls.

Billions of bits of data traveled to the Professor through hundreds of miles of fiber-optic cables—an information network that snaked its way through every room, every vent, every wall.

Poised like a spider in a technological web, the Professor surveyed his domain from the center of the vast complex. From behind sealed doors and coded locks, he could access any accumulated data, observe any experiment, and issue commands with the flick of a switch or the utterance of a spoken order.

What interested him now, of course, was Subject X.

Through the monitor, the Professor viewed the arrival of the second medical team. With a hiss, a pressurized door opened, and the group moved in to replace the preparatory staff. The members of this new team were clad in the same bulky environmental suits, not to protect them, but to shield Subject X from the threat of contamination—a necessary precaution.

The task of this second team was to fit Subject X with a variety of biological probes designed to monitor bodily functions, along with hollow injection tubes sheathed in Teflon. These tubes were crucial to the success of the adamantium bonding process.

The Professor's long-fingered hands—the hands of an aesthete, he liked to think—played lightly across a custom-made ergonomic keyboard only he could decipher. Abruptly, the ubiquitous whir of air-scrubbers and the constant hiss of the climate-control systems were drowned out by snatches of conversation and ambient sounds transmitted from the medical lab.

Scrolling data vanished from the supplemental view screens, to be replaced by images of men in protective suits crowding around the simmering, transparent coffin.

Dr. Hendry, the team leader—his environmental hazard suit marked with a broad green stripe to signify his status—studied Subject X through the opaque fluid.

"Who shaved the patient?"

At Hendry's side, a man raised his hand. "I did."

"What did you use, poultry shears?"

"What?"

"Look at the man." He pointed to the lone figure in the clear, rectangular tank.

Behind his faceplate, the other man seemed perplexed. "That's really weird. I shaved him twenty minutes ago, and he was as smooth as a billiard ball . . ."

"Could have used a haircut, too," observed another member of the team.

The physicians and specialists took their positions around the Plexiglas, gazing mutely at the figure inside. The pale pink male form was swathed in bubbles. His raven black hair drifted around his head like a storm cloud.

A flexible steel breathing tube looped down from a wheezing respirator to a mask that completely covered the subject's nose and mouth. This technological umbilical cord also contained various sensors, tubes that supplied nutrients, and needles to administer drugs, if necessary.

The silence was broken at last by a trundling medical cart pushed by a nurse clad in the same bulky gear worn by the others. On the cart's antiseptic surface sat an array of surgical probes resembling medieval torture devices more than any modern medical implement. Each gleaming probe was comprised of a hollow, razor-sharp stainless steel spike—some as long as six inches, others as short as an inch. A long, flexible tube was attached to each spike's base, along with wires to channel biological information to various monitoring devices.

Many of these probes would be used to measure and evaluate the subject's mundane bodily functions—heart rate, blood pressure, basal metabolism, body temperature, electrolyte balance, respiration, hormonal activity, digestion and elimination, and brain functions. Others would be used for more arcane purposes.

As the Professor remotely observed the procedure, the team leader began to attach the first probe. Reaching into the simmering stew, Dr. Hendry plunged a slender four-inch spike directly into the brain of Subject X through a hole drilled into the cranium above the left eye.

A flurry of movement erupted inside the tank. The medical team was taken by surprise when the subject jerked once, then opened his eyes and stared up at them, seemingly aware.

"Back away from the subject," Dr. Hendry commanded, even as he stood his ground.

The subject's eyes appeared focused and alert, though the pupils were dilated. Subject X tried to speak as well, but the sounds he made were muffled and incomprehensible behind the bubbling respirator and whirring machinery.

"The goddamn tranquilizer is wearing off." The neurologist's tone was critical.

"We pumped enough into him to stun an elephant!" said the anesthesiologist defensively.

"I can't believe it, either, but look at his brain wave patterns."

The neurologist stepped aside to display the encephalograph's readout to the rest of the team.

"You're right." The anesthesiologist could hardly believe it. He had never seen anything like it. "The subject's still in a fugue state, but he's regaining consciousness—despite the sedatives."

"Okay, I want Thorazine. Four hundred and fifty

CCs. Stat." Dr. Hendry extended his hand for the hypo-dermic gun.

His surgical assistant lifted the injector, loaded a plastic vial of the powerful drug into the device, then hesitated.

"Are you sure about the dosage?" the assistant asked weakly. "Thorazine is going to mess up his brain functions something awful, and 450 CCs . . ."

The timid voice trailed off, but the meaning was clear. The serum could kill the subject.

Dr. Hendry gazed through his faceplate at the ghostly silhouette thrashing inside the coffin-shaped tank. The subject's chest was heaving, his jaw moving behind the breathing mask.

"If he comes around, he's going to mess us up something awful," Dr. Hendry replied.

"But that's a huge dose—enough to finish him, maybe . . ." The anesthesiologist's voice wasn't as weak as the assistant's, but it faded, too. He'd felt obligated to say it, though he knew it didn't matter. Not with Hendry in charge.

Watching from his sealed chamber, the Professor grunted in irritation and keyed the intercom. When he spoke, his sharp tone thundered inside the medical lab as well as the team's environmental hazard helmets.

"Administer the Thorazine at once. In the dose Dr. Hendry prescribed. The patient must not awaken. Not again."

Hendry snatched the hypodermic gun away from his assistant and plunged the injector into the churning tank. The hypodermic hissed, and Subject X tensed as a violent spasm wracked his thick frame. Soon, however, the subject's eyes closed and his respiration and heart rate slowed.

"He's out," said the neurologist.

"Blood pressure normal. Heart rate normal. Breathing is shallow, but the respirator will force sufficient oxygen into his lungs," the anesthesiologist noted with relief.

Inside the helmet, Dr. Hendry tried to shake the perspiration out of his eyes. "For a second there, I thought we were going to have to release the cyanide."

"Then we'd know how good these hazard suits really are," someone quipped.

The attempt at humor broke the tension of the moment, but the laughter was forced.

"Continue the procedure," the Professor's voice commanded.

Dr. Hendry lifted his eyes to the ceiling as if searching for the invisible cameras that recorded every step of the delicate process. After his assistant slapped a long probe into his gloved hand, Hendry reached into the boiling mixture and plunged the needle-sharp skewer directly into the subject's abdominal cavity.

Again, Subject X tensed as tremors rocked his muscular frame.

The Professor keyed his intercom. "There's been another spike in brain wave functions," he said, observing the data on his private touchscreen monitors.

This time, Hendry backed away from the tank with the rest. "What should we do, Professor?"

"I want you to use the biodampeners to inhibit Subject X's brain functions . . ."

The anesthesiologist spoke up again. "But Professor, we've already administered enough Thorazine to—"

"—stun an elephant, yes. But the sedative does not

seem to be effective," the Professor murmured. "As you can plainly see, Subject X is hardly . . . placid."

Hendry signaled another member of his team. The man stepped forward, cranial probes in hand. The rest of the staff retreated to allow the specialist enough room to work. But before he attached the probes, the psychiatrist spoke.

"If you wish, we can activate the Reifying Encephalographic Monitor. Interface with the brain should be very simple while the subject is unconscious . . ."

"That won't be necessary," the Professor replied. "The dampeners will suffice, for now."

The psychiatrist accepted the answer without argument and went to work.

"Will you be joining us in the medical lab, sir?" Hendry asked.

"Shortly, Dr. Hendry. Shortly . . ."

Within a few minutes, all the cranial probes were in place and the devices activated. The readouts indicated that the biodampeners—tiny devices that emitted low-level electromagnetic waves to short circuit brain activity—had done the trick. Subject X would not awaken now. Not until they wished it.

"You may proceed," said the Professor.

Satisfied that the preparatory procedures were at last back on track, the Professor switched off the audio feed, though he allowed the video images to continue to play across the monitors.

As he shifted in his chair, the Professor's arm accidentally brushed a bulging personnel file, which sent a stack of yellowed newspaper clippings fanning across his desk.

MERCY KILLER "QUACK" ELUDES FBI. read the sensational headline emblazoned across one clipping. Next to the headline, a grainy black and-white photograph displayed a bearded man with a round, almost cherubic face. The caption read:

DR. ABRAHAM B. CORNELIUS NOW A FUGITIVE FROM JUSTICE.

With a weary sigh, the Professor stuffed the clippings back into the file and set them aside. Keying a recording device built into the console, he began to dictate in a slow, clear voice.

"This is a memo to the attention of Director X. Date, current . . . I have met with Dr. Cornelius at the designated location . . ."

Designated location? The Professor found himself musing. *A ridiculous euphemism for the sinkhole of urban blight where the fugitive scientist had fled in an effort to avoid capture, imprisonment, and perhaps execution.*

"The meeting was cordial . . ."

If one can call the threat of blackmail cordial.

". . . and Dr. Cornelius expressed an interest in our project and its ambitious goals . . ."

In truth, Cornelius was desperate to escape punishment. In the United States, the authorities dealt harshly with murderers— especially those who'd taken the Hippocratic oath.

"Dr. Cornelius has willingly agreed to our terms for employment, and seems grateful to be of further service to the science of medicine . . ."

As if he had a choice.

"However, I question whether Dr. Cornelius is the optimum candidate for such a critical position in this experiment. In the past he's demonstrated a disturbing propensity for independent thinking, as his crimes suggest.

"I also doubt his expertise will be required. There will

be no tissue rejection, of that I am certain, and Dr. Hendry concurs. My bonding technique will be sufficient to sheathe Logan's skeleton, I assure you."

Ridiculous of the Director to equate Dr. Cornelius's skills with my own. There is no comparison. I am an architect of the flesh, an artist, a visionary. Cornelius is merely a skilled practitioner of a single discipline. Can Director X not see the difference?

"Surely other researchers in the field of immunology are equally qualified and have much less . . . questionable backgrounds?"

The Professor keyed off the microphone. With a frown, he carefully reconsidered his statement and paused with a thought.

If I object too strongly, Director X will question my motives, even my loyalty. Perhaps it is better to be gracious and diplomatic, to accept this interloper as I accepted Ms. Hines. They can both be disposed of later, when their services are no longer required . . . In the end, only results matter.

The Professor keyed his microphone.

"Erase memo back to the word 'employment.'"

The recorder hummed, reversing itself.

"I feel that Dr. Cornelius will be a valuable addition to this project," the Professor continued. "His credentials are impressive . . ."

But he's certainly not a genius . . .

". . . I am sure that he will be able to assist me greatly in the coming months . . ."

Though I neither want nor require an assistant, no matter how qualified Director X feels this man is. Did the artist Michelangelo require an assistant to paint his vision of The Creation on the ceiling of the Sistine Chapel?

". . . This project is far from completion, and there is much work to be done . . ."

Did God require an assistant or additional help to fashion the universe? I think not.

"And, of course, Ms. Carol Hines, formerly of NASA, has also proved herself to be a valuable asset . . ."

The woman is acceptable, even if Director X thrust her upon me. To her credit, Ms. Hines required no additional training, and has assumed her duties immediately upon arrival.

"She comes highly trained by the National Aeronautics and Space Administration, and is proficient in the use of the REM technology—one of a few capable specialists in the world . . ."

Better still, the woman is malleable and easily led; the type who would provide an invaluable service and expect little in return. Best of all, she would ask no questions—the perfect drone, a worker bee. Certainly not a queen . . .

"Both individuals have arrived at the facility, and are settling in."

And Dr. Cornelius had better hit the ground running, or he is less than useless to me, and to the experiment . . . I'm already impressed with Ms. Hines's dedication and her considerable skills. But I shall reserve my judgment of Dr. Cornelius until I observe the man in action . . .

"I shall file an additional progress report of success or failure, after the adamantium bonding process is completed. Until then . . ."

The Professor added his cyber signature, then keyed off the microphone and slumped into his chair. His thoughts were troubled.

If only men were as predictable, as tractable as the elements.

As a scientist, the Professor knew with certainty that the molten adamantium bubbling in the vats below him would melt at a precise temperature. He also knew that the same substance would harden with the tensile strength greater than a diamond when cooled. He knew the precise composition of the resulting alloy on the molecular level. He understood how the various elements would bond and what configurations the electrons would take as they circled the atoms. Yet he could not predict with any kind of certainty how one of the lowliest animal wranglers in his facility would behave under the precise circumstances for which he'd been trained.

The Professor leaned back in his command chair and gazed, unseeing, at the flickering monitor.

Meanwhile, inside the medical lab, activities continued apace. The technicians had finished placing the probes and were draining the coffin-shaped container. The valuable fluid would be pumped into a stainless steel vat, where it would be cleansed of impurities and stored for use in subsequent procedures.

Subject X would spend the night in a carefully controlled holding tank, in an electronically induced slumber. His vital signs and brain activity—what there was of it—would be monitored by a medical staff separated from the subject by an impenetrable wall of Plexiglas. Chemical compounds, fluids, and basic nutrients would be added intravenously as needed.

On the console, another flashing light indicated that the procedure had ended. The Professor watched the medical team file out of the lab, stripping off their environmental hazard suits and mopping their sweating brows.

His console buzzed and the gray, patrician features of Dr. Hendry appeared on the central monitor.

"The probes are in place, Professor. No indication of infection. No threat of rejection. Vital signs are all quite positive."

"Very good," the Professor replied. But the team leader did not log off.

"More to say, Dr. Hendry?"

The man on the monitor cleared his throat. "I spoke with the new immunologist," he said.

The Professor raised an eyebrow. "And?"

"I'm impressed by his work, but not by the man. Dr. Cornelius's theory is sound, and he seems to have solved one of the most intractable problems of the bonding process . . ."

"I sense more than hesitation in your tone, Dr. Hendry. You may speak candidly."

"He's a common criminal," Hendry said, agitated. "He's violated the ethics of his profession. Can't we utilize his work without actually employing him?"

"The procedure is experimental, much can go wrong. It's better to have Cornelius here in case unexpected complications arise."

"But—"

The Professor cut him off. "It's out of my hands."

Hendry frowned. "I . . . understand."

"Very good. Carry on."

With a touch of a button, Hendry's face vanished, to be replaced by an endless parade of scientific data crawling across the monitor. The shift in focus pleased the Professor.

The certainties of the physical world and the comprehensible workings of advanced technology are infinitely preferable to the unpredictability of human thoughts and behavior.

Illogic and ambiguity had always troubled him, and the Professor longed to purge humankind of useless emotions and wanton desires. Control of the human mind was the key—but absolute control had never been achieved. Until the development of the Reifying Encephalographic Monitor, it had never been possible.

Until now, the limits of the REM device had not been explored, not even by its inventors. NASA used the innovative device for training purposes, or to stage virtual reality drills. But the Professor knew the machine was capable of so much more.

They call themselves scientists, yet they behave like children, playing with a loaded weapon, never realizing its potential . . .

"Sniveling cowards, the lot of them . . ." the Professor muttered.

With the REM device, mastery of the human mind was within his grasp—no thought would remain secret, no desire hidden. Every hope, dream, fear, or rage could now be monitored, controlled, measured, and evaluated. Memories could be erased, personalities altered, false recollections implanted to replace real experience.

In the Professor's own estimation, the genesis of the technology behind the Reifying Encephalographic Monitor became a testament to the timidity, the lack of imagination, and myopia, which plagues the scientific community.

Brain Factory, a video game company in Southern California, pioneered and marketed the first, primitive REM as a novelty device. However, early product testing proved too dangerous for human subjects. The Consumer Products and Safety Administration stepped in and banned the use of REM technology for any entertainment purposes and other commercial usages.

Several researchers in the fields of psychology subsequently recognized the potential of the breakthrough technology in the treatment of mental disorders. But instead of embracing this area of study, the American

Council of Concerned Psychiatrists spoke out against the REM device being used "until such time as further testing could be completed."

Of course, no further testing would be possible without funding, and psychiatrists and academics—fearing obsolescence should the device live up to its vast potential—blocked any grants for research projects using the Reifying Encephalographic Monitor.

At that point, Brain Factory fell into bankruptcy, and made a bargain basement deal with the United States government. With a new infusion of cash, Brain Factory went on to produce *It's Clobbering Time* and *Fing Fang Foom*—two of the hottest computer games in the world. In exchange, the Central Intelligence Agency, SHIELD, and the National Aeronautics and Space Administration received exclusive rights to the use of the Reifying Encephalographic Monitor for "research and training purposes."

Though he did not know how the CIA or SHIELD ultimately utilized REM technology, the Professor discovered that NASA had squandered the greatest scientific breakthrough in the history of brain research by using the REM as a teaching tool. Instead of tapping the machine's mind control powers to exert total mastery over its astronauts and NASA researchers, they limited themselves to using the device as if it were a textbook, for simulations and training exercises.

The Professor would not be fettered by the same restraints. In the coming months, he fully intended to test the limits of the REM machine's untapped potential on Subject X. It was not enough to transform the subject's body. His mind must be restructured as well. The ultimate mastery of Logan became the Professor's goal. He knew it was only a matter of time.

The Professor knew that the physical form had certain limits, vulnerabilities. Bones—even ones sheathed in adamantium steel—had limits, too. And chemically enhanced muscle and sinew could still tire or fail.

But a mind reduced to a beast-like state of consciousness—devoid of fear and doubt and desire, stripped of memory and emotion, and unfazed by the dread of personal extinction—would never waver. In its pristine purity, such a mind would experience no pain, suffer no discomfort, feel no remorse.

Burn away the chaff, rip away the superficial layers of humanity and unleash the savage, unreasoning animal that lurks behind the civilized facade of every human being.

Then I will mold that animal into Weapon X—the deadliest implement of war ever forged.

But unlike the Supreme Being who gave humanity life, I will not make the mistake of bestowing free will on my creation. Weapon X will be nothing more than a tool to do my bidding. An extension of will, yes. My own.

3

The Wrangler

The man pulled the leather parka snug around his neck as a chilly blast whistled through the pines. With every step, the autumn snow crunched under his boots. Rabbit tracks crisscrossed the trail, and overhead a raptor cawed as it drifted in lazy circles on the thin mountain air.

The trail he followed ended abruptly, with a five-hundred-foot drop. In the river valley below, the rushing waters churned blue-green foam and the skeletal brown trees wore an uneven dusting of white. From a distance, the snowcapped peaks of the Canadian Rockies shimmered orange and yellow in the hastening dawn.

For a long time, the man stood on the precipice and gazed at the breathtaking vista. His blue eyes shone in the morning sun, face ruddy from the cold. Sandy hair ruffled under a wool cap, obscuring a gauze bandage that covered a two-inch gash across his forehead.

Too soon, the peace of morning was shattered by an electronic chirp. The man grabbed the communicator tucked next to a holstered Colt in his belt.

"Cutler here . . ."

"Playtime's over, Cut. You have to come home now."

Cutler ignored the jibe. "What's up?"

"Deavers wants you in his office ASAP."

"Roger that."

"Looks like the major's got a job for you—"

Cutler cut him off and pocketed the communicator. He turned his back on the dawn and without a second glance, retraced his own footprints along the trail. Through tangled brush and dense pines, he noticed barbed wire and electrified fencing—the first indicator of civilization. Soon he was close enough to read the bright yellow signs posted every few yards:

NO TRESPASSING

DANGER!

The signs were printed in English and French. A few were even printed in Blackfoot Sioux, the dominant language of the Native American population in the region. No one was permitted to approach this complex. Few even knew it existed.

Cutler followed the fence until he reached a security gate, where he slipped his identity card through the magstripe reader and entered his code on the keypad. Above his head, face-recognition technology confirmed his identity while a retinal scanner photographed his right eye. Two seconds, three, and Cutler heard the beep. The gate opened.

Inside the compound, no guards were in view—only more security cameras, X-ray sensors, and magnetic scanners. As Cutler crossed a barren stretch of frozen ground, an animal stench floated down from the pens. He heard snorts and grunts, too. Mercifully, the wolves had stopped howling soon after the sun showed itself.

Hiking beyond the concrete kennels and steel cages, Cutler headed toward a modern glass-and-steel structure that dominated a low rise. The four-story building was topped by conical microwave towers and spidery satellite arrays. Beneath were five levels of steel-lined tunnels, laboratories, workrooms, and storage chambers—including a moderately sized adamantium smelting facility on the deepest level. The underground maze had been bored out of solid granite, expanding beyond the limits of the deceptively modest surface structures. So extensive was the complex that an on-site fission reactor had been installed to provide for its energy needs.

Pushing through the glass double doors, Cutler found himself flanked by an armed security team—the same men he saw every day. Per established security protocol, they checked his ID and scanned his fingerprints.

"Out for your morning constitutional?" a guard asked.

Cutler nodded.

"I think nature boy was writing poetry. Sunrise, purple mountain's majesty, and all that crap," said another, his tone less friendly. "Makes me wonder how the hell a guy like Cutler gets Class A security clearance in the first place."

"Same way you did, Gulford. I won a contest."

A few moments later, Cutler entered Major Deavers's sparse office. The major's back was to him. He swiveled from his computer terminal and brusquely waved toward a cushioned chair. He wore a tense look on his face.

"I'll stand," said Cutler.

Despite their differences in rank, neither man saluted. Technically, they were no longer in the Canadian Defense Forces, so the acknowledgement of rank was not required.

"You're the security chief as of this morning," Deavers told him. "At 0830, Subject X is to be moved from the holding cell on Level Three to the main laboratory."

Cutler silently cursed.

"The subject is sedated and ready to go," the major continued. "Anticontamination protocols are in place, so please wear your environmental hazard suit. Don't bother with a weapon, though—Subject X is down for the count, and guns make the docs nervous."

Deavers rose. The man was ten years older than Cutler, and a head taller, too. Salt-and-pepper hair, always cropped short. Jawline smooth as a baby's ass. Even his khaki green coveralls, standard issue around the compound, appeared crisply pressed.

"And clean up your act, will ya, Cutler? Shave, comb your hair, take a shower. The Professor is going to be in the lab today and he likes his staff to look sharp."

Cutler turned to go.

"One more thing," said Deavers. "Take Agent Franks with you—"

Cutler stared for a moment. "Why do I have to break in the new guy? I'm no tour guide."

"Because there's no one else available," Deavers replied. "Most of the staff is tied up with this morning's experiment. The Professor's ordered double security for the rest of the day, and Erdman's still in the infirmary from that altercation in the parking lot the other night—"

"Couldn't be helped, sir."

"—and Hill was medivaced out of here last night. Gutted by a cougar that escaped from its cage. Docs give him a fifty-fifty chance to pull through. Either way, he won't be back anytime soon."

Cutler blinked. "I didn't know."

"Look," Deavers said. "Agent Franks is a real bright kid. You'll like him. He's friendly and eager and a born volunteer. Rice just briefed him on data retrieval and security protocols, and Franks got high marks. Show him the ropes and he'll lighten your load."

"Is that all, sir?"

"No. Keep the new kid away from me. I can't stomach Boy Scout types. Got too much on my plate to babysit a newb."

"Yes, sir. That's my job."

Deavers turned his back on Cutler, his gaze returning to the computer screen. "Get out of here!" he barked, not looking again in Cutler's direction.

Dismissed, Cutler showered, shaved, and hooked up with Agent Franks in the ready room. The fellow had a boyish face and wide brown eyes. He wasn't too obvious as he checked out the cuts and bruises on Cutler's face.

As they suited up, Franks peppered Cutler with questions.

"Is it true the guy I'm replacing was mauled by a grizzly bear?"

"Don't worry," Cutler replied with a slight smile. "That was a few weeks ago, before we worked all the bugs out of our animal control procedures. Now we've got professional animal handlers on staff, so we don't have to deal with bears anymore—"

"Thank God."

"—just the big cats."

"Cats?"

Cutler's smile widened greatly. "You know about them . . . lions. Tigers. Leopards . . . cats."

"Cats? Bears? Who needs all these wild animals, and why?"

Cutler's grin disappeared. "You'll find out soon enough."

Many minutes passed in silence as the men donned their complicated environmental hazard suits.

"Big turnover rate around here?" Franks asked at last, lifting his helmet and testing the communicator.

"They come and go," Cutler replied. "This place has only been up and running a year, and the research they do . . . well, let's just say it keeps changing direction. And like I said before, there are a lot of bugs to be worked out."

Franks pointed to Cutler's bruises. "So what kind of 'bug' ripped into you?"

From the very moment Cutler and his group brought Logan in, the medical team complained about "the subject's" condition. Nobody seemed worried about Erdman, though. He was only coughing up blood from a broken rib that had pierced his lung.

Cutler and Hill had barely placed the unconscious Logan in the tank before technicians swarmed all over him. A man in a doctor's smock shaved the subject while a vile-smelling, antibacterial immersion fluid was pumped into the decontamination tank. Then the doctors began their preliminary examination.

The chief physician appeared the most displeased. "Looks like your boys got a little enthusiastic," said Dr. Hendry, frowning as he indicated the subject's swollen jaw and bruised throat. He gritted his teeth in annoyance.

Major Deavers nodded. "He put up some resistance when my men brought him in last night."

"And your thugs saw fit to rough him up, eh, Major?" Cutler, fresh from the infirmary where his forehead had been sewn shut, worked his jaw, teeth grinding up his obscene reply.

"They had to jostle him a bit," said Deavers, not even glancing in Cutler's direction.

Cutler turned and left the lab. It was bad enough Hendry and Deavers saw fit to talk about him as if he hadn't been standing right there, as if he were one of their research animals, incapable of comprehending human conversation—though he should have been used to that kind of treatment by now, especially from the academic types crawling all over the compound. But he'd be damned if he was going to stand there and listen to Hendry call him a thug.

What I am is a professional, as much of a pro as anyone else in this damn facility.

For more than a decade he'd trained to become a soldier, one of a very few highly-skilled professional warriors who possessed both a background in special operations and field experience in both spy craft and unconventional warfare. As a former member of Canada's Joint Task Force Two, Cutler's military and counterterrorism training had lasted longer, and been far more comprehensive, than the commonplace schooling of these degree-heavy eggheads that cluttered up Department K's labs, cafeterias, and dormitories. And Cutler was willing to bet that his expertise was far more valuable, too. Especially these days.

Hendry and his fellow quacks wouldn't even have their prize "Subject X" if Erdman, Hill, and I hadn't risked our necks bringing him in. And I'd sure love to see Dr. Hendry try to take down a mark as tough as Logan without messing up a hair on the precious subject's head.

To be fair, Erdman and Hill did more than mess up Logan's hair. They'd almost killed him. Cutler touched the bandage on his forehead and wondered how such a routine assignment could have gone so wrong. . . .

A simple shoot-and-snatch. "Spy school stuff," the Major had called it. Three agents on a lone mark. "Pop him, pack him, bring him in—and don't let any damned civilians see you do it," he said.

They'd caught up with Logan the night before, outside a church-run dive on the edge of town. They followed him to a local gin mill and waited in the bar while their man consumed at least a fifth of whiskey in under an hour.

A lesser man would've been intoxicated—if not falling-down drunk. Cutler had been impressed when Logan walked a straight line across the icy parking lot without a single stumble.

As Logan climbed into his car, they made their move. Hill was handling the tranquilizer gun. Erdman and Cutler were responsible for the snatch. It was Hill who'd pulled a Murphy when he alerted the target to their presence by uttering his name.

"Mr. Logan . . ."

Hill said later, in the debriefing with Major Deavers, that he'd wanted a clear shot.

You were standing, like, five feet away, Cutler thought in disgust. *How much of a clear shot did you need?*

From behind the wheel of his convertible, Logan looked up just as Hill pulled the trigger. The dart struck him in the shoulder as he attempted to rise. A moment later, Logan's legs gave and he toppled out of the seat.

Erdman caught Logan before he hit the pavement, then grunted under the man's weight. "Help me with him. He's real heavy for a little guy."

Suddenly, Logan's eyes opened and he lashed out. The blow sent Erdman reeling back with two broken ribs. When he landed, his head cracked against the ground.

With a roar, Logan tossed Hill out of the way, then leaped onto Erdman's chest. As he pummeled the helpless man, Erdman curled into a defensive ball.

"Get him off of me!" he howled between pain-wracked coughs.

Cutler grabbed Logan's hair and yanked his head back to expose his throat. A blow to the jaw, followed by another to the solar plexus, knocked some of the fight out of their mark. As Logan folded, Cutler loomed over him, fists raised, waiting for an opening, or for the sedative to take effect.

He thought he was alert, but Cutler never saw the blow that got him—only an explosion inside his head, and his own blood staining the snow.

As Cutler went down, Erdman rose, cursing and spitting. He leaped onto Logan's back and wrapped his powerful arms around the man's throat. Gritting his teeth, Erdman squeezed.

"Didn't you get him with that stupid stun gun?" he growled at Hill through blood-flecked lips.

"Of course I did!" Hill cried. "Point-blank."

Cutler stumbled to his feet. Through a bloody haze he saw that Logan was weakening—either from the sedative or from Erdman's choke hold. Though Logan purpled from lack of oxygen, he fought on relentlessly.

Hill hefted the stun gun. But instead of reloading, he

turned the weapon around and used the handle to pistol-whip the struggling man to the ground.

"Wait!" Cutler shouted. "If you kill him, he's use-less."

But Hill was full of adrenaline—too pumped to stop now. He hit Logan again and the man's head lolled.

"Major's not going to like this," Erdman wheezed. "He said no body damage."

"Sure," said Hill. "But the major didn't say what a tough son of a bitch this guy was gonna be!"

Hill raised his fist high, but Cutler blocked it. "Enough, Hill. He's out cold."

Logan slid to the icy ground. He didn't move again.

Cutler pocketed the gore-soaked stun gun and shook the blood from his eyes. He checked out his partners. Erdman, ghostly pale, was doubled over and clutching his side, his breath a gurgling wheeze. Hill was still twitching from the fight, a ball of raw energy. Cutler tried to calm him.

"Let's get Logan into the van before someone sees us and calls this in."

He and Hill carried the listless body to the waiting van. Erdman limped at their side, pausing to spit a wad of blood and saliva.

Then Erdman spoke, his weak voice a wet wheeze. "This one here . . . watch him, Cut . . . he's trouble . . . and a whole lot tougher than he looks. He's one vicious son of a bitch."

"Let's pressurize the suits," said Cutler, tapping the control pad at his wrist. "You first, Franks."

Cutler's voice boomed inside the other man's helmet, and Franks adjusted the volume. Then he tapped the keypad on his own wrist until tiny red digits appeared, counting down from ten.

At zero, Franks heard a sharp hiss and his ears popped. The environmental hazard suit seemed to tighten around his waist, armpits, and shoulders as the joints vacuum-sealed. The surge of claustrophobic, suffocating panic passed quickly as the rebreathing system kicked in and cool air filled his helmet. Before proceeding, Franks waited patiently for a second digital readout to verify the suit's integrity.

"Sealed," he declared when the light flashed green.

Cutler sealed his own suit, then both men stepped through a Mylar quarantine barrier into an adamantium-lined holding cell. Once inside, Cutler introduced Franks to Subject X.

Logan—scalp freshly shorn, unrecognizable—drifted in a swamp-green chemical solution behind the translucent walls of the holding tank. An oxygen mask covered his face, intravenous tubes snaked into both arms. His head wasn't the only part shaved—not a hair remained on his entire body. Follicles had been replaced by hundreds of probes that projected like porcupine needles from Logan's arms, legs, torso, throat, and groin.

Long copper needles penetrated the corners of his eyes, which were taped shut. Many more spikes pierced his ears, nose, and even his brain through holes drilled into the temple and at the base of the skull.

"Cripes, he looks like a goddamn pincushion," Franks said as he circled the tank. "Who the hell is he?"

Cutler paused. "A volunteer," he said.

Franks studied the silhouette bobbing in the tank, then shook his head. "There isn't enough money in the whole wide world to get me to volunteer for this shit."

"Maybe he didn't do it for the money."

"You're right," said Franks. "This guy's probably a soldier, just like us. Maybe he's a hero or something—an astronaut, maybe. He looks like a bodybuilder to me. Check out those arms and that chest. He's one tough-looking guy. A freaking gorilla on steroids . . ."

To Cutler, Subject X seemed smaller now than last night in the parking lot. A lot less formidable, too.

As Franks paced the length of the holding cell, he noticed a team of technicians in lab coats observing their actions through a Plexiglas window overhead.

"We're supposed to move this guy, right?" said Franks, trying to ignore the audience. "So how are we going to get him out of that stupid tank?"

"We don't, Franks. We load the whole tank—subject and all—onto a flatcar."

"A what?"

Cutler opened a wall panel to display a stainless steel vehicle that resembled an armored golf cart. With a whine of servomotors, Cutler guided the flatcar out of the battery-charging unit and over to the bubbling tank.

It took several minutes to show Franks how to operate the flatcar, and where to hook the tank's life-support systems during transport.

"I sense you've done this before," said Franks.

Cutler nodded.

"So hero here isn't the first volunteer. There were others . . ."

Franks was fishing. Cutler wasn't biting. Not until he knew the guy better, trusted him not to shoot off his mouth.

"He's the first human," said Cutler.

Franks grinned. "Mystery solved . . . That's the reason for all those wild animals."

"Drop it, Franks. We've got work here."

Under Cutler's supervision, Franks backed the flatcar under the holding tank and activated the electromagnetic clamps that held it tightly in a magnetic grip. The tank settled in, the flatcar groaning under its weight. As the vehicle rumbled to the exit, fluid sloshed inside the crystalline coffin and the subject bumped against its transparent walls.

Cutler glanced at the digital readout on the flatcar's control panel and noted with satisfaction that life support was working normally. Then he checked his watch.

"I've got twenty minutes to get Subject X down to the main lab, so I'll see you later, Franks."

"Can't I go with you? Where are you going?"

"That's 'need to know.' And you don't need to. Your security clearance ends at the elevator, so turn around and follow the yellow signs back to the changing room. Don't open any other doors or you'll violate security protocol, and you wouldn't want to do that on your first day—makes a bad impression."

"No, sir . . . I mean, yes, sir . . ." Franks turned to go, little-kid disappointment on his face.

"Hey, Franks. If you're bored, go see Major Deavers. I'm sure he'll find some action for a Boy Scout type like you."

The main laboratory sat one level above the adamantium smelting plant in an area approximately the size of an airplane hangar. Typically, only a small portion of the massive space was in use at any one time, with the rest of the level dark. However, when the elevator doors opened, Cutler was astonished to find the enormous floor fully illuminated. The entire lab had become a hive of frantic activity.

Flashing red lights hit Cutler's eyes as he exited the elevator. WARNING. ZONE UNDER QUARANTINE. Red-light procedure required environmental hazard suits be sealed and pressurized before personnel entered the area. Cutler was all set.

He moved forward into the steel-lined, dome-roofed cathedral—a space hollowed out of solid bedrock. At least fifty physicians, medical assistants, computer technicians, and various specialists, all clad in the same pressurized suits as Cutler's, crowded around an enormous holding tank in the center of the floor.

That tank was empty now, but it was easy to guess who the guest of honor would be. Cutler squired Logan forward, guiding the rolling flatcar toward the center of the lab. When the medical team saw him, they rushed him like sycophants swarming a red-carpet celebrity.

His escort duties fulfilled, Cutler was shuffled aside, the hardest shove coming from his favorite scientist—Dr. Hendry, the same doctor who'd called him a "thug" and complained about Logan's condition when they'd first brought him in.

In a hurry to check the subject's medical status on the display panel, Hendry's voice sounded shrill over the headsets. "Heart rate, normal . . . Respiration is normal . . . Blood pressure is normal. Okay, people, let's get him to the tank, stat."

A team of technicians wheeled the flatcar to the base

of the mammoth tank, where a waterproof hatch on the larger vessel yawned. Using a Plexiglas sluice, the medical team attached the smaller holding tank to the larger vessel.

Finally, a bubbling green biological soup was pumped into the larger tank. After a few moments, the level in both containers was equal. As the fluids merged, the technicians literally floated Logan from his holding tank into the larger container.

A specialist squeezed through another hatch—a neat trick in a bulky EH suit—and splashed into the containment tank beside the unconscious man.

First, he attached Logan's intravenous tubes and respirator to the systems built into the larger tank. Then he used a handheld sensor to check the status of the hundred or more probes piercing the subject's body—one probe at a time. The process took many minutes, and several probes were flagged and replaced by another specialist who had also squeezed into the tank.

Finally, the two men gave the doctors a thumbs-up and climbed out. The hatches were sealed behind them and more fluid flowed into the tank until it was near to brimming with a bubbling green liquid. As the two technicians headed for the changing room, small robots scooted across the polished metal floor, cleaning the chemical trail the men left in their wake.

Banks of computer terminals clustered around the central containment tank hummed and ticked as their systems began to interface with the probes in Logan's body. Consoles surged with energy and monitor screens began crawling with indecipherable data that flowed endlessly.

Moving unnoticed among the sea of physicians, technicians, and specialists, Cutler spied some new faces in the observation booth—an enclosed gondola ringed by catwalks that hung from the high stone roof over the center of the lab.

Behind a glass partition, a short, stout, middle-aged man with a full brown beard and thick glasses watched the containment procedure with interest. His hands were thrust into the pockets of a stained lab coat. From a distance, Cutler read his name on the security clearance tag: DR. ABRAHAM B. CORNELIUS.

The name sounded familiar, but Cutler—a news junkie—just couldn't place it.

Next to the middle-aged man sat a petite young woman in a pale green smock. Though she had plain features, even from this distance Cutler could tell she was intelligent and intense.

Or, more likely, compulsive and driven, like most of the eggheads around here.

As she punched keys on a small handheld computer, the woman pushed a wisp of straight, brown hair away from her elfin face with an impatient gesture.

Yep. Compulsive and driven, Cutler decided.

He turned his attention to the ceiling, where a two-ton metal cap alive with arcane technology was lowered by stout steel chains. As the heavy lid clanged into place, technicians climbed aboard to connect yet more pipes, tubes, and sensors.

"The containment tank will be sealed in five seconds," a disembodied voice warned. "Four . . . three . . . two . . ."

With a roaring hiss that reverberated throughout the vast domed chamber, the airtight seal was activated.

"Containment tank sealed and pressurized," declared the disembodied voice. "Venting now . . ."

Rushing air ruffled papers and buffeted the staff as the atmosphere in the main lab was sucked away, to be replaced by pure, filtered air. The vented gasses exited into biohazard tanks that were disposed of in accordance with the rules and regulations of Canada's Environmental Protection Agency.

In a few minutes, flashing red lights shifted to green. The voice spoke once again: "Main laboratory decontaminated. You may now depressurize your suits."

The group immediately broke their pressure seals and removed their helmets. Many began to strip away their protective clothing as well. Amid sighs of relief and celebratory laughter, they inhaled cool, fresh air, mopping sweat from their brows or scratching some persistent itch that had been tormenting them.

Cutler removed his own helmet and gloves and tossed them onto a conveyor belt. Others did the same. The belt carried the gear over to a dumbwaiter, which transported the contaminated clothing to a sterilization room on another level.

Suddenly, Dr. Hendry's voice hissed a warning to his staff. "Heads up, gentlemen. The Professor is arriving."

Cutler had never seen the famous Professor up close. Curious, he turned to watch the Professor glide into the lab. Already, Dr. Cornelius and the anonymous woman had exited the booth and moved to the main floor. Now they watched with the others as the master of this facility, and the genius behind this experiment, moved among them.

"How is the patient?" the Professor asked.

"I'm told he has a few injuries," Dr. Hendry replied haltingly, his tone deferential.

"Is he severely damaged?"

Hendry shook his head. "Not at all."

"Any deep cuts? Abrasions . . . We can't afford leakage."

"I understand," said Hendry with a nod. "We plugged him up pretty tightly. Teflon patches around all the probes, sealing the entry wounds. The subject's mouth, nostrils, ears, and anus are all surgically sealed, and a catheter is blocking his urinary tract."

Abruptly, the Professor turned to address another. "Good morning, Dr. Cornelius. Are we set to begin?"

As they spoke, Cutler noticed that the Professor treated Dr. Cornelius with a measure of respect—a deference he apparently reserved for a select few. Dr. Hendry was one. Now, apparently, this Dr. Cornelius merited equal treatment, which both surprised and impressed Cutler.

As the conversation degenerated into technobabble, Cutler shifted his attention to the woman. She listened in rapt attention to the two eggheads as if she were listening to the spoken word of God.

Cutler shifted his feet in an effort to catch her attention, and the woman turned her forest green eyes in his direction. He locked stares with her, gave her a polite nod, a small smile.

To his surprise, the woman looked right through him, as if he wasn't there. Something about her unblinking, almost vacant gaze disturbed him.

Finally, the Professor dismissed most of the staff.

"Everyone not a part of this phase of the experiment is to depart the lab immediately," he commanded.

Most of the milling crowd quickly moved toward the elevator. Cutler joined the crush.

As he pushed his way into the crowded car, he couldn't help wondering just what the Professor and the rest of these mad scientists had in store for that poor sucker floating in the tank.

4

The Fugitive

Someone is watching me. I can feel the eyes. Curious. Penetrating . . .

For many minutes, Dr. Abraham B. Cornelius resisted the urge to wipe his forehead, beaded ever so lightly with sweat.

Just like on the courthouse steps . . . all those camera lenses pointing . . . reporters barking questions . . .

The dampness increased. Dr. Cornelius could feel it all in his caramel-brown beard, his mustache, his eyebrows. And worst of all, his forehead felt slick now with perspiration. *Obvious perspiration.*

Is that what they're looking at? Or are they thinking the same thing as the people in that courthouse crowd, the ones who'd pointed and whispered, "That's him. That's the one. Cornelius, that doctor who murdered his wife and child."

Dr. Cornelius could hardly stand it. Dipping into a pocket, he pulled out the handkerchief he always carried—the one his wife had embroidered in the corner with a delicate C. Pretending his glasses needed cleaning, he made a show of wiping the bottle-thick round lenses, then, ever so casually, he dabbed the sweat away, offhandedly, indifferently.

Eyes watched me then. I could feel them. Like I can feel them now. But perhaps they're only speculating. Perhaps they don't know. Or if they do, they don't know everything . . .

Hands thrust back into the pockets of his wrinkled white lab coat, Cornelius put back his treasured handkerchief and surveyed the faces of the men and women around him in the pressurized observation booth.

Which one of these people is staring? Or are they all watching? I need to know . . .

On his left stood Carol Hines. No M.D. following her name, no title of any kind. Yet after watching the frenzied pace at which she'd been working for the past few days, Cornelius could only assume her expertise was vital to the success of the experiment.

The petite Ms. Hines had a smallish face and wore her hair in a severe, almost boyish style with thick, straight bangs. She might be described as attractive if her features weren't constantly pinching with impatience and dissatisfaction—nothing like his tall, slender wife, a dedicated scientist who had an easy laugh and whose face, even when working intensely, had reflected exhilaration, enjoyment, even delight.

At the moment, Ms. Hines's intense green eyes were fixed not on him but a large liquid crystal display panel of a handheld device. Unblinking, she tapped the keypad with robotic efficiency, her face an agitated frown.

When Dr. Cornelius was introduced to Ms. Hines several days ago, she'd hardly even glanced at him, and she'd barely looked in his direction since.

Clearly, she's not the one . . .

Cornelius next turned his attention to a medical technician hunched over a terminal near the observation window. The man had hardly taken his eyes off the monitor since Cornelius arrived. He seemed transfixed by the medical data streaming into his terminal from the lab below.

Abruptly, the man looked up. Cornelius steeled himself to meet the recognition, the accusation—but the technician looked past him to the digital chronometer on the wall.

Cornelius shifted his attention to another technician, this one wearing a headset and microphone. The man was on his feet, dividing his attention between two ticking digital display panels on the console and the activity on the other side of the glass.

Until a moment ago, the main laboratory had been filled with a lethal antiseptic gas that created a germ-, virus-, and bacteria-free environment with near-genocidal efficiency. This draconian measure was performed to protect Subject X from the threat of contamination during the prebonding preparation and transferal period. Now that the subject was fully immersed in a sterile suspension fluid, the lab was being vented of the toxic gasses.

As the technician watched, his digital readout measured the rate and amount of sterilized air being pumped back into the massive space. The display next to it measured how much poison was being sucked out. When both displays glowed green, the technician spoke into his headset.

"Main laboratory decontaminated. You may now depressurize your suits."

Cornelius joined the others at the window to peer down at the laboratory floor. The relieved medical staff were stripping off their bulky environmental hazard suits, then tossing them along with their helmets and gloves onto a fast-moving conveyor belt.

Among the group, Cornelius spied a stocky, power-
fully built young man with dirty blond hair and attentive
blue eyes. His ruddy face upturned, the young man was
openly staring into the observation booth.

He's the one . . . the one who's been looking . . .

Cornelius sensed intense curiosity behind the man's
stare, but no hint of recognition, accusation, or emotion
in his neutral expression.

*He's some kind of policeman, though . . . after a year on the
run I know the stare of the law when I see it. A fed, or ex-mili-
tary, maybe. Or he's a private security guard. But not a clock
puncher.*

Cornelius knew he was right. A year on the run gave
him a sixth sense for such things.

Suddenly, an alarm bell sounded inside the booth.

"Depressurizing. You may now proceed to the laboratory floor."

Behind them, a heavy steel hatch opened with a sharp
hiss and Cornelius moved to the exit with the others.
Outside the booth, a narrow catwalk with a mesh steel
surface ran for many meters; under it, a drop of fifty meters or more.

Cornelius noticed that the air had a faint chemical
taint. It stung his nostrils, and he wondered briefly if the
lab had been thoroughly purged of the toxic disinfectant,
or if there was a fatal malfunction in the venting system.

*Have I traded the possibility of one gas chamber for another?
A lethal injection for a lethal atmosphere?*

White-knuckled hands clutching the guardrail, Cornelius followed Carol Hines along the catwalk, then
down a steep flight of grated steel steps to the main floor.

Moving among the doctors and technicians, Cornelius felt more at ease—hidden in plain sight, anony-

mous in a sea of earnest faces too wrapped up in their work to pay much attention to him.

Then, like a royal herald, Dr. Hendry spoke. "Heads up, gentlemen. The Professor is arriving."

Along with everyone else, Dr. Cornelius turned to greet his master, his keeper, the man who'd promised him protection from the law—as long as he gave his all to this unprecedented undertaking.

Walking erect as a proud general surveying his militia, the Professor moved among the members of his staff, meeting their eager, respectful gazes with an air of polite but indifferent superiority. Occasionally, the Professor paused to address a technician about a specific issue. His face remained impassive as he listened to the reply, and he usually moved on without comment when he'd heard enough. The Professor did not waste words.

It was the same the first time I met him. Why is he treated with such reverential awe by these people? I know what power he holds over me, but what about all the others? Can they all be volunteers? Did they all willingly commit to this bizarre experiment?

Before being "recruited" himself, Dr. Cornelius had encountered the Professor only twice before, yet each chance meeting came at a crossroads in his own life.

Their first encounter occurred many years before, when Dr. Cornelius was poised on the brink of professional triumph and personal happiness.

It seemed so long ago now . . . like another lifetime. No. Like another man's life. . . .

With a wide grin, the dean of the medicine department greeted Dr. Cornelius at the door, pumping his hand like a lost brother. Before a hundred colleagues, he gave a glowing introduction to an internationally diverse audience that included Cornelius's former teachers and fellow pupils from his medical school days.

It was simply the most gratifying moment in his career. To return to his adopted country, to his alma mater, to present to the world his successful results after years of struggling—years that in many ways had already been rewarded, in Cornelius's own estimation, by the beautiful woman who watched him from the front row.

"As a researcher, and an esteemed member of the academic community both here in Canada and in the United States, Dr. Cornelius is known to us all as a revolutionary thinker within the field of immunology," the dean declared. "But Abraham Cornelius refused to allow his accomplishments to end there. He returned to his native country and received a degree in molecular biology *and* the first-ever doctorate in the field of biomedical nanotechnology."

Amid all the cheers and applause, Cornelius felt humbled by the effusive outpouring of support from his peers.

"On this momentous day," the dean continued, "Dr. Cornelius has returned to our school of medicine, to outline a series of new techniques and technologies for the suppression of the body's immune system during transplant procedures previously considered impossible. It is my privilege and pleasure to introduce to you, Dr. Abraham B. Cornelius."

Cornelius rose, nodding at the warm applause, then, standing before an international audience comprised of specialists in the fields of transplant surgery, neurological function, and bionic limb replacement, he presented his theories.

"I believe that the threat of tissue rejection that followed many transplant procedures will soon be a problem of the past . . ."

For the next eighty-five minutes, he discussed several nanomedical devices that he'd developed—along with innovative surgical procedures that would open up new avenues in the repair and replacement of damaged organs, muscles, even nerve tissue.

"Soon, programmable microscopic devices injected inside the human body will fight infection, destroy cancerous tissue without damaging healthy cells, and wage battle against the body's own immune system after transplant surgery."

When the seminar ended, practically every member of the audience rushed the stage to extol the limitless potential of Cornelius's groundbreaking research. Many, including the dean of medicine himself, urged Cornelius to begin testing human subjects as soon as possible.

"Oh, well, that will have to wait," Cornelius told the audience during an impromptu question-and-answer session. "I'm not sure I'm ready for clinical trials quite yet. Perhaps in a year. More likely two. I'm still trying to complete the animal testing. Then I'll have to correlate my findings, write a new paper, and present what I hope will be positive results. Of course, there is also the ever present issue of funding—or the lack thereof."

His colleagues smiled at that, having faced the same hurdle. Then Cornelius touched the shoulder of the woman who stood at his side. She smiled and wrapped her arms around his waist.

"And because my former assistant, Dr. Madeline Vetri, has just consented to be my wife, I will also have to pencil in a wedding and a honeymoon. I'm told by the bride-to-be that attendance at both is mandatory."

Madeline laughed and poked his arm.

Opposites attract, they say, and Dr. Cornelius and his fiancée could not have seemed more different. She was French-Canadian, he a U.S. citizen of Irish-Jewish descent. Plain-faced and slightly paunchy, no one would ever mistake Abraham Cornelius for a movie star, while Madeline Vetri was easily the most attractive woman in any room. Her long, lustrous hair was raven black, in contrast to Cornelius's own tangled brown mop, and she was as slim and tall as he was short and stocky—even in low heels she stood nearly a head taller than him. And while his manner was quiet and reserved—a harsh critic might even say dull—Madeline's every gesture brimmed with grace and vivacious energy.

More applause and more congratulations greeted the joyous announcement—then ceased abruptly. At the entrance to the auditorium, a buzz of excitement erupted.

"It's the Professor," someone murmured and all eyes turned.

"Welcome, sir . . ." called the dean with a respectful nod as the man they called the Professor glided down the center aisle.

It was as if the Red Sea parted. Physicians, researchers, academics—all stepped back in quiet awe as the Professor passed. Finally, the man halted in front of Dr. Cornelius.

"I've read your paper," he said without preamble, and without extending his hand. Behind his angular glasses, the Professor's eyes were unreadable, dead flat.

"Your work shows potential, Doctor. And much promise for future scientific pursuits. But I must concur with my colleagues—"

The Professor's cool gaze took in the woman at Cornelius's side.

"—when they say you should put aside any . . . distractions . . . you may have in your personal life and concentrate solely on clinical trials. Anything else would be counterproductive, a waste of time."

His declaration complete, the Professor licked his thin lips. To Cornelius, the gesture seemed vaguely reptilian.

At his side, he felt his fiancée tense. He squeezed her hand, turned his head to meet her eyes, reassure her. The Professor's statement was galling—but when Cornelius turned back to demand an apology, he was gone.

"Good God, who was that ridiculous man?" Cornelius asked the dean, who guided him away from the others before answering.

Dr. Cornelius was shocked to learn the Professor's identity. Forgiving the insult to his fiancée would not be easy, yet he couldn't help but feel uplifted. His research had just been endorsed by one of the most brilliant scientists since Albert Einstein.

"Good morning, Dr. Cornelius. Are we set to begin?"

Revived from his reverie, Cornelius managed a wan smile. "Good morning, Professor. Yes, I believe everything has gone quite smoothly. It certainly looked that way from the observation booth."

The Professor stood, emotionless and unreadable, his hands clutched behind his back. "And your nanochips are ready for injection?"

Cornelius directed the Professor's attention to the tank.

"Right there, Professor . . . inside that blue container."

He pointed to a teardrop-shaped metal jar roughly the size of an average household aerosol can. It was attached to a long injection needle situated among a cluster of them located on the ceiling of the holding tank.

"Should we begin the process?"

"Whenever you are ready, Professor. The nanochips will be injected directly into the heart simultaneously, so the microscopic devices will be dispersed throughout the body quickly. The chips should fuse with the subject's bone in less than a minute."

The Professor barely nodded, then drifted away to interrogate another member of the team. Like yes-men around a winning candidate, the crowd followed. Only Carol Hines remained at Cornelius's side. For the first time since they'd met, she showed a glimmer of interest in something that did not involve her REM machine.

"An injection straight into his heart?" she asked. "What are you pumping into Subject X, anyway?"

"A silicon-based chip with a coded memory—several million of them, in fact. Each one creates a microscopic valve that will adhere to the tiny sinuses in the bone. The valves are self-sustaining and can even use nutrients absorbed by the body to replace the ones that malfunction or wear out."

"You mean they reproduce?"

"Precisely."

"I see . . . And your goal with this?"

"Well, the first objective is to sheathe the subject's skeleton with adamantium steel, to increase bone mass and tensile strength. But because bones are living organisms—and vital organs in their own right, since bone marrow manufactures blood—they cannot be completely coated with steel, or the bones would die and so would the subject."

Carol Hines nodded. "You need pores—holes that will allow blood to pass through the steel barrier?"

"Exactly."

"And the nanotechnology creates these pores?"

"More accurately, it replaces them," Cornelius explained. "Human bones already have tiny pores that permit fluids to pass. My chips will seek those out and replace their function once the adamantium bonding process has been completed."

Despite his reservations about the project and his suspicions about the Professor, Cornelius was astonished to find that the work of the last few days had stimulated some of his old love for scientific discovery. And it didn't hurt that the usually reserved Ms. Hines had suddenly taken an interest in his area of expertise. It had been so long since he felt needed.

"Well, I have my doubts," said a loud voice in a decidedly hostile tone. "In fact, Dr. Cornelius, I fear your technology will do more harm than good. Why are you so certain that these nanochips of yours will not degrade the integrity of my adamantium bone sheathing?"

Dr. Cornelius met Dr. Hendry's skeptical gaze with a very stern one of his own.

"For one thing," Cornelius replied, "my nanochips can withstand the destructive power of white-hot molten adamantium because they are actually three times more resilient than the steel itself. So the question you should really be asking, Dr. Hendry, is will your adamantium degrade the integrity of my nanotechnology?"

Hendry stood his ground. "What do you conclude?"

"An unequivocal no. Why? Because these two very complex processes are complementary—"

"Complementary or contradictory?" snapped Hendry.

"—which means that despite their obvious differences, the two technologies will work together to achieve a single goal—to make the subject's bones virtually indestructible."

"I'm reassured to hear you say that," Hendry replied, his tone still skeptical. "Some of us here in Department K have devoted years of our lives to this project. We want nothing more than for the Weapon X project to succeed."

Cornelius raised an eyebrow. *There* was the resistance. Right there. He was the new guy, the star exchange student from lands unfamiliar. He had come into their midst with little warning, carrying a briefcase of breakthrough research—and they resented it, to a man.

"Surely, you understand our trepidation," Hendry continued. "After all, we wouldn't want our efforts—all of our hard work—to be jeopardized by the use of a reckless and untested technological process devised by a . . . a newcomer."

Cornelius tried not to laugh out loud. *Newcomer, indeed.* "The Professor has expressed the utmost confidence in my technology," he said evenly.

Hendry moved to reply, but was interrupted by a booming voice from a loudspeaker.

"The bonding process will begin in thirty minutes. All personnel take their positions and commence prebonding procedures."

Dr. Hendry instantly wheeled around and strode away. Dr. Cornelius had intended to escort Ms. Hines to her workstation, which was located next to his. But when he turned in her direction, he found nobody there.

• • •

In truth, Cornelius wondered why he even had a work-station during this procedure—and so close to the Professor's own that it made him uncomfortable. It was like having the front row seat in a class taught by a particularly exacting teacher.

It's not like I'm drowning in work . . .

It had taken Dr. Cornelius all of five minutes to interface his computer with the biological monitors embedded in the subject's body. Now, with nearly twenty minutes to go before the bonding process commenced, he had absolutely nothing to do.

For Cornelius, most of the really intensive labor took place during the distillation of the liquid silicon solution, and the chemical processing that crystallized the substance, which helped encode the programming onto the molecules themselves. Once the nanotechnology was formulated and vacuum-sealed in a sterile vessel, Cornelius's job was pretty much over.

After the nanochips were injected into Subject X, they were out of anyone's control. In the bloodstream, their internal programming would take over. All Dr. Cornelius could do at that point was monitor their progress.

So why am I here? Not even the inestimable Dr. Hendry— the Professor's own right-hand man—has such a choice seat for this critical experiment.

Of course, Dr. Cornelius was aware of one skill he possessed that would prove useful. If his nanochips completely failed, he could unleash a synthetic hormone of his own invention into the subject's body. This substance would essentially "kill" the nanochips, which would then be filtered out of the body by the liver, to be eliminated like waste matter. If that happened, it would spell certain doom for the experiment—and for Subject X.

Without holes in the poor bastard's bones, he will die. Slowly, painfully, his skeleton will asphyxiate while the rest of his body withers from a dearth of whole blood.

But why dwell on the negative?

Cornelius never wanted to be a part of this research. His intention always had been to help humanity, to cure disease—not to create some kind of superweapon. Not to turn a man into a killing machine. An unstoppable tool of war.

Unconsciously, Cornelius began to massage his temples as a pain bloomed behind his eyes.

How the hell did I end up with these people? Doing this kind of work? Trapped in this place?

After the triumphant conference at McGill University's School of Medicine, Cornelius's time had been absorbed by his intense research and, of course, his wedding. He had put the unpleasant encounter with the Professor out of his mind until the second day of his honeymoon, when a very expensive bottle of Taittinger's Blanc de Blanc was delivered to his stateroom aboard the cruise ship *Delphi.*

"BEST WISHES FOR A HAPPY MARRIAGE," read the card. It was signed by the Professor.

Recalling the man's negative reaction to his pending marriage, Cornelius was surprised to learn that the Professor was capable of such a magnanimous gesture.

He considered mentioning the gift to Madeline, but the memory of the man's distasteful conduct at the conference stopped him. Cornelius tore up the card and flushed it down the toilet. Later that night, they celebrated their marriage by finishing the Professor's bottle of champagne in a single sitting.

During that extraordinary week, Madeline Vetri-Cornelius conceived their only child. A boy was born nine months later, christened Paul Phillip Cornelius after Madeline's father, a noted architect in his native Quebec.

Then came the agony, and there began a downward spiral. A disease that robbed him of all his joy, and the madness that resulted in murder . . .

Half a year later, after the indictment on a charge of double homicide had been handed down, Cornelius, rather than face a prison cell or executioner, became a fugitive. His lawyer had convinced the judge that bail was uncalled for, that an esteemed member of the medical community was not a flight risk.

But Cornelius fled just the same.

Months later, he'd begun to live what he thought was an anonymous life in a small trailer park outside of Syracuse, New York, when he received a package. No stamps on the outside, no postmark, either—which meant that the plain brown manila envelope had been stuffed into his mailbox by hand while he was working the graveyard shift at a local medical supply warehouse. The label was addressed to Ted Abrams—the name he was living under at the time—but when he peeked inside, it became obvious that the unknown sender knew his true identity.

Cornelius's first impulse was to hide from the truth. He hurled the envelope into a corner. With shaking hands, he brewed his morning coffee, toasted two stale slices of bread. Temporarily soothed by the caffeine, he retrieved the envelope and spilled all of its contents on the table next to his plate.

Inside were more than a dozen newspaper clippings

culled from wire service stories that had been filed over the past eighteen months. The stories all covered the same subject—the phenomenal rise and precipitous descent of Dr. Abraham B. Cornelius, from esteemed immunologist to fugitive double-murderer.

The envelope also contained a note written in large, almost childlike block letters:

YOU ARE BEING WATCHED. AT 11:00 P.M. TONIGHT YOU MUST BE WAITING IN FRONT OF THE MAIN MUNICIPAL LIBRARY IN BUFFALO, NEW YORK. IF YOU ATTEMPT TO FLEE BEFORE THIS MEETING TAKES PLACE YOUR LOCATION WILL BE LEAKED TO THE AUTHORITIES. IF YOU FAIL TO ATTEND THIS MEETING YOUR LOCATION WILL BE LEAKED TO THE AUTHORITIES. IF YOU AGREE TO THESE TERMS CALL THIS NUMBER NOW.

A telephone number had been scrawled in red ink below the message. Of course, there was no signature.

Is it blackmail? But why not just demand money? What's the reason for this secret rendezvous crap? Why the hell do I have to drive to Buffalo for a goddamn shakedown?

He stared at the remains of his morning coffee, cooling in the cup, the butter congealing atop the dry bread on his plate. Hesitantly, Cornelius lifted the receiver and dialed. A phone rang once. Then a male voice answered with two words.

"Wise decision."

The line went dead. Cornelius slammed the table with his fist. Enraged by the crass manipulation, and at being treated in such a disdainful manner, he immediately redialed the number.

This time, he got a recorded message stating that the number was no longer in service. He tried a second call, a third, a fourth—with the same results.

That afternoon, as wan yellow rays streamed through the dirty windows of his trailer, Cornelius tossed and turned in his narrow bunk. At five o'clock, he rose. Plenty of daylight was still left in the summer afternoon, and Cornelius weighed his options over another pot of coffee.

Finally, decision made, he showered, shaved, packed a small bag with a few necessities, and left the trailer without a second glance. He was due at his warehouse job in an hour, but he would not show up tonight, or ever again. Cornelius knew that no matter what happened at this forced meeting, he would never return to Syracuse.

As he drove to Buffalo, Cornelius noticed a storm was brewing in the darkening sky. By the time he arrived, the clouds had cut loose and the city turned gray under the gloomy downpour.

While waiting under a lamppost in the rain, Cornelius heard the clock on a nearby steeple strike eleven. He looked up to see a figure emerge from the watery curtain. Cornelius wondered if it was the person he was supposed to meet, or just a bystander.

Maybe the man should have given me a code word or something, so I'd recognize him as the genuine blackmailer.

Despite his misery, Cornelius managed the slightest chuckle.

A secret code. How ridiculous. And wouldn't that make this absurd espionage melodrama complete?

No code word was necessary, as it turned out. The man walked right up to Cornelius and lifted his head. As a brief waterfall ran off the tan wide-brimmed hat, Cornelius recognized the sharp refined features of the Professor, his square glasses speckled with raindrops.

"Professor, I—"

"Don't speak. Just listen carefully. I have a proposition for you. Do not tell me how grateful you are. Not now. Not ever. For what I offer you is not charity."

"What do you want from me, then? I have no money, no reputation. What can I possibly—"

"I have need of your special skills," said the Professor. "That is all you are required to know for now."

"But—"

"If you accept my proposition you will be spirited across the Canadian border within the hour," the Professor continued. "If you turn me down, you are free to go with the assurance that I will not expose you to the authorities. But bear in mind, doctor, that it is only a matter of time before the Federal Bureau of Investigation catches up with you."

The Professor paused to let his words sink in.

"By the way, congratulations are in order." The Professor's eyes were empty, dead flat as on the day Cornelius had first met him. "Did you know that you have made the FBI's Ten Most Wanted list? The press release was issued just yesterday."

The news had not yet reached Cornelius. His guts twisted at the very thought.

The Professor leaned closer, until Cornelius could feel the man's breath on his cheek. "And did you know that the Syracuse branch of the FBI has been alerted to your presence within their jurisdiction? They staged a raid on that trailer you call a home . . . and at that warehouse where you work. If you weren't here with me, you would be locked up in a cell by now."

Cornelius felt the panic quickly closing off his throat. He needed air. The Professor was crowding him, pushing him.

"What's your offer?" Cornelius snapped back. "I want to hear all of the details before I accept your, or anyone's, job. I'm going with the highest bidder."

The Professor seemed surprised by the doctor's obvious ploy—an attempt to regain a measure of control. A small smile lifted the edges of his thin lips. Under the glare of the street lamp, the Professor's grin reminded Cornelius of a bone-white skull.

"Come, come, Dr. Cornelius. Don't be ridiculous . . . Do you really believe you have any choice in the matter?"

"Professor? Dr. Cornelius? We can begin the procedure now."

The Professor nodded to Dr. Hendry, then faced Carol Hines. "Has the REM interfaced with the subject's brain?"

"Interface has been achieved, Professor," she replied crisply.

"Dr. MacKenzie, deactivate the brain dampeners."

With the flick of a switch, the psychiatrist cut off power to the generators, and the steady stream of ultrasonic energy, precisely tuned to a frequency that paralyzed Logan's brain, abruptly ceased.

"I detect a slight spike in the subject's brain activity," Dr. MacKenzie warned immediately.

"It's an error," said Carol Hines.

"You're sure of that?" MacKenzie shot back, the shock of red hair on his head bristling. "There can't be a glimmer of brain activity—not even dreaming—or the subject may be able to cling to certain facets of his personality even after conditioning."

"It's an anomaly," Hines insisted. "I've seen this phenomena before. Spikes occurred with test subjects at NASA, usually when their sleep was interrupted."

"What could cause such brain activity?" replied MacKenzie.

Hines shrugged. "There are several theories, Professor," she replied. "We might be seeing random electrical activity inside the hypothalamus—the area of the brain that controls bodily functions—or continuing chemical reactions within the pituitary stalk. But, of course, that's only conjecture."

The Professor seemed satisfied with her explanation, though Dr. MacKenzie remained unconvinced.

"The waves I saw on the monitor suggest activity in the cerebral cortex," the psychiatrist insisted. "Most certainly not random electrical or chemical activity."

MacKenzie glared at Hines, who stood her ground. It fell to the Professor to break the impasse.

"What do you see on the encephalographic monitor now, Ms. Hines? Dr. MacKenzie?"

"Interface with the REM has been achieved," said Carol Hines. "As of now, there's no brain activity we don't control."

MacKenzie hesitated, then nodded. "The screen is blank . . . now. Perhaps Ms. Hines is correct in her assumptions."

The Professor waved his hand. "Very well, then. Proceed."

"Stage One, people. Prepare to inject the nanochips," Dr. Hendry said, eyes on Cornelius.

Dr. Cornelius tapped the keyboard and his program sprang up on the monitor. Hunched over the terminal, he entered the code that released the injector.

M-A-D-E-L-I-N-E

The screen blinked: CODE ACCEPTED.

Then: INITIATING INJECTION PROCEDURE.

Finally, the monitor flashed: READY FOR INJECTION.

Cornelius reached for the control, then paused, his beefy index finger poised over the release button.

A moment passed. Then two. Still Cornelius held back.

Suddenly impatient, the Professor rose out of his chair. "Doctor . . . proceed."

Cornelius felt the man's eyes on his back—staring . . . always watching—and he punched the key.

A hydraulic whine from inside the bubbling tank, and a razor-sharp needle came out of its sheath like a cat's claw. Down it came until the tip caressed pale flesh.

Then the pointed tip plunged through muscle and bone, deep into Logan's beating heart. The figure in the tank jerked once, then thrashed about in a long, continuous spasm—an unanticipated reaction that set alarms ringing on a half-dozen monitors.

Specialists and physicians darted between terminals and the lab filled with excited voices.

Then Cornelius heard it, or imagined he did. A human cry that tore at his insides. A wail that drowned out the alarms and the shouts of the medical staff. The tremulous screams of a pain-wracked child, shrieking in uncomprehending agony.

5

The Mission

Logan was falling, tumbling through a black void. A sustained blast of frigid wind battered his body and roared through his mind. He reached for memories, something to hold on to.

Nothing there.

Panic rushed in to fill the void.

The storm has me. The whirlwind.

He moved his fingers, toes, and found himself enveloped in a smothering technological cocoon. He heard the rasping noise of his own breath, hot behind an oxygen mask that muzzled nose and mouth. He turned his head—to bump against the walls of a climate-controlled cybernetic helmet. On the other side of the visor, only darkness—and then a blinking cursor, flashing an inch from his left eye.

Logan watched as the computerized Heads Up Display cycled through its initiation sequence, then interfaced with a geopositioning satellite in Earth's orbit. Two seconds later, the HUD projected a map grid of the terrain below on the inside of his visor.

Logan recognized the grid, the map, the all-too-familiar terrain, and his memory flooded back with crystal clarity.

Must have bumped my head . . . knocked me for a loop . . .

As the parameters of the mission poured back into his mind, critical data scrolled across the visor. Wind velocity, airspeed, external temperature—a chilly seventy degrees below zero—his rate and angle of descent, longitude and latitude. The altimeter told Logan that he was in free fall from an altitude of thirteen thousand meters.

Somewhere above him—and probably miles away by now—the unmarked MC-140 he'd jumped from was on afterburners in a race for the border. They probably had a couple of North Korean MIG-22s chasing their tail, too. Logan silently wished the pilots luck getting home.

Only sixty-three seconds of free fall to go. At six thousand meters, the wings of the High Altitude Wing Kite harness would automatically deploy and the repulsors would fire to slow his descent. Until that time, Logan would continue to drop like a stone.

He noted the local time: 0227—the middle of the night.

"Terrain and objective," he said in a voice dry and raspy from the pure oxygen he was gulping.

The grid shifted. Outlined in sharp detail, Logan saw the digital silhouette of rugged hills and a narrow road that wound through them. To the north, an artificial lake restrained by a concrete dam. At the foot of the dam, a hydroelectric plant surrounded by double and triple fences, watchtowers, several wooden structures with detached latrines—probably barracks—and an antiaircraft gun emplacement.

Finally, Logan spied his objective—a collection of cir-

cular structures on the banks of a shallow river created by
the dam's runoff. The three- and four-story structures
appeared to be fuel storage tanks. But why store fuel near
a hydroelectric plant? It's the water that turns the generators; no oil was needed.

More ominous, reports confirmed that dead fish had
been turning up downstream, where the runoff from the
dam flowed into a larger river. JTF-4 Intel believed that a
toxic substance was the cause—a chemical, biological, or
possibly nuclear pollutant. Intelligence concluded that
the pollution came from the supposedly innocent power
plant, which meant it was generating more than electricity. The North Koreans were probably producing weapons of mass destruction at that site as well. Canadian
Intelligence wanted to know what types of weapons, and
in what quantities—which is why Logan and his partner
had been sent on this mission.

On his visor, hovering over the glowing map, Logan
saw a second blip. Invisible to the naked eye, another figure plunged through the night not so very far away—
Neil Langram, Logan's partner. The two men would
come down in separate landing zones, then rendezvous
on the ground.

A muted alarm sounded inside Logan's helmet, and
his training kicked in. He stiffened his spine and threw
his arms over his head as if he were high-diving into the
dark, shining waters far below. Spine rigid, he spread his
arms and legs wide to form the letter X.

The second alarm. Logan braced himself, muscles
tensed, as the readout counted down.

FOUR . . . THREE . . . TWO . . . ONE . . .

With a sudden jolt, the "wings" deployed. Leatherlike
membranes of a frictionless fabric burst out of hidden

seams under Logan's arms, along his torso, down his legs. Flexible ribs inside those wings instantly filled with compressed air, giving the membrane shape and creating an airfoil.

But by design Logan was still falling headfirst, as his rate of descent had hardly slackened. If Logan tried to catch wind and level off now, the HAWK harness would be ripped away by the stresses and he would plunge to his death.

A blinking cursor. Digital numerals. Another countdown.

Then the Stark Industries Mark III Repulsor units kicked in. Each of the six saucer-sized, disc-shaped devices was capable of firing three one-second bursts before their energy supply was exhausted—more than enough to slow Logan's descent.

But when the units fired, Logan felt a sharp, stabbing pain, like a knife plunging into his heart. He folded in agony and fell even faster. Alarms sounded in his ears, and the noise merged with the wind's howl. To Logan, black night seemed to turn a phosphorescent green.

Suddenly, an explosion in his head—a red haze of pain. A moan was ripped from Logan's lips. Through the agony, he wondered if his harness had somehow malfunctioned.

Soon, the anguish receded and Logan was able to concentrate. He fought for more control of the now-aerodynamic full-body flying suit against the shifting air currents. After some effort, he managed to level off at about two thousand meters. He was gliding parallel to the horizon at roughly three hundred kilometers per hour.

"Target."

Instantly, a flashing pipper appeared on the map grid,

highlighting a point on the slope of a low hill above the dam and the hydroelectric plant. Logan was still several kilometers away. He switched to infrared mode and suddenly he had a rouge-tinged panoramic view of the surrounding countryside.

"Telescopic mode . . . magnify . . . magnify . . . stop."

His telescopic night-vision visor revealed every detail on the ground below. Though he was still far away, Logan could make out vehicles parked near the top of the dam and a previously undetected security gate. And in the valley below the dam, Logan could see guards manning the watchtowers, and other uniformed men with dogs walking the perimeters on both sides of the fence.

Moving his arms, he slipped into a descending glide, occasionally adjusting for wind shear or updrafts caused by the hills.

To Logan, this was the only good part of a HAWK harness drop—flying like a bird on fluttering wings . . .

As he approached his target, Logan knew the fun was about to come to an end.

His plan was to buzz the facility in an effort to determine the quality and strength of the security forces. Then, if all went according to plan, Logan would find his landing zone, land without detection, make his way down the hill, across the dam, down the valley, over the fence and into the hydroelectric plant—all while avoiding contact with the guards, the dogs, and any minefields or electronic surveillance systems that might be installed around the complex.

"A freakin' cakewalk," Langram had called it.

Roger that.

Logan noted that the other blip was above and behind him now—Langram, still on target. Logan knew his partner would soon break off, to land on the opposite side of the lake. That way, if one of them were caught or killed, the other could complete the mission.

He and Langram would maintain a strict radio silence during the entire operation. They would not meet until they were among the storage tanks, or maybe not until they reached the extraction point after the mission was all over.

Of course, if things go really bad for either one of us, we won't be meeting at all.

Suddenly, a powerful updraft pushed Logan several hundred meters off course. Logan manipulated the HAWK's twin repulsion jets—activated by sensors in his gloves and a button in the palm of each hand—to compensate for the wind shear. Within seconds he was back on course. His computer control system took over to keep him on target.

Logan marveled at the quality of this new device, and how user friendly the next generation of HAWK harness had become.

Not like the bad old days.

Logan recalled that the first prototypes of the High Altitude Wing Kites were exactly that—powerless gliders made of leather, canvas, and spandex, deployed from standard form-hugging SHIELD battle suits. Those early models were not very reliable and lacked the amenities of the improved versions. Logan wondered how he'd gotten by without a pressurized helmet, heating unit, HUD, wireless computer control, GPS system, infrared night-vision visor—or even the repulsion units.

The current HAWK even eliminated the threat of radar detection. Sheathed in nonmagnetic, wave-absorbing composite material—a flexible version of the coating used on stealth aircraft—Logan and Langram were invisible to all forms of electronic detection and hi-tech surveillance.

Of course, one improvement had yet to be made. No one at SHIELD R&D had devised a way to make landing a HAWK harness easy. Logan hadn't used one in a couple of years and regretted it, for as the ground hurled up to meet him, he began to wonder if he still had the chops to pull off a smooth touchdown.

"It's easy to land a HAWK. Even a four-eyed yahoo can find the ground in one of these birds," Nick Fury once told him. "It's making that landing without cracking up that's tough."

A smirk tugged his thin lips. Logan could almost smell Fury's cheap stogies.

You'd think a guy neck-deep in covert ops could get his hands on some contraband Cuban Monte Cristos.

Logan concentrated on his approach. After calibrating the wind and angle of descent, the HUD displayed the flight pattern to the landing zone. But, first Logan wanted to make that reconnaissance pass over the power plant.

Like a silent, invisible wraith, Logan dived lower and lower. Finally, he raced parallel with the horizon, less than sixty meters above the ground. He passed over a steel fence and shot over a guard tower—low enough to see inside. He observed a few tired guards, teacups, and a knot of men playing dice.

Tempted to land right now . . . these guys are hardly awake. I could drop down and find out what's in those tanks within five minutes . . . but that would be wrong.

Logan had his orders. He was to land in the hills, bury his suit, and make his way down to the facility on foot.

Anyway, if it's too easy—where's the fun?

Racing silently over the hydroelectric plant, he noticed that a hangar-sized double door was open, a cluster of workers lounging just inside the pool of light. Beyond the plant, the area around the storage tanks was dark. Even in infrared mode, most of the details were lost in shadows.

Finally, Logan banked and headed for the gray, featureless wall of the dam. He bent his head back and spread his arms as wide as he could, to create more wing surface and lift. Then he fired the repulsion jets.

He rose like a bottle rocket over the dam. He spun in the air, then zoomed low across the dark water, his black suit shining like sealskin under the spray.

Logan fired the repulsors one last time, cleared the shore, and raced up the slope. Ahead of him, the designated landing zone—a barren stretch of brown Korean hill that had been deforested to make way for power lines still under construction. As he approached the LZ, Logan noticed thick stumps sticking out of the ground and several fallen trees blocking his path.

In preparation for the landing, Logan bent the harness to slow his airspeed. At eighty kilometers-per-hour, he loosened the harness so that he'd be ready to punch out of it the second he spotted a fairly level piece of real estate.

Landing in a HAWK harness was roughly the same as jumping out of an airplane with a parachute, then unbuckling that chute about ten or fifteen meters above the ground and falling the rest of the way. The landing tended to be hard, and you didn't always end up on your feet. Most guys curled into a ball and rolled until they came to a stop.

Not Logan.

As his visor ticked off the altitude in meters . . . 50 . . . 40 . . . 30 . . . 20 . . . his airspeed was reduced to less than forty kilometers per hour.

Logan threw his legs forward and punched out of the harness. The wings disengaged, folding like a crushed butterfly in his wake. He hit the ground running, rolled three times, and hopped to his feet. But the momentum he'd built up in the descent was still pushing him. Ahead, Logan spied a fallen tree in his path. Just as he leaped over the obstacle, a silhouette—human—rose from behind the log.

It was too late for Logan to stop. He slammed into the stranger and heard a muffled cry. Hurling out of control, they both tumbled down a steep slope in a cloud of dust.

The alarms had been silenced. Calm had been restored. Subject X now drifted motionless, the spasm subsided. Technicians and doctors moved about the room, recalibrating instruments and rebooting key computer systems.

"We'll lose a little time, Professor. It's unavoidable," Dr. Hendry said, face grave. "The technicians will have to get the computers back online. Restore function in some of the probes. But for now, Subject X has been stabilized."

The Professor barely nodded before facing Dr. Cornelius. "The nanotechnology. Is it functioning?"

"The process is complete, the silicon valves are working like the real things," said Cornelius. "You can see them on this full-body ultrasound . . . the tiny black specks on the skeleton . . ."

The Professor glanced at the image, then raised an eyebrow. "And you are absolutely convinced that your nanochips did not cause the subject's seizure?"

"Not a chance," Cornelius replied with more confidence than he had ever felt.

"Then we must turn to you, Ms. Hines," the Professor hissed. "What is your theory? What do you think went wrong?"

Carol Hines swallowed nervously. "I . . . I still believe we're dealing with random electrical impulses in the hypothalamus. It's man's basest instincts—the 'lizard brain'—fighting for survival in the very face of extinction."

"Poetic rubbish," Dr. MacKenzie scoffed. "There was obviously brain activity going on somewhere in the cerebral hemisphere. The subject was experiencing random memories, a total recall of some past event, the pangs of birth—whatever."

"Nothing like that showed up on the monitors," Hines insisted.

"We both saw the spike," MacKenzie replied, "only you dismissed it as an anomaly."

The Professor lifted his hand to silence the argument. "What does it mean, Doctor?"

MacKenzie faced the Professor. "The REM failed to completely interface with the subject's mind. There was a hole in the system, a flaw in the program. Some of Logan's—I mean, the subject's previous personality was exerting itself."

MacKenzie turned his back on the Professor to face the man in the tank. He tapped the glass as if it were a fishbowl.

"Something was going on inside that head of his. Subject X is not ready to surrender his identity . . . not yet," MacKenzie stated. "I'd stake my reputation on it."

The Professor placed his hands behind his back and paced around the laboratory. "This presents us with a small dilemma. Two of my associates disagree about a critical phase in the Weapon X program. We are at an impasse. How are we to proceed?"

MacKenzie stepped forward. "I've done everything in my power to keep Subject X under control. We experienced no difficulties until the brain dampeners were deactivated. I suggest we go the chemical route—Pheno-B. Three-point first dose, more if needed."

MacKenzie stared a challenge at Carol Hines. She met his gaze, then faced the Professor. He was staring at her, too.

"I'll reboot the REM mainframe," she said. "And start the interface from scratch. It's possible . . . maybe it's possible . . . that a step was overlooked."

MacKenzie, smug in victory, turned his back on the woman.

"The reboot should take about an hour," Carol Hines continued. "And we can try again."

"One hour, then," the Professor replied. A moment later, he was riding the elevator to an upper level.

With the Professor's departure, Dr. Cornelius approached Hines's workstation and touched her arm.

"Don't feel too bad," he said. "Stuff happens . . . delays . . . mistakes . . . errors in calcultion. Nobody's perfect. Bet this kind of thing went on at NASA all the time."

Carol Hines tapped her keyboard without looking up.

"Anyway, the Professor was in a quandary, and he went with Dr. MacKenzie . . . you can't blame him for—"

"For what?" she interrupted, looking up at him. Her thin face was flushed under her severe haircut. "For listening to the person with the most letters after his name?"

Cornelius shook his head. "You've got it all wrong, Ms. Hines. The Professor went with the technology he trusts, not the man. His decision had nothing to do with advanced degrees, or the fact that MacKenzie's a doctor. It's just that he's used Pheno-B before, but never the REM."

He could see he'd reached her and that she was paying attention to his words.

"If you'll recall," he continued, "the Professor was looking to blame my nanochips for Subject X's strange reaction."

Cornelius was relieved to see the lines on her face soften.

"And in case you haven't noticed before," he whispered conspiratorially, "there's a certain Dr. Hendry who's got it in for me. So don't feel too persecuted just because the project's headshrinker doesn't like you. I'm beginning to think everybody involved in this project is up the proverbial creek without a paddle."

6

The Experiment

From his chair, the Professor lifted a pale hand. "Let's make history."

The clatter of keys and the echo of voice commands came next. Inside the massive space, scientists and technicians had set to work.

"Feed."

The command came from Dr. Chang, a metallurgist known for his work with special alloys. Chang was hunched over a full-body monitor beside a two-tiered portable pumping station set against the bubbling tank.

"Conductive feed," said the tech assistant seated right below the metallurgist, at a second workstation.

Behind leaded glass at the base of the pump, steam hissed as liquefied adamantium flowed from the holding tank into the feeder tubes that snaked into the subject's containment unit.

"Steady . . . adamantium breakdown twenty-nine in one, sir," Dr. Chang warned. "I'll compensate."

The Professor shook his head without an ounce of concern. "It'll reduce. No problem."

Chang nodded. "Feed."

"Steady . . ."

"Feed."

"Cardiotach?" asked the Professor.

Carol Hines was about to glance at the heart monitor when Dr. Hendry barked, "High. Higher than we expected."

The tank looked like a simmering glass kettle; the figure inside bobbed as a cork would in boiling liquid. Subject X would either make scientific history or die a burning death.

Dr. Cornelius watched the procedure with tense anticipation. The room smelled more like a steel smelter than a medical lab or a makeshift operating room. An odor of burnt metal hung in the air, and in the last few minutes the temperature on the floor had increased several degrees. The reason for both: the holding container at one end of the room, glowing crimson-hot behind a thick wall of leaded glass. Inside, hundreds of pounds of molten adamantium steel were pressurized and primed to pump into the subject's body.

Cornelius knew that adamantium was the hardest substance in the universe. Developed in the 1940s by Dr. Myron MacLain, a United States government metallurgist, the alloy was created using a mixture of several top-secret resins including an infusion of the mysterious substance vibranium. In its liquefied form, adamantium was only malleable for approximately eight minutes, and only if maintained at a constant temperature of fifteen hundred degrees Fahrenheit. After four hundred and eighty seconds, the alloy would not bond to any other substance. This meant that any interruption during the critical pumping stage would be catastrophic.

Around Subject X's tank, the team supervised all facets of the process at computer terminals and medical monitors. One sound rose above the white noise of whirring machinery: the beep of the machine that measured heart rate, breathing, body temperature, and other body functions.

Dr. Chang's hands continued to play on his keyboard. Inside the leaded glass, the cloud of steam dissipated. "Steady . . ."

"Feed . . ."

"Suffusion enacting . . . now!"

The activity in the tank increased exponentially. As molten metal filled the feeder tubes, they superheated, then quickly transferred that thermal energy to the fluid inside the tank. In seconds, Subject X was totally obscured by a boiling chemical stew.

"Steady . . ."

"Feed."

At the monitor, Dr. Chang watched the molten adamantium seep into the subject's skeleton. On the ultrasonic image, it appeared as if the ghostly gray-white bones were being coated with black paint.

On his own display panel, the Professor magnified that same image several hundred times to observe the surface of the right femur. It was clear from the ultrasound that the nanochips were protecting the delicate fissures in the bones as well as the veins and capillaries that ran through them.

Cornelius watched the same data on his monitor and felt a mixture of triumph and relief. A few years ago, he believed that the process he just witnessed would be impossible. But the sheer vision of the Professor, the immense scientific progress of the program, and its vast resources made anything seem possible.

"Steady . . ."

"Things are going well, Doctor. I'm pleased."

It took a moment for Cornelius to realize the Professor had addressed him.

"Feed?"

"Suffusion?"

"Steady. Both steady," Dr. Chang replied, pushing a shiny black strand of hair away from his face.

As Cornelius watched, living tissue was being bonded to a metal alloy to create the world's first truly bionic organism. It was indeed history in the making, and Cornelius was moved to speak.

"This is an extraordinary experiment, Professor. I'm honored to be a part of it."

The Professor's thin lips curled into an expression more like a sneer than a smile. "Of course you are, Cornelius."

"Cardiotach?" This time it was the metallurgist who called for an immediate update.

Hendry shook his head. "Not good . . . I guess it's ANS."

"Feed."

Dr. MacKenzie spoke for the first time since the bonding procedure began. "Let's up the Pheno-B. Two points . . . no, one. Any more and he'll have beans for brains."

"Is there any reason for concern?" The Professor directed this question to the psychiatrist, but it was Hendry who answered.

"I don't believe so, Professor. You chose Subject X for his rather remarkable stamina. What we're getting here is his autonomic nervous system kicking in. He's a hard fellow—even unconscious."

"Chelation beginning," said Dr. Chang.

The mass of roiling bubbles around Subject X expanded outward as he began to thrash violently, bumping up against the glass walls.

"What was that?" the Professor demanded.

"Resistance, sir," MacKenzie replied.

"He's pulled a feeder tube!" the metallurgist cried. "Cut the flow to tube Nineteen B, use backup tubes A and C to compensate."

"Compensating."

"Maintain."

"Damn . . . resistance. More resistance," said Hendry, anxiously.

"Equalize."

"Feed."

"Impeded."

"Feed backup channel."

"Balance imminent," spoke the metallurgist. "Steady . . . steady . . . balance achieved."

The thrashing subsided. Molten steel continued to be pumped into the subject's twitching flesh.

"How's the REM interface holding up?" asked the Professor.

"It's at one hundred percent," Carol Hines replied. "I upped the amps to short out the subject's autonomic nerve functions. I believe that has corrected Dr. Hendry's ANS problem."

"Hendry . . . ANS?"

Hendry looked up from his monitors. "Subsiding, Professor. Nearly normal."

"Cardiotach, Miss Hines?"

She hesitated before answering, surprised that the Professor had called on her again. "Rising rapidly, sir. As of now, the heart rate is 198 per minute and increasing."

The Professor gritted his teeth. He found the subject's accelerated heart rate troubling.

"Diagnosis, Dr. Hendry?"

"Sir, I believe the nanotechnology is at fault—"

"Now, wait a minute—" Cornelius protested.

The Professor lifted his hand. "Clarify, Dr. Hendry . . ."

"On the ultrasound monitor, you can see gray flecks covering the skeleton which Cornelius tells us are his nanochips. Well, look at this—"

A magnification of the subject's heart muscle revealed the same gray-black specks lining the interior of all four chambers.

"I believe Dr. Cornelius's programming was incorrect. The nanochips treated the dense heart muscle like bone, with predictable results."

Cornelius was speechless. *Could I have been so wrong?*

The Professor frowned and spoke tersely. "Ms. Hines, would you please access the subject's medical profile and history? I studied it long enough, but I could have missed something."

"On-screen, sir," Hines said.

"Detail any cardio-abnormality."

"None, sir."

The Professor gazed in silence at the figure adrift in the tank. When he finally spoke, his tone was rueful. "You're really letting me down here, Cornelius. Why didn't you prepare for this in advance?"

Cornelius stared at the image. His nanochips still clustered around the valves—doing who knows how much damage to the subject's heart—when they should have been long gone.

Hell, they were long gone a few minutes ago. Why did some of them end up back inside his heart muscles?

"I thought I'd prepared for everything, Professor. But who could have foreseen this?"

The metallurgist interrupted them. "Sir, the rate of adamantium absorption should be twenty-four in one—"

"Of course."

"It's fifty-three in one, sir . . . and increasing."

For the first time since Cornelius met him, the Professor appeared baffled. He immediately called for an explanation from Carol Hines.

"It seems that Subject X's highly accelerated heart rate is draining the adamantium reservoir at three times the estimated speed of absorption," she explained.

An alarm sounded, interrupting them. Dr. Hendry analyzed the problem without looking up from his monitor.

"The subject's thrashing again. And there is some leakage in the tank. I detect trace amounts of adamantium."

"The damaged tube?" Hines offered.

"No," Hendry said at once. "The leak is coming from the subject's pores. He's passing adamantium through his sweat glands."

The Professor was suddenly alarmed. "Rejection?"

"More likely . . . elimination," Hendry replied. "His liver, his lymph nodes—they're dealing with the metal as they would a bacterial infection or a toxin. Some of the alloy is being filtered out, passing through his skin. Not enough to worry about, but . . ."

"This guy's liver functions must be phenomenal," said Dr. MacKenzie. "So efficient I doubt our boy can get drunk even if he wants to. That could also explain his resistance to drugs."

"My God! It might also explain the nanochips lodged in his heart," Cornelius declared.

"Explain, Doctor," said the Professor.

"The subject has phenomenal stamina, right? And we can see that his immune system is amazing, too—"

"Your point?"

"Those chips didn't travel to his heart on their own, and their programming wasn't flawed. They were forced back into the bloodstream by the subject's immune system!"

Cornelius whirled to face Hendry. "What's the white blood cell count inside the subject's heart?"

Hendry tapped his keyboard. "Elevated . . . Abnormally high, it's as if—"

"As if he's battling an infection." Cornelius faced the Professor. "That means his immune system was strong enough to kill a percentage of my chips, which are now being passed out of his body like waste matter, through the sweat glands."

The Professor digested the information. As his mind turned, his glasses seemed to dance with reflected light.

Dr. Cornelius glanced at the cardiotach, noting that the heart rate had stabilized.

"I can assure you that there'll be no further problems, Professor," he said. "Subject X's heart rate can't possibly go any higher or he'd be . . . well, a superman or something."

The Professor's head jerked as if stricken by Cornelius's observation. His pale flesh turned bone-white, and though he didn't speak, the Professor's jaws moved behind thin lips.

"We're going to pass the equalization point, sir. We'll

have to compensate on every channel," Chang's assistant warned.

Dr. Hendry was also perplexed. "So soon?"

"Astonishing," said Cornelius.

The technician paused, looking to the Professor for a decision. But Cornelius could see that the scientific genius was paralyzed, unable to take action, unable even to speak.

Cornelius stepped forward. "Refeed, then," he commanded. "On every channel."

Dr. Hendry blinked, but said nothing.

Guess I'm in charge—for the moment, Cornelius thought. *And if that's the case, I say we push the envelope . . . to the max. If this guy Logan can swallow so much adamantium without so much as burping, who knows what else he can do?*

"Feed?" the technician asked for confimation.

"Feed on all channels," said Dr. Chang, glancing at Cornelius.

"Compound feed. Maintain at Level Two."

"What's causing this, Doctor?" The speaker's hand dug into Cornelius's shoulder like a talon.

"Your guess, Professor, is as good as mine," Cornelius replied. "We've pumped enough Thorazine into the subject to drop a bullock, so the problem is obviously more than a cast-iron constitution or an auto-nervous anomaly."

"Doctor?" It was Carol Hines, her green eyes looking past the Professor to Cornelius. "I've some interesting data for you."

Cornelius—with the Professor in tow—approached the woman's terminal.

"According to Medfax, Subject X has been shot at least five times and survived each attack. Four to the trunk, one to the leg. He's also suffered a number of grave injuries."

Cornelius shrugged. "Tough geezer . . . We know this, Hines."

"But the bioscans, the ultrasound, show neither epidermal nor internal scar tissue. None whatsoever."

"Cornelius, didn't you say that the subject was hurt last night?"

"Yes, Professor." *Well, Hendry actually said it. I only saw some of the injuries.*

"Then where are his wounds?"

That gave Cornelius pause. He glanced at the figure in the tank, too shrouded in bubbles to make out details . . . only pale flesh, black hair drifting like a tattered banner.

"Hines, do you have any readings?" Cornelius asked, still staring at Logan.

"I have a trace," she said. "Some clotting around the mastoid. But an hour ago he had a dislocated jaw, cuts, abrasions. Now there's absolutely nothing."

Cornelius and the Professor mulled over the information as Carol Hines continued her report. "On the board there's a direct linear equation between the phenomenon and the intense cardio-activity. And . . ."

She hesitated.

"Well, I don't know how important this is . . . Seems silly. But Mr. Logan's hair has almost entirely grown back again in just twenty minutes. We shaved him a number of times. This anomaly was attributed to the tank's synthetic embryonic fluid."

The lab became very quiet as all eyes shifted to the subject in the tank. Only the steady beep of the biomonitors broke the silence.

"We seem to be in the midst of something unprecedented," Cornelius declared in an almost reverential tone. "Our Mr. Logan is somewhat more than human."

"Okay, I have to rethink this fast," said Dr. Hendry, who had joined the huddle. "If the patient's wounds are now healed, his heart rate could drop—be prepared to de-escalate at a second's notice. That's option one."

"What if the heart rate starts to climb again?" Hines asked.

"We go to option two," Hendry said. "If the rate continues to rise, pump equivalent noripenephrine to its ratio . . . but keep me informed of all changes."

Nobody was talking about killing Subject X anymore, Cornelius noted. *Probably because it's clear that whatever we do probably isn't going to hurt the guy, let alone kill him. At this point, I'm not sure anything we do can harm him . . .*

"Dr. Chang, Ms. Hines? Is the adamantium reservoir sufficient for all this . . . additional activity?"

"Sufficient at the current rate, Dr. Hendry."

Hendry slapped the console. "Not good enough. Go to reserve."

Carol Hines shifted her gaze to the Professor. "I'll need authorization from—"

"You have it, madam. Go to reserve adamantium, now."

The Professor's command was shouted over his shoulder as he strode to an access door leading to an auxiliary lab.

"Professor," Cornelius called. "I could use your advice on . . ."

The door closed shut. The Professor left without a word.

Dr. Cornelius scratched his bearded chin. "How do

you like that? We're in the middle of a crisis and he walks out."

What in blasted hell could be so important?

The Professor seethed. *That fool Cornelius wants my advice? Has he forgotten that he's here to give counsel, not receive it? I am the master here.*

Inside a small containment area off the main laboratory, the Professor closed a heavy hatch and activated the magnetic clamps to lock out the rest of the world. Behind him, a terminal automatically sprang to life. He began to punch a code known only to him into the desktop communicator, but suddenly paused. The Professor noticed his hands were shaking.

Absurd to be this rattled, he told himself. *I haven't been this unsteady since I began pulling the strings instead of being pulled by them.*

He completed the code and waited as a satellite picked up the feed and scrambled the communication.

"Speak." The voice on the other end echoed faintly, mildly distorted by a constant electronic hum.

"It is I," the Professor began.

A split-second delay as the transmission was coded. "You risk much by contacting me, Professor . . ."

"Yes, I know. But I have something to say—"

"What is so important that you choose to break established communications protocol?"

"The operation is proceeding right now—"

"And going well, I trust?"

"Yes—"

"Subject X will survive the bonding procedure?"

"Of course he'll survive it," the Professor stated, his

agitation increasing. "That's the point. You knew that Logan was a mutant."

Silence.

"This fact comes as quite a surprise," the Professor continued, his voice tight. "Why did you not inform me?"

"This conversation is risky, Professor. For both of us."

"No one can hear me. I'm in a sealed lab down the hall—"

"You should be with your patient."

"I can see the operation on a monitor. I must insist that you hear me out—"

The Professor sensed the Director was irritated by his call, but he had to press on. "Logan is a mutant. He has a superhuman power to regenerate damaged tissue. He is practically immortal, and yet you don't inform me of this important factor?"

"That information was available to me, it is true. But Logan's mutant status was classified—on a need-to-know basis—and you, Professor, did not need to know."

"I'm in there with that backwoods Cornelius and my staff, and this, this girl—practically a typist—discovers the truth about Logan by pushing a few buttons on her blasted computer!"

"Your point?"

"It makes me look like I don't know anything. I had to leave the operating room in case they asked me any questions about it. I felt like a fool!" The Professor hated himself the moment he'd confessed it. His voice betrayed him as a whiny child and he was repulsed.

The Director chuckled. "You sound angry, Professor."

"Yes . . ." He forced the calm back into his voice. The control. "You could say I'm a bit put out."

"But according to you, the procedure is going as planned."

"You don't understand . . . I'm supposed to be in control of these people. How can I give even an illusion of that if I'm not thoroughly briefed by you?"

Silence.

The Professor sought to quell his anger. He knew Director X did not like emotional displays, nor did he respect weakness. When the Professor spoke again, his voice was steady, devoid of expression.

"Do you not trust me?" he asked, then immediately regretted asking the question. *Damn it!*

The Professor hardly listened to the reply, for the Director's response was unnecessary. Of course Director X did not trust him. The mere fact that the Director withheld such critical information about the subject spoke volumes to the Professor regarding Logan, the experiment, the Director's priorities, and the Professor's own place in the scheme of things.

"I see," said the Professor at last. "Then I have one last question."

"Yes?"

"What else do I not know about Experiment X?"

This time, there was no reply. The Director had ended the call.

Back in the laboratory, the rate of adamantium bonding had increased threefold. Dr. Chang suggested that a leak might be the culprit, so Carol Hines and Dr. Hendry searched their monitors for evidence of one.

"The channels are sufficient, Doctor, but there's an excess drain at . . . wait a moment . . . at the *flexor brevis— minima digiti* section."

Cornelius's first-year anatomy classes were too far behind him. "Plain language, please, Ms. Hines."

"Sorry. The hands and wrists, sir."

Cornelius stood behind the woman, gazing at the monitor. He glanced at Hendry, hoping for answers. But the man's angular face and square jaw were tense. It was clear he didn't know what to make of the alloy leakage, either.

"Not much of this so-called leak is showing up in the tank," Cornelius observed. "Less than one part for one hundred thousand. But the adamantium has to be going somewhere. It can't be collecting at his wrists—what would it bond with?"

Cornelius shook his head. "We're going to need some advice on this . . . Anybody know where the Professor is?"

Blank stares.

"No? Have him paged, then."

After a moment, loudspeakers boomed with an exasperated voice. "Cornelius? What is all the fuss?"

Cornelius looked around for a communicator, then spoke. "Professor, where are you?"

"What do you want, Doctor?"

Cornelius realized that the Professor could hear everything. *This lab is obviously bugged. How many other rooms are wired? Are they watching us right now?*

"We have a new problem," Cornelius began. "Could you return to the operating room?"

"I'm busy . . . What is the problem now?"

"There's an excess adamantium drain to the *minima . . . flexor*—the hands and wrists. We can't account for it and we're unable to stop it from occurring."

A long silence followed.

"Uh, Professor? Did you hear me?"

"Of course."

"Well, then—"

"It's all part of my program, Cornelius. Do you think I don't know what I'm doing?"

"No, sir. Of course not—"

"Continue with the procedure, and the wrap-up when the bonding is completed."

"Then you won't be returning to the lab?"

Another long silence. This time, Cornelius realized the Professor had cut him off.

Carol Hines looked up at Cornelius. "And the leak, Doctor?"

"It doesn't appear life-threatening, nor is it interfering with the procedure, so we're going to ignore it. Let's finish this up, shall we? We'll try to find out what happened with the leakage in the post-op examination and evaluation phase."

The intercom buzzed, the sound filling the cramped quarters, waking the man in the bunk. Cutler sat up and punched the button. "Cutler here," he said, rubbing his eyes.

"Your Boy Scout has been camped outside my office for the last few hours," Major Deavers barked. "Your idea, I presume?"

Cutler chuckled a bit. "Just wanted Agent Franks to familiarize himself with all the personnel and procedures around here."

"Franks is on his way to the main lab to pick up Subject X. Meet him there. This time, you won't need EH gear."

"So the operation's over?"

"And the patient has apparently survived. Go get him, then escort Subject X to a new holding facility—Lab Two."

Cutler nodded and keyed the intercom. "No containment facilities there. That means the patient's out of the soup?"

"Yeah, for good. He's going to maximum security bio-monitoring cell for post-op surveillance. Some technical types will be there to meet you and hook him up."

"Roger that. Out."

Cutler stepped into his standard-issue green overalls and brushed back his hair with his hand. Then he exited his quarters and rode the elevator down to the main laboratory.

When the doors opened, Cutler noticed that the huge tank was completely drained of fluid. Wires lay coiled at the bottom of the tank. Like fairy dust, twinkling silver specks of hard adamantium dotted the inside surfaces of the Plexiglas walls.

Next to the tank, in a powered wheelchair, Subject X slumped, head tucked into his hairy chest. Logan was naked and still damp from the post-op chemical bath. His hair hung down in wet ringlets.

Cutler did a double take. *Wasn't he shaved the last time I saw him? Strange.*

Agent Franks stood over the subject, a look of disgust marring his young face.

"Sickened?" Cutler asked as he sidled up to the young officer.

Franks shrugged. "Kinda, I guess. He's still got all those probes and wires sticking out of him. That's gotta hurt."

"Doesn't look like he's feeling much pain. Bastard's zonked. Out like a light."

"Geez, look at this," said Franks.

Cutler circled the chair to find thick wires coiled around a hook on the seat back.

"All those wires are still plugged into him," Franks said.

Cutler nodded. "Let get the subject to Lab Two. The medicos are waiting. Maybe then we can call it a day."

7

The Mutant

A thousand nails grinding into my back. My arms. My legs. Gouging. Slashing. Burning . . .

Logan slid helplessly down the crumbling slope. Roots and jagged rocks shredded the flight suit and ripped into his flesh. Loose stones battered his helmet in a clattering wall of noise. His cracked visor shimmered with psychedelic light—bright visual chaos from his malfunctioning Heads Up Display. And in his grip, tight against the skin of his tattered stealth suit, Logan clutched the black-clad stranger in a bear hug.

Blind, deaf, and unable to stop his precipitous tumble, Logan risked losing his captive to rid himself of the useless helmet. But when he let go, the stranger hung on, arms around his neck. Logan's fingers fumbled with the latch at his throat. With a hiss, the helmet detached. Blinking against a tide of dirt that pummeled his eyes, Logan spied a tall shape looming in the darkness.

He seized the handle of the Randall Mark I at his belt. As he tobogganed toward the tree, he tore the all-purpose knife free of its Velcro scabbard. Then he stabbed outward.

A hollow thud as the seven-inch blade bit deep into

the wood—then a jolt that nearly tore the handle from his grip. The earth disappeared under him in a shower of rocks and dust. Logan's feet dangled over an abyss. Hundreds of feet below, the man-made lake shimmered in the pallid moonlight.

Logan gripped the knife with both hands while his captive held on to him. Muscles straining against their combined weight, he hung for a moment—long enough to feel a warm, wet stream of sweat course down his ravaged back. Then Logan slowly hauled them both onto a ledge formed by the tree's twisted roots. As he swung his leg over the edge, his captive squirmed up over his shoulders and around the tree. Turning, the shadowy figure helped pull Logan the rest of the way, then collapsed into a heap at the base of the tree. Panting from the strain of saving both their lives, Logan lay on his side. When the figure rose, Logan reached up and closed his fingers around the stranger's arm.

"You. My prisoner," Logan snarled in passable Korean.

To his surprise, there was no resistance. Instead, the stranger used the other hand to pull away the dark commando mask. Logan stared up at almond-shaped eyes filled with concern.

"Are you hurt?" the woman whispered, kneeling at his side.

Logan recognized her accent and hissed a reply in the woman's native tongue. Japanese. *"O-namae wa?"*

"English, please, Mr. Logan," she said in a voice barely above a whisper. "General Koh has deployed hundreds of audio sensors in these hills. If we are heard, better to be in your language than mine. Many of Koh's agents understand Japanese."

Logan grunted and rolled onto his back. Then he

winced and sat up. Even in the dim light, the woman could see the dark stain on the ground where he'd collapsed.

"You're hurt . . . bleeding."

Logan shook her away. "Give me a minute and I'll be all better." His tone was edged with bitterness, and the woman gave him a curious stare, her small, round face washed in the moonlight.

Then she rose, and Logan watched as she inspected the harness and belt that circled her trim, formfitting night camouflage suit. A lot of equipment had been hung on the woman's diminutive frame, and from the expression that marred her dainty features, some of it had been lost.

"You still haven't answered my question. How do you know my name, but I don't know yours?" Still on the ground, Logan cautiously unzipped the sheath of the Heckler & Koch G36 strapped to his leg. The woman detected the move and drew her own weapon—a sleek black USP 45 Tactical.

Big toy for a little lady.

She noticed his reaction, and a smile touched her full lips. "I am Agent Miko Katana, Japanese National Police, Tokyo Prefecture."

Logan blinked in surprise. "A cop? You're a cop!"

"Hardly a cop, as you say," she replied. "I'm a member of the Special Assault Team."

"You're still a cop. So explain to me, Officer—what the hell is a Japanese detective doing in the middle of North Korea?"

"The same thing you are doing, Mr. Logan."

"And what would that be?"

As he spoke, Logan freed his automatic rifle and

placed it on the ground—far enough away to gain some trust but close enough to grab if he needed to. Miko understood the gesture and holstered her Tac.

"Truce, Mr. Logan?" she said, brushing aside straight hair that fell around her pixie face in a silky black curtain.

"Maybe," he replied, rising. "But only if you'll tell me where you got my itinerary."

"Itinerary? That is very funny."

"Cut to the chase or I'm cutting you loose, Agent Katana," growled Logan, no longer amused.

Miko frowned, then spoke. "French intelligence has been operating a deep mole inside of Canada's military community for a number of years. At times they share information with SAT. Nothing of much consequence, usually. But two days ago, a GIGN operative in the South Pacific tipped us off to your mission, provided the details—"

"What kind of details?"

"We know there is another operative involved," she replied, "Agent Neil Langram. We know the location of your landing zones, your time over target, and your final objective. We also know how and where you'll be extracted when the mission is concluded."

Logan considered her story. *The woman could be bluffing, but I doubt it.*

France's Groupe d'Intervention Gendarmerie Nationale was one of the most active counterterrorism forces in the world. Unfortunately, they weren't always on the same side as the Canadians, and it bothered Logan that the French learned about his mission, then passed on the details to a third party.

"What you just told me is a keg of political dynamite waiting to explode—if it's true," hissed Logan.

"Why would I lie?"

"Why would you tell the truth?"

"Perhaps as a gesture to gain your trust, Mr. Logan. Perhaps because I require your help."

Logan picked up his G36, twirled it, and thrust it back into its holster. "Now, why would I help you?"

"Does it matter to you that lives hang in the balance? That an entire nation may be at risk?"

"Probably not."

The woman's expression hardened, her tiny hand caressed the handle of her automatic.

"Mr. Logan, I do not care how you feel or what you believe. You must help me get inside the complex below before it is too late . . . if it is not too late already."

"Abe . . . Abe, please . . . Please, wake up . . ."

Dr. Cornelius heard his wife's plea, but her voice—like her image—seemed spectral and very far away.

"It's Paul . . . he's crying again. His fever is raging. I'm afraid he'll burn up," Madeline cried. "We have to take him to the emergency room. We must go now!"

Over the sound of his wife's sobs, Cornelius heard the agonized scream of his infant son. Suddenly on his feet, Cornelius found himself moving in slow motion, his legs hindered as though he were running through an ocean of glue.

"I'm coming!" he pleaded, pushing against the clinging tide.

But no matter how he struggled, how he raged, Cornelius's every step forward seemed to carry him back. His heart pounded against his rib cage, threatening to burst. He redoubled his efforts, yet his legs failed to carry him to his child.

Finally, Cornelius burst through the sea of milky fog to reach his son's bedroom. The colorful wallpaper glowed in front of his eyes like a hundred computer screens; the toys hanging over the crib looked ominous, twisted—long steel spikes, six-inch hypodermic needles, blood-flecked surgical probes.

When Cornelius stared down into the crib, Paul Phillip, his son, was gone. In the boy's place, Subject X—his flesh pierced with a thousand steel thorns—lay on bloody sheets.

Cornelius heard a scream and bolted upright. A pen slipped from his limp hand and clattered to the floor. He reached up to adjust the mashed glasses on his face, then tossed them on the keyboard in front of him. Rubbing the sleep out of his eyes, he pushed himself away from the computer terminal.

Must have been more tired than I thought . . . Passed right out.

The intercom buzzed only once. On his monitor, Cornelius saw the pinched face of an earnest young technician who was manning the observation booth adjacent to Lab Two. Cornelius didn't know the name of the young technician working "status tech" and it didn't matter, anyway. Wearily, the doctor pulled on his glasses, then punched the key.

"Cornelius here . . . Status?"

"Resting, Doctor. But he's on the ground, not on his cot."

The technician tapped a key, and the view from Lab Two filled the monitor. Cornelius saw Logan sprawled out on the floor on top of a bed of coiled tubes and wires—eyes closed, chest heaving. Body hair now covered the subject's chest, arms, legs, genitals. On the right-hand side of Cornelius's screen, a toolbar supplied real-time data on the subject's temperature, respiration, blood pressure, heart rate, and electrolyte balance.

"S'okay. Anything to report?" Cornelius could see the young man was concerned about something, though the readings were well within the normal range.

"No, sir . . . except . . ."

A complication? Absolutely impossible. Subject X was making a remarkable recovery.

"What?"

"Well, you know," the technician began. "Looks like this guy's really been through the mill."

"Uh, yeah," Cornelius replied.

What does this technician want me to say? Cornelius wondered. *That I feel bad for the subject? That I think it's wrong to put another human being through this kind of torment? That the Professor is inhumanly cruel? The Weapon X program misguided and sick?*

"Keep a close eye on him," Cornelius said before ending the transmission. *So I don't have to.*

Dr. Cornelius glanced at the digital clock. *It's three in the morning. Jesus. No wonder I'm so exhausted. Maybe I should call it a night?*

He rose and stretched his back, which had been bent over the computer terminal when he'd fallen asleep. He reached out to power down his workstation when the intercom buzzed again.

Stifling a yawn, Cornelius answered.

"Doctor? He just woke up." This time, the technician sounded nervous.

"How does he look?"

"Like cow flop, Dr. Cornelius."

Logan appeared on Cornelius's monitor. Subject X seemed to be in the same position as before, only his eyes were open and staring blank and unseeing, at the opposite wall.

"Is he moving?"

"No. Just staring."

Better leave my terminal active, Cornelius decided. *Just in case something really does go wrong.*

"Okay," Cornelius told the younger man. "Keep monitoring. Call me if anything happens. Out."

Cornelius kicked off his shoes and stripped off his lab coat to drape it over his chair. Then, still fully clothed, he stretched out on the bunk, tucked his glasses into his shirt pocket, and closed his heavy eyes.

Almost immediately, he slipped into a deep, dreaming sleep . . .

"So, Clete. You've seen the results. What do you conclude?"

"Do you really need a second opinion, Abe?"

Dr. Cornelius nodded. "I'm a research scientist. You're the practicing physician. Now, what's your diagnosis, Doctor?"

Dr. Cletus Forester pulled thick bifocals from the pocket of his pale green lab coat. Holding them to his face without opening them, he studied the results of a battery of tests he'd performed. Unfortunately, they mirrored the first set of charts provided by the child's pediatrician.

"The, er . . . patient's white blood cell count is far higher than normal, even for a child five times the boy's age," Dr. Forester began. "If you didn't know this from your own work, your pediatrician probably told you that children have lousy immune systems—which is why they're sick all the time."

"But not Paul?"

Forester shook his head. "Your son is different. His antibodies are through the roof, and they're busy little bastards, too—killing everything in sight. Persistent generalized lymphadenopathy is present—"

"Those lumps on his neck, under his arms?" Cornelius asked.

Forester nodded. "The groin, too. The lumps haven't shown up on the boy's skin yet, but they will soon. Only a matter of time. You say the fever is chronic?"

"Above one hundred at all times—but spiking to one hundred and two or even one hundred and three at night," Cornelius replied.

"Night sweats?"

"Every night, practically. Some mornings the sheets are soaked. My son . . ."

Cornelius paused, biting back emotion. When he spoke again, his tone was neutral. "Paul sheds fluids as fast as I can pump them into him. When the bad bouts occur, he's on an IV constantly. Even then, his electrolyte balance is totally shot to hell."

"There are signs of connective tissue disease," Forester added.

"Systemic lupus erythematosus?" Cornelius said, surprised. "So Paul's crying might be related to joint or muscle pain . . . damn . . . I never considered the possibility of lupus."

Dr. Forrester slowly shook his head. "Not lupus. Not precisely. Something like systemic lupus erythematosus. Something we've never seen before."

Cornelius, lost in thought, rubbed his chin. "I was reluctant to use painkillers, but now . . ."

"Use painkillers. Alleviate the boy's suffering," Forester said.

Cornelius looked up. "But there must be more I can do . . . a treatment to reverse the organ damage? Maybe a synthetic antibody to fight the antibodies he's producing . . ."

"Look, I'm sorry to tell you this, Abe," Forester said. "But, to be blunt, you're grasping at straws. You've obviously arrived at the same conclusion I have, or you wouldn't have sought a second opinion."

Cornelius looked up as if stung. "What are you saying, Clete?"

"We . . . we both know that your son's condition is fatal . . . that it's only a matter of time."

Cornelius looked away. "I haven't accepted that prognosis."

"Come on, Abe!" Forester cried. "Paul's immune system is forming antibodies that are attacking the cell nuclei. His DNA. RNA. Cell proteins. Phospholipids. It's only a matter of time before the organs are degraded and fail . . . one by one. Maybe three months. Four at the outside."

Behind his bottle-thick glasses, Cornelius's eyes burned. "I haven't given up. Not yet."

"But there's no cure—"

"I'll find one."

"—And probably there will never be a cure," Forester insisted. "In any case, it would take years, maybe decades, just to isolate the underlying cause of the condition. And more years trying to find a treatment to alleviate the suffering, never mind a cure."

Forester placed his arm on Cornelius's shoulder. When he spoke again, it was as a friend, not a physician. "Abe. Listen to me and accept what I'm telling you for your own good.

"The patient . . . your son, Paul . . . doesn't have decades, or even years. Prepare yourself for the worst. Grieve when the time comes, and get on with your life."

It seemed as if he'd just closed his eyes for a moment when the intercom buzzed again.

Cornelius rolled off the bunk and stumbled to the terminal. He keyed the speaker, then fumbled with his glasses.

"Doctor?"

The same technician, now looking positively frantic.

"Yes . . . Status. What is it?"

"He's moving now."

"Violently?"

The technician paused. "He just leaned forward a bit."

You woke me up for that? Cornelius thought.

"Status . . ."

"Yes, sir."

"You don't have to tell me every time the patient shifts weight."

"Yes, sir . . . sorry, sir." The technician vanished.

That's it, Cornelius concluded. *After twenty-two hours on my feet, I need some rest.*

Cornelius stooped over the keyboard and pounded out a short message instructing the status tech to direct all inquiries to the Professor for the next two hours.

If the tech wants to go into panic mode before his shift ends, Cornelius figured that the Professor can deal with it.

But before he could power-down his terminal, Cornelius received yet another call.

"Status?" he answered.

"The patient's fine, sir. But he seems alert now."

Cornelius was suddenly wide awake. "He's aware?"

"He's just staring at his hands."

"Hands?"

"Yeah. The wires on his hands."

Cornelius recalled that Dr. Hendry put post-op bioscan monitors on the subject's hands in an effort to find out where the extra adamantium ended up collecting. Both Hendry and Chang feared that Subject X would lose mobility in his hands if too much adamantium accumulated around the delicate bones of his fingers.

"I'd better come over," Cornelius told the man. "Call the Professor. Have him meet me there. Out."

"I have desperate need of your help or I would not ask, Mr. Logan," Miko Katana said. "Lives hang in the balance—"

"So you mentioned," Logan replied. "But you'd better preach to the choir, 'cause I'm not buying."

"Please, Mr. Logan, hear me out before you judge."

Standing on the ledge that hung over the dam and the man-made lake, Logan faced the woman, eyes level with hers.

"Two weeks ago, a Japanese research scientist was kidnapped while visiting Seoul. SAT intelligence uncovered evidence that the man was snatched by agents working for General Koh because of the knowledge the scientist possessed."

"Knowledge of weapons, no doubt," said Logan. "It's

no secret that the North Koreans have a nuclear program up and running. It's a delivery system they lack—rockets and missiles. So let me guess—the missing scientist is a rocketry expert? A whiz at telemetry? Is that what you're hinting at?"

"I am not at liberty to discuss the doctor's work."

"Lady, you're not giving me squat."

"I am telling you what you need to know—nothing else."

"So basically you want me to help you get inside that facility—but you won't tell me why beyond some bullshit about people in danger. Then, once we're inside, we're supposed to find some guy who has been kidnapped, but you won't tell me who he is or why he was snatched. And you keep talking about some guy named General Koh, who has a hand in all of this—yet I never heard Koh's name in any of my intelligence assessments. Who is this Koh?"

"General Koh is a Japanese problem that does not concern you," she replied.

Her answer didn't surprise him. "Look, babe, I've got to know a bit more."

But Logan's demand was met with a wall of silence and an unwavering stare. Time was ticking by. Logan would soon be behind schedule—and his tardiness would jeopardize the success of the mission, putting Neil Langram at risk, too.

"Okay, you win," Logan said at last. "You can come with me, but only because I'm lonely."

And because your team obviously has better intelligence than mine. And in the spy game, knowledge is power—the kind that can save your life.

"Thank you, Mr. Logan. I promise I will not compromise your mission, even if it jeopardizes my own."

"Fair enough."

Miko Katana reached for a pack at her belt. "Before we start, let me patch you up. You must be in terrible pain."

The woman stepped around Logan and examined his blood-stained back. But when she began to clean his wounds, Miko got a huge surprise.

"I . . . I do not understand. A few minutes ago, your back was covered with lacerations. Now your wounds are nearly healed!"

"It's like I told you," Logan replied. "Give me a couple of minutes and I'll be all better."

"This is not normal," Miko replied.

"Yeah, tell me about it."

"But how do you do this?"

"Good genes," Logan said with bitterness.

Miko accepted his explanation and set out to clean the wounds that remained. When she was done, Logan tore off the remains of his high-tech stealth suit, then popped open a metal canister that had been hooked to his belt. He dumped a tight black bundle the size of a bar of soap into his right palm. As he worked it in his hands, the bundle expanded until Logan finally shook it out. When the formfitting camouflage suit was completely unfurled, Logan stripped off the rest of his gear and donned fresh clothing.

While he changed, Miko shyly averted her eyes. She cautiously crawled to the very edge of the cliff to observe the dam through miniature binoculars.

"See anything?" Logan asked as he snapped his utility belt around his waist.

"Just normal activity. The North Koreans do not seem to be aware of our presence."

"That's great," said Logan as he hefted his G36 and fed a round into the chamber. "Because I've had just about enough surprises for one night."

8

Unforeseen Consequences

Despite the hour—nearly dawn—sleep eluded the Professor, as sleep always had, since early childhood. He sat rigid and alert on his ergonomic throne, grateful for the timelessness of his command center, where he could ignore the twenty-four-hour cycle and utterly dispense with the sleep ritual—at least until physical and mental exhaustion forced him to retreat into dreamless slumber.

Fortunately, that happened with less frequency. In the past few months, as the Weapon X project came to fruition, he marveled at how much more he was able to accomplish without the need for sleep. How uncluttered and crystallized his thought processes had become without the uncontrolled fancies of dreams or nightmares.

The entire Weapon X program would have been impossible without my sacrifice, my constant vigilance, the Professor reflected. *All I ever wanted was success—which is why the Director's reckless action is such a betrayal.*

Flickering unseen on his central monitor were images from Lab Two, where Subject X lay in a post-operative stupor. The laborious procedure had gone well—so well that the Professor didn't need to look at the medical data to know that his patient would make a full and rapid recovery.

That issue was never in any doubt. The patient was destined to survive because Director X stacked the deck to ensure success. *Perhaps I should thank him . . . Thank him for jeopardizing the project, years of work. Thank him for his lies, his treachery.*

But no thanks were possible. The Professor felt only a huge burning rage.

Why did the Director exclude me from such a critical decision? Why risk a rigidly structured experiment by adding a wild card— a mutant? Who knows what variables have been added to the equation? What surprises might be buried in the subject's DNA? What unforeseen consequences may arise?

As a scientist, the Professor understood that the most important factor in any experiment was total control of all its aspects. Nothing could be left to chance.

But with his careless decision, the Director has wrested that control from me.

The Professor's intention was to develop a procedure to turn human beings into weapons of terror—the first step toward creating an entire army of mindless supermen under his rigid control. But now he didn't even know if his process worked on humans, because it had only been attempted with a mutant.

The only way I can salvage what remains of this project is to seize control of the reins once more—find a way to reassert my will, my vision of the Weapon X program . . . which means I will have to take complete charge of the psychological conditioning phase of Subject X through my own surrogates.

Of course I will have to push aside Hendry, MacKenzie, and anyone who has resisted my ideas and questioned my vision.

The Professor clenched his fists in a vain effort to still his quavering hands. He couldn't keep them still.

Look at me now, he thought without a trace of self-pity. *I am incapable of controlling my own reflexes. How can I hope to regain control of the experiment? Of this facility? Of Weapon X?*

The sudden buzz of the intercom startled him, shattered his intense concentration.

On the central monitor the image of Subject X—now conscious—was abruptly replaced by the apprehensive face of a very young technician, eyes wide behind delicate glasses.

"Uh, Professor, sir? This is the status tech worker at Lab Two."

"Yes, what is it?"

"Dr. Cornelius asked me to—"

Suddenly the youth on the monitor began to babble. "Oh God! Oh my God!" he howled, eyes wide.

"What is it, man?" the Professor demanded, jumping to his feet.

"Blood," the technician gasped. "Something's happening . . . oh God. More blood—it's spurting out of his hands!"

Behind double panes of three-inch-thick Plexiglas, a technician frantically pounded a keyboard. His mouth gaped, his jaws moved, but his shouts were muted by the observation booth's soundproof walls.

Inside Lab Two, Subject X thrashed on a bed of tangled wires and coiled tubes, writhing in paroxysms of relentless, stabbing torment. What began as a dull ache in his wrists had rapidly detonated into intolerable agony. Now Logan's hands twitched uncontrollably, and the thick muscle that sheathed his wrists burned and quivered under bruised, tortured flesh. On his corded biceps, veins bulged until they threatened to burst.

Teeth gritted, an animal moan escaped his blood-flecked lips. His arms jerked in violent spasms that yanked a battery of medical probes from his flesh. Sparks rained down from shorted monitors and shattered probes. Logan's arms flailed wildly, splattering a crimson spray on walls, ceiling, Plexiglas panes.

As he staggered to his feet, beads of sweat appeared on Logan's forehead and neck, to run in rivulets down his torso. He reeled at his first halting step, his joints afire. Heart pounding at an inhuman rate, the veins on his forehead, neck, and forearms swelled and then throbbed. Blood started from his gums, his nose. Red stained his cheeks, as blood flowed like tears.

Finally, Logan dropped to his knees and threw back his head. His mouth gaped, and in a spray of blood-foamed spittle he unleashed a howl of mortal anguish.

"Status . . . where is Cornelius?"

As he spoke, the Professor attempted to pull up images from Lab Two, but something—probably the subject's thrashing—had shorted out much of the system. The only camera he managed to activate projected a red smear—its lens splashed with blood.

"Oh God, sir! I need help here. I'm all alone. I'm not trained for this."

"Listen to me, man!" barked the Professor. "Patch me into your monitors. I want to see."

"Yes . . . yes, sir."

A moment later, Subject X appeared on the Professor's monitor. Logan was on his knees, probes ripped free to dangle from the ceiling, the walls, like chains in a dungeon. A hundred wounds seeped black blood. Shattered probes protruded from his spine like porcupine needles.

Despite the horrific tableau, the Professor dispassionately observed that the subject's mouth was open in what he presumed was a sustained scream.

How tragic that the sound system has failed. I must remember to view the surveillance tapes later . . . listen to his shrieks . . . assess the level of pain he experienced.

The panicked voice of the tech interrupted his thoughts. "Sir . . . should I go in there and help him?"

"Uh—" *Intriguing idea.* "No. Not yet, Status."

"But he must be in terrible pain, sir."

The Professor smiled. "Yes. I think you are right."

On the monitor, Logan was still on his knees, his face buried in his chest, fists clenching and unclenching spasmodically. The subject screamed again and stared in dazed horror at his own wrists.

Suddenly, the Professor's ears were battered by Logan's inhuman howl. Impressed that the anxious technician had managed to restore the sound as well as the visuals, the Professor quickly lowered the volume, then looked back at the screen.

The image came as a shock. Awestruck, the Professor cried out. "Look at that!"

At Logan's wrists, on the backs of his hands, anguished flesh began to bulge and stretch. He doubled over, the movement tearing out the last remaining medical probes in a fountain of blood. As the subject's cries intensified, the Professor lowered the volume again— thankfully not enough to miss the wet, ripping sound of three razor sharp points bursting through the epidermis of the mutant's hand.

Over the auxiliary monitor, the Professor heard the technician scream like a child.

"You said you're all alone in Lab Two, didn't you?" asked the modulated voice.

Pause. "Yes, sir."

"I'll summon a security team." The Professor opened the glass hood that covered the emergency alarm, fully intending to alert Major Deavers to the potential crisis. But as his finger hovered over the red button, the Professor discovered that his formerly shaky hands were now as steady as a rock.

"God! He's got . . . nails . . . spikes coming out of him. Right out of his hands! What do I do?" the technician gasped.

"Stay calm. Help is on the way."

The Professor's eyes remained locked on the figure in Lab Two. Three clawlike appendages—a total of six of them now—protruded from each of the subject's hands. About thirty-one centimeters in length, slightly curved, and coated with adamantium steel, the claws appeared to be sharp-edged.

Where did they come from? How firmly are they rooted to the subject's skeleton? Does he control the deployment of his claws, or is their extension a reflex action?

So many questions . . .

One thing the Professor knew for certain. *Those . . . claws . . . no doubt caused Subject X excruciating agony as they extended.*

"God, Professor, more blood. He needs help, right now."

"Listen to me," the Professor commanded. "Do you . . . do you have access to the patient's cell from the observation booth?"

"Yes, sir, I do."

"And you're sure the subject needs medical assistance?"

"God, he must!" the technician replied.

"Then you should go in there and try to help the poor man."

A long pause. "Yes . . . I'll do that, sir. If . . . if you say so."

"I believe you should," said the Professor. "And be sure to close the security door after you enter the cell. Just to be safe."

On the auxiliary monitor the Professor saw the technician nod, his face ashen.

"Good lad . . . run along."

Dr. Cornelius stopped at the dispensary for a cup of coffee before heading down to Lab Two. As he waited for the pot to brew, he attempted to contact the observation booth on the wall intercom.

"Status? Status? This is Cornelius. Come in . . ."

No reply, so he beeped the booth again.

Come on, Status, you've been bothering me all night. Why won't you pick up now?

Cornelius began to worry after three attempts went unanswered. At the very least, Status Tech was violating the project's protocol by ignoring his call.

Cornelius spun on his heels and hurried out of the dispensary without his coffee. The aroma had attracted two members of the security team, who were due on the outside perimeter for the sunrise shift change. Both were swathed in Kevlar body armor, though the older man neglected to don his helmet.

"You and you!" barked Cornelius. "Come with me!"

"Yes, sir," Franks replied crisply.

"Something wrong, sir?" asked Cutler.

Cornelius shrugged. "Could be. I don't know for sure. Please just stick close."

The guards followed him into an elevator. They rode down to Level Two in silence, though Franks and Cutler exchanged anxious glances when they discovered their destination. They'd been on Level Two hours before, delivering Subject X to the technicians.

Sure enough, Dr. Cornelius led them to Lab Two, though he paused at the security door.

"The lab worker here, what's his name?"

"Not sure, doc," Cutler replied. "Cal or Cole or something."

"He's new, sir. Just met him today," said Franks.

"New?" Cornelius was perplexed. "If he's new, then he shouldn't be in this section."

Cornelius punched the security code into the keypad and entered the observation booth, Cutler and Franks bringing up the rear. The doctor was surprised to find the booth empty, the power off save for dim emergency lights. The monitors were blank, and a smell of ozone and burnt plastic hovered in the air. On the other side of the Plexiglas wall, Lab Two was pitch-black.

Cornelius bit back a curse. "If he left without authority, I'll have that kid's hide for a drum." He scanned the console, searching for a light switch. Cutler found it first.

As the lights came up, they heard a sudden scream that ended abruptly in a wet gurgle.

On the other side of the Plexiglas, in the center of the lab, the missing technician lay sprawled on a bed of coiled tubing, shattered electrodes, and twisted wires. Blood spurted from his mangled throat. The man's eyes were pleading, his arms and legs twitched as his lifeblood pooled around him.

Hunched over his victim as if he were watching him die, Subject X stood—bloodstained and naked. His corded arms outspread. Protruding through bloody holes in both hands—six curved adamantium steel claws.

"Good Lord! What the hell happened here? This is horrific!" Cornelius exclaimed.

"He's dead, he's dead!" cried Franks, averting his eyes.

Only Cutler kept his senses. He triggered the alarm and activated the security system, which sealed all the doors between levels. But even through soundproof walls, the men in the booth could hear the Klaxon's wail.

Franks slowly backed away as the figure on the other side of the Plexiglas locked eyes with him. "Is that him? Is that Subject X?" he stammered.

"It's Subject X!" Cornelius cried. "That's my patient, but God . . . what's happening to him?"

"He murdered the boy," said Cutler. "He's covered in blood. Used those knives coming out of his hands."

Behind his thick, round glasses, the scientist's eyes narrowed curiously. "They look like claws."

"He looks like a rabid animal," Cutler shot back.

Franks stepped up. "Sir, we'll get guns and blow the thing away."

"Too late for that," said Cornelius. "Too late for anything."

"You're right," said Cutler. "It is too late. That son of a bitch is about to come right through the panel."

Cornelius snorted. "Ridiculous. That's four inches of Plexiglas. He's tough, but—"

The clear plastic wall exploded outward, showering Cornelius, Cutler, and Franks with a pelting crystalline hail. From the middle of the whirlwind, a howling figure leaped into the observation booth to face them. Cutler heard an angry snarl as Subject X dropped into a crouch, ready to spring.

On his central monitor, the Professor watched the chaos in Lab Two with joy. The frantic cries of Cornelius and the security men were music to his ears.

"It's Subject X! But God . . . what's happening to him?"

"He murdered the boy . . . covered in blood. Used those knives . . . out of his hands."

The auxiliary monitors scattered around the console provided real-time windows to the manic activity in other parts of the facility. From Level One Security, Major Deavers and a team of wranglers hurried to the elevator. In the OR, physicians and technicians assembled to deal with the emergency medical needs of Subject X.

". . . look like claws . . ."

"He looks like a rabid animal . . ."

". . . get guns and blow the thing away . . ."

"Too late for that. Too late for any—"

The Professor touched a button and cut the audio, his hand as steady as the finest surgeon on his staff.

Weapon X is already a success, the Professor realized. *The subject has more potential for mindless violence than even I imagined or ever could have hoped.*

Logan's primary instinct . . . perhaps his only instinct . . . was for destruction. When he viciously slashed that technician's throat—an innocent who only tried his best to alleviate the subject's pain—Weapon X acted on instinct, unclouded by mercy or reason. In a word, the subject's performance was . . .

"Magnificent."

• • •

"Out of the booth!" Cutler cried as he threw himself between Franks and Cornelius and the rampaging Logan. Franks dived for the exit before the last pieces of Plexiglas tinkled to the floor. But Cornelius froze, eyes wide with surprise behind bottle-thick lenses, and Logan whirled to face the bearded scientist.

With a guttural roar, Logan raised a clawed hand to strike Cornelius down. But before he could deliver the fatal blow, Cutler leaped on his back, locked his legs around Logan's neck, and seized his clawed arm with both hands.

"Move!" Cutler roared as he struggled to take Logan down.

Transfixed, Cornelius didn't budge. As Logan strove to free his upraised arm, Cutler felt his grip on the madman slipping. With a roar, Logan reached up and yanked the man off his back. Spinning helplessly, Cutler rolled over the computer terminal and through the remains of the shattered window. He landed on his back, hard. He tried to rise but fell again, his head lolling against the bloody carcass of the murdered technician.

Logan advanced on Dr. Cornelius. Face-to-face, their eyes locked, and Cornelius braced himself for the fatal strike. It never came. Instead, Logan's legs gave out and he reeled. With a final moan, Logan tumbled to the steel floor and lay still. Cornelius dropped to his knees beside the subject and touched his wrist to check for a pulse—only to recoil as the adamantium claws retracted, vanishing under folds of the subject's flesh.

The security door burst open. Weapon drawn, Major Deavers rushed in. Backing him up was Agent Franks and a team of animal handlers, electroprods crackling in their gloved hands.

Cornelius raised his hand to stop them, then placed two fingers on Logan's throat. "The subject is alive—barely. But all of his life-support systems have been torn away. We have to get him to the OR, stat, or we'll lose him."

To the doctor's surprise, the wranglers pushed him aside and seized Logan with rough hands. Using wires and tubes from the shattered medical probes, the guards hog-tied the unconscious man, ignoring Cornelius's protests.

Finally, the scientist spied the tag on Major Deavers's body armor. "You! Are you in command?" Cornelius barked.

"Yes, sir," Deavers replied gruffly, his voice echoing behind the clear face mask.

"I want you to take control of your boys, then take Subject X to the OR for evaluation. Time is of the essence. With his life support gone, he doesn't have long."

Deavers looked past Cornelius to the mangled corpse on the floor. "What about him?"

Cornelius faced the technician, then lowered his eyes. "There's no hurry . . . he's gone."

Deavers's eyes burned, but he bit back a response. Then he turned to face his men.

"Put him on a gurney and take the bastard to the OR," Deavers commanded. "Restrain him well. And if he wakes up—or even snores—shock him with your prods."

Two burly handlers tossed Logan onto a gurney, strapped him down, and wheeled him out. Meanwhile,

Major Deavers and Agent Franks entered the lab to check on Cutler.

"He's out," said Deavers. "Doesn't look bad, though."

Deavers slapped Cutler awake, and when the man opened his eyes, the major shook his head in mock sympathy. "On your feet, hero," said Deavers, offering his hand.

Cutler took it, pulled himself erect, and shook his head to clear it. "What hit me?" he moaned. "And do I look as bad as I feel?"

Major Deavers directed his attention to the corpse sprawled on the floor in a darkening pool of his own blood.

"You look a hell of a lot better than that guy."

"If I had known what you were really up to, Professor, I might be very upset with you."

Cornelius sat in the shattered observation booth among shards of Plexiglas and smashed consoles, cradling a cup of lukewarm coffee in his trembling hands.

"Possibly," said the Professor. "Though I never hid the true nature of the project from you. Rather, you chose not to discuss the more controversial aspect of the program with me. Thus, I felt you were not ready to accept certain . . . ugly realities."

"I thought you were trying to create some kind of superbeing. A . . . a supersoldier or something. Surely you've heard of that program, back in the 1940s?"

"Of course."

Cornelius put the cup to his lips and gulped loudly, draining it. He wiped his mouth with his shirtsleeve, then frowned. "I've helped you to create a monster, not a superbeing . . ."

"No, not a monster exactly—"

"To hell with that! It's a mindless, murdering animal."

"Well, yes. But we can make him behave."

Cornelius almost laughed. "Behave? Good God, Professor. It slaughtered an innocent boy in there."

Without looking, he pointed to the dark stain on the floor of the now-empty lab. "Then it came after me and the guards—straight through that blasted window as if it wasn't there."

In an uncharacteristic gesture, the Professor laid a comforting hand on his colleague's shoulder. "You must have been terrified, doctor," he crooned sympathetically.

"You don't know the half of it."

Oh, but I do, the Professor silently countered, bowing his head to hide the slightest of smiles. *And I'm delighted by your reaction. I can only imagine how those who confront a fully trained and conditioned Weapon X will feel! No nation, no power, could stand up against such might.*

The Professor withdrew his hand. "But in the end you weren't hurt, Doctor, so let's not overindulge ourselves, hmm?"

Cornelius placed the cup to his lips, found it dry, and set it aside.

"Logan could have killed us all. I met his eyes for a second . . . filled with hate and fury. But I couldn't tell if it was some animal bloodlust, or horror at what we have done to him."

All we've "done to him" is free the untamed, unchecked beast inside, thought the Professor. *A beast that will soon be trained like a circus animal to perform on cue.*

The Professor watched as Cornelius rose and crossed the booth, to replenish his cup from a near empty pot. "And then what happened, Doctor?" he asked encouragingly.

"Then, with his life supports torn away, Subject X went down . . . collapsed. Those terrible knives—"

An extraordinary adaptation, those claws, the Professor privately marveled. *A dazzling evolutionary leap—*

"—sunk back into his body."

Stealthy. Lethal. The perfect weapon for Weapon X.

"And I thanked God for my good fortune."

A pity I hadn't thought of such an innovation first. We might have been better prepared for it . . .

The Professor shifted impatiently. "Well, you have survived to tell your tale. Now we should consider—"

"But the boy is dead, Professor."

"Yes, it's very tragic. Whatever could have possessed him to leave his booth?"

Cornelius shrugged. "I don't know. He must have seen the danger. But still, we have to answer for it."

The Professor frowned. "How so, Doctor?"

"Well, the police, obviously . . . and what about the boy's family?"

"Surely you do not want the police involved? Asking questions? Prying into people's lives? Your life? Why, if that happened, I'm not certain I could ensure your safety, Dr. Cornelius."

"That hardly matters now," Cornelius replied, surprised because he meant every word. After facing Logan's wrath, his terror of imprisonment had evaporated.

The Professor studied his colleague, puzzled by his change of attitude. "And I thought we'd won you over,

Doctor. Convinced you not to squander your scientific knowledge. Impressed you with our steadfast dedication."

Cornelius lowered his eyes. "I've had enough."

Not until I say you have. But finessing is obviously required. How very tiresome . . .

"Fortunately, I don't believe police involvement will be necessary," the Professor replied, ignoring Cornelius's statement. "The boy's relatives can be compensated. Secured, let us say."

Cornelius wasn't listening. He fumbled with his coffee, the bitter brew staining his lab coat.

To vent his impatience, the Professor swept the Plexiglas debris from the top of the computer monitor. "Doctor. I realize you must be feeling a little estranged from me just now, so perhaps it is time to induct you further into my program . . ."

Cornelius looked up. "Program?"

Always the soft touch, then the iron hand.

"Yes . . . but first I will require your explicit trust. Do I have that, Dr. Cornelius?"

The doctor's jaw moved a second before a sound emerged. "I . . . I don't know. There's a lot—"

"That I will explain."

He's disoriented, the Professor observed. *Looking for direction . . . leadership. Now the iron hand.*

"Your trust, Doctor," the Professor repeated. "I require it. Offer that trust and I shall accept."

"Well," Cornelius said in a whisper. "Okay, then, if you want . . . I trust you."

The Professor licked his lips. "Thank you for that."

"You're welcome, sir."

"Tell me, Doctor, are you familiar with the term *Homo superior*?"

Cornelius shrugged. "As in master race or something?"

"To some extent. But no . . . I mean mutant." The Professor paused to reactivate the blood-flecked monitor. "Mutants aren't human, Dr. Cornelius, they are *Homo superior*. Subject X is not human. He is, therefore, *Homo superior*. Look here—"

The Professor replayed the final moments of the status technician's life.

"What do you see?"

Cornelius was repulsed, yet scientific curiosity compelled him to watch. "What do you think?" he said angrily. "I see a wild beast that was once a man."

"Very well, Cornelius. I accept your assessment. Yet I see a man as ever he was, but with his subconscious stripped bare. Cut from his very soul and scored to the bone. Our friend has come into his own at last. For that we should rejoice. We are transforming him—architects of Logan's mind, body, and soul."

Cornelius scratched his chin, unnerved by the Professor's thin smile. "The experiment. The adamantium bonding process. Are you saying it mutated him into this infernal thing?"

"No, Doctor. You must understand that this 'infernal thing' is what the patient has always been. A determinedly violent individual pummeling his way through a purposeless life."

As the Professor watched the endless replay loop on the screen, his eyes were filled with something that resembled pity.

"Imagine such a life, Cornelius? One day distinguished from the next only by the changing patterns of bruises and blood from last night's drunken fight. But then, inexplicably, the wounds are healed and gone before noon and his first beer . . ." The Professor shook his head. "How sad. Why, I doubt if he even suffered hangovers."

The intercom buzzed.

"The diagnostic tests have been completed, Professor," Dr. Hendry reported. "We are assessing the results now. It will be a few hours. Perhaps by noon."

"And the subject?"

"He's been placed in maximum security. Lab Five, Level Five. A team is monitoring his activities."

The Professor's delicate hands tapped the keyboard and the murderous scene on the monitor shifted to a real-time image of Logan in another cell, awake and struggling against the bonds that restrained him from head to toe.

"Think of it, Dr. Cornelius," the Professor continued. "All his years, Logan has endured this . . . madness. Suffering a destiny that tore at him from his guts outward. Battling a fate decreed him by nature—a curse not unlike the scourge of lycanthropy in the Middle Ages. Do you even know Logan's history?"

"No," Cornelius replied. "Only . . ."

"Only that he was kidnapped for the purposes of this highly advanced experiment, correct?"

Cornelius nodded.

"Yet that did not trouble you?"

"I . . . I thought he was a criminal or something. I figured that the REM machine was part of the process . . . to rehabilitate Logan. To make him a better man."

The Professor threw back his head and laughed. "You have stumbled upon the truth, Doctor, for it is my intention that Mr. Logan be fully rehabilitated."

Cornelius could not tear his eyes away from Logan on the screen. "You were saying . . . his history, Professor?"

"Logan became a government agent and was ideally suited to the dangers of his activities. He had nothing to lose—not even his godforsaken life." The Professor faced Cornelius. "You saw the Medfax yourself, Doctor. Shot several times. Stabbed and beaten in the course of duty. Recklessly seeking the honor of dying for his country. How pitifully desperate he must have become."

On the monitor, Logan managed to free his arms. As they both watched, he began to tear at the thick cables that circled his waist.

"But now his demon is free," said the Professor. "Released by the intervention of Project X. His double identity—tormented mutant and secret spy—has been eradicated by the REM device. It's been supplanted by the superego, and all of Logan's primal instincts are focused and resolved. Do you understand?"

"I'm not sure I—"

"Before he became clay in our hands, it was as if Logan did not exist, anyway. He had no family. His body never aged, he carried no scars to remind him of past mistakes. Only his memories told him he was alive at all, and those memories caused him nothing but pain and endless suffering."

The Professor moved closer. "Logan's curse was to live on, while past friends, lovers, wives—perhaps even sons and daughters—aged and died before his eyes. Imagine such loneliness?"

"Yes . . ." Cornelius answered without a moment's hesitation.

Of course you can, the Professor recalled, then continued.

"How many times must he have considered suicide? Yet even death was denied him. No wonder he sought escape in alcohol. It's as if Logan understood that a retreat from the ego—the death of the 'I' and all of its memories—was his only chance at salvation."

"Yes, I do see, Professor."

"Of course you do, Doctor. And what you're looking at right now is Logan stripped of ambiguity, of emotion. What you see is the most formidable tactical weapon ever conceived."

"The knives, then, in his hands," said Cornelius. "Pure adamantium . . ."

"They're not knives, Cornelius—they're claws! And already Logan knows how to use them."

As they watched, Logan extended his talons and severed the last of the cables restraining him to the bunk. He sat up, claws fully extended.

"Are they asleep in that booth?" the Professor muttered as he punched the intercom. "Security!"

"Security here."

"We need the gas now, in Lab Five."

"We're waiting for Dr. Hendry's authorization . . ."

"You have mine," the Professor cried. "Haste! Haste! He's almost on his feet."

"Copy."

As Logan rolled off the bunk, a cyclone of yellow gas was blasted into his face from nozzles hidden in the walls, the floor, even the ceiling of the cell. Choking, he went down on his knees and clutched his heaving chest.

"Oh my God," gasped Cornelius.

Logan's mouth gaped, and a green bile erupted from the back of his throat. He hit the floor facedown, but twitching arms and legs quickly tossed him onto his back. Finally, Logan gagged like a beached shark. As he slipped into unconsciousness, the claws slowly retracted into his flesh.

Cornelius sank into a chair, transfixed by the image.

"A necessary action, Doctor. You saw what happened."

"Yes . . . but . . . I mean . . ."

"Spit it out, man. I'm open to suggestions."

"Can't we treat him better than this? He's still human, isn't he?"

The Professor considered his words. "In some way, perhaps. But your earlier description was more apt. 'A mindless, murdering animal,' I believe you said."

"Yes . . . I suppose so . . ."

"And this is why I am depending upon you, good doctor." The Professor rested his arm on the other's shoulder in what he imagined was a paternal gesture.

It made Cornelius's skin crawl.

Cornelius closed his eyes to banish the image on the screen, only to find Logan's face seared into his brain like an afterimage, as if he'd stared at the sun too long.

"In truth, Subject X is not so very different than your

amazing nanochips," murmured the Professor. "He was created for a specific purpose. Now he must be restructured. Trained. Then programmed."

Cornelius opened his eyes. Logan seemed to stare up at him through the screen.

"You can do all of this," uttered the Professor. "Manipulation of the mindless, Dr. Cornelius. It is your calling."

9

Revelations

Carol Hines traced the curved adamantium blade with her left hand.

Magnificent.

In her mind, this was an unprecedented achievement.

The Professor had created an entirely new biological defense mechanism within the subject organism through the use of technology—totally bypassing the vagaries of the natural selection process. Amazing.

She shifted her wide green eyes to a second X-ray, this one taken laterally. It revealed a mysterious knot of muscle and cartilage in the forearm that held the claws in place. The muscle also served as a sheath when the blades were not in use.

Amazing architecture.

The claws appeared both lethal and efficient. To Carol, this configuration alone was a testament to what could be achieved when total discipline and a single vision were imposed on a scientific community in unison.

A true triumph of the will.

Like a patron of the arts, she moved from image to image, studying each of more than a hundred X-rays and ultrasounds wallpapering the medical conference center.

Behind her, more personnel began to file into the room, answering the Professor's summons, as she had, to attend this emergency meeting.

Carol Hines paused as a particular image caught her eye—an electron microscopic photograph of the surface of the subject's unbreakable steel claw.

No sword-maker in ancient Japan could have forged so perfect a blade.

At a magnification of more than one hundred thousand times, not a flaw, not a ripple could be found in the sleek, glassy surface. And the subject's claws were twice as dense as tempered steel.

Virtually indestructible, thanks to the adamantium alloy . . .

A resin replica of the subject's blade configuration had been cast while he was unconscious. It now hung from surgical wire in the center of the wall display.

Carol Hines couldn't resist the urge to touch one shaft of the three long, slightly curved blades, to imagine the cold-cast resin's dull edges were really a steel alloy and sharper than a razor.

I had my doubts about the Professor, Carol admitted to herself, *especially after he seemed to freeze in panic during the bonding process. But it's obvious he truly had a vision of what Subject X was to become. And that vision has come to pass . . .*

"Pretty remarkable development, eh, Ms. Hines?"

She turned to find Dr. MacKenzie, the staff psychiatrist, standing at her side.

"I never imagined such a thing was possible," she replied, awe in her voice.

"If I were a Freudian, I could make much hay out of this particular configuration," MacKenzie chuckled as he rubbed the side of his red beard. His face was florid, his shock of red hair uncombed. The doctor had obviously been up much of the night, along with everyone else. But the lack of sleep hadn't affected his jovial nature.

Carol Hines offered MacKenzie a reserved smile. "What is your discipline, doctor? Which psychological theory do you expound?"

"In my golden youth, I was a student of Alfred Adler—a fact you probably could have deduced yourself."

"That seems intended as a very witty remark. I'm sorry, but I don't understand the reference."

"Well, Ms. Hines, Adler believed that the sense of inferiority rather than the sex drive is the fundamental motivating force in human nature. Feelings of inferiority, conscious or unconscious, combined with defense mechanisms are often the cause of all psychopathological behavior, in Adler's opinion."

"I still don't understand."

"Since you arrived with that magic machine of yours, my services as staff psychiatrist are no longer deemed important. Hence my own feelings of inferiority."

"I'm sorry, but—" Ms. Hines began again.

MacKenzie threw up his hands. "No, no, please don't apologize. You misunderstand me. I readily surrender to your expertise, Ms. Hines, and truly hope that you assume all of my responsibilities in the very near future. To be frank, I've had my fill of the Professor. And of Project X."

After MacKenzie's impromptu admission, they stood in silence for a moment, viewing the images as others moved around them.

"Any idea why this meeting's been called?" MacKenzie asked when they were more or less alone.

"I was about to ask you the same question," she

replied. "Perhaps it might have something to do with the violent incident last night in Lab Two."

"Possibly . . ."

MacKenzie sounded doubtful. In her heart, Carol Hines harbored doubts as well. Something was in the air. A whiff of change that she had sniffed before. She sensed the same tension, the same confused feeling she'd experienced at NASA after the last space shuttle accident—a feeling of chaos, mingled with the knowledge that certain individuals had lost power and prestige within the organization while others had gained it.

The difficulty for me, she recalled, *was trying to figure out whose star was on the ascent, and whose was falling like space junk.*

Institutional chaos and ambiguity eroded one's sense of purpose, fostered doubts, diminished productivity.

No one is immune. Not even a scientist like my father—his doubts led to alcohol abuse and worse.

Carol believed in focusing on the task, not the politics swirling around it. Better a worker bee than a queen. Better to keep ones head down than get it chopped off—like my father's, when a drug he developed failed to pass Federal Drug Administration approval.

The drinking, the violence got much worse after that. But at least the beatings stopped when I reached adolescence, won a few science fair prizes. Yes, the beatings stopped, but not the abuse . . .

A cluster of technicians jostled them, and MacKenzie and Hines moved to a quiet corner to continue their conversation.

"Quite impressive how you reasserted control over Logan after last night's incident," MacKenzie told her.

"It was very simple," she replied. "Subject X has already been conditioned to accept the REM interface. It gets easier each time you use the device."

"I did notice the same spike in brain activity during the initial interface—more chemical activity?"

"I don't believe Logan was on a trip down memory lane, if that's what you mean."

"You're certain, Ms. Hines?"

"I think we've covered this ground before, Doctor." MacKenzie grinned, relishing the verbal sparring. "Anyway, Ms. Hines, that machine of yours has turned out to be the only means of controlling the subject. Drugs like Thorazine and Pheno-B, technology like the brain dampeners, even knockout gas have all proven ineffectual in the long run."

"Yes. Dr. Hendry did mention that the subject was gassed."

"Indeed." MacKenzie frowned. "A whopping dose, too. Enough to subdue an elephant for a week. Subject X woke up in twenty-eight minutes. By then, you had your machine attached and the interface put him down for good."

"Actually, I doubt Subject X was ever really 'awake' or 'conscious' as we understand the terms. His individual consciousness—his ego—has been completely eradicated. His memory, all traces of his former personality have been wiped away. The subject is a blank slate."

"Someone smashed up Lab Two, Ms. Hines."

"More like some*thing*. Subject X was acting purely on instinct—lashing out as even an insect will do if its survival is threatened."

"Hmm. I wonder if Logan felt threatened . . ."

Carol faced him. "I've heard whispers that someone—one of the status technicians—got injured. Flown out to a hospital this morning. Needs intensive care."

"Interesting . . ."

"You don't think so?"

MacKenzie shrugged. "I was outside this morning. I try to get out every morning—even we pale-skinned academics need a little sunshine now and then."

Carol Hines raised an eyebrow. "And?"

"We had quite a bit of snow in the last couple of days. A few inches at least. This morning the helipad was still covered."

The sharp whine of electronic feedback interrupted them. Then the amplified voice of Dr. Hendry called the meeting to order.

"Can we all take a seat, please? The Professor would like to brief us on some . . . recent developments."

"Excuse me, Ms. Hines," MacKenzie said. "I must join the rest of my staff in the orchestra pit."

The clatter of folding chairs filled the room until everyone found a place. Carol Hines sat alone, surrounded by empty seats.

Despite the post-operation incident in Lab Two, there was a general feeling of confidence among the staff. When the Professor stepped up to the microphone, he was greeted by a wave of applause that he immediately swept aside. As he began to speak, two men stood with the Professor—Dr. Hendry on his left and, on his right, Dr. Cornelius.

"As we move into Phase Two of this experiment, I have found it necessary to reevaluate the core members of the team and shift some of the responsibilities to other members. This new hierarchy I have formulated will be permanent . . ."

Suddenly, the room felt very uncomfortable. Colleagues exchanged puzzled glances, wondering about the long-term ramifications of the unexpected managerial shake-up. Only Carol Hines appeared completely unfazed. She alone was not caught totally by surprise.

"As of today, Dr. Cornelius will assume overall responsibility for the next phase of the operation," announced the Professor.

A wise choice—the best the Professor could make, she thought. Hendry had neither the proper attitude nor true dedication to the project. He questioned every idea that was not his own and spent too much time defending his sandbox to be an effective leader.

"Dr. Hendry will move into a support staff role, though he will still be responsible for the subject's overall health as well as the future physical conditioning of Subject X."

Murmurs intensified until the Professor paused, waiting for complete silence.

"Dr. MacKenzie, our staff psychiatrist, will retain his current title. But he and his staff of psychologists will now report to Ms. Carol Hines, our REM technician."

Carol blinked in surprise. Then her eyes met Dr. MacKenzie's. The man offered her a sly smile and a salute.

"This change is necessary for the success of the psychological conditioning process and is in no way meant to impugn Dr. MacKenzie's reputation as a physician or his participation in the experiment. This change was only made because the REM device will play a critical role in the next stage of Project X—the retraining and reprogramming of the subject—and Ms. Hines is our resident expert in that technology."

The Professor paused to scan the sea of anxious faces.

"Now I will turn over the floor and this meeting to

Dr. Cornelius, who will outline the next stage of our on-going experiment in much more detail . . ."

"Have a good lunch, Cutler?"

"Yes, sir. Thanks for asking."

Cutler stood at attention before the major's desk. He'd shown up in his boss's office wearing crisp new overalls, fresh from Supply. He chose overalls because they were the only regulation gear bulky enough to cover the bandages that swathed his torso.

The major glanced at the after-action reports he was holding, then tossed them aside and rested his hands on his desk.

"Good work, Cutler. Both Franks and doctor-what's-his-name said you saved their bacon. But you should have called for backup before entering Lab Two, not after. Next time you might end up with considerably more than a few stitches."

"A dozen stitches, sir. And I won't make that mistake again."

"No, you won't. You're on light duty for a week."

"Come on, Deavers—"

"Seven days. Starting now."

"What do I do, sweep the halls?"

"You're going to review all current security proce-dures, double-check the cameras and motion detectors, test the alarms, and then implement a complete lock-down of the entire complex by midnight."

"Now, why would I implement a lockdown, Major?"

"Because the Director ordered one, that's why. All personnel, without exception. Until further notice."

"What happened? World War Three?"

"Management happened," Deavers replied. "I got the coded message this morning. Supplies come in, nobody goes out. End of story."

"Why do I get my day ruined?"

Deavers laughed. "Hey, you're not the only one. Rice is working on a complete communications blackout, including Internet and phone access—you should hear the egghead's bellyaching. And poor Franks is on perimeter duty, walking the fence in the snow and freezing cold for the next ten hours."

"Yeah, the lucky bastard," said Cutler.

The thoughts played through his mind in an endless loop as Cornelius lay sleepless on his bunk.

Beast . . . once a man, but scored to the bone . . . animal now, no longer human.

Dr. Cornelius had fallen asleep listening to the jumbled, chaotic voices recorded during and after Logan's violent episode in Lab Two. Now they mingled with his own conflicted thoughts.

He has claws, but he's still a human being . . . No, not human. Homo superior. *Logan must be superior. With those spikes embedded in his cheeks, the corners of his eyes, his brain. He'd be dead if he wasn't a freak of nature . . . a mutant . . .*

Cornelius sat up and deactivated the recorder. Chest heaving, heart pumping, he found himself doused in a cold sweat. He fumbled for his glasses, then he checked his watch.

Quarter of seven . . . but is it morning or afternoon? In this damn place, there's no way to tell. Been days since I saw the sun . . .

He rolled off the bunk and crossed his tiny quarters to

the computer terminal. Next to the black screen, a digital clock read 0647, military time.

"It's early morning," he groaned. His voice sounded strange as it echoed in his ears.

His movements had activated the room's overhead lighting, and the computer terminal also sprang to life. The intercom buzzed a moment later.

"Cornelius here . . ."

"Good morning, Doctor," said the status tech. "The Professor wanted me to tell you he will attend the experiment this morning."

"What time?"

"0800 in the main lab."

"What about the HDTV screen?"

"Up and running. Ms. Hines is going through the checklist now, but the screen has already been connected to and interfaced with the REM. Everything should be a go."

"Thanks, Status. Out."

Need some coffee . . . have to fortify myself for the day ahead. The day I play Dr. Frankenstein. The day I create a monster . . .

But instead of hurrying to the cafeteria, Cornelius sat down at his desk and reviewed the latest data on Subject X.

The indications are all positive. No sign of rejection—Logan's superimmune system was overridden long enough for the bonding to take place. Now that system has reasserted itself, and Logan has made a recovery in record time. No aftereffects, no scars, no wounds—except where our probes remain in place.

He rifled through pages and pages of information to find the blood test he'd ordered yesterday. He found the results near the bottom of the file, and eagerly scanned them. At first glance, Cornelius was disappointed. Logan's blood was unremarkable in every way. Type O negative. Normal white blood cell and platelet counts. Plasma normal, too—a little heavy on the trace minerals, but that could be due to the massive amounts of adamantium being pumped into him.

All normal . . . and yet Logan's blood can muster itself into a bacteria- and toxin-fighting substance as powerful as the Professor's cherished Weapon X.

Cornelius was ready to toss the blood test aside when he noticed something unusual about Logan's white cells.

As an immunologist, Cornelius knew that normal humans had several different types of white blood cells. But one type—neutrophils—is dominant. Neutrophils are quite good at attacking invading bacteria, but that's pretty much all they do.

Another type of white cell, the lymphocyte, is more powerful and much more versatile, though there are far fewer of them. Lymphocytes fight more than bacteria—they battle all foreign substances, including poisons, and work with the immune system to combat infection in a manner not yet fully understood.

While Logan's overall white blood cell count was within the normal range of one to two percent, his lymphocyte count was off the charts. Not only that, but the hematologist had noticed certain anomalies in the shape and size of Logan's lymphocytes. They were larger and had some "additional structures as yet unidentified," according to the man's cryptic notations.

Could this be the secret of the subject's phenomenal immune system? Cornelius wondered. *Could it be something so simple? So basic as a white blood cell? If so, then vaccines for a hundred—no, a thousand diseases might be isolated and synthesized through a thorough study of Logan's unusual blood.*

Only then did the realization come. *This . . . this is a seminal find. As fundamental as the discovery of penicillin.*

Cornelius suddenly found himself shaking with raw emotion. He tore off his glasses and tossed them onto the table. Then he covered his eyes.

Good God . . . if I'd had access to Logan's blood a few years ago, I could have easily synthesized a vaccine for my son's disease. I've found the secret—the cure—too late to do any good.

If only I'd found Logan then, Cornelius despaired, *everything would have been different. My son's suffering would have ended. Paul could have lived a normal life, and my wife, Madeline, would be alive today.*

His hands came away wet with tears.

Maybe they were tears of hope, because if Cornelius's work was successful in the past, no one would have had to suffer like Paul—ever again.

Yes, the Professor will have his monster, his killing machine, his goddamn Weapon X, because I'll be the one to create it for him.

But in return—for my own part in this hellish, twisted experiment—I will pick the Professor's brain for all his knowledge, his techniques, and then use Logan as a guinea pig in an effort to alleviate human disease and suffering, to find a panacea, a universal elixir that will cure every single disease forever.

Cornelius prayed that the ends justified the means.

CARDIO-INHIBITOR, MS. HINES . . .

When he heard the booming voice echo through the night shrouded valley, Logan melted into the shadows under a tall pine, dragging Miko Katana down with him.

"What is it?" she mouthed silently.

Logan tapped his ears like she was crazy. Surely she'd heard it, too. How could she miss that sound?

They scanned the woods around them, which were fairly thick now that they'd reached the base of the hill. They had moved close enough for Logan to smell the water, though the lake and the dam beyond were still invisible through the dense foliage.

Cautiously, Miko drew her infrared lenses—Logan's had been destroyed with his helmet—but after a careful scan, she saw nothing.

"Sorry," Logan whispered as softly as the wind in the trees. "Thought I heard a voice or something. Maybe I hit my head harder than I realized."

"No problem, I could use a rest."

Miko drew a pocket-sized GPS system. But before she activated it, he stopped her. "The dam is that way— less than a kilometer," he gestured with his thumb. "The road's over there. Maybe five hundred meters. Beyond that, the lake."

"How do you know this?"

"Brought up on the frontier. Didn't have GPS. Not even a compass. Just the sun. Moon. Stars. And instinct."

"Your 'instincts' are well honed." She tucked the device away. "To the road, then?"

"Let's parallel the road until we get to the main throughway over the dam, then it's back into the woods. Then we head to the complex right below."

When they set off this time, Miko took point, weapon drawn. Logan let her go.

After my foul-up back there, she'd rather trust her own ears, he thought ruefully. *Or maybe she's got something to prove.*

Though Miko's Tac was equipped with a noise suppressor, if she actually had to pull the trigger, no amount of shooting would save them—they would be hunted down like imperialist running dogs. It had happened to Logan before.

Fifteen minutes later, they reached the road—a wide dirt trail sprayed with oil tar to keep the dust to a minimum. On one side of the road ran a drainage ditch deep enough to hide in if they had to. On the other side, a sharp drop to the lake below, where moonlight shimmered off the rippling black water. Across that lake, a black ridge rose as high as the one they'd just ascended.

There was no sign of traffic along the winding road, or the dam beyond. There were only the aircraft lights twinkling on the pinnacle of the dam's tall superstructure.

Miko pushed forward, but Logan stopped her.

"I presume you think your missing scientist is inside that complex, am I right?"

Miko looked at him through a curtain of hair. "What is it your American celebrities say? No comment."

"That's Hollywood. I'm Canadian."

"I cannot tell you because I do not know, Mr. Logan," she said.

"Fine, because if you did plan on rescuing him, think again. Unless the guy has sold his services to the North Koreans, and then faked his own kidnapping—"

"An impossibility, Mr. Logan."

"—he's not cooperating with his captors. And that means the North Koreans had to soften him up a bit . . . so that he'd see things their way." Logan paused to let his words sink in. "Chances are good that even if you find him, he'll be in no shape to travel—let alone make a break."

Miko walked silently for a few steps. Then she whirled around to face him.

But as she opened her lips, Logan silenced her. "Listen!"

At first, she heard only the water. Then a flapping sound—a steady beat that echoed off the hills.

"Go! Get down," Logan whispered, pushing her into the ditch. She landed in thick grass and a shallow puddle of stagnant water. Logan dived in next to her.

The pounding became a steady roar as the helicopter rose over the ridge on the other side of the lake. Miko cautiously peered above the edge of the trench, then used her night-vision binoculars to identify the vehicle.

"An MD-500 helicopter," she told him. "North Korean military markings . . . North Korean Special Forces, to be precise."

"Damn."

"Something is suspended from its nose. Not a weapon but—"

"Get down!" rasped Logan, pulling her back into the ditch just as the spotlight stabbed through the darkness. But not in their direction. Instead, the spotlight played across the opposite slope. "Don't like the look of that," snarled Logan.

The chopper hovered over the hill, shaking the branches as the spotlight probed the ground between the trees. Soon, a second helicopter roared across the lake, joining the hunt. And on the road at the base of the hill, more activity—a convoy of vehicles raced from the dam. The helicopters still hovered in place. Several armored cars and a Russian-made armored personnel carrier rumbled ahead.

"Langram. They're looking for my partner," said Logan, face grim. "Hope he makes it."

Then a new sound—more beating rotors—this time coming from behind. They ducked their heads as two more helicopters roared over the ditch, bright white lights tracing the ground, following the road.

"They're on to us. They have to be," said Logan. "Must have tracked us as we came down. Don't know how, but—"

"Logan, more vehicles on the road!" Miko shouted. "They're coming from the dam, driving right for us!"

10
Illusions

"Cardio-inhibitor, Ms. Hines."

Tapping, and then she looked up, bright green eyes on Cornelius. "Activated."

They all stood in the west corner of the main lab, which was now dominated by a digital screen the size of a wall. In the middle of the room, Subject X lying naked on a technological "table" mounted atop an array of computers and diagnostic machinery. Carol Hines sat at a terminal, inches from Logan's head.

"I don't understand the point of this twenty-four-hour delay, Doctor," the Professor grumbled. Hands in his pockets, he leaned over the edge of the massive medico-diagnostic tub. Logan lay in its sunken center, sprawled on a bed of wires and tubes.

"Ms. Hines and I have determined that all of Dr. MacKenzie's conditioning techniques will most likely fail," said Cornelius. "We have decided to take a different approach using the REM device."

"But it took MacKenzie years to develop his data, formulate effective surgical techniques," countered the Professor.

"His data was based on human subjects. Logan is

Homo superior, which renders the good doctor's advance research moot."

"Surely Logan has the same psychological makeup as anyone. The psyche is formed by experience and conditioning. He probably thought he *was* human until he discovered the truth."

Cornelius shook his head. "Dr. MacKenzie was relying on brain surgery, detaching the hippocampus, rewiring the prefrontal lobe, severing the hemispheres. But with Logan's healing abilities, it's possible he could regenerate the damaged brain tissue—"

"Preposterous!" snorted the Professor.

Carol Hines spoke up. "But Professor, with all due respect, we've already learned that Logan can regenerate damaged nerve tissue—something impossible with a normal human being. Why not total restoration of his brain functions, too?"

"And there are also risks of side effects," Cornelius added. "The hippocampus is particularly sensitive to global oxygen deprivation. Epilepsy could result."

"I see." The Professor rubbed his chin. "Logan would certainly not be a reliable or effective weapon if he suffered chronic seizures."

Cornelius nodded. "Worse than that, there's the possibility of anterograde amnesia. How could Logan accept conditioning if he lost the ability to form new memories?"

The Professor's eyes remained focused on the subject. Cornelius sensed he was still unconvinced.

"There are other factors," Cornelius warned. "The subject is still aggressive despite ego eradication."

"Reason?"

"Chemical reactions have been ruled out. No metal poisoning is present, no schizoid chemical imbalances we can detect."

"Perhaps it has something to do with pain," said Carol Hines.

Both men faced her.

"What if the organism itself were experiencing a kind of recognition—a memory, if you will—of the pain experienced during the bonding process?"

The Professor scoffed. "Memories reside in the brain, Ms. Hines, not in the individual cells."

"Whatever the cause," Cornelius declared, "his brutish impulses have become greatly exaggerated since the adamantium bonding process began."

"And this . . . treatment . . . will correct that situation?"

"No, Professor. Hardly," Cornelius replied. "But it should give us a real knowledge of Logan's mental stress dynamics and a better understanding of his current capabilities, such as his retention of language skills, his recognition of symbols . . ."

The Professor's eyes narrowed. "I hope this isn't a waste of my time, Cornelius. We should've begun reorientation by now. What's the point of this weapon if we can't control him?"

"But we can control him, somewhat." Cornelius handed the Professor a spidery headset and microphone. "Use this. It's a direct link to his cerebral cortex."

The Professor seized the device with greedy hands. "With this I can speak to him? Control him?"

Cornelius shrugged. "Suggest, perhaps. Control? I don't know."

Carol Hines tapped her keyboard. Cornelius threw

various switches. The console on the medico-incubator activated with beeps and dings as vital signs were monitored.

Cornelius directed the Professor's attention to the giant HDTV monitor, now rippling with silent static.

"Ms. Hines has interfaced successfully. The REM is digitally coding the electrical impulses inside of Logan's brain, and will translate them into digital images."

"Remarkable."

"Indeed, Professor. We can actually watch Logan's dreams," Cornelius told him. "What you'll see on the big screen will be in direct relation to your spoken words. Tell him he's eating, and you might see a sizzling steak. Tell him he's flying, and you may see the image of a bird, an airplane—"

"I understand, Doctor," the Professor barked impatiently as he raised the microphone to his lips. "Logan," he began in a commanding tone. "You are in my control, Logan . . ."

"Yes, like that," said Cornelius. "Speak clearly and slowly. But you shouldn't use his former name, sir. It probably wouldn't mean a thing to Subject X at this stage, but we are trying to eradicate the previous markers of his life."

"Yes. Quite so," the Professor replied.

"Ms. Hines, we'll need an exacting flow of adrenergics as soon as possible," Cornelius cautioned.

"It's all in the system, sir," she replied. "I programmed it myself. For the most part, it was pretty straightforward."

"Splendid."

They looked up when they heard the Professor's sonorous voice.

"You are a beast," he said. "You are an animal born to serve . . ."

Cornelius and Ms. Hines exchanged glances.

"You have one master—and it is me. You will do anything I say—"

"Uh, Professor?"

"Yes? What?" snapped the Professor.

"We . . . We haven't begun yet, sir," Cornelius explained. "The link hasn't been activated."

The Professor pursed his thin lips. "Then please get on with it already, Doctor."

Cornelius gave Carol Hines a signal, then ran down the checklist in his head. "Set three of six in post-adamantium cell-bonding process. Stress and engram block and block complex. Language and symbol comprehension scan. Feed interface with the monitor. Two way communication. Have all that?"

"Yes."

"Proceed, Ms. Hines . . ."

She tapped the keyboard with machinelike precision. Cornelius stepped up to the Professor, who watched the whole process with predatory eyes.

"Pardon my suggestion, sir," he began, "but it might be advisable to avoid any directives to the patient during these tests. The psychotechnics of the situation warrant caution, as—"

The Professor cut him off. "Thank you for your suggestion, doctor. Have you any more?"

"No," Cornelius replied. "I guess not."

A sudden pop, then Carol Hines's console sparked. "Oh!" she cried, jumping back. Smoke and more sparks emerged from behind the faceplate of her terminal.

Then a thunderous, crackling roar—screeching like

feedback magnified a hundred times—as the electronic systems overloaded and shorted out one by one.

The Professor tore off his headset, but the noise was filling the lab as well. He howled and covered his ears.

"Overload!" Cornelius cried, his voice lost in the racket.

The fire extinguishing system blasted flame-smothering halon gas that quickly doused the electrical fire brewing inside of the computer, but the damage had already been done.

"Hines! Do something!" Cornelius cried. "Cut off the power!"

"I'm trying," she said as she pounded the keys. Finally, she located the audio cutoff and the deafening noise ended as abruptly as it began. Only an insistent fire alarm could be heard reverberating through the corridors outside the sealed laboratory.

Another electronic pop, then a crackle of static—this time from behind the massive HDTV monitor.

"What was that?" the Professor cried as the wall screen sprang to life. Projected on it, a roiling purple haze, like psychedelic smoke. "And what's that on the screen?"

Carol Hines glanced at the monitor, then down at her smoldering terminal. "We're getting some sort of internal feedback, sir," she reported. "The interface is—"

She squealed and pulled her scorched fingers away from the console. "The imaging is so powerful, it's burning circuits," she cautioned. Her statement was followed by another automatic blast of frigid halon.

On the wall screen, three curved, bone-white spikes rose into the frame. Each structure had a raw, jagged, unfinished look. Several times the digital image froze and began to break up, only to reconstitute, sharper than before.

"Something's wrong here," said the Professor as he stepped back from the monitor.

The spikes became ribs that morphed into spinal column, hip bones, a skull. Then a booming voice filled the lab with a single word: "PAIN!"

Cornelius tore his eyes away from the screen. "Okay. Shut it down. Shut it all down. We'll clean up the mess, check the data preps and find out what the hell went wrong."

A sudden, incomprehensible scream of baffled rage echoed off the walls.

"Ms. Hines, I said shut it down!" Cornelius cried.

"I . . . I can't, sir. There's no response!"

"I'M HURTING . . . PAIN!"

On the screen, the image of a skeleton was fully formed. Wild eyes glared with hate from dark sockets. Gnashing teeth turned to fangs as spikes sprang from every bone, every rib.

"WHAT HAVE YOU DONE TO ME?"

"If you can't cut the monitor, will you please cut the damn audio so I can hear myself think?"

Carol Hines met Cornelius's angry glare with a look of fear. "The audio feed is not activated, Doctor. It's malfunctioning. I shut it down already."

Cutler was manning the security command center when the fire alarm went off in the main lab on Level Five.

As per established protocol, he sealed off the floor from the rest of the underground complex. With the clatter of keys, the fireproof hatch closed automatically, the ventilation system shut down, and the elevator cars ascended to the surface and disgorged their passengers before powering down.

Cutler was about to alert the emergency response team when they contacted him.

"Anderson here. I've got a halon gas release in the main lab. Heat sensors indicate the fire is extinguished, but there's smoke so I'm dispatching a security team."

"Who's with you?"

"Franks and Lynch."

"Arm yourselves with tranquilizer guns. Sidearms with live ammo, too. Kevlar body armor. Helmets and visors."

"Come on, Cut. It's a fire, not a war."

"Don't be too sure," Cutler shot back. "There's another experiment going on down there. The Professor and his team are working on Subject X."

There was a pause before Anderson replied. "Okay, I'm calling for immediate backup."

Cutler grinned. "Great. I'll be right down. Over."

Cutler was halfway out of his chair when a firm hand pushed him back down. Another reached over his shoulder and keyed the intercom back on.

"Major Deavers here. Listen up, Anderson. I want you to call Rice or Wesley if you need help. In the heat of the moment, Agent Cutler probably forgot that he's been assigned to light duty. Over . . ."

The Professor stared at the monitor, transfixed. A grinning death's head stared back at him.

"PAIN! WHY PAIN?" the voice raged.

"This is unbelievable, Cornelius," the Professor cried, hands covering his ears. "You must stop it. Stop it now!"

"I can't. We're not sending. We're receiving." Cornelius looked up at the screen. *"He's* in control."

Then he turned. "Hines. Can you get Logan under control?"

Green eyes wide, she glanced away from the horrific image on the screen, hand covering her heart. "No, sir, Dr. Cornelius. I . . . I can't do a thing."

When Hines looked back at the screen, the bulging eyes seemed to stare back at her. Fearfully, she slowly stepped away from her console. She bumped against the diagnostic table.

A thick, muscled arm shot out of the high-tech sarcophagus, fingers curled into a grasping claw.

"PAIN!" roared Logan as he reached for Carol Hines.

"Doctor—help m—" Her frantic plea was cut off as Logan's fingers closed around her throat.

Still clutching the helpless, choking woman, Logan tore an intravenous tube from his neck and stared into Hines's terrified face.

"YOU! YOU GIVE PAIN TO ME . . ."

Her frail fingers clawed at Logan's hand, nails breaking as she tried to pry open his grip. Logan shook her as she pleaded for her life with gasping sobs. "No . . . oh, no . . . oh God, no . . ."

"PAIN . . ."

While Cornelius called for a security team, Logan struggled to rise against the wires, tubes, and restraints that held him to the diagnostic table.

The sound of the fire alarm mingled with the loud howl of the security alert, creating a chaotic cacophony. Suddenly, a very stern voice broke through the clamor.

"Logan! Leave that woman alone, you animal."

It was the Professor, eyes burning behind his square lenses.

He's mad, thought Cornelius. *He hasn't seen what Logan can do . . .*

"This is your master! You are in *my* control," the Professor bellowed. "You have no will but to serve me! Your master . . ."

A guttural snarl rumbled in Logan's throat. He locked eyes with the Professor and tossed the woman aside like a rag doll.

Carol Hines sprawled to the floor, unconscious or worse. Despite his fear, Cornelius dropped to his knees at the woman's side and dragged her back, away from the raging wild man.

"Stay where you are!" the Professor shrieked as Logan reared up from the table, tearing away the last of his restraints and ripping out tubes and wires. As he crawled off the recessed slab, a security team burst through the door, tranquilizer guns ready.

Before the Professor could retreat, Logan vaulted. Fingers reached for the man's throat, and the Professor fought in vain against Logan's choking grip.

"Guards, tranquilize Logan now!" Cornelius cried, still cradling Carol Hines in his arms.

But Agent Franks hesitated. "We might hit the Professor."

"Just shoot, damn it! SHOOT!" screamed Cornelius.

With the Professor still struggling in his grip, Logan spun around to face the guards. Hair wild, eyes wide, Logan howled and stomped his feet at his new foes, snarling like a trapped animal.

A third guard—Anderson—barked a command from the corridor. "Fire! Fire now!"

The shots were not loud—just a sibilant hiss accompanied each gas-propelled tranquilizer dart as it burst from the tube, followed by a wet smack as it impacted. The darts peppered Logan in the throat, chest, face, and belly. But he did not go down.

More shots, Anderson adding to the volley with his own dart gun. Finally, without a sound, Logan fell backward, into the incubator tub. His legs twitched as powerful nerve suppressants made their way into his bloodstream and then dispersed throughout his body.

Carol Hines lolled on a chair, eyes fluttering. Then she coughed and held her head in her hands. Cornelius faced the others. "Professor," he called. "Are you all right?"

Cornelius saw the man stumbling to his feet, clutching his throat. His face was ghostly pale, and Cornelius feared the Professor was about to collapse, too.

"I didn't hit the Professor, sir," Franks babbled to Anderson. "I know it."

The Professor coughed, then his eyes focused on the now unconscious Logan and he snapped.

"Kill him!" he shouted. "We must kill Logan now!" The Professor lunged at Franks and tried to tear the tranquilizer gun out of the agent's grip. "He's a wild animal! We cannot control him!"

Franks pulled away and the Professor spun around and lunged at Anderson, trying to rip the automatic pistol from his holster.

"Give me that gun," the Professor demanded as they grappled for the weapon.

"I can't do that, sir," cried Anderson, trying to fend off the man without hurting him. Suddenly, Cornelius threw himself between the two men.

"Professor, calm down now. You don't know what you're saying."

Wild-eyed, the Professor clutched the lapels of Cornelius's lab coat. "That beast tried to kill me. Didn't you see?"

"Yes. Yes, of course," said Cornelius. "But you're just in a state of shock right now, that's all."

The Professor muttered something unintelligible, and Cornelius grabbed his arms to steady him.

"Guard," Cornelius called over his shoulder. "Get some medical staff in here. Stat."

"Yes, sir."

"Doctor!" The cry came from Carol Hines, standing near the diagnostic table.

Cornelius raced to her, the Professor following reluctantly. They watched in awe as pinpricks of blood spouted from Logan's forearms. Then, the adamantium claws slid out from their sheaths, to gleam bloodstained-silver in the lab's dim light.

SNIKT! The sound of the claws silenced all.

"It's alright. He's totally sedated," Cornelius whispered. "That's some sort of random impulse we're seeing—a reflex. Good thing it didn't happen when he attacked you, Professor . . ."

"Oh God!" gasped Hines. "Look at the screen!"

Logan's violent thoughts flashed on-screen. Framed in splashes of clotted crimson, the face of the Professor dominated the digital frame—mouth open in a frozen shriek, glasses pierced by razor-sharp claws, the eye sockets gaping, bloody pits.

Cornelius looked away. "Well," he said in a weary voice. "I guess we've all had enough for today. Turn off the monitor, Ms. Hines . . ."

• • •

She winced when his hands touched her throat.

"Sorry to startle you, Ms. Hines, but I must examine the injury."

"Of course," she replied, staring straight ahead as he circled her, fingers probing her neck, shoulders, ribs.

At last, Dr. Hendry removed his hand. "No soft tissue damage on your neck. Just some bruising. Nothing a little makeup wouldn't hide, eh?"

"I don't wear makeup."

"Yes. Quite. That bruise on your rib may smart, but nothing is broken."

He stepped over to the sink and washed his hands. She pulled up her green smock to cover her nakedness. Hendry dried his hands, then opened a glass cabinet filled with plastic bottles. "I'm going to give you a mild painkiller, and an analgesic to reduce the swelling."

"Thank you. How is the Professor?"

"Resting comfortably, I hope. Dr. MacKenzie is handling his treatment. Most likely all the Professor needs is rest. He's a workaholic. And speaking of sleep, would you like something to soothe your nerves?"

"I'm fine. I can't take a nap now, I have duties to perform."

"You seem to be holding up well, Ms. Hines. It must have been quite a shock—Subject X attacking you like that."

"I thought he was going to murder me . . . and the Professor."

"Yet I doubt that was Logan's intention, at least in your case. If he wanted to kill you, Logan could have broken your neck with one hand, as easily as you or I break a pencil."

She faced him. "Thank you for that comparison, Doctor. It's an image I'll cherish."

Hendry laughed. "A sense of humor, Ms. Hines? Who knew?"

She slid off the diagnostic table. "Can I go now?"

"First I'd like to ask a question. You don't have to answer if you don't want to."

She raised an eyebrow, but said nothing.

"I couldn't help but notice old scars on your abdomen. They look like chemical burns. And you've had a surgical procedure, too. One not listed on your charts . . ."

"Chemistry set. I was accident-prone as a child."

"I . . . see. And the surgical procedure?"

"Emergency appendectomy when I was fourteen. I guess I forgot to list it when I filled out my personnel file."

"Not to worry," Hendry replied. "I'll fix that oversight right now."

"Then I can go?"

Hendry nodded. "Light duty for a day or two. Cold compresses to relieve the swelling. And if you have trouble sleeping, give me a call."

After she left, Hendry went to the computer and pulled up the personnel file for Carol Hines. On her health chart, he entered the results of the examination. Then he scrolled down to the "Past Medical History" section of the woman's profile. Under "Prior Surgeries" he deleted "none" and then typed: *Surgical procedure, approximate age 14. Cesarean section?*

"You're gonna fall out of your seat, Cutler!" Deavers barked.

Cutler straightened up in his chair and took his feet off the terminal where they'd been propped, then spun to face Deavers. "They teach you that in management school?"

"What?"

"Sneaking up on people."

"I've got my eye on you, Cutler, if that's what you mean. And I think you're enjoying this light duty thing way too much. Consider yourself active—as of now."

"That screw-up in the lab last night got you spooked, too? Should have let me get in the mix."

Deavers closed and locked the security command center hatch, then sat down across from Cutler. "You got that right, Cut. Since I lost Agent Hill, this place has been going to hell. Last night, Lynch and Anderson behaved like amateurs, and Franks is as green as grass. Nearly dropped the Professor with the tranquilizer gun instead of the resident menace, Logan."

"Sorry I missed it."

"Well, you won't miss the next mess, because you're back on the active list—as head of tactical security."

"I don't want Hill's old job," Cutler shot back.

"Why not?"

"Because I don't want to end up in intensive care like Hill. I am not an idiot, Deavers!"

Deavers leaned close and spoke barely above a whisper. "Listen, Cut. Things are only going to get messier around here, and soon. We've got a house full of mad scientists and one very dangerous monster. I need your help to keep this place together."

"No way, Major."

"Come on, Cutler. You're the best I've got, even if you

are an insubordinate son of a bitch with a chip on your shoulder. You also seem to be allergic to authority."

"Nice to see you drop that 'big boss' facade, Major. Makes you seem almost human. Did you give the same pep talk to Rice?"

"Rice is no longer my problem. He's been transferred to data control and information security, permanently. Orders came down from the Director."

"I love management."

"So what will it be, Cutler? Are you gonna do the right thing for once and stop being a pain in my ass?"

Cutler spun in his chair. "I'd really hate to leave this here comfy security booth, but I've got to tell you the truth, Deavers."

"What's that?"

"You had me at 'son of a bitch.' And I do love to wear those spiffy Kevlar battle suits."

After her examination, Carol Hines hurried back to her cramped quarters in the section of the complex known as the Hive.

By the time she'd reached her room, her heart was racing. She didn't calm down until she'd locked the door behind her and curled up on her bunk.

I certainly handled that badly, she thought. *I'm sure Dr. Hendry is a capable enough physician to know that my scar isn't from a simple appendectomy.*

She tore off her smock but tossed it in the corner, then stood before the mirror, examining her wounds— new and old.

I do everything I possibly can to forget my past, and my own body betrays me. It's like a map that leads perfect strangers to long-buried nightmares.

She covered her ears in a vain attempt to shut out the voices in her head that had been echoing for years.

"Your medical history has revealed a . . . psychological malady that forces us to decline your application for top secret security clearance, and deny you a position at the National Security Council. Very sorry, Ms. Hines . . ."

"Dear Ms. Hines: We regret to inform you that the National Aeronautics and Space Administration only considers applicants in top physical condition for astronaut training. Your prior condition forces us to remove you from consideration."

"Anyone who has attempted suicide—even in the turmoil of early adolescence—probably won't pass the stringent criteria of the United States Air Force Space Command . . ."

The fools. I never attempted suicide. I was young. Afraid. I only wanted to be rid of the . . . thing . . . in my womb. I never intended to harm myself . . . only it.

Yet her past dogged her for years, denied her opportunities within the research community. And when she finally did land a job at NASA, it was as a low-level training specialist, not the position she most coveted—astronaut.

It's not as if I didn't have the intelligence and the skills. I was an honors student by the time I was twelve. My father used to call me his "little scientist."

My father treated me special, too. Stopped beating me. Started to take an interest in my studies, my science projects.

Life became tolerable after I brought home that first science fair prize in third grade—almost idyllic, until . . . the accident, a few years later.

That's what my father called it. The accident. Like it was no-

body's fault. Like it just happened—sort of like a storm, or an earthquake.

But if it was an accident, why did I blame myself?

In spite of her resolve, Carol felt a wetness on her cheeks. She wiped her eyes with the palms of her hands and buried her head in her pillow. As she slipped into a troubled sleep, she thought she heard the voice of her long-dead mother . . .

"Your father is going to be so proud," Mrs. Hines said. She held a report card in one hand, her third drink of the day in the other. "My goodness. Only fourteen and already a whiz in advanced chemistry."

If my mother wasn't already half-tanked, she might have noticed that I was as pale as snow. But Mom only concentrated on the slip of paper.

"Can I go to the garage now?" Carol asked.

"Not until you get out of your school uniform, young lady—you just about burned the color out of your last smock with those chemical experiments of yours."

"Yes, Mother."

Upstairs, Carol stripped away her clothes and studied her reflection in the mirror. She imagined that her belly already protruded—her mother had even remarked at breakfast that she seemed to be gaining weight.

A neat trick for someone who throws up practically every morning . . .

It wasn't as if she was too young to know what was happening to her body. Even if she didn't grasp the truth at first, Carol Hines was an honors student and knew how to do research. As soon as she suspected the truth, she went to the library and took out every book she could find on the subject.

She knew every aspect of the biological process she

was going through. And more, so much more, too, because "Daddy's little scientist" had studied heredity. She found out that if the parents were a near genetic match, if the bloodlines were too closely related—cousins, perhaps—then there was a much higher probability of genetic abnormalities and inherited diseases. Cystic fibrosis. Down's syndrome. Friedreich's ataxia. Hemolytic anemia. Hemophilia.

The thought of having a disabled child horrified her. *How could Daddy's special little girl give birth to something that was malformed? Defective? Imperfect?*

Daddy loved perfection—didn't he tell her that himself? The night he was drinking while helping her with her homework. The night she sat too close to him. He always told her to keep her distance, but that night she felt her father's perverse love . . .

She carried a monster in her belly.

So before her father came home, before supper with the family, Carol Hines went down to the garage and mixed up something special with her junior chemistry set.

"Do what you oughta, add acid to water," her father used to say with a big laugh.

That night, in the garage, she mixed the acid but dispensed with the water. Instead, she used the corrosive on herself in a desperate, misguided attempt to burn the abomination she carried out of her womb . . .

A buzzing inside her head—the intercom—made Carol Hines bolt upright in her bunk.

"Hines here."

"Ah, so you *are* at home," Dr. MacKenzie said jovially.

"I went to see Dr. Hendry. And I felt a bit tired after . . . after what happened this morning."

"Understandable," MacKenzie replied. "Unfortunately, we have need of your skills. Subject X is thoroughly sedated, but the drugs are quickly wearing off. Dr. Cornelius has attempted an interface with that machine of yours, but he does not have your deft touch."

"Problem?"

"We're getting those pesky brain spikes again. And with all that happened today . . . well, you see our dilemma."

"I'll be right there. Over."

More responsibility . . . But I never, ever wanted to be in charge. Just do my job, keep my head down, so it won't get cut off.

She rose and dressed in one of her array of identical green smocks. Without glancing into the mirror, she left her quarters and followed the maze of corridors that led to Logan's cell.

A maze . . . this place is becoming another maze, just like NASA. The Professor promised me a place where pure scientific pursuit was the goal; a place free of judgment, petty bureaucratic politics.

But it was all lies.

Already the bureaucratic infighting has started, and Dr. Hendry is snooping into my past—no doubt in search of ammunition he can use to destroy my career, destroy me.

I wonder. Have I traded one maze for another?

Carol Hines felt lost.

11
Prey

"I count two four-wheeled APCs and a big job—looks like a knockoff of a Soviet BTR-60. Eight wheels, search-light on top, maybe six men inside with a driver. You can count on a dozen soldiers coming right for us."

Logan crawled back into the drainage ditch and handed Miko the night-vision binoculars. Behind them, the sound of beating blades echoed off the hillsides as twin helicopters with searchlights scoured the valley.

"We can't go backward, either. It's only a matter of time before those 'copter jockeys figure out I've made it to the road. They'll hunt us like a pack of wolves."

"So we are trapped."

"I'm trapped," said Logan. "I'm betting they don't even know you're here."

In the moonlight, he saw her frown.

"Why do you say that?" she asked.

"Because all the leaks are coming from my end. You knew about the mission. Why not the Koreans?"

She couldn't argue with Logan's logic, so Miko didn't try. "What do you have in mind?"

"Can you find that clearing in the foothills where we rested?"

"*Hai*, easily."

"Meet me back there in two hours."

"But what about the helicopters? Surely they will be searching the hills as well as the road."

"They won't be looking for me by then."

Miko shook her head. "You are not thinking of surrender?"

Logan laughed. "No way. I'm not crazy. I've got a better idea. I'm going to let them kill me."

She blinked. "Are you insane?"

"I don't like this any better than you. I've been shot before—didn't much care for the feeling. But this is the only way out that I can see—for both of us."

Realization dawned on Miko's face. "This is wrong. You could really die."

"You saw the way I recovered from that fall down the hill. I can heal, faster than any . . . human."

"But machine guns, bayonets . . . won't they finish you off or capture you if they find you are alive?"

"They won't get near me. I'll show my face, let them pop off some shots, then I'll tumble into the lake. If they're still looking for me tomorrow, they'll be dragging the pond, not scouring the hills, where we'll be safe."

"And after we rendezvous?"

"Face facts. No matter what, the mission is over—"

She tried to object, but he cut her off.

"—because we lost the element of surprise. They're going to double security. Triple it. And it's worse if they managed to grab Langram. They'll beat or drug the truth out of him in a couple of hours, so the extraction plan is compromised. If that happens, we'll both have to take your ride out of here."

Miko's face was grim. "Can we not stay together?"

"And risk both our lives?" Logan shook his head. "This is a much better plan."

He peeked over the edge of the trench. "They're less than a minute away. Get down into the ditch and crawl on your belly until you can make a clean break for the tree line."

He turned away to watch the road.

"Logan . . . I—"

"You got something to say?"

"Good luck," Miko whispered. Then she was gone among the tall grass. The rustling sound of her retreat was soon drowned out by the noise of the vehicles bumping along the rough road.

As Logan scrambled up the side of the trench, he freed the G36 strapped to his leg. A man seated in the top hatch was playing the searchlight in the ditch ahead of him. Logan carefully averted his eyes to retain his night vision. When the searchlight stabbed upward, into the tree line, Logan noticed a glint of moonlight off glass, and smiled. The BTR's armored windshield visors were up, the bullet resistant windows exposed. He quickly switched magazines.

These guys seem pretty cocky. But a Teflon-tipped titanium shell should ruin their day—and punch a huge hole right through that windshield.

As the eight-wheel personnel carrier rumbled closer, Logan suddenly lost his nerve. His heart palpitated, he broke out in a cold sweat, and doubt flooded his mind. When he threw the safety, his hands seemed unsteady enough to spoil his aim. Logan felt short of breath as he beat back rising panic. For the first time in a month, he had the urge to drink himself into a stupor, to sink back into a bottle, where he'd lived for far too many years.

Beat back the fear. Swallow it. You can take a bullet, you can live with the pain, Logan told himself.

But another part of him wanted to turn tail and run like a rabbit, to dive back into the ditch and crawl away from this place on his belly.

He started to rationalize his thoughts. *It's not fear, it's what you do with it. No matter what, I'm in control of the situation and I'm not running.*

That thought seemed to calm him, and Logan took several slow, deep breaths as the BTR rolled within range. When he glanced down at his hands again, they were as steady as a statue's.

Now the ten-ton personnel carrier was close enough to shake the ground under his feet. Logan saw that it had raced a little too far ahead of the other two vehicles—a break for him. Logan rose out of the ditch and stepped into the middle of the road.

The man in the top hatch was busy scanning the woods to the side, so it was the driver who spotted Logan first. The vehicle slowed, and its driver barked something to his comrade in the hatch.

Logan stood, left hand raised in mock surrender, right hand hanging at his side, the G36 tucked behind his leg. He slouched his right shoulder, hoping they'd think he was injured. The man in the top hatch swiveled the searchlight to frame Logan in its beam.

Bad idea. You die first.

Logan's arm shot up and the G36 coughed. The titanium shell exploded the searchlight into a shower of glass and fiery sparks. The man behind the light flew out of the hatch the instant the nearly expended shell caught him under the chin. His entire head disappeared in a shower of blood and fractured skull pieces. The headless corpse dropped onto the back of the BTR like a bag of dirt.

Logan could see the pale, frightened face of the Korean behind the wheel, illuminated by the dashboard light.

Now you.

Arm outstretched, Logan pumped off a second shot. The windshield splintered into a spiderweb, splashed dark crimson.

Suddenly, the BTR lurched forward as the driver's dying spasm punched the gas pedal. Eight tires squealed and dug into the dirt as the vehicle shot forward, an electrical fire streaming from the broken light on top.

Logan hesitated for a fatal instant and the armored frontal plate struck him full on, lifting him off his feet and tossing him halfway through the now-shattered windshield. As two Korean soldiers tumbled out of the rear hatch, the BTR-60 lurched off the road, bumped down a sharp incline and over a low cliff. Engine running, wheels turning, the vehicle hit the lake with an enormous splash.

Cutler doused cold water on his pallid face. Cheeks stinging, he wiped away the last traces of shaving cream and studied his reflection. With his index finger he traced the scar that divided one eyebrow with a faint white line—the result of his scuffle with Logan the night he, Erdman, and Hill snatched the man.

Seems like a lifetime ago.

Time, Cutler knew, passed slowly in lockdown.

The last six weeks seem to have stretched time to the point that

I can't remember when I wasn't living in this Hive, doing this same rotten job day in and day out.

He pulled a comb through his damp, sandy hair—noticing for the first time a touch of white at the temples. He turned away from the bathroom mirror and reached for his uniform. A piece of paper fell out of the pocket and drifted to the ground. Cutler picked it up and read it.

MEMO FROM THE DIRECTOR TO ALL PERSONNEL
RE: Security Measures

DUE TO SECURITY CONCERNS AND SEVERAL DANGEROUS EXPERIMENTS THAT WILL SOON BE CONDUCTED INSIDE THE ABOVEGROUND FACILITIES, ALL PERSONNEL ARE TO MOVE TO QUARTERS ON LEVELS TWO AND THREE OF THE UNDERGROUND COMPLEX, EFFECTIVE IMMEDIATELY. PLEASE BE ADVISED THAT YOU HAVE TWENTY-FOUR HOURS TO PACK AND PREPARE FOR THE MOVE. SEE YOUR DORMITORY SUPERVISOR FOR SPECIFIC ROOM ASSIGNMENTS.

That memo was dated four weeks ago. Twenty-eight days ago . . . six hundred and seventy-two hours ago . . .

Except that down here there's no day, no night, no sense of time passing. And everyone is living this way, now that the aboveground facilities are completely deserted.

I don't think I've seen the sun, except on guard detail, for almost a month. But at least I can get out once in awhile. Not like the docs, the technicians.

For the last fifteen days, double duty had become the norm, with all researchers working double shifts, technicians a sixty-five hour week. Tension was running high, and Cutler's security teams had to break up two fights in the cafeteria in just the last five days.

And yesterday that shrink MacKenzie warned me that sleep disorders were becoming more common because of sun deprivation.

Cutler wondered how much longer the lockdown could continue until there was a breakdown of discipline—or an open revolt.

His gloomy thoughts ended when he heard the intercom.

"Cutler. It's Deavers. My office. Ten minutes."

"Roger tha—" The line was already dead.

He dressed, locked his quarters, and headed to the elevator. On the way, he noted that the recessed lighting on much of his level had failed—the third time in a month. It should have been fixed, but the maintenance staff was overtaxed, so they claimed.

Or maybe they're on an unofficial strike since that incident at the beginning of the week. Either way, I'm going to have to kick some butt to get this place in shape.

Cutler entered the elevator and rode up to Level One with Carol Hines. She held her straight brown hair back with one hand while holding a PDA in the other. Her face was pinched in a frown of concentration that consumed her, and she never looked up from the illuminated dial for the entire ascent. When the doors opened, she bolted for the diagnostic lab. He headed in the opposite direction, to Major Deavers's office.

Cutler entered without knocking. Deavers gave him a lemon-sucking look.

"The eggheads want the wolves this morning. I've alerted the handlers and they're ready. Now I've alerted you."

"What do they want us for?"

"You're in charge of Subject X. Two-man team, with a third for backup. Tranquilizers only. No live ammo."

"I'll go myself, and take Franks. He's learned the ropes, he knows how to obey orders, and he can keep a cool head, usually. I'll bring Lynch for backup."

"What about Anderson? Erdman?"

"Erdman's off duty, and has earned the rest. Anderson's been real sloppy lately. Almost got himself cut to pieces by a perimeter laser he 'forgot' to deactivate before he headed outside for guard duty."

Deavers frowned. "Anderson was sharp enough to stop that escape attempt on Monday. The Director would've had our heads if there'd been a breach of security."

"Anderson got lucky. Or maybe he was just pissed off because he didn't get a cut of the bribe."

"How stupid do those guys in maintenance think we are?" Deavers asked. "Trying to buy their way aboard the supply chopper. As if we wouldn't notice . . ."

"They weren't thinking straight. Cabin fever. This lockdown has been tough on everyone. I'm surprised there hasn't been more trouble."

"Especially since we're short of experienced security personnel. We've got fifty-five armed guards in this facility—you'd think more than eight of them would learn how to handle the subject."

"For the record, we're down to seven who can do that. Hill's gone, remember?" said Cutler. "Let's face facts, sir. The rest of the guards, they just don't want to learn. Logan—Subject X—has them all spooked."

"Can you blame them?" said Deavers. "He gives *me*

the creeps. With those wires and machines coming out of his head. That thing over his eye, the battery around his neck. He looks like the walking dead, like some kind of a robot zombie . . ."

Logan thought he was dead when the BTR smacked into him. The G36 flew out of his hand and clattered away, to be crushed under the tractor-sized front wheel. As eight tons lifted him off the ground, Logan was hurled through the cracked windshield by the momentum. Then the vehicle swerved off the road.

Torn and bloody from a dozen lacerations, Logan rolled inside the vehicle, to land in the lap of a headless man—the driver, his brains decorating the compartment. Vaguely, as if from a great distance, Logan heard cries of panic, then felt fresh air pimple his skin as someone opened a hatch.

Soon after, the heavy armored vehicle struck the lake. The jolt threw Logan against the dash just as a blast of water surged through the window. The torrent buffeted him as the compartment instantly flooded, but the frigid water stung Logan back to consciousness.

Battered by the mini-tsunami, Logan opened his mouth for a deep breath and gagged on water. He nearly passed out again—wanted to pass out, into the comforting warmth of oblivion—but he fought against the suicidal urge. He forced his eyes open and tried to orient himself. He got a little help from the vehicle's interior lighting, which had not yet shorted out. Though hindered by water that still gushed into the passenger bay of the fast-submerging vehicle, Logan knew he would get out.

While the BTR sank front-first, a booted foot connected

with Logan's shoulder and he grabbed it. His captive carried him upward, and all the way out of the driver's compartment—into the rear of the armored carrier.

Suddenly, Logan's head broke the surface and he sucked air. Right next to him in the fast-flooding compartment, a Korean officer sputtered and choked as he treaded water. Logan recognized the other man's rank by the bugle draped over his right shoulder—the North Koreans still used bugles to issue commands in battle. When the man saw Logan, he shouted something incomprehensible and fumbled for the pistol on his belt.

I'll have to shut him up quick or he'll tell his pals that I'm still alive. Can't let him get away.

Logan grabbed the man by the throat and pushed him under. Already the water level inside the compartment had risen to the edge of the rear hatch. Soon Logan would have to get out or be sucked under with the BTR.

Outside, searchlights already played on the water, and Logan could hear the men on the road calling for their stricken comrades. Making a clean break was not going to be easy.

Meanwhile, the man struggled against Logan's grip. Still forcing the officer's head under the surface, he reached down with his right hand and yanked the Model 1 fighting knife from his belt. Logan stabbed out once, twice. After the third thrust, the Korean went limp in his grasp and Logan released the man.

The water bubbled up to his chin. Logan took a deep breath just as the tail end of the fighting vehicle slipped beneath the liquid darkness. He held on to the hatch, waiting until he was two or three meters under, then he kicked outward in an attempt to swim as far away as he could get from the sinking hulk before the undertow dragged him to his doom. Ultimately, Logan was able to clear the wreck and swim away.

He kept on swimming, just under the surface of the black water, until he could no longer withstand the lack of oxygen. As spots blotted his vision, Logan cut the surface and gulped air. A hundred meters away, he watched North Koreans scurry down to the shoreline to rescue their comrades.

Exhausted and relishing the air, Logan deduced that there was a current, because he was being carried slowly toward the dam. He lay on his back, floating, until the chattering voices faded, the glare of the searchlights dimmed, and even the beating of the helicopter blades was muted. Then he swam to the shore, crawled out of the water, and scrambled up the incline. Unnoticed by the soldiers, he crossed the road and ducked into the trees, then ran deeper into the woods until he reached the foothills. Finally, when he was sure he was not being pursued, Logan slumped down behind a tree to rest.

Gasping, he checked his condition. His second battle suit, like the flesh on his back, his thighs, and his torso, was in tatters. He'd probably left a trail of blood all the way up the hill, but hoped the North Koreans were too sloppy to notice. As he tore a chunk of material from his camouflage suit, Logan cursed.

That's the second set of duds I lost tonight. At this rate, I'll be butt naked by morning.

Suddenly, he felt like laughing.

Hell, at least I didn't get shot.

He checked his watch. Barely thirty minutes had passed since he parted company with Miko. He now had ninety minutes to circle around the mess on the road and climb the hill to meet her.

Groaning, seeping blood, and shivering from the wet and the cold, Logan stumbled to his feet and pressed on.

Fifteen minutes after his meeting with Deavers, Cutler took Franks and Lynch to the surface, where they walked the ground that was going to be used for the morning "experiment."

The sun had just risen, a dull yellow ball over the mountains. And though it was cold and getting colder, Franks was as eager to get outside as Cutler. Lynch did nothing but complain because he'd been on duty all night and now he had another eight-hour shift because of the scheduled experiment.

The ground in question was a parcel of rolling, snow-covered land within the compound. A bevy of two- and three-year-old saplings and a few reedy pines dotted the topography. The entire area was encircled by double four-meter walls of chain-link fencing that would be electrified for the actual experiment. Already the technicians and sound men had set up remote cameras and microphones on steel posts planted deep into the frozen ground, high up in the trees, and on top of fence posts.

The trio circled the perimeter, double-checking to make sure there were no gaps in the fence where a wolf—or Subject X—could slip through and escape. Halfway around, they came to a tall, barred gate with multiple layers of steel fence beyond. From somewhere inside that prisonlike maze, they heard howls and angry snarls of a pack of timber wolves.

"What's got 'em so stirred up?" asked Lynch.

"We're downwind," Cutler replied. "They can smell our scent. It's driving them nuts."

"Geez," said Franks. "Why are they acting so aggressive? It's like they want to kill us or something. That pack sounds as if they're ready to rip us apart."

"They're starving," Cutler replied. "Maddened with hunger. Once they're out of those cages, they will drag down anything that moves, regardless of size."

"What the hell do those eggheads need starving wolves for?" Franks asked, shivering against the cold.

"They're going to put Subject X inside this fence, then let out the wolves and film the whole thing."

Franks whistled. "What's the point?"

Cutler shrugged. "Your guess is as good as mine," he said with disgust.

Miko burst from cover when she saw Logan struggling up the slope. She raced to him and took his arm.

"Lean on me," she whispered, and he willingly slumped against her slight but strong frame.

They stumbled up the hill and into a crude shelter Miko fashioned from pine branches. Inside, she snapped a chemical glow stick and laid Logan down on a bed of moss and leaves.

Her face was full of concern in the dim light. "I feared you would never return," she said as she stripped off his clothing and cleansed his wounds for the second time that night.

"Told you . . . I could take it," he wheezed, choking back a dry cough. Her cool hands felt soothing, but soon Logan began to shiver.

"Here, drink this," she said, thrusting a warm flask into his hand. He gulped the hot tea gratefully.

"Nifty device," he said, admiring the flask's battery-operated heating element. "You're just a bundle of tricks."

She smiled. "Unfortunately, the tea is instant."

"Never tasted better in my life."

After a few minutes, Logan felt revived. He propped himself on his elbows. Miko lurked at the entrance to the makeshift hut, NV binoculars to her eyes.

"What do you see?"

"Nothing. No one suspects that we are here. The soldiers are convinced that you died in the lake. They pulled several of their comrades out of the water—dead and alive. From what I could understand, some of their men are still missing."

"Lost my Heckler & Koch."

"Yes. One of the soldiers found the remains of your weapon on the road. He took it with him when they left."

"And Langram? Did you see anything or anyone on the other side of the lake?"

Miko lowered the binoculars and faced him. "They captured your friend. Soldiers brought him down from the hill. His arms were bound and they . . . mistreated him. He was placed inside an armored car and driven in the direction of the dam. I am sorry."

Logan was quiet a long time, his face grim. Finally, he spoke. "Maybe we can rescue him. We have a chance. They think I'm dead and they don't even know about you."

Miko's face was tense. "But even if we could find him in that complex and manage to free him, where can we go?"

"We evacuate with your team. Where are they picking you up? Is there a specific time, or do you have to summon an extraction?"

"I . . . I have no way out," she confessed. "I had planned to get out with you, after my own goal was accomplished."

"What are you, a kamikaze? Did your government send you on a suicide mission?"

"My government . . . my superiors . . . don't even know I am here. I took on this mission by myself. For personal reasons."

To her surprise, Logan threw back his head and laughed until he was wracked by a coughing spell.

"Are you all right?" Miko asked, springing to his side.

"Swallowed a little too much of that lake," he said, feeling a pleasing warmth creep through him as she stroked his head. As drowsiness began to claim him, Logan chuckled softly.

"A renegade, just like me, huh? Shoulda guessed."

Miko smiled down at him through a tumble of hair. "Mr. Logan, you do not know the half of it."

"If I felt better, I'd make you tell me the whole story . . . but right now . . . I'm too damn tired."

"Then sleep, Logan-*san*. You need rest. You are only human."

As Logan's eyes closed, he whispered a reply. "Only human? I wish, Miko . . . I wish."

Though the sun had risen, the surface temperature had dropped precipitously since their trip outside at dawn. Despite clear skies, a frigid Arctic wind howled down from the north. Right now it was a few notches below zero degrees Celsius, and dropping steadily.

Swathed in several layers of undergarments, his uniform, and a cocoon of Kevlar body armor, Cutler still shivered against the cold. Blasts of chilly air blew under his helmet so that his breath turned to vapor. And even though it offered no protection from the cold, Cutler didn't dare remove his helmet. The danger was too great.

With a long electronic staff, forked on one end and attached to a battery pack on the other, Cutler carefully directed Subject X across the snow-covered expanse to the middle of the fenced-off perimeter. The electroprod—dubbed a "pitchfork" by the handlers—deadened Logan's senses yet allowed him to be led about on his own two feet. "Like walking the dog on a leash," Lynch quipped as they prepped for the experiment.

Cutler wasn't sure what the docs had done to Logan in the past six weeks or so. He didn't look brainwashed—more like brain-dead. He figured Logan's senses must be numb or the cold would be getting to him, because the "subject" was stark naked in the snow, covered only with Teflon "sensor ports" embedded in his chest, neck, arms, and torso, where surgical probes had been inserted.

As Cutler led Logan to the designated area, Lynch and Franks followed a few steps behind, ready to take the subject down with tranquilizer guns at the first sign of rebellion. But Logan remained docile, his bare feet shuffling zombielike through the snow, dragging dozens of wires and tubes in his wake like shackles on a felon.

"Right here," said Lynch, digging his booted foot into a mound of snow stained with blue dye.

"Where are the goddamn techs?" Cutler demanded. "Logan still has to be hooked up."

"Here they come," said Franks.

Two technicians, bundled in ill-fitting Kevlar body suits and dragging too much equipment, set to work as soon as they arrived. They began by hooking the loose wires to a computer terminal buried in the snow at Logan's feet.

"What's that?" asked Franks.

The man kneeling at Logan's feet looked up. "This box is a wireless link to the computers in the lab, including the REM device. These feeder cables will keep our boy docile until the docs decide it's time to turn him loose."

"Yeah, when these wires get unplugged—watch out," warned the other technician.

"Seen him in action yet?" Cutler asked.

"Just heard rumors," the tech on the ground replied as he tested a circuit.

"I've seen him in action," said Franks. "And I plan to be long gone when they unleash him."

"Hey, Dooley," said the man in the snow. "This wrangler's seen Subject X in action."

Franks turned red. The man called Dooley turned and thrust a pocket-sized computer into the agent's hand.

"What's this?"

"The feeder cable release control. When Doc Cornelius gives you the word, you press this button and the monster is loose."

"Man, why me?" Franks asked.

"You're a wrangler, ain't you?"

Meanwhile, the technician activated the wireless box at Logan's feet, then entered a code into the keypad on top.

"Okay, Agent Cutler," he said, rising. "Remove the electroprod, then move back to the shelter."

With trepidation, Cutler deactivated the staff and detached the twin prongs from the magnetic locks embedded in Logan's temples. To his relief, Logan acted the same as he had throughout the entire process. From the moment they came above ground to the time they hooked him up to the box, Subject X didn't even blink, just stared straight ahead, eyes unseeing.

The security team backed away from Subject X, tranquilizer guns held ready. At sixty meters they turned and bolted for the concrete surface shelter near the wolf cages. They would wait in that compact bunker cluttered with communication's equipment until their services were required again.

The technicians joined them a few minutes later—after all the connections had been tested, the cameras and sound systems activated, and Logan subjected to a final stage of "preparation." The techs stripped off their gear and took their places at the communications console. Cutler and Franks grabbed some coffee from a flask and peered at Subject X through a narrow slit. Franks held the feeder cable control like it was a bomb he'd prefer to get rid of. Lynch, uninterested, curled up on a bench and took a nap.

Outside, the subject stood stock-still, legs braced, up to his calves in thirty centimeters of powdery snow. A brisk wind stirred Logan's hair, and carried the scent of warm blood to the wolf cages.

Almost immediately, the animals howled in anticipation as they moved around in a frenzy, hollow-eyed with feral hunger.

"Amazing work, Dr. Hendry!" exclaimed Dr. Cornelius. "Subject X has increased his muscle mass by a third and lost more than a third of his body fat in just under six weeks. Your chemical treatments are nothing short of miraculous."

Dr. Hendry waved Cornelius's compliment aside and grinned. "It was a thorny problem, but all it took was a fresh approach to figure out a solution."

They stood in the main lab, near a buffet table laden with a continental-style breakfast. Two dozen doctors, researchers, and technicians had worked through the night to prepare for this day's critical experiment. It was Dr. MacKenzie who took it upon himself to arrange for breakfast to be delivered by the cafeteria at dawn.

Carol Hines sat near the two doctors, a cup of tea cooling at her side. She paid no attention to their conversation as she ran down the complex programming checklist in her lap.

"I'm surprised you didn't use steroids," Cornelius said between bites of cheese Danish.

"No, no. Steroids are quite unsuitable. The results of steroid use are temporary, and there are far too many harmful side effects."

"So how did you solve the problem?"

"Once the researchers at Johns Hopkins University determined that the protein myostatin limits muscle growth in humans, it was fairly simple for me to devise a specific enzyme to block that protein, allowing Subject X to bulk up in record time."

Cornelius looked forlornly at his own belly, which protruded over his belt. "Man, you've got to let me try that stuff, Doctor."

"Good morning," the Professor announced as he entered the crowded lab. Dr. Cornelius turned, a Styrofoam cup of hot coffee in one hand. Hines looked up from her chart as the Professor crossed to their side.

The Professor directed his first query to Ms. Hines. "So this may be the big day, eh?"

"We're hoping so, sir," she replied.

"Good, good . . ." He turned. "Dr. Cornelius. Do you have anything for me to review?"

Cornelius gulped down the last of his Danish. "Well, we believe we've overcome the supraendocrine gland problem."

The Professor was impressed. "How so?"

"A simple trabeculae matrix," Dr. Hendry interrupted. "It was staring us in the face the whole time."

"But you've got it now," said the Professor.

"We believe so, sir," Cornelius replied. Not an endocrinologist, he was taking his cue from Dr. Hendry.

"Excellent work," said the Professor. "Have you released all of Logan's feeder cables?"

"Not yet, sir."

"Then do it now, Dr. Cornelius. Let the experiment begin."

Cornelius nodded, then faced the rest of the staff. "Everyone to your places," he commanded. "Experiment two of six to commence in two minutes."

Hines took her seat at the REM workstation and unlocked the controls of the device. Her face was placid as she faced them. "I'm ready."

"Biomonitors ready," said Dr. Hendry.

"CAT scan ready!" called Dr. MacKenzie, his red hair wild and uncombed.

"Cameras ready . . . audio ready," crackled voices speaking from the communications bunker on the surface.

Cornelius leaned over his terminal and keyed his mike. "Wranglers, release all cables and reel them in."

"Copy, sir," Franks replied.

On the wall-sized HDTV screen appeared the image of Logan, immovable in the center of the snowy expanse as the feeder cables dropped from his chiseled body.

The Professor, eyes locked on the screen, sat down behind the central terminal and licked his lips.

"Now, Dr. Cornelius. Show me what Weapon X can do."

12
Predator

"Three . . . two . . . one. Set. This is Experiment Two of Six. Defense."

Dr. Cornelius paused to scan the lab. "Everything check? Cameras? Monitors?"

"Fine," said Hendry. Other voices muttered affirmatives.

"Dr. Cornelius."

"Yes, Professor."

"Mr. Logan—"

"Subject X," Dr. MacKenzie corrected. "He no longer has a name."

"Subject X seems to be covered in ichor."

"Sheep's blood, sir," Cornelius explained. "Quicker scent. We want the wolves to act aggressively."

"I see." The Professor's eyebrows rose. "Ingenious. Lovely."

For many minutes, the figure stood like a monolith in the vast frozen expanse. Carol Hines found herself listening to the sound of the wind transmitted by the speakers, drawn to the image of Subject X on the screen. More minutes passed, filled with the sounds of ticking monitors, hushed voices. The howl of the wind was joined by the howl of the wolves.

While technicians calibrated their instruments, Cornelius helped himself to a third cup of coffee. Time seemed suspended as more checks and rechecks were carried out.

Finally, Carol Hines spoke. "He's been out there in subzero weather for more than twenty minutes. Can't we get on with this?"

Cornelius lowered his cup without tasting it. "We are following procedures, Ms. Hines."

Over the speaker, the cries of the hungry wolves intensified.

"Readings, Dr. Hendry?"

"Heartbeat, pressure, all okay."

"Maybe we should have him do some stretches, loosen up. Cold muscles can get pretty stiff," the physical therapist suggested.

"Not his muscles," Hendry replied. "They are conditioned to perform at the optimum level despite cold or long periods of immobility."

Over the blaring speakers, wet snarls mixed with angry barks. The animals were getting impatient, lashing out at one another in their zeal for fresh kill.

"He can hear them?" asked Cornelius.

"Yes, sir. I'm sure of it," said the audio technician, speaking from the bunker outside. The voice link was crystal clear. "We can hear the wolves behind a half foot of concrete without the sound system. If Subject X can't hear them, he's deaf."

"Yet there is no adrenal rise . . . odd," muttered Cornelius.

"Not odd at all," declared the Professor, eyes bright

with anticipation. "It means that your reprogramming has worked, Dr. Cornelius. Weapon X feels no fear."

Cornelius gazed at his screen. "Prepare to release the gate."

"Roger," said the voice of an animal handler positioned inside the animal control compound on the surface.

"When did the animals last eat?" the Professor asked.

Cornelius shrugged. "Don't know. Handlers?"

"Copy," the animal handler replied. "Chart says about six days ago, sir."

"Well, gee, they can have my Danish."

The voice came from the status tech station, followed by some laughter. The Professor turned in his chair and glared at the offender.

"Release the gate," said Cornelius.

The visuals were split between two cameras. On the big screen, the laboratory staff simultaneously watched the wolves bursting through the open gate and Logan standing rigid in the snow.

"He's not reacting."

"Give him a chance, Cornelius."

"I mean there's no blood pressure rise, no increase in heart rate."

The timber wolves scrambled across the snowy field, paws churning up great gouts of snow. The alpha male leaped ahead of the pack, a one-hundred-seventy-pound, red-brown brute with a long, foam-flecked snout and a lolling tongue. Scrawny from lack of food, the wolf's wiry muscles rippled under its ruddy fur.

"God, he's not moving," whispered one of the techs.

"Is he alive?" the Professor demanded.

"Yes, of course!" Cornelius cried.

"But he's not moving."

"Good God . . ." Carol Hines averted her eyes.

As the wolves surged ahead, the camera switched back to single screen—the animals were so close to the subject that they were both in the same shot.

The Professor's face was grim. He focused his harsh glare on Dr. Cornelius. "Do you have data for me?"

Cornelius, eyes on the screen, shook his head in bafflement. "He's just . . . not reacting."

"Blast!" The Professor jumped up from his chair and approached the screen. "Is it a physical disability?" he asked. "The claws, perhaps?"

"No, I doubt that." Cornelius faced Dr. Hendry for validation, but the other seemed to be too busy to notice.

"If his claws function, then why doesn't he use them, Doctor?" asked the Professor.

The wrangler cried out, "They'll rip him to pieces!"

At last, Hendry looked up, to meet Cornelius's desperate eyes. "He won't be able to heal if he's torn to bloody chunks," said Hendry.

Cornelius spun around to see Carol Hines's face turned away from the monitor. "Hines, do your job!" She turned back to the monitor, fingers poised over the keyboard, her face red.

"Up the response column now!" Cornelius commanded.

Carol Hines programmed the new data into the transmitter, hit the send key, then watched the screen.

Somewhere in Logan's deadened brain, a switch dropped—a chemical rush that kick-started a slumbering portion of his mind. A burst of electrochemical activity in the left prefrontal cortex stimulated Logan's aggression, and a glimmer of awareness flickered behind his unblinking stare. The spark lasted a split second—long enough for Subject X to hear, see, smell, and comprehend the danger.

But the wolves were already on him. The alpha leaped off the snow and slammed into the mutant and the others surrounded him. Jaws clamped on legs, on arms, dragging Logan to the ground. . . .

Slavering, snapping jaws. Hot, foul breath. Teeth digging, tearing, ripping. Vicious.

Logan swam through a sea of nightmarish images and woke up fighting—arms waving blindly as he fended off phantom predators. With a cry he sat up in a bed of leaves and moss. He opened his eyes to blinding sunlight, until the appearance of a silhouette dimmed the bright glare.

"Who—"

Two fingers gently covered his lips. "Hush, Logan. You are safe," a quiet voice soothed.

"Miko?"

"Hai."

Logan blinked. "Must have been dreaming," he muttered, the terrible images fading like wisps of morning fog.

She stared at him, her expression curious.

"Do I look that bad in the morning?" he growled, looking away.

"Not at all. You look perfectly fine. And there is the mystery."

"Yeah, well . . ."

"You fell into a deep sleep. I thought you had gone into shock. Then I thought you were dead," she said, her tone muted. "But as I watched you in the morning light, I observed that gaping wound on your chest."

With the tip of her index finger, Miko gently touched a spot between his pectorals. "Open and bleeding last night. Healed by morning. Now not even a scar."

He stared straight ahead; she settled on the ground next to him. "Anyone else would be dead."

"I'm not like anyone else."

She waited, silent. Finally, he spoke. "Have you ever heard of mutants, Miko?"

"*Hai.* But to be truthful, I never thought mutants were real. Just a superstition, like moving things with your mind, or EPS—"

"You mean ESP. Extrasensory perception."

She nodded.

"Well, mutants are real. I know because I'm a mutant. I found out—never mind how—just a couple of years ago. Knowing changed me, but not for the better."

"Yet your abilities? Surely you've had them for a long time?"

He faced her. "I always knew I was different, even as a kid. People treated me differently, too. Like they knew there was something unnatural about me."

"Alienation. Everyone feels that way when they are young."

"But I'm not young, Miko. If I told you how old I am, you wouldn't believe me. Don't you see? There was something different about me. I never got sick like other people, wounds healed quickly. But it wasn't until I went to war that I found out how different I really was . . ."

"You are immune to disease and do not age at all. How is this a problem?"

"It's a problem. Watching someone you love grow old and suffer and die while you remain forever young . . . Yeah, that's a problem—"

She winced at the comparison. "I see. Like watching a parent die?" she whispered.

"Yes. Like a parent. Only it's your lovers, too. And even your children, if you had any . . ."

He pressed his fists to his temples and closed his eyes. "And I don't even know why I'm different. I was trouble for everyone around me since the day I was born. I don't deserve this 'gift.' Why me?"

"When there is no answer to a question, why ask?" Miko replied. "But now I understand."

"Do you? Can you?" he shot back. "I've lived in Japan. I am familiar with your language, your society, your ways. The Japanese stake a lot on conformity. In your world, I would be even more of a misfit. Someone like you could never understand that."

Miko shook her head. "Do not be so sure, Logan-*san*. I also know what it is like to be an outsider."

"What, you flunked third grade?"

"Have you ever heard of comfort women?" she asked.

"Like prostitutes?"

"Not prostitutes, Logan. Slaves to their Japanese masters. In World War Two, soldiers took thousands of women from their homes and used them. My grandmother was a comfort woman, taken from her farm in Korea by a high-ranking officer, brought to Tokyo to be his mistress. My mother was their child."

As Miko spoke, she played with a ring on her middle finger. "After the war, the Koreans did not want these women back because they were considered defiled. Many had borne half-Japanese children. Such children are shunned in both countries, as are their descendants, even today, in these enlightened times."

The sound of a passing jet fighter high overhead made

them pause. The aircraft vanished as quickly as it appeared.

"You say you know Japanese society, Logan-*san*," Miko continued. "Do you know that mixed-race children are excluded from the best schools, no matter how talented or intelligent we may be? Did you know that we are relegated to the lowest positions in Japanese corporations— salaryman or secretary—never to rise higher?"

"So you ended up in civil service?" Logan asked.

"Yes. The SAT accepted me because I was useful. I had skills they needed—I spoke Korean like a native, could pass for a Korean if necessary. Something I have done in past assignments."

"But you're not on assignment now?"

"No, Mr. Logan. I am here on my own, on personal business."

"And that personal business is inside that complex at the base of the dam?"

"*Hai.*"

"It's a sure bet Langram is there, too."

"Last night you said you were going to rescue your friend."

"I intend to go after Langram. It's such a stupid, suicidal move, the Koreans might just fall for it. You can come with me and finish your personal business as long as it doesn't interfere with mine. Or you can try to get out of North Korea on your own."

"I will come with you, Logan. When do we go?"

"Tonight, after it gets dark. It'll take us an hour to get past the dam, another two to get down the hill and inside."

"Until then?"

"We eat, Miko. Then we rest. It's gonna be a long night."

"You have an appetite?" Miko asked.

"Yeah. After one of those healing comas, I wake up hungry as a damn wolf."

"They're eating him alive!"

"I'm getting no response," cried Cornelius. He pushed Carol Hines out of the way and started banging on her console. "He should have been triggered. We've lost it."

On the screen, the wolves were a snarling, squirming mass swarming over the struggling mutant. Subject X fought back weakly as ripping claws and gnashing jaws closed on his unprotected belly and slashed at his throat.

Suddenly, Cornelius looked up from the REM console. "It's coming through. The epinephrine is rising . . ."

The Professor appeared at his shoulder. "Eighty-six . . . ninety percent . . . ninety-five . . ." The man clapped his hand on Cornelius's shoulder. "He's fighting back!"

A moan of agony blared from the speakers. On the screen, Logan's right forearm emerged from the sniveling, slavering pack. The groan became a frightful roar of rage and defiance. Suddenly, the wolves reared back, yelping, their muzzles flecked with blood, as three adamantium claws sprung from Logan's ravaged flesh.

"Listen to that feral roar. Gentlemen, we have succeeded!"

"I don't think that sound is bloodlust, Professor," Dr. Cornelius said. "I think it's pain."

A welter of blood poured from the claw extraction

points, rolling down Logan's outstretched arms as he stumbled to his feet.

"Splendid." The Professor nodded his head, adjusted his square glasses. "It will make him all the more savage."

Over Logan's roar, the scientists heard a snarling whelp that made them wince. Logan burst from the middle of the barking curs. The alpha leaped at his throat. With an uppercut that impaled the animal and lifted it over his head, Logan slashed the wolf in half at the torso—severing its spine in a chopping gesture that neatly divided the howling creature.

Hot, steaming blood rained down on Logan, saturating his face, neck, torso. He ducked a leaping female and thrust his right arm back to pierce the skull of another male.

Carol Hines averted her eyes as Logan disemboweled a yelping she-wolf, then slammed its broken, writhing body against another. Though she avoided the image, Hines could not block out the gruesome sounds—barks, howls, grunts, whelps, and whimpers of animals suffering, dying . . .

"Readings, Cornelius," the Professor commanded.

"Heart rate just shot off the scale, Professor. And you don't want to know the high levels of adrenaline, epinephrine, serotonin. Phenomenal stress level. He could burn out."

"Is that likely?" the Professor asked, alarmed.

"I don't know," Cornelius answered truthfully. "The metabolics alone . . . it's beyond human. And the wounds he's already received . . ."

"Those wounds haven't slowed Logan yet," noted MacKenzie.

A half-dozen dead wolves sprawled on the ground.

Others gasped their last frost-steamed breath. A few struggled in the slippery muck, dragging broken limbs, their entrails staining the snow yellow-brown-red.

Then a sustained howl pierced the air as Logan pinned the alpha female to the ground with the claws of his left hand while using his right to cut the flopping bitch to pieces. Blood and gouts of fur and flesh flew with each brutal swing, yet no mortal blow was struck. Logan was deliberately prolonging the creature's agony.

"He's far more bestial than those he's slaughtering," Cornelius observed.

The Professor was all smiles. "What a perfect choice Logan was," he declared with smug satisfaction. *And how foolish of me to doubt the Director.*

Carol Hines appeared behind them, her eyes fixed on the screen. "Professor, can't we stop it now? Save the animals that remain? It's just senseless slaughter."

The Professor was shocked by her suggestion. "I think not, madam. I am enjoying this far too much. Let the animals save themselves. Survival of the fiercest. It's nature's violent way."

"Professor, I've got a fluorescent analysis now, and a CAT scan," called Dr. Hendry. "Would you like to see them?"

"Just give me your results on the scan."

"Activity in the left prefrontal cortex—" began Dr. MacKenzie.

"Ah, I see—the part of the brain that seeks vengeance," the Professor interjected.

"You are correct, Professor," MacKenzie replied. "It's also the part of the brain that is active when people prepare to satisfy hunger, a craving. Hunger and the lust for revenge are hardwired—and appear to be related."

"And the fluorescent analysis?"

"On-screen," said Hendry.

A square section of the violent images on the screen froze, broke away, then filled the entire monitor— Logan's raised right arm, claws extended.

"Yes. Can you hold on that?" the Professor asked.

The screen went blank, then the same picture reappeared—but as an X-ray image. Logan's claws and adamantium bones silver-white; vessels, tendons, muscles a medley of muted grays.

"We need more detail," the Professor complained. "Give me a re-emission on the osteograph."

"One second," said Hendry's assistant.

The image morphed, then melted into a blur. "Bring it in to either hand," instructed the Professor.

Suddenly, the image of Logan's clawed right hand filled the screen, bones still silver-white, but nerves, veins, tendons all shaded a multitude of hues. The image was three-dimensional, and as they watched, Dr. Hendry shifted the perspective so they could view the anatomy in action from every conceivable angle.

"Look at that," the Professor cried. "The perfect synthesis of human trabeculae and adamantium. Bone, bonded to the hardest metal in the world, inside the body of a berserker."

The Professor stepped up to the screen as if he were about to embrace the image. "Logan. Weapon X. The perfect fighting machine. The perfect killing machine."

Dr. Hendry interrupted the Professor's revelry. "There is some excessive distortion in the metacarpals. That could be the cause of the subject's pain upon extrusion, as Dr. Cornelius suggested."

"How so?" It was Carol Hines who asked.

"The adamantium appendages seem to cause him discomfort as they activate," Hendry told her. "Some of it is undoubtedly due to the damage the adamantium prostheses cause to his own skin as the claws rip through, but he may also be experiencing a general ache, similar to a child who is teething."

The Professor faced Hendry. "You'll look into that?"

"Yes, Professor."

"Good. Then take us back to the battlefield."

With a beep the image vanished, to be replaced by the prerecorded scene in the bloody snow. The sound returned as well, though the howls and cries of the wolves had been silenced forever.

Logan stood, legs wide, in the center of the bloody tableau, arms outstreched and dripping hot gore.

"Program complete," Cornelius announced. "We seem to have gone through all our wolves."

Carol Hines turned away from the screen.

"A total massacre. Splendid. This exercise couldn't have gone better," said the Professor. "And look at Logan! I think he wants more. Do we have more?"

"No," said Ms. Hines.

"Pity . . ."

Then a long, continuous canine howl echoed throughout the lab; an alarming sound that sent shivers of superstitious dread down the spines of civilized, educated scientists and researchers. The cry was feral, animalistic—yet somehow ominously human.

Cornelius spun to face the Professor. "Good God. He's roaring like an animal."

"Ah! And you thought it was just pain that made him cry out, Cornelius—but no." The Professor stood, fist clenched in front of his face as he stared at Logan's image on the screen, listening to the sustained bestial bellow.

"The wolves would kill for food, or territory, perhaps," said the Professor, his voice rising in intensity. "But this mutant . . . this living weapon . . . his passion is the *fear* of his prey. He finds relish in the odor of blood. Fear is the key. Fear is his motivating factor."

The Professor's rant ended as did the mad howl. Instantly, the laboratory grew quiet.

The Professor turned to address them all.

"Despite his original protestations, his struggles against us, I know we've done Logan a great favor," the Professor declared. "His most bestial needs are about to exceed his most primitive dreams . . . In our service, of course."

He faced Cornelius. "You can turn him off now, Doctor."

Cornelius returned to his console as Carol Hines resumed her position behind the REM keyboard. They both prepped their systems for powering down.

On the screen, Logan dropped to his knees, where he swayed as the claws slid back into their sheaths. Then, without a sound, he toppled face-first into the bloody snow like a puppet whose strings had been severed. Legs jerked like the spasms of the dead, and Logan flopped in the wolf guts and settled on his back.

"Wranglers?" Cornelius radioed.

"Copy," Cutler replied, his voice tense—an effect of the scene he'd just witnessed from the bunker.

"Bring Logan in."

Suddenly, the Professor stepped forward. "Please cancel that order, Cornelius."

Cornelius wondered why he had just been overridden. But he knew better than to question the Professor's command. *Better to take a diplomatic approach.* "Cancel . . ."

Then Cornelius turned. "I'm sorry, Professor," he began. "I thought we were done for the day."

"We are."

"Then?"

The Professor turned his back on the screen and walked to the exit. "Leave Logan out for the night," he called over his shoulder. "I like the idea of him resting in his own gore. He needs to become one with the guts of his glory."

"But it's fifteen degrees below Fahrenheit out there," Cornelius protested. The winter day was so short, the sun was already beginning to set behind the mountains.

"All the better. Toughen him up, eh?" The Professor paused at the door, then turned to face Cornelius again. "You can monitor his vital signs from here, can you not?"

"Yes, of course," Cornelius replied.

"Splendid. Then we've accomplished much this day. Good evening to you all."

"You are now guests of the provisional military government. Though you are Western oppressors . . ."

The Professor heard the harsh voice. Authoritarian. Insistent. A barking horn of spartan bravado.

Don't bother me now. Too much to do to be sidetracked by ancient history.

He'd worked through the night, then all the next day. As night fell again, he'd returned to his technological lair to review unending loops of data. Sleep was an illusion, a distant oasis that provided no rest, no peace. Instead, he sat erect in his command chair, as he had for endless days.

"Once the interrogation is complete, you will both be released. Nothing will happen to you or your child as long as you . . . cooperate fully."

Annoyed, the Professor tossed his glasses onto the console. A road map of thin, red lines marked the whites of his eyes. He rubbed them with long-fingered hands.

I know I'm right . . .

Fear is the key.

Control Logan's fear and you control his aggression. Control his aggression and you control him. And then you have the perfect killing machine. The perfect defense . . .

"Do not fear for your boy . . . He will survive as long as you please us. I hear he is quite intelligent, your son. It would be a shame if something happened to him . . . to you both . . ."

Go away.

"Not until I've gotten what I want from your mother, boy. Not until she pleases me . . ."

The faces were around him again, circling like the wolves stalking Logan. Cruel. Feral. Savage. Mocking. And one face above all . . .

Colonel Otumo.

At eight, the Professor was small and wiry for his age. His father was a renowned epidemiologist, his mother the heiress of a Vancouver business empire. They'd journeyed to Africa to do good works, to help the impoverished, cure the sick.

Noble sentiments wasted on savages . . .

Father was somewhere in the jungle, inoculating tribesmen's children in remote tribal villages. He and his mother had remained in the capital city, a rude former colonial town built on the shore of a muddy African river. While his father was gone, a military coup had cast the West African nation into bloody chaos.

Pale, terrified, he hugged his mother's skirt that night. Trembling behind oversized glasses, watching tanks roll through dusty streets, soldiers beating back unarmed men and women. He heard shots, saw panic, smelled burning tires and the stench of fly-specked, bloated bodies rotting in the tropical heat.

When daylight came, so did martial law. Police and bureaucrats from the overthrown regime were captured and herded off to a sports stadium. Firing squads worked all day and through the next night.

That second night, the hotel's thin door bulged. The tromp of heavy boots on wooden floors, locks kicked through, servants and hotel workers beaten and shot. He'd run to his mother's room for safety. Colonel Otumo had already arrived with his officers.

Tall. Beige uniform. Crisp and pressed. A soldier.

Father had told him soldiers were like policemen—men to be trusted. Respected. Here to serve and protect.

"Where is your husband, the Western doctor? . . . That answer is not sufficient . . . What is your reason for coming to our country? . . . No, that is a lie. You represent the criminal interests of the North American colonial powers, no use denying it . . ."

At first, the men acted somewhat civil—Otumo most of all—Oxford-educated, well-spoken, he could discuss William Blake's poetry, British history, Marxist economics, or methods of torture with equal eloquence. But all too soon the polite conversation turned completely brutal.

An eight-year-old could barely understand the events

unfolding. He knew the soldiers were cruel and loud, his mother sobbing and afraid.

As day turned to evening once again, the soldiers took his mother away. She kissed him and told him to be brave . . . that she would be back with him soon, and forever. He tried to follow, crying, screaming, but the other soldiers laughed and beat him down with their rifle butts.

After that, he lay on the floor, listening as, from another part of the hotel, his mother's sobs, her pleas, finally her screams, broke through the black night. Meanwhile, the soldiers . . . did things to him. Things he did not understand. They did things to his body that hurt so much he retreated into his mind until he was far away. In a vast desert, alone. What was happening to him couldn't be happening, and so he watched as if through a glass, or a camera, or another person's eyes.

Morning brought a blast of wind and beating blades. The helicopters descended from the high clouds in the African sky. Men in black-skinned suits carrying big guns blasted their way through the hotel. The guard sitting over him rose to flee but was shot through the eye. Then, for the second time in twenty-four hours, men burst into the room. A man picked him up off the floor.

"You're safe now, boy. Understand? Safe," he said in a thick British accent. The man pulled off his hood. "I'm a soldier, son. Here to rescue your mother and father. Do you know where they are?"

Dumbly, he pointed down the hall. The men moved through the building, shooting and knocking down doors.

"Oh God," someone choked. "She's in here."

"Mother!" he'd cried, hurling himself down the hall.

"Don't let him see her!"

But he was too determined—a small animal squeezing between giraffe legs—and he did see her, sprawled on the bed, before they picked him up and carried him away.

In the helicopter, he sat mute, listening to the British soldiers speaking over the command net.

"Why did they do that to her?" a soldier whispered when they thought he couldn't hear. "Why'd they cut off her—"

"Quiet! The boy," hissed the officer.

"But why, sir?"

"Colonel Otumo calls it tribal justice. When his troops attack a rival clan, they . . . mutilate the women that way. So they can never suckle their young or bear more children . . ."

"What's going to happen to the boy?"

"Found his father in the jungle. Be here later today. They're going back to Canada, I'd reckon . . . no point in staying here."

When he saw his father that day, he said nothing. When they flew back to Canada, he didn't speak. When he turned nine, his father sought help.

"Despite his terrible trauma, your son exhibits a phenomenal intellect. He's a perfect candidate for our school. He's brilliant, IQ among the top one percent, and he's at just the right age to absorb knowledge without effort."

"I only want the best for my son . . . he's been through so much."

"At our academy, your son will be surrounded by peers. Boys of a gentle, academic nature who'll understand his . . . intensity. The trauma he experienced."

So his father shipped him off to a boarding school, then married his nurse.

In school, he missed his mother, he drew pictures of soldiers, hung them by his bed like talismans to ward off evil, taped them to the ceiling above his head. He lay awake, telling himself that one day he would have his own soldier to protect him from all the bad things.

As he matured, his reserve increased. He stuttered. He felt afraid of everything. He exhibited violent tendencies.

His father found another boarding school, where he arrived at fourteen. But the new school was far less . . . accommodating.

"Big brain, stutter for us. Ca . . . ca . . . can you do th . . . th . . . that?"

My tormentors. The mocking Greek chorus that was my peers.

Finally, one of the older boys found him in an empty classroom and just touched him.

"My God. The police at Bedford Science Academy. Disgraceful," said Dean Stanton to his father.

"That poor boy. What did my son do to him?"

What did I do? I took the scalpel I was using to dissect a formaldehyde-drenched frog and hacked at his face, again and again. And when I was done, under all that blood, I saw what I'd done . . . what I wanted to do to Colonel Otumo's face.

"You understand, Doctor, that we have to cover this up. The school's reputation must not suffer."

"But the victim—"

"His father will understand. A graduate. School tradition and all. But we'll have to send your son away, perhaps to a school in Switzerland. In any case, he can never return to Bedford. We cannot let this incident mar our reputation."

"But what about the victim?"

"The family, of course, will demand a financial settlement. But I'm sure your wife's fortune—"

"My late wife's fortune."

"Indeed. Your fortune will surely cover the expense."

My education continued, unmolested. I had discovered the secret . . . the key to controlling humans.

Fear was the key.

With Weapon X, the ultimate soldier, the key is in my hands.

"I didn't like spending the whole goddamn night in this freezing bunker, that's for sure," Lynch said for about the hundredth time.

"Come on, Lynch, you're giving me a headache," said Franks, who was already suited up.

But Lynch wouldn't shut up. He just kept talking and scratching his growling stomach. "Figure it out, Cutler— triple duty—that's double-time-and-a-half for the last eight-hour shift. Can't wait to see Deavers's face when I put in that overtime requisition."

Cutler had done his best to ignore Lynch since dawn, but he was only human. "Don't spend it yet. We might be in here all day, and all night tonight, too. That means no breakfast and no lunch—and you without a bag of chips."

"Don't even say that. Don't even, Cutler." His voice went up an octave. Cutler had suspected that Lynch was suffering from cabin fever before they'd got trapped in the bunker. Now he was sure Lynch was losing it.

Can't blame him. Stuck in this bunker for twenty hours now, waiting for the eggheads to decide what to do.

"Don't get your underwear in a bunch over your beloved junk food, Lynch," said Cutler. "If you've got the munchies, you can always take your chances outside. Go on, walk right past him to the fence. Hell, Logan might not wake up."

Lynch slumped on the bench where he'd spent most of the night. "I may be hungry, but I ain't crazy, Cutler. That's your vocation."

Cutler turned his back on Lynch to stare through the narrow view slits. Logan had spent the night laying in the now frozen gore, wolf carcasses stiffening around him. For all he knew, Subject X was dead.

A blessing, after what I saw . . .

Cutler was still processing the senseless scene he'd witnessed the day before. He couldn't figure out how that butchery could have anything to do with research, with knowledge—with creating the perfect weapon.

It wasn't an experiment. It was more like an atrocity, a massacre. Blood sport, not science.

Franks looked up at Cutler, his youthful face curious. "Was he like that when you brought him in?"

"Who?"

Franks gestured with his chin. "Logan. Weapon X. Word is you and Erdman and another guy brought him in. That he was a wanted criminal or something—wasn't a volunteer at all."

Cutler saw no point in lying. "He was tough. Gave me this—" he pointed to the scar that cut his eyebrow in half and divided his forehead. "Guess I had it coming, though, seeing what they have done to him so far."

The intercom buzzed, and the communications console came to life. One of the technicians rose from the corner where he'd been curled up and kicked his friend.

Yawning, they both crawled into their seats and flipped a few switches.

Lynch poked Franks. "This is it, kid. We're going home."

The intercom crackled to life. "Wranglers?"

"Cutler here."

"This is Cornelius. Bring him in."

Lynch slapped his knees and started to suit up. Franks and Cutler strapped on their helmets. Before they went out, Cutler tested the power on the electropod.

"Ready?" said Cutler at the hatch. Franks nodded, face grim. Lynch cradled the tranquilizer gun. "Let's go," he barked.

Cutler threw the latch and stepped outside. The cold hit him like a fist and the wind howled loudly—he hadn't noticed it was blowing from inside.

Franks came out next, and Lynch brought up the rear after he'd secured the hatch behind him. The technicians inside the bunker hardly seemed to notice they'd gone.

"Stay back about fifteen paces, Lynch. Franks and I will come up on either side."

"Roger that, sir."

The morning was overcast, the mountains shrouded in haze. As they crossed the snowy expanse, the hoarfrost crunched under their heavy boots.

"God, look at that," whispered Franks. He stared down at something red and bloody in the snow. Cutler refused to look. The wolves were all dead, their carcasses frozen solid. Solidified blood smooth as wine-colored glass and slippery under their feet. Franks slipped and Cutler shot him a look. "No sudden moves," he yelled.

But Cutler himself nearly jumped backward when he saw Logan's open eyes. They stared at the sky as if he were watching clouds. Franks and Cutler moved to surround him.

Cutler positioned the control prongs over the magnetic clamps in Logan's temples. Then he flicked the button. The magnets locked with a click loud enough to be heard above the howling wind.

With a gentle tug, like pulling the reins of a horse, Logan sat up, then rolled to his knees. Cutler brought the pole up and over his head stepping around the subject, per protocol.

When Logan finally stumbled to his feet, Franks moved in with the leash and clamped it around the mutant's throat. Logan didn't even blink. Still, as a precaution, Lynch aimed the tranquilizer gun at the small of his back.

Cutler gave Logan a push, which caused the mutant to lurch forward, shuffling stiffly toward the pen and the underground elevator beyond.

13

Golem

"Dr. Cornelius, sir? Sorry to disturb you—"

The astonished technician stood with a stack of files in his hands, staring in muted shock at the patchwork man sprawled on a steel operating table.

"Huh? I can't hear you." Cornelius shook his head and tapped the mask-and-visor combination that muffled his hearing. The tech had found the doctor surrounded by several assistants, stooped over Logan, Cornelius's face inches from the subject's.

"I said I'm sorry to disturb you," the tech repeated, speaking loudly. "Dr. Hendry wants you to have the results of yesterday's brain angiography, along with the figures on the blood gas test from the diagnostic lab."

Cornelius paused, scalpel in hand, though he barely glanced up from his task. "Great. Um, just put them on the pile," he mumbled.

"Sir, ah, Dr. Hendry wanted me to tell you—"

"Just give me one second," said Cornelius.

The tech watched as the doctor pierced the corner of Logan's right eye, then slid the scalpel down all the way to the base of the man's nose. Cornelius jumped back as a spurt of black blood narrowly missed splattering his visor. The gash he made was deep enough to expose bone.

As blood bubbled up from the wound and pooled on the yellow stain-resistant surface of the operating table, an assistant in a gore-spattered lab coat placed a small diamond drill in Cornelius's hand.

Using a laser dot projected from a ceiling-mounted surgical scope as his guide, Cornelius activated the power tool and drilled a small hole into the subject's exposed skull, right below the eye socket. Bits of bone flecked Cornelius's visor. As the shrill, dentist-chair whine filled the room, a pink-tinged tear rolled down Logan's cheek. An assistant quickly wiped it away with a cotton swab.

"Careful, Dr. Cornelius," warned Carol Hines, seated at the CAT scan monitor a few feet away. "No more than two centimeters into the brain pan or you risk damage to the nerve cluster."

"Done." Cornelius pulled back and cut the power. He set the drill aside and faced the tech. "You had a question?"

The technician nodded. "Dr. Hendry would like you to suspend the blood anomaly test until after this phase of the experiment is complete. He says since the lockdown his resources are limited, and the hematologist has been tied up for three days—"

"I know how long he's been tied up," Cornelius snapped. "I'm tired of waiting for results from that 'expert' as well. So what's Hendry's point?"

"He . . . Dr. Hendry said he needs the hematologist for his own work. Said if you told the specialist what you are looking for, the work might go faster."

As he spoke, the young tech's eyes never strayed from Subject X on the table.

"If I knew what I was looking for I'd have found it myself!" Cornelius replied.

"Sir? Is that what you want me to tell Dr. Hendry?"

"No. Tell Dr. Hendry that he and his staff are not here to question my requests, only to fulfill them. Tell him to remember who is in charge."

As the technician backed out of the lab, Cornelius angrily returned to his work. He snatched a long copper probe from his assistant's hand. Then he looked up at Carol Hines. "Ready?"

"Ready," she replied as she adjusted the angle of the real-time brain scan.

"That's fine, Ms. Hines. Freeze that image." Cornelius watched a monitor embedded in the wall. "I can see the nerve cluster quite clearly."

Stooping over Logan again, Cornelius slid the long needlelike probe through the fresh-drilled hole and into Subject X's brain with a single smooth thrust.

Cornelius stepped back as the assistant moved in with Teflon thread to seal the flesh around the protruding probe. With the procedure completed, Cornelius tore the hot mask from his face. Unlike his two assistants, who were clad head to toe in laboratory whites, Cornelius wore only a gore-streaked surgical apron over his shirt, vest, and tie. It made him feel like he'd just stepped out of a Victorian novel—a harried London physician, perhaps, or an East End slaughter-man . . .

"Stitch him up," Cornelius tossed over his shoulder. "I'm back in fifteen."

As he went, Cornelius snatched new files from the top of the teetering stack, leaving a bloody thumbprint on the cover sheet. He wiped his sticky hands on his apron, then strode into an adjacent lab, where he tossed the files onto an empty desk and doused his hands at the sink.

Somewhere in the back of his mind, Abraham B. Cornelius, M.D., was disgusted by the sloppy surgery he'd just performed—operating without anesthetic, without sterile implements or sterilized conditions. He doubted he'd even remembered to wash his hands after breakfast and before he'd begun working hours earlier.

My techniques these days are positively medieval, he thought, *but in the end, it really doesn't matter. Sepsis has no more effect on Logan than a mosquito bite.*

In the past weeks, as the Professor pressured Cornelius and Hines for faster results, Cornelius was forced to take shortcuts. One of the first protocols he'd dispensed with was sterile lab conditions.

Too damn many operations happening for such safeguards. Two this week, three last—and that doesn't even count minor procedures like the one I've just performed.

Retraining and reprogramming Weapon X wasn't Cornelius's only goal, either. He'd decided to launch his own private quest to unlock the secret healing potential of Logan's blood.

But as he leafed through the latest report, he discovered that the hematologist was no closer to explaining the "unusual structures" or the "curious proteins" found in Logan's blood than he'd been eight days ago.

The electron microscope might help, but Hendry has booked that facility solid. He's keeping me away from his precious toy out of spite, I'm sure of it.

Cornelius slammed the cover on the files and pushed them aside. With conditioning trials about to begin, he knew he would have even less time to devote to the study of Logan's phenomenal immune system. Performing tasks assigned to him by the Professor ate up virtually all of his waking hours.

Perhaps when this preposterous Weapon X program is back on track—when the Professor has made Subject X his walking, stalking, killer-on-a-string—then I can catch a break, do the real work with Subject X. The work Logan was born for . . .

Over the speaker, a soft-spoken command interrupted his desperate thoughts. "Dr. Cornelius, please report to Lab Seven at once . . ."

"Hey, Rice! Where're you going?"

Communications Tech Rice spun around to find a man approaching him from the opposite end of a darkened corridor.

"Is that you, Cut?"

Cutler emerged from the shadows a moment later. Rice recognized him and visibly relaxed.

"You looked spooked, Rice. What're you up to? Feeling guilty?"

Rice shook his head. "Thought you might be the Professor, that's all. He's been riding our butts for a week now. I don't think that guy ever sleeps. And with this big remote guidance test tomorrow, the whole communications department is working double time to get the technology up and running. The job stinks, man."

"Yeah, we miss your sunny disposition down in security," Cutler replied. As he spoke, Cutler located a precise point on the steel wall and slammed it with his fist. The lights in the corridor sprang to life, bright enough to cause both men to blink.

"A two-billion-dollar complex, and the lights don't work," said Rice. "This place is falling apart."

"You seen Anderson?"

"Yeah, this morning, with Subject X."

"That's what I thought," Cutler said. "I go in to prep Subject X for the 0800 experiment and find his cell empty."

"Doc Cornelius called for him at 0430. Anderson was on duty and brought Logan down to the lab himself."

"Without adequate backup. And Anderson never entered the transfer on the docket or wrote it up in the roster. That's three security protocol violations. And to make it worse, until I ran into you I didn't have a clue where Logan was. How good a security chief does that make me?"

Rice chuckled. "About as good as the last one, I reckon."

"Don't ever let Deavers hear you say that. I'm his second choice."

"Hell, Cut, I wouldn't have chosen you at all."

The Professor entered the lab at 0759. He wore a crisp, white lab coat over his tailored suit, a clipboard tucked under his arm. With relaxed confidence, he stepped up to the operating table.

"How are we proceeding, Dr. Cornelius?"

"Spinal codes are in," Cornelius reported. "It's just a matter of final sensor grafts now."

The Professor stared down at the unconscious Subject X. Logan lay flat on his back on the adjustable operating table. The probes Cornelius had placed in the subject's brain now had huge feeder boxes connected to them. The devices dangled from Logan's cheeks, under eyes that had been sewn closed with surgical thread. Bundles of fiberoptic wires threaded their way in and out of the subject's flesh through punctures at each of Logan's critical nerve clusters.

His forearms were raised and locked into restraints, hands open. Each finger had a long electromedical probe embedded at its base that stuck in the air like an antenna. Thin fiber-optic cables ran between his fingers like delicate webbing, and thicker bundles of Teflon-coated wires snaked in and out of the muscles in his forearms like artificial veins.

More wires were being added to Logan's feet, ankles, and behind his knees by a group of technicians supervised by several of Dr. Hendry's staff physicians. Electricians and communications specialists primed a thirty-pound battery and hooked it up to a steel cybernetic helmet married by wireless connection to Carol Hines's Reifying Encephalographic Monitor.

The Professor tapped the microwave-receiving box dangling from a thick wire bundle attached to the base of Logan's spine.

"And the distribution of the signal? What is our range?" he asked.

"About a three-mile radius, sir," Cornelius replied.

The Professor frowned. "But that is so very limited, Doctor. Is that all you can give me?"

"Professor, if you want a puppet, you have to have strings." It was clear from the doctor's tone that Cornelius saw the remote control phase of the experiment as a waste of time and effort.

The Professor's frown increased. "Yes . . . indeed . . . I do want a puppet, as you put it. But my design specifically called for a radius of at least ten miles."

Cornelius nodded impatiently. "I know that. But the

batteries are just too heavy. I don't know why we couldn't have stayed with the on/off system, anyway. Weight wasn't a factor, because we didn't need batteries for that."

The Professor focused his cold eyes on his colleague. "I will have my way on this, Cornelius. A ten-mile radius."

Cornelius met the Professor's gaze for a moment, then relented. "Okay. Load him down. See if I care. You can turn him into a traveling radio station if you like."

Hearing the short-tempered exchange, Carol Hines looked up from her terminal, then quickly averted her eyes.

"Your dissent is noted, Dr. Cornelius. But let's not be testy, hmm?" The Professor's tone dripped with condescension.

Cornelius's attention was focused elsewhere. "Those braces can only keep the incisions open for so long, you know," he barked at a member of the surgical team.

The tech, face covered with a surgical mask, nodded. "Yes, Doctor. I can see that clearly. The flesh is actually forming around the clamps here."

"Then work faster, man."

"Any problems, Ms. Hines?" asked the Professor.

"Computer indicates leakage of semen and marrow into the intracellular fluids."

One of the surgeons cursed. "You heard the computer," he said to the technicians. "We're losing goop here. Keep those holes plugged and move with more expedience."

One of the surgeons freed Logan's hand and laid it flat on the table. "Give me a right stem, short fiber," he called.

"Short fiber right stem is on ninth," his assistant replied.

Suddenly, Logan moaned.

"Good God, he's coming around!" cried the Professor.

"Don't get jumpy, Professor," Cornelius said. "We have to keep him floating so that we can trace the relay flux in his nervous system. If he were out, some critical synapses wouldn't be firing."

The Professor visibly paled. "Do you mean he's conscious?"

Logan groaned again, his head rolling to one side.

"Yes, partly," Cornelius explained. "Maybe a little too conscious. Add two millimeters of Pheno-B."

"Yes, Doctor," a surgeon replied. A moment later, the man slipped a hypodermic needle into Logan's carotid artery.

The Professor's interest seemed suddenly piqued. "So Logan can feel what we're doing to him, eh?"

Cornelius nodded, face grim. "Most of it, yeah. I don't like it, but it can't be helped. Of course, Ms. Hines will soon wipe any and all memory of this . . . procedure from Logan's mind. But right now . . . well, the poor guy's in a lot of pain."

As if to emphasize Cornelius's words, Logan moaned twice, the last a keen of agony.

"Pain is a principal of life, Dr. Cornelius," the Professor declared. "Not that I subscribe entirely to the dictum."

"Of course," Cornelius muttered, trying to turn his mind away from this aspect of his work. But Logan would not let Cornelius forget his torment. The subject's head moved from side to side as the groans continued.

"Four more millimeters of Pheno-B," Cornelius commanded. "And try to keep him from shaking or he'll damage some of the delicate connections."

Subject X began struggling weakly against his restraints. His head lolled to the side and his mouth opened. Logan gagged, then ejected the contents of his stomach. A green bile, followed by a spray of saliva and blood, spattered the table.

"Readings, Hines?" Cornelius called.

"Sensory cortex monitor is overloaded, Doctor. There are no readings."

"Good God . . . off-the-charts pain." Cornelius leaned close to Logan's head, muttering. "Poor son of a bitch is unconscious at last. I hope he finds some peace in his dreams."

Son of a bitch . . . Some peace in his dreams.

Logan heard the voice as if it were next to his ear. He opened his eyes, but the only person who could have spoken was curled up beside him on the pine branches, fast asleep. *Could be the North Koreans on the hunt?*

Better check.

He rose slowly, trying not to disturb Miko, crawled to the hut's entrance, and gazed outside. The sky was clear and cloudless, the late-afternoon sun stabbed down through the thick pines in yellow and-orange columns of light. A few birds sang in the tree; an errant breeze stirred the branches. Otherwise there was only silence in the approaching twilight.

Must be crackin' up . . . hearing voices this whole mission . . .

Then, as Logan strained his ears, he heard another sound—engines in the distance, muffled by the trees. He ducked back into the shelter and gently shook Miko awake.

"There's activity down on the road. I'm going for a quick look," he whispered.

"What kind of activity? Men? Vehicles? How do you know?" she asked, instantly awake.

Logan popped a garment can, worked the material until it expanded, then stripped off his rags and slipped into his last battle suit. Like the others, it was formfitting, with a splinter camouflage pattern ideal for blending into the surrounding forest.

"We should stay together," Miko said.

"No," he told her. "I can travel better alone. Rest up, we're taking off in a couple of hours. I'll be back in thirty minutes or less."

He took Miko's binoculars and handed her his remaining firearm, a lightweight M9 Beretta. Perfect for a HAWK jump because of its compactness, the M9 didn't have enough stopping power to satisfy Logan, who preferred bladed weapons, anyway.

Logan tucked the Randall Mark I fighting knife into his boot and from Miko's belt took a second, long-bladed weapon, which he wielded like a sword. Without a backward glance, he slipped through the opening and was gone. She watched as he darted down the slope and melted into the long shadows of the fading day.

Among the trees, the sounds went dead, but Logan could make out engine noises in the distance, and soon he heard human voices calling across the water. He emerged in a clearing that gave him a view of the road and lake beyond. An armored personnel carrier and two Chinese-built trucks were parked below. He counted three men around the vehicles; twelve more by the lakeshore, including an officer. A small boat was trolling back and forth close to land. Three soldiers aboard tossed hooked ropes into the water.

On closer examination, Logan spied skid marks on the tarred road and wheel tracks in the dirt—this was the spot where he'd ridden the BTR-60 to its watery grave. The Koreans were dragging the lake for their missing troops. This wouldn't have bothered Logan except for one thing—if they dredged up the dead officer, the Koreans would realize the man had been stabbed, not drowned. They might deduce that Logan had survived the plunge, or they might just figure he died in the fight and his body was still at the bottom of the lake. Of course, the soldiers would keep looking. And when they didn't find Logan's corpse, all hell would break loose.

Either way, time was running out. He and Miko would have to move now, before the Koreans realized they were here. But as Logan turned to ascend the slope, he heard more voices—these coming from the woods on either side of him.

Then he heard a noise that galvanized him into instant action—the sound of barking dogs . . .

They sat Subject X in a chair. Spine straight, head erect, breath shallow, he was naked except for hundreds of multicolored wires that dangled from his body like feathers. Eyes stitched shut, nose pinned, mouth plugged, the cobra-hooded mane of wild black hair his crown, Logan resembled the mummy of a savage warrior king prepared for a ceremonial funeral.

A thirty-pound battery, which powered the adamantium-plated cybernetic helmet that sat at the subject's feet, hung from his neck like an unwieldy medallion. When hooked to the electrodes in his temples and the relays below his eyes, it would filter everything Logan saw, smelled, or tasted through the virtual-reality processor inside the helmet.

The Professor stood close to Subject X, examining the inputs and the raw, puffy flesh around them. "So, have the sutures healed?"

"Not all of them, Professor. But enough for the purpose." Cornelius glanced at his watch. "Or we could wait a few more minutes, if you prefer."

The Professor, hands folded behind his back, shook his bald head. "No, no. Let's get on with it, Cornelius."

Cornelius rubbed his chin. "Okay, the cables are a problem. They are clumsy and bulky, but can be reduced eventually. The power source—that unwieldy battery—is temporary, of course."

He crossed the lab to stand near the surgical team assembled behind the remote control transmission terminal. The actual manipulation of Logan became the responsibility of one of the communications specialists— a technician named Rice, who sat behind a large control panel.

"In the coming weeks, we'll try to compact the boxes, but I can't guarantee that." Cornelius tapped a key and a perimeter map appeared on one of the overhead monitors. Overlaid on that map was a red circle.

"We're looking at the range of these devices displayed over the test field," Cornelius explained. "For anything over a hundred and fifty yards, we'll need to use the helmet device to pull in the signal. The cybernetic circuitry inside that steel dome dramatically increases the range."

The scarlet overlay expanded until it almost filled the

screen. Then the monitor went black, and Cornelius faced the Professor. "Other than that, we're in business."

"And what is the range, Cornelius?"

"A little over nine miles, sir." Cornelius could feel the Professor's displeasure. But he was too tired, and too disgusted with the work to really care.

The Professor snorted, then faced Rice at his terminal. "And the control console here. It isn't based on my original design."

Cornelius nodded. *A joystick*, he thought ruefully. *The Professor wants a goddamn joystick, as if Logan were some kind of video game character.*

"You wanted the extra power, Professor," he replied. "We had to modify the control surfaces to achieve it."

Cornelius tapped Rice. "Staff, show the Professor the layout of your top board."

"Sure, okay," Rice replied, rising. "It's easy, sir. These button codes are based on your data. You press them in sequence. Forward, back—"

"And the levers are controls. I understand," the Professor said tersely, annoyed that a mere tech should brief him on technology he had actually pioneered.

"Give us a brief demonstration, Rice," Cornelius directed.

"It isn't necessary," said the Professor. But to his chagrin, the impertinent technician pressed on.

"Watch," said Rice as he tinkered with the controls. Logan's arm twitched, then the flesh on top of his hand bulged from within.

"You got full articulation of the claws," prattled the staff tech. "Like this little piggy went to market—"

The first claw emerged.

"This little piggy stayed home—"

Two more steel claws emerged in a welter of blood.

The Professor shoved Rice aside. "I get the idea, and your entertainments are extremely out of place."

"I . . . s-sorry, Professor," Rice stammered.

"I hardly need instructions on how to operate my own device." The Professor touched the controls, then toggled the levers. "Yes . . . watch this . . ."

Logan jerked to his feet, then tottered unsteadily— two steps forward, one back. With each grotesque lurch, the dangling wires whipped and the battery clattered along the floor.

"You see, Cornelius, how the naturalistic movements imitate the human . . ."

"Yeah, yeah, I see that . . ."

"And how discreet adjustment creates the effect—"

Suddenly, Logan spun with such force that the heavy battery yanked him off balance. His legs became tangled in the cables and wires and he tumbled to the floor like a stumbling newborn.

The laughter of the staff caused Cornelius to wince. While he understood that the pressure on them had been mounting through weeks of lockdown and hours of difficult surgery, he thought the humor misplaced.

"*Shut up!*" the Professor shouted with more passion, more rage, than Cornelius had ever seen the man exhibit.

"Sir, I'm sorry—"

The Professor turned on him. "Cornelius, your staff are absolute fools. Ignoramuses."

Cornelius faced the medical staff. "Okay, boys, that's it. Get out of here."

"Yes, get out, buffoons!" the Professor barked. "This

is a scientific endeavor and should be treated with the proper gravity. I . . . I've never been so insulted."

"Please, Professor," Cornelius said curtly, in spite of himself. "Dr. Hendry's medical staff did a good job and you got what you wanted."

Except for Logan, still sprawled on the floor, Cornelius and the Professor were alone. Cornelius poured a cup of coffee.

"Here, take this," he insisted, thrusting the cup into the Professor's hand. "And can we just call it a day? It looks to me like you haven't had a rest since the Weapon X project began."

"No!" the Professor shot back. "We've accomplished nothing today. The experiment is not over, Cornelius. I have to know for sure if it's safe."

Cornelius glanced at the man on the floor. Logan looked dead; even his chest barely heaved. If it wasn't for the continuous beep of the heart and respiration monitors, the doctor couldn't be sure there was any life left in that tortured frame.

"He's safe," Cornelius said softly. "He's wired and shut down. Let it go, Professor."

"You misunderstand. I meant if *I* am safe, you fool. Me! Subject X tried to choke me to death. Remember?"

"Look," Cornelius explained. "When the power is on, you've got him by the tail. When it's off—like now—he's just dead meat. You wanted it, you got it."

Then he turned his back on the Professor and walked to the exit. At the door, Cornelius paused. "But you have to be sure, right?" he said with a weary sigh. "So go, Professor. Spit in his eye. Then you can be sure."

He opened the hatch.

"Where are you going?" demanded the Professor.

"I've had enough of this circus for one day," Cornelius replied. "I'll send in the wranglers to clean up the mess. See you tomorrow."

When the hatch closed, the Professor looked down at Subject X. He watched Logan's chest rise and fall for a few moments. Then, tilting the coffee cup, the Professor poured the scalding contents over Logan's upturned face. Black liquid splashed and beaded, leaving red blisters that quickly faded to white, then pink, under the Professor's relentless glare.

With a final kick to the subject's rib cage, the Professor turned his back on Logan and strode out of the room, satisfied now that it was safe. Despite the pain and the humiliation he'd just administered to the once fierce and independent Logan, the mutant didn't even flinch.

Cornelius did it, the Professor thought triumphantly. *The reprogramming worked. Now I control Weapon X. . . .*

14

The Hunt

"Catch," hissed Logan, tossing Miko the binoculars.

He'd almost arrived at the top of the hill, to find Miko already clad in her formfitting camouflage suit, waiting behind cover, Tac drawn. Logan had been about twenty paces from her when he'd heard the barking dogs and the sound of voices.

"My gun," Logan loudly whispered.

Miko drew his M9 from her belt and tossed it down to him. The clips followed.

"Go," said Logan, pointing to the woods behind her as he tucked the weapon into its holster. "Take off up and over the hill, circle around the soldiers and the dogs. I'll lead the hunters away from you for as long as I can, give you a head start."

"But—"

"Don't argue. The dogs have already got my scent. Move before they catch yours. Head for the complex, bust in. Do your business and then rescue Langram if possible. If they get me, I'll do what I can from inside."

The sound of beating blades cut through the dusky sky.

Logan cursed. Helicopters meant they must have found that dead officer . . .

Miko turned her eyes upward, then looked down at him. "Logan, fight. Do not surrender."

He glanced over his shoulder. The dogs closed in, their barks louder, more insistent. "I may not have a choice. Now take off!"

Without another word, Miko turned and raced up the slope, to vanish among the low-hanging pines. Logan hopped over the rotting trunk of a fallen tree and ran in the opposite direction. As he ran with leaps and bounds down the hill, he also moved away from the dam and the dogs and soldiers who pursued him. He knew that in the long run, flight was hopeless. He had few escape options—trapped in the middle of enemy territory. The North Koreans had the home ground advantage.

With helicopters and searchlights and dogs, with soldiers and armored cars, it was only a matter of time before the hunters caught up with him.

As the stalker's bare feet silently padded through the snow, a motion detector caught the movement, and a camera quietly focused its lens on the subject. Even in the dusk's deepening shadows, the camera effortlessly followed the hunter as he tracked down his prey.

"He's within one hundred meters of the target now—" Cornelius looked away from the HDTV screen to glance at his watch. "At three minutes, precisely."

The Professor watched the monitor, anxious to assess his creation's performance. "Rather impressive," he muttered, chin resting on his long-fingered hands.

"Camera five on subject," a video tech called.

"Switch to camera eight and bring him in close."

"Switching."

A frontal shot of Subject X appeared on-screen. Naked from the neck down but for the batteries and microwave receivers clustered around his waist, Logan's head was completely encased in a gleaming cybernetic helmet. Wires dangled from the headpiece to cocoon his torso. Most of the embedded feeder connections that sent signals directly to the subject's nerve clusters had been removed, to be replaced with a less cumbersome wireless system that allowed for freer movement.

"Ninety-seven yards at three minutes twenty-seven seconds," Cornelius announced.

"He's downwind," observed the Professor. "He has the scent."

Over the constant howl of the wind, the microphones picked up the *snikt* of the adamantium claws sliding from their sheaths.

"Claw extrusion, right hand. Some blood release is evident," noted the Professor.

"We need some kind of terminals there," said Cornelius. "Something to keep the flesh apart. Make a note, Ms. Hines."

The woman looked up from her REM monitor. The mind machine was running on automatic, at maximum output, sending a preprogrammed signal to Logan's brain. Carol Hines was receiving only limited feedback from the information the subject was processing, but it was enough to deduce his next move.

"Less than fifty yards now," Carol Hines said. "It appears the target is coming toward our subject, not moving away . . . his heart rate is elevated. Adrenal rise with carpal flux—"

"Left claw extrusion."

"Camera ten, please . . ."

"This is it," Cornelius declared. "Keep the brain monitors up and running. We won't get a second chance . . ."

Carol Hines began speaking into the voice log on her terminal. "Mister Logan. Set . . . I mean, Subject X, Set Twelve . . . Stimulus response quarry one, duration from zero four minutes and twenty-one seconds—"

The grizzly bear emerged from behind a copse of leafless trees, lumbering forward on its short hind legs, forearms spread wide, claws bared, snarling.

With a string of hot drool dripping from its snapping jaws, the creature grunted a challenge, then roared angrily when the human stood his ground.

Without the benefit of a preprogrammed command, Subject X deftly avoided a swipe from one massive paw, crouching low to duck the blow, then slipping around the beast to administer a few stabbing jabs to the creature's torso.

Moving in front of the bear, Subject X thrust with his right hand, the adamantium blades sinking deep into the raging beast's rippling red-brown flanks.

The grizzly whirled, off balance. Logan saw the opening through the lenses of the virtual-reality visor—the signal dispatched to the brain by direct optic nerve inputs. Logan drew back his right arm for another thrust. The steel claws plunged through fur, hide, flab, and muscle, directly into the creature's heart.

Jaws gaping, lips flecked with gore, the bear's roar of defiance faded into a wet gurgle in its throat as it choked on its own blood.

Subject X brought up his left arm for a quick, slashing

cut, and the bear's head literally leaped from its shoulders and spun away, to tumble into the bloody snow, eyes staring blindly.

A fountain of arterial blood gushed from the stump, steaming in the cold. The headless body of the bear wobbled and Logan drew back his right arm in a shower of gore. Without the indestructible claws to prop it up, the grizzly's carcass slumped to the ground at Logan's feet.

Subject X stepped forward, looming over his vanquished foe, ready to deliver the *coup de grace*. But except for its dying spasms, the decapitated bear did not move. Even the black blood ceased to flow as the damaged heart ceased to beat.

Programmed goal achieved, Logan stood stock-still, arms wide, legs braced, steel claws dripping gore, as if someone had turned him off. According to the readings Carol Hines was receiving, Subject X had lapsed into a kind of mind loop. His brain remained active yet not fully conscious.

"Superb. Bravo!" the Professor cried. "An utterly impeccable killing. The time has come, Cornelius. The weapon is primed and perfect. He's ready for his first mission."

The statement shocked Cornelius. *No,* he thought in a panic. *You can't take Logan away from me now. My study of his immune system will be over before it's begun . . .*

Though his mind raged, outwardly Cornelius remained calm, arguing logic that the Professor could understand. "I'll agree that the demonstration was impressive, Professor. But the transmitters limit his effective range . . . and they're so cumbersome. And the helmet cuts his vision—"

"Thirty percent, both sides," offered Carol Hines.

"—and the transmission lag delays his responses for what could be a critical split second in a tight situation. Worse than anything are those bulky battery packs. They're nearly ten pounds apiece, and the microwave receiver weighs even more. Everything's so clunky and in the way."

Carol Hines glanced at the screen. "Shall I retract his claws, Doctor? Or wait?"

"Yes, go ahead, Ms. Hines."

"I agree that it's not optimum, and it's not what we planned," said the Professor. "But we do have the weapon in our control, correct, Doctor? Ms. Hines?"

Cornelius nodded.

"As long as Logan's brain is subject to the REM waves, he is under our control," said Carol Hines.

The Professor's eyebrow shot up. "A qualification, Ms. Hines?"

"Merely an observation, sir. The Reifying Encephalographic Monitor is an effective tool, but it must be utilized properly."

"Explain."

"Well, Professor . . . the REM sends out frequency-specific brain waves that interfere with the normal functions of the right and left frontal cortex of the brain."

"And that's what makes Logan docile? Controllable?"

"Not precisely, Professor. The REM device takes control of the subject in three stages. In its initial phase, the waves effectively deactivate the right and left frontal lobes of the brain—cutting the subject off from all memory, emotion, self-awareness, and the ability to distinguish between the real and vividly imagined experience. Though hearing is unaffected, the proximity of Broca's area—the part of the brain that controls speech—means that Logan's vocal abilities beyond the most rudimentary are also eradicated."

"We don't need him to speak, Ms. Hines. We need him to hunt, to kill," said the Professor.

"Yes, sir. During the second stage, the REM destroys or suppresses the subject's actual memories and replaces them with false memories and experiences we create ourselves. At NASA, the implanted memories were used as learning tools, a kind of virtual reality exercise to teach pilots of space shuttle emergency procedures. We went no further than that because of certain unforeseen side effects."

"No one told me about any side effects," grumbled Cornelius.

"We're well past that stage, Doctor, so the question is moot. Please continue, Ms. Hines."

"In the case of Weapon X, the implanted memories will be used to manipulate him, make him believe things that aren't or weren't true, in an effort to make his mind more . . . pliable. We can manipulate his fear, paranoia, activate feelings of vengeance, anger, rage . . ."

The Professor tapped his chin impatiently. "Yes, I understand, Ms. Hines. Get to your point."

"We are now in the middle of the third stage of the subject's retraining—the critical command-and-control phase—but psychological integration is not yet complete, which means that Logan is not yet completely under our control."

"But he obeys our commands. What am I missing?"

"Once the third phase is complete, Weapon X will be self-sufficient. He will not need the REM waves to keep him in thrall because his own brain will be programmed to obey without them. But right now, the subject still needs the microwave receivers and a power source. If the brain waves generated by the REM device cease to reach his brain or if the batteries fail or something breaks down, then we will lose control of the subject."

"He'll go wild? Attack?"

"Not likely, Professor. Probably he will simply shut down, or fall into a mind loop similar to the state he reverts to after a training session. There is danger only when a modicum of someone's personality, their individuality, survives the initial phase of REM integration. That can cause conflicts in the id, the subconscious, that can result in explosive bouts of violence."

"So he's safe?"

"Yes, Professor. In the case of Subject X, I'm positive we've utterly eradicated his personality. Nothing of the man called Logan remains in his mind."

While Carol Hines spoke, Cornelius buzzed the wrangler pen.

"Cutler here."

"Bring the subject."

Cornelius swiveled his chair to face the Professor. "You see our situation, sir. Logan is working—but not to optimum potential. Not yet. I think that with a little more psychological—"

The Professor cut him off. "No. No more psycho-anything. I want action now."

"Action? Chopping a grizzly into bloody pieces—that's not enough action for you?"

The Professor's eyes narrowed. "I didn't create this weapon to be some imbecilic game warden, Cornelius."

"So what are you saying here?"

The Professor shifted his gaze to the screen, where Logan waited docilely while the wranglers approached him.

"I am saying that our killer is ready."

"But it isn't all cut-and-thrust, Professor. A bit more time to eliminate some of the kinks in the system, that's all I'm asking."

"No. He is ready," the Professor repeated in the tone of a spoiled child.

"Ready for what?"

"The great test, Doctor." The Professor spun to face Cornelius. "What is the most dangerous game of all?"

Cornelius blinked. "Bengal tiger?"

"Man, of course."

Cornelius stared at the control console, face grim.

Pretending to work, Carol Hines and Technician Rice listened intently to the exchange.

"Well, we don't have any humans in stock right now," Cornelius said at last.

"Then we'll have to get some, won't we?"

Cornelius's eyes flashed in anger. "You're not serious, of course."

"On the contrary, Cornelius. I'm deadly serious."

"My God," the doctor protested, appalled. "If you think I'll sit at these controls and make Logan . . . that's complete madness. Do you know what you're saying?"

"I always know what I'm saying, Cornelius. So I'll brook no arguments." The Professor turned his back on the room and strode to the door.

"We're . . . we're not finished with this debate," Cornelius rasped.

But the Professor entered his own world. He stopped listening to Cornelius. His focus was on Weapon X and the grand experiment he was about to conduct.

"I will be in my control room," the Professor declared as the hatch closed behind him.

Logan was fairly certain Miko had gotten away clean. That knowledge kept him going, even after he heard a second helicopter join the hunt.

Every step I take leads them a step farther away from Miko . . .

Twice Logan took time-consuming detours and double-backs to avoid large clearings where he could be seen from the air. He knew from experience it would be better after dark, when the choppers would have to use searchlights.

But all this running is for nothing if those helos are equipped with infrared or thermal imaging. They will find me easily once it gets dark . . .

For now, Logan ran as quietly as he could, until the only sound he could hear was his own breathing and the distant baying of dogs. No matter what happened, he was determined to go down fighting.

After all, why make it easy for them?

As the yellow sun sank low on the horizon, Logan broke out of a wall of pines as straight as telephone poles, their lower trunks mostly stripped of branches. Just ahead, a narrow stream of clear, icy water tumbled down the rocky slope to the lake far below. Without breaking stride, he plunged into the shallow pool, shivering as he slathered mud on his face, his hands, to hide what the splinter camouflage did not. He even rubbed the brown sludge into his hair in an effort to dull the sheen. Though he'd gotten a severe buzz cut before the mission, two days had passed and he now had a full head of long hair again.

Logan followed the stream for about a kilometer—an old but effective trick to throw the dogs off his scent. He knew that the bloodhounds would soon find his trail again, but he hoped the search would slow them down. Sometimes bloodhounds would be distracted by other animals, but these hills have been purged of all wildlife by the starving population in the area. Logan hadn't seen any creatures larger than a bird or insect since he'd arrived.

More and more, the landscape—brown grass, sloping hills climbing to jagged mountain peaks, forests of gaunt, tall pines—reminded Logan of the Canadian Rockies where he'd grown up. Logan found himself reaching back through a century of memories and experiences to conjure up every trick of woodcraft he'd learned from the Blackfoot Indian trackers he'd known in his youth.

When he reached a rocky area where he would leave scant footprints, Logan exited the stream and sprinted through the forest. The foliage was denser here, so as he swept past, Logan was careful to bend branches rather than break them, crossing more hard ground than loose soil, more rocks than mud. For an instant, memory carried him back, until Logan felt like the boy he'd once been—a wild youth on an even wilder frontier.

In the gathering gloom, Logan glanced at the fluorescent glow of the chronometer-and-compass combination on his wrist. According to their original plan, Miko should be slipping past the dam about now and making her way down the valley to the top secret complex below—if she hadn't run into trouble, that is.

Suddenly, Logan paused to listen to an insistent beat of distant propellers. Down among the trees, the sound was muffled and he could not decide what direction the noise came from.

It was sheer instinct that threw Logan to the ground a moment later. It was training that made him press himself into the dirt as a helicopter passed directly over his head at an altitude of less fifty meters.

Son of a bitch! Didn't even see it coming.

The thick trees hid Logan well, but he knew they also obscured and distorted sound, which aided his pursuers.

He lay on the ground for a few minutes, heart racing from the close call. Finally, Logan heard the dogs yelping in confusion behind him. They had lost his trail, for now at least.

Logan rolled to his feet and began to move swiftly between the trees again, this time keeping one eye skyward to scan the breaks between the branches for any sign of pursuit. But soon the sun set behind the mountains and the valley became shrouded in deep shadows.

Just when Logan thought things would get easier, he burst through the tree line into a vast clearing. At the same time he heard the roar of an engine and the beat of blades. He ducked back into the trees and peered cautiously through pine needles. Within a minute, an MD-500 arrived overhead, its searchlight cutting an arc through the twilight. Illuminated by the glare were hundreds of ragged stumps that used to be trees. About a hundred meters away, a steel tower bristling with cables punctuated the clearing. The power lines ran up the slope to another tower, then over the hill.

Across the wide, desolate swath—perhaps three, maybe four hundred meters away—more forest, more cover. Behind him, Logan heard the dogs again. They had picked up his trail and were closing in.

The bastards have been herding me all along . . . pushing me to this clearing where their helicopter gunners can pick me off. All those guys in the chopper have to do is wait for me to make a break for it.

Too bad for them I'm not that stupid.

Patiently, Logan watched the single chopper cruise up and down the clearing, its searchlight effectively covering every inch of ground. He used their light to scope out the landscape, but the results were not promising. There were no ditches, no dips or rolls in the ground to hide behind, and absolutely no vegetation beyond some ankledeep brown grass and hundreds of tree stumps sticking out of the earth like grave markers.

From somewhere in the night, Logan could hear the echoing beat of the second helicopter.

Sounds like it's covering the road. Which means it will take a couple of minutes to get here if there's trouble.

Logan knew time was running out. He would have to act now or risk capture. Longing for the stopping power of his familiar Colt, Logan drew his Beretta, checked the clip, and flicked off the safety. Then he hunkered down in a bed of pine needles and ignored the sound of the approaching dogs as he waited for the helicopter to make another low-level pass.

Logan's patience was rewarded a few moments later. The MD-500, moonlight glinting off its bubble canopy, swept overhead. A column of light stabbed down through the trees, and Logan had to slip deeper into the brush to avoid its glare. As the helicopter passed over his hiding place, Logan discovered there were two men on-board—the pilot and a soldier armed with a sniper rifle. The gunner's door was open, and the man's foot hung out of the cabin, to rest on the landing skid.

They're not looking for a prisoner, Logan realized. *They're planning to gun me down from the air.*

The dogs were close now. He had perhaps ten minutes, no more than fifteen, to make a move before the hounds sniffed him out. As the helicopter circled the top of the hill for another pass, Logan took several deliberately slow and calming breaths.

Then, when the helicopter was almost on him, its searchlight beam rippling along the uneven ground, Logan burst from cover and ran right into the middle of the clearing.

Cutler didn't like the way Subject X was behaving.

Something about the bear hunt had gotten under Logan's skin. Though he looked like a walking dead man, he sure wasn't acting like a zombie tonight.

When the wranglers found Subject X, he loomed over the dead grizzly, muscles twitching. Lynch said that he was shivering from the cold. Of course, he had a point. Logan was naked, and it was more than ten below zero. But the cold had never bothered Subject X before, so Cutler couldn't understand why it would affect him now.

To Cutler, Logan's sudden jerks and ticks more resembled the actions of his boyhood pet, a dog who flopped and twitched when he was in the throes of a dream. At one point, as Cutler was about to connect his electroprod into his helmet port, Logan shook his head like a horse wildly flapping its mane.

The prod locked into place on Cutler's second try

and he carefully steered Logan toward the pens and the elevator. But they hadn't walked more than ten meters before Logan paused, seemingly reluctant to move forward. His helmeted head lifted, as if scanning the darkening sky.

Cutler pushed, and Logan shambled ahead. But his steps were hesitant, and instead of dropping his shoulders under the weight of the heavy cybernetic hardware, Logan jerked it from side to side as if he were alert and watching.

"Cuff him," Cutler commanded.

"Come on, Cut. He's a freakin' zombie, wh—"

"I said cuff him, Lynch. Don't make me give a command twice."

"Cripes, okay." Lynch pulled the plastic flex-cuffs from his belt and fit the bracelet over one forearm, then brought it back and snapped it to the other wrist. Logan didn't resist, but Cutler still would've liked to look Logan in the eyes, which were totally obscured by the heavy adamantium helmet.

The handcuffs seemed to have done the trick, however, for Logan remained docile on the ride down the elevator. At the door to Lab Two, Cutler was greeted by Anderson, who was waiting for him and dressed in full body armor.

"What are you dressed for, the winter ball?"

"Major's orders, Cut. Deavers wants you in his office, pronto."

"Can't the boss wait until I get Logan locked down for the night?"

"Sorry, Cut. Major says now, and hop to it. The Professor just laid some big experiment in our laps. Deavers says it'll take all night to get things prepped for tomorrow."

Cutler cursed and thrust the electroprod into Anderson's hand. "Watch him closely. Logan is acting funny tonight."

"You mean funny like in the lab the day they made him walk? Rice showed me the tape—hilarious."

"Just watch him, Anderson. And don't get sloppy."

As he headed for the elevator, Cutler ripped off his helmet and ran his hand through his sweaty hair. Without shedding his armor, he rode the elevator to Level One, lost in thought.

Another goddamn experiment. I wonder what that crazy egghead Professor has in store for Logan—and for us now.

The men in the chopper saw Logan as soon as he broke from cover. The aircraft immediately swerved to intercept the exposed figure that raced across the clearing.

Logan zigzagged to avoid the shot he had learned would come, his spine tingling in anticipation. He had learned from hard experience that you never hear the shot that gets you, so when the supersonic blast shocked his ear, he knew before the tree stump exploded in front of him that the sniper had missed.

As the chopper rolled over him, Logan tumbled across the ground and slammed into the shattered stump. At the speed the helicopter was traveling, he knew the sniper would only get one shot on the first pass. But Logan also knew that the pilot would not make that mistake again. His second run would be low and slow, giving his partner time to aim.

While the chopper made a circle in the sky and came back at him, Logan extended the M9 with both hands and waited for the approach. His breath came in ragged gasps as he fought back panic, especially at the moment when he had to close his eyes against the searchlight's glare or risk losing his night vision.

As the MD-500 leveled off, the searchlight dipped, and Logan opened his eyes to see the sniper lean out of the canopy. He quickly calculated the range, then adjusted the handgun and fired three shots in quick succession—all of them directed at the pilot.

A spark erupted as the first shot glanced off the bulletproof canopy; then another flash followed as the glass cracked. The third shot dinged off one of the blades as the pilot swerved to avoid Logan's fusillade. His maneuver was so abrupt and unexpected that it jolted the sniper out of his seat.

As the helicopter spun away, Logan watched the sniper air-swim all the way to the ground. He heard a loud crack, like a branch breaking under ice, as the sniper shattered his spine on a tree stump. The rifle landed next to its owner, and Logan took off across the clearing to retrieve it.

The helicopter pilot must have summoned help, for Logan heard the sound of another engine approaching the area—still out of sight, but coming on fast. Meanwhile, the pilot of the first helicopter regained control of his aircraft and was scanning the ground with the searchlight, looking for his fallen comrade. As Logan watched the copter's approach, his foot caught something and he went down.

He spit dirt and stared into the face of the dying

sniper, now draped like a broken doll over the stump. The man's eyes moved from side to side. He made a gurgling sound, but with a shattered spine he wasn't getting up. So Logan didn't waste time finishing him off. Instead, he fumbled on the ground until he found what he'd tripped over—the sniper rifle, its scope shattered, the barrel bent. Logan cursed and tossed the useless weapon aside.

He ducked behind the dying man as the helicopter flew overhead. But this time, the searchlight played across the tree line at the edge of the forest—the pilot had obviously lost track of him. After the chopper raced by, Logan went through the sniper's belt. He found a Chinese-made pistol and a high-explosive grenade.

Logan tucked his M9 into its holster and leveled the more powerful Chinese handgun at the returning helicopter. The chopper bore down on him. Its searchlight reached out to pin Logan in its dazzling brilliance. The beacon made a nice target, even with his eyes half-closed, and Logan aimed for the light. He emptied the magazine with quick, successive shots. In an eruption of sparks and broken glass, the light went dim.

The helicopter still approached, moving under forty kilometers per hour and less than fifteen meters off the ground. Logan discarded the empty handgun and pulled the pin on the grenade. As the helicopter roared over his hiding place, Logan tossed the explosive through the sniper's open hatch.

The pilot saw the lobbed weapon bounce into his cabin. Losing control of his aircraft, he struggled to find the explosive before it detonated. The aircraft veered wildly as the man seized the bomb and tossed it out. The grenade blew up just inches from the landing skid, its explosion jolting the aircraft.

Unfortunately for the pilot, the helicopter's wild trajectory had carried him into the path of the power lines. The whirling blades cut through the electrical cables and the fuselage slammed directly into the tower.

In a magnesium white flash of crackling power, the MD-500 disintegrated, showering burning debris down onto the barren field. The explosion washed over Logan, heat scorching his flesh and setting his hair afire. He rolled to extinguish the flames, then jumped to his feet as a second helicopter dived low over the trees and raced toward him.

The familiar chatter of an AK-47 greeted Logan. Bullets rained on him from above. He would not be able to avoid automatic weapon fire for long. As the chopper rushed to cut him off, Logan ran back into the forest, even though the sound of the dogs was nearly as loud as the helicopter overhead.

At the trees, Logan was suddenly pinpointed by a huge column of light—a third helicopter had arrived. Logan zigzagged out of the brilliance even as he heard the crack of a rifle. He threw himself to the ground as the searchlight beam passed over him, illuminating two infantrymen with rifles aimed in his direction. Logan drew his Beretta and squeezed off two quick shots. Both men went down in sprays of blood.

Logan jumped to his feet and literally dived into the woods. As he hit the ground between two thick tree trunks, the butt of a rifle slammed against his head and the tip of a bayonet pierced his guts. He howled as the man holding the bayonet stepped out of hiding to drive the blade deeper into his belly. With the knife pinning him to the ground, more soldiers, like a wave, rushed to his side and pummeled Logan with their rifles.

Someone barked an angry command and the soldiers drew back. An officer leaned close to Logan's face, screaming threats in Korean. Feigning unconsciousness, Logan reached down with a bloody hand and slipped his fighting knife from its sheath.

One more kill and I won't go to hell alone . . .

Logan lashed out, and rammed the four-and-a-half-inch blade into the man's throat. The knife just stuck in his Adam's apple. A quick slash and the officer's arteries parted. Hot blood spattered all over Logan as the Korean fell away.

The pummeling resumed, more savage than before, until Logan mercifully slipped into darkness.

"Come on, Anderson, let's get the Professor's zombie strapped down. The cafeteria closes in ten minutes and I want a hot meal. They're serving steak and fries tonight."

Using the prod, Anderson guided Logan into the diagnostic chair. Without bothering to restrain the subject's arms, as required by security protocol, Anderson started to detach the cybernetic helmet. Lynch watched him curiously.

"Prof says to remove the dome but keep him wired on the points," said Anderson.

"So we should leave the batteries on, then?"

"Yeah, I guess so," Anderson replied as he detached the visor and reached for the helmet. "And set the in-line alarm, right?"

"Guess so," said Lynch. "Okay, alarm set."

As the helmet was lifted, there was an explosion of awareness inside of Logan's benumbed brain. One thought flickered through his semiconscious mind.

One more kill and I won't go to hell alone . . .

"I don't know about this, Ms. Hines."

Cornelius stood in the center of the lab, shoulders hunched. "First I'm told we're creating a kind of super-soldier with Experiment X. Then it turns out he's some sort of mutant animal thing, so the adamantium bonding and the agony he endured in the process sends him cuckoo . . ."

Working beside Carol Hines at the REM terminal, a brain specialist from Dr. MacKenzie's staff paused to listen.

Cornelius, oblivious, continued his diatribe.

"Now the Professor's talking about the 'perfect killing machine' and all that most dangerous game crap, as if this poor guy is some kind of assassin or something. It's like, what is this weapon going to protect us from, the Commies?"

Cornelius frowned. "I never intended to build weapons. I got virtually blackmailed into this whole affair, you know. No . . . I guess you don't."

Carol Hines turned to the specialist. "Why don't you take your coffee break now, John?"

"But I'm on duty until—"

"Take a break, John."

The man nodded, then departed in a rush. When he was gone, Carol Hines swiveled in her chair to face Cornelius.

"I'm not too big on soul-searching," he told her. "But I've got some responsibility to humanity . . . and I don't have murder inside me, Ms. Hines . . . No matter what you may have heard. I'm not a killer. I'm not like the Professor."

Carol Hines remained silent for a long time. When at last she spoke, her voice was soft but determined.

"If you need me, Doctor, I will support you. In anything you decide to do."

Cornelius opened his mouth to reply but was interrupted by a shrill and sudden wail.

"The alarm!" he cried. "On source, Ms. Hines."

The woman swung around and hit the source button. On the gigantic monitor, the interior of Lab Two—Subject X's cell appeared. Logan was standing, helmet gone, claws extended. His left arm was poised to strike, and from the steel claws on his upraised right arm a dead wrangler dangled limply, leaking gore like a fresh side of beef on a meat hook.

15

"The alarm is coming from Lab Two. It's Mr. Logan. He's loose."

Carol Hines had managed to keep the fear out of her voice but not her eyes. She gawked at the security monitor, watching as Logan drove his left fist into a second guard—impaling the body, his gleaming claw points springing through the victim's back, rendering the man as inert as a rag doll thrown on a pitchfork.

Cornelius lunged for the intercom, punched the button. "Professor! Professor!"

"What is it, Cornelius?" The Professor's tone was saturated with the annoyance of a superior unexpectedly disturbed by an inferior.

"You maniac!" Cornelius roared. "The 'most dangerous game,' you said. Now you're using our own security personnel as guinea pigs? How could you? You're insane."

"What?" The Professor turned to face his own monitor. On the screen, Logan was pummeling the exit door. "This is not my doing, Cornelius. I am not in control!"

The alarm became a blaring Klaxon, filling the complex with its shrill, urgent wail.

Cornelius adjusted the intercom, sent his voice over every channel, shouted the warning to every level. "All security to Zone Two. Weapon X has escaped."

Cutler was just approaching the door to Deavers's office when the storm began. He turned and tore back to the armory, expecting to meet at least fifty guards on site—SOP for a call like this one.

"Professor," said Cornelius over the direct link. "My emergency shutdown is not functioning. Use your command center monitor controls to shut off the power."

"I'm trying, Cornelius. The cutoff is not working. I think Logan's batteries are still engaged."

"What happened to your fail-safe, Professor?"

"It isn't working, I tell you. Logan's helmet is off, but some fool left the power packs in place. He's moving at will, out of control, and he's not receiving our signals."

On the Professor's monitor, Logan tore up the security door with the ease of a jaguar shredding human flesh, his adamantium claws passing through stout steel. Stepping through the debris and into the corridor, he confronted a young technician moving equipment from one lab to another. A single elegant slash and the man went down in a widening crimson pool.

Two guards armed with tranquilizer guns rushed through the corridor. Their radios crackled. "We got three men down and two active. Request permission to shoot."

"Of course, man, shoot!" The Professor's superior tone had disappeared, replaced with a voice near panic.

A ceiling-mounted security camera relayed the action that played on-screen for Cornelius, Carol Hines, and the Professor. Two guards in the foreground fired continuous bursts of sedative darts into Subject X. Logan treated them like school yard spitballs. He brushed away the bothersome projectiles and continued traveling.

All of the guards backed away, slowly at first, then faster. "Security . . . We need live ammo down here. Repeat. We need—"

In one fluid movement Logan speared the first guard, the unbreakable claws penetrating Kevlar, fabric, tendon, and bone. Effortlessly, he tossed the pierced carcass over his shoulder. The second guard's gun he knocked aside as claws slit open the man's heart and lungs. Over the loudspeakers, gurgling screams horrified listeners throughout the research complex.

In the main lab, where Cornelius foolishly assured himself that the darts were enough to stop the subject, scientific bewilderment supplanted near-hysteria.

"Sir, how could this have happened?" he asked the Professor, his voice relaxing into a respectful, dispassionate tone. "Logan was harnessed up, how could he—"

"It's not over," Carol Hines interrupted. "The tranquilizers appear to be noneffective."

She glanced up from the REM console. Cornelius met her eyes: Fear had seeped back into them, along with something else—something resembling excitement.

Hines had discovered that although Subject X could not be controlled by the scientists, he could still be monitored by them. Constant data streamed into Hines's REM machine, giving her a clear readout of Logan's actions and his present capabilities. One thing was more than apparent to her—his brain activity, which was supposed to be suppressed, began running at full throttle. Logan became sentient. Fully aware, his mind morphed into a smart bomb fully engaged.

Cornelius slammed his console. "This is crazy, Professor. Can't you do something?"

"My system is down. I've no control over Weapon X whatsoever," repeated the Professor.

"Then who does?" Cornelius demanded.

"Yes . . ." the Professor murmured. "Who does, indeed?"

Behind the Professor's frightened gaze came a mysterious realization. Whatever it was, he didn't voice it to Cornelius.

"This is an emergency," Major Deavers interrupted over the intercom, his voice anxious, reaching. "I'm losing men in Zone Two. I need an advisory on this—"

In the armory, thirty-three guards had assembled. Cutler found them not suiting up, but gaping at the security monitor.

Friggin' amateurs.

"Who's down?" he barked.

"Anderson and Lynch in Lab Two," said Erdman. His face was a pale round surface cratered with worry lines. "Pollock and Gage in the corridor."

Cutler watched the playback. "Who's the other corpse?"

"Some technician. Poor son of a bitch got in the way of that psycho lab rat," Erdman told him.

Cutler turned to the rest. "Gear up. I'll break out the live ammo—"

"Deavers is still waiting for the Professor's authorization on that," said Erdman.

Cutler sneered. "Screw that shit! I'm authorizing live ammo—I'm taking no chances."

As the men strapped on Kevlar body armor, Cutler punched in a multi-number code on the wall-mounted keypad and yanked open the door to the weapons bay. The guards clustered around him while he passed out the serious muscle—Heckler & Koch UMP .45 caliber submachine guns with 25-round magazines.

On his monitor, Cornelius watched Logan cleave through an airtight hatch in less than a minute. The door was made of two-inch carbonized steel. It failed to matter.

"Professor," called Cornelius through the intercom, "can you seal the corridor from your remote location?"

"Seal?"

On the smaller monitor, Cornelius saw the pinched face of the Professor blanch a pale, pasty color.

"Yes. Contain Logan inside of Zone Two?"

The Professor sputtered. "I . . . I . . . Nothing is functioning here. And you . . . you saw what he did to that hatch . . ."

"Please," Major Deavers bawled over the intercom. "Will one of you give me a directive here? Professor? Dr. Cornelius? Dr. Hendry? We got a world of trouble coming down. Over."

"Can you close any part of Zone Two from your command center, Professor?" Cornelius repeated, trying to break through the Professor's stunned paralysis.

"Sir," Carol Hines interrupted. "Logan is moving away from Lab Two. Approaching Zone Three and D-Block."

Cornelius and Hines shared a look and the very same thought—

Dr. Hendry and his staff are in D-Block.

"Security! Move to D and Zone Three," Cornelius cried into the intercom.

"He's entering the service tunnels," Carol Hines warned next.

Cornelius began to sweat. "If he gets in there, he could go anywhere. Even to the surface."

"Doc!" It was Major Deavers. "I got five men down. We're gonna need more than tranquilizers to handle this situation."

Cornelius didn't answer. For a moment, his attention was wholly diverted by the puzzling sight on his small monitor. The Professor was having an animated conversation over a secure frequency. Cornelius listened intently. The conversation might be one-sided for his ears, but he had to hear it—

". . . Are you aware of what's happening at this time?" the Professor was asking.

"Dr. Cornelius? This is Deavers. Do you copy?"

Cornelius cursed. "Yes," he told Deavers. "I . . . uh, I copy."

"We can't take him without artillery. Do you understand?"

"Yes . . . yes," said Cornelius, still trying to listen in on the Professor's private communication.

". . . That is correct," the Professor was saying on his end, "Experiment X is out of my control. Running amok, you might say . . ."

"Ms. Hines," Cornelius snapped, pointing at the Professor on the small monitor. "Who is he talking to?"

"Computer shows exterior unit, sir. Satellite transmission can't be traced. He's obviously forgotten to turn off his intercom, doesn't know we can hear him."

". . . Precisely . . ." continued the Professor. "Killing

everyone in sight . . . But you see, Logan is fully harnessed. Yet my control panels are inactive . . ."

"Doc! Professor!" yelled Deavers. "For crying out loud! You gotta authorize weaponry. I got men down there—two of them. Trapped in Level Three by the sealed hatches. Logan's blocking the security ladder and they have to get past him to get out. They're armed with tranquilizer guns—goddamn peashooters. They haven't got a chance in hell."

Cornelius shifted his gaze to the monitor tracking Logan. The pair of security guards moved cautiously through a dim access tunnel. They looked like sewer rats to the scientist, foraging rodents, and Cornelius suddenly realized that's exactly what they were. Crawling without forethought, without higher intelligence, without any better awareness than the hapless vision provided by the weak, battery-powered beams of their flashlights dancing on the walls and ceiling. Before Cornelius could cry out, a stab of light pinned Logan, who was crouching against the wall like the higher form he was, like all higher forms who need do nothing more than wait for their traps to spring.

The moment the guards saw Logan, they nervously raised their tranquilizer guns.

"Don't fire! Don't fire!" Cornelius screamed. "Deavers, get your men out of there. Now!"

Too late. The sound of the firing darts, like toy popguns, reverberated off the tunnel's close walls. Screams came next, echoing down the metal-lined underground tube in shrill, earsplitting waves, as Logan charged.

"Security Zone Three!" Deavers screamed. "Get out of the tunnels—"

Logan struck the first guard in the abdomen. His

adamantium claws plunged through Kevlar and flesh with equal ease. When the claws were withdrawn, they left a cavity so large the man's intestines flowed onto the floor in a steaming pink-and-yellow mass.

As the second guard turned to flee, a slashing cut severed his left shoulder from his torso. The appendage slid sideways to the floor; still twitching as it hit the ground. Barely alive, gushing black blood, the hysterical guard crawled out of camera range.

Logan did not pursue.

"Oh God," rasped Deavers "That was Conran and Chase."

In the armory, the security men reacted to the butchery with revulsion and rage.

In his command center, the Professor continued to drone on, still oblivious to the fact that Hines and Cornelius were listening in. His conversation became background music to the mayhem.

". . . We are losing our security guards somewhat precipitately . . ." the Professor shared with his satellite uplink.

"Professor," called Cornelius, finally breaking in, "I need your clearance to issue the men firepower. Do you read me, Professor?"

". . . Given this . . . I'd like to ask . . . do you have a hand in these occurrences?"

Cornelius turned to Hines. "He's not listening to me. I think he's lost his mind."

Carol Hines did not respond.

"Ms. Hines?"

She appeared to be hypnotically focused on the data streaming into her Reifying Encephalographic Monitor.

"Carol!"

Carol Hines looked up, her face hopeful. "Sir, I think I've found something important."

Cutler had organized the men into what he hoped was a formidable enough force to counter Weapon X.

Because of the tight quarters they would be forced to fight in, Cutler had only issued fifteen UMPs to those he judged to be his best men—personnel with years of military experience, or those who kept their heads despite the chaos going on around them. Among that group was Agent Franks.

"Stick close to me as we go into action," Cutler said to Franks as he thrust the weapon into the agent's hands.

The rest of the guards were outfitted with short-barreled M14s, semiautomatics that had a much slower rate of fire than the machine guns. Right now, Cutler judged his men too jumpy to work effectively without close supervision, so he figured that the less bullets flying, the less chance of friendly-fire injuries.

And how many bullets is it gonna take to stop Logan, anyway? Cutler speculated. *He's only human—well, sorta . . .*

Now, armored up and armed, Cutler led his men into the service tunnel above Zone Three. Once inside, he formed them into a phalanx—a wedge-shaped formation with the highest concentration of firepower at the apex.

"I'll take point," Cutler said, hefting his UMP.

"No, I'll take point," said Erdman, stepping into position.

"What's the problem, Erd? Don't trust me?"

"I do trust you, Cutler. That's the reason I want to take point," Erdman replied. "Major Deavers is vacillating, trying to convince the eggheads we should be armed. But you took charge, made sure we were armed despite what the mad scientists want. That makes you the only leader we got."

Then Erdman grinned behind his visor. "Anyway, I want another shot at that bastard."

Cutler relented and moved to the right flank.

"Okay. Move out."

"Mr. Logan has breached three zones and is now within two hundred and twenty yards of the Professor's command center on Three and C-Block," said Carol Hines.

"Jesus." Cornelius rubbed the back of his neck. Sweat was trickling from every pore of his body, his brown beard felt like it was crawling with insects.

"And it is not a coincidence, sir," continued Hines. "I've traced his movements from the holding bay at Lab Two. He has made a definite path to the Professor's quarters."

"I don't know, Ms. Hines. Doesn't seem logical. How could Logan know where the Professor is?"

"You'll recall that he just hunted down a bear in less than four minutes, Dr. Cornelius. Our Mr. Logan has shown uncanny tracking abilities."

"But that was a controlled situation, Ms. Hines."

Carol Hines glanced at the small monitor, where the Professor continued his strange conversation. "And who says this isn't a controlled situation, sir?"

". . . I see, I see," said the Professor. "Sort of biting the hand that feeds, eh? . . . A clean sweep, as it were . . . get rid of the deadwood, eh?"

Cornelius activated the intercom. "Security? Major Deavers? Break out the big guns. Shoot to kill."

"Did the Professor okay it, then, Doctor?" Deavers asked.

"No," Cornelius said as he watched Logan's swift progress toward the Professor's sanctum. "But he won't mind, believe me. And make that on the double, okay? Over."

Deavers signed off, leaving only two pronounced sounds over the general hum of the equipment in the lab: the ticking of Hines's monitor and the droning voice of the Professor.

". . . There is just one thing . . . let me ask . . . should I leave now, or should I take refuge here while—as you put it—Weapon X clears the deadwood . . ."

Cornelius stared at the madman on the screen, having a polite conversation while chaos swept through the entire complex. As he watched, the Professor's chair exploded upward. A clawed forearm ripped through the steel plates from the floor below.

Screeching, the Professor fell as Logan moved through steel and concrete, slashing his way up, reaching for purchase and the chance to find his hated prey.

Cornelius took a startled step back from the monitor. "Good Lord. We've got to do something."

Ms. Hines stood, hugging herself, face tense. "The security force is almost there, sir. They should be able to handle it."

"But we should help him, too . . . shouldn't we?"

Carol Hines could not reply. She began to sob with terror as she listened to the Professor's shrieks. Cornelius stepped closer to her, but when he reached out to put his arm around her shoulders, she shrank from him.

"Don't touch me! Don't ever, ever touch me!" she shouted, trembling uncontrollably.

• • •

The guards exited the service tunnel on Level Three.
The elevators were shut down and the stairwells sealed,
per emergency security procedures. Fortunately, there
were no innocent civilians wandering the corridors. If
anyone was here, they were probably quivering behind
sealed hatches.

The alarms still blared, however, and the din was becoming a distraction. "Why doesn't somebody cut that
damn thing off?" Altman complained.

"Can't," said Cutler. "Only our pal Deavers can turn it
off, from the security command center."

A voice crackled in their helmet receivers. "This is
Deavers to all security units. Assemble immediately in
the armory, where heavy weapons will be issued."

"Speak of the devil," whispered Altman.

Erdman tapped the headset in his helmet like he
couldn't believe his ears, then turned to the men behind
him and slightly lifted his Heckler & Koch UMP .45 caliber submachine gun. "That's our major. On top of the
situation, as usual."

Laughter followed from a few of the men, but most
were too nervous to respond. They had all seen what
happened to Anderson and Lynch, to Chase and Conran.
They were filled with dread but weren't about to admit
it, least of all to their comrades.

On the right flank, Cutler played lieutenant to Erdman's tough sergeant, letting Erd shoot the orders and
prop up the men's spirits while he focused on the overall
strategy—what there was of it. He decided now was a
good time to report to "management."

"Cutler to Deavers. Come in . . ."

The major reacted as if he'd heard the voice of God. "Cutler! Are you in the armory?"

"Just finished issuing heavy weapons. Sir? Could you cut that damn alarm?"

"Alarm? Yeah, sure, the alarm." A moment later, silence descended like a forest snowfall.

"Where are you, Cutler?" Deavers asked, some of the old authority returning to his voice.

"We're moving toward Level Three, Zone Three now."

"How far are you from C-Block?"

Cutler raised his hand to Erdman, who halted them all. "Major," Cutler replied with a whisper. "We're right outside of C-Block now. What's the situation?"

"Weapon X is—"

Deavers's reply was cut off as they heard a scream, followed by the Professor's panic-stricken pleas. "Help me! Help . . ."

"—coming for the Professor," Deavers said. "He's—"

Cutler cut the major off, then used his master communications code to cut off Deavers's transmission from the rest of his crew, too. He looked up, to see Erdman staring at him with curious eyes.

"Deavers isn't down here, so he's not in charge anymore," said Cutler. "I'm calling the shots."

Erdman nodded approvingly, then turned to face the others. "Let's move it."

The hatch to the Professor's command center was closed but not locked. On the opposite end of the corridor, the second entrance was ajar, according to the real-time images coming through to Cutler's helmet screen.

"This is it," said Cutler. "We're going through both doors at the same time. Erdman, take ten men and circle to the other entrance. You got fifteen seconds to get into position. Now go!"

As they hustled around the corner, Cutler faced the rest. "You," he called to Franks. "Take these men and block the exit to this level. If Weapon X gets through us, it's up to you to take him out."

"But Cut—"

"Now!"

Franks turned and led nine relieved security men to the elevator shaft on the opposite end of the long corridor.

Cutler faced the dozen men still with him. "Five seconds," he whispered as he silently unlatched the hatch and popped it open a crack. "Three . . . two . . . one . . . Go! Go! Go!"

Cutler slammed his shoulder against the heavy steel hatch, and it swung open. He leaped over the threshold, UMP raised.

The Professor was on the floor, pinned helplessly under the weight of his ergonomic command chair, which had been uprooted from its mounts in the floor. A giant hole yawned where Logan had burst through. Wires dangled and sparked in the opening.

Agent Abbot came in right behind Cutler. "Where's the bastard?" he cried. "Where's Weapon X?"

With a feral roar, Weapon X leaped to the floor directly in front of them—he'd been lying in wait among the heating and air ducts over their heads.

"Look out, Cut!" Abbot shouted, shoving him aside and raising his UMP.

But Logan was faster. With a slashing backhand, he knocked the machine gun out of Abbot's grasp. Then he brought down his right, claws extended. The adamantium steel cut through helmet, skull, and brain, dividing the agent's head into four neat slices, like a ripe watermelon on a cutting board.

Abbot's legs kicked out and he slammed onto the deck with a clang. Cutler rolled away from his comrade's twitching corpse as Weapon X lunged for him, claws striking sparks from the metal floor.

Then Erdman burst through the other hatch, UMP blazing. At least three shots danced across Logan's naked torso, each followed by an explosion of gore. But Weapon X didn't even flinch as he spun to face his newest foes. With a single quick stroke, Logan decapitated Erdman. The head bounced off the wall, the body took one final step forward before it toppled. Dying spasms pumped off three more shots, which blew out monitors and shattered computer consoles.

Behind Erdman, another guard pumped three shots into Weapon X at point blank range, forcing him back.

"Get the Professor outta here!" Cutler screamed as he struggled to his feet. Two men raced past him, then a third and fourth. One dropped to the Professor's side while the other three struggled to lift the heavy chair and drag the shrieking man out from under it.

"It's okay, Professor," a guard said in a voice loud enough to be heard over the chaos. "We've got you now. You're going to be all right . . ."

More shots, ripping into Logan, tearing the command center up in a shower of sparks.

"He . . . he tried to kill me," the Professor cried. A bullet bounced off the wall and sent debris spilling onto the Professor's upturned face. He howled as his glasses were knocked away. "My glasses . . . can't see."

"I got them, sir," said the guard leaning over him, his voice echoing behind his visor.

The Professor slipped his rectangular-rimmed glasses on, but suddenly, he heard a hollow, meaty sound. The man looming over him stiffened and his eyes rolled up in his head. He opened his mouth and blood burst from it, to coat the inside of his visor. The guard slumped over him, the weight of his dead body and the Kevlar armor he wore crushed the Professor.

With a strength borne of desperation, the Professor pushed the corpse aside. He reached up his hand to grip the edge of his command-and-control console.

A silver slash. For a long, agonizing moment, the Professor's world was defined by pain—sudden, excruciating, all-consuming. Reflex made him yank his arm back. Through tearing eyes, he saw the stump gushing gore, cleanly severed at the wrist.

"My hand!" howled the Professor. Then, as his own blood splashed his face, rage replaced anguish.

"Kill him! Kill!" shouted the Professor. "Destroy Weapon X now!"

Strong arms grabbed his torso as two guards dragged the Professor out of the command center, into a side corridor.

Meanwhile, Cutler watched as the guards, firing and moving forward with precision, forced Logan to give ground until his back was against the wall. But as they aimed their machine guns to finish him off, Weapon X surged forward unexpectedly, disemboweling a guard who was foolish enough not to retreat.

Cutler, seeing his men die one by one, threw himself into the fray, only to be knocked aside again. He tried to

get a clear shot at Logan, but the fighting was too close.
Weapon X seemed to be completely covered by a mass of
squirming, fighting guards struggling vainly to bring him
down.

"Did you get the Professor out?" Cutler cried. "Did
you get the Professor out? Come in. Answer me, somebody. What's going on?"

"Professor secured," came the reply. "He's okay."

Cutler heard other voices as well. Shouted commands, screams of pain and surprise.

"Target's all over the place . . . No clear shots . . .
Get back . . . Too late . . . Losing men . . . Goddamn
monster . . ."

Cutler watched as Altman was lifted off his feet by
claws embedded in his torso. Logan slammed the man's
head against the ceiling with so much force, his Kevlar
helmet shattered. When Altman hit the ground, his broken face stared up at Cutler, nose twisted, eyes askew,
like the face on a Picasso painting.

*Over a dozen body shots, no effect. It's a stupid, senseless mas-
sacre. Fuck!*

Cutler keyed his communicator. "Fall back, everybody. Fall back . . . into the corridor . . ."

To Agent Franks's surprise, the elevator doors on Level
Three opened. Dr. Cornelius and Carol Hines hurried
out, intent on reaching the Professor's command center.

"Whoa!" Franks cried, stopping them. "You can't go
that way. You're heading for a firefight." As if to punctu-
ate his words, Cornelius and Hines heard multiple shots,
shouts, and screams.

"Damn it," Cornelius said in frustration. "Aren't you
going to do something?"

"I have my orders," Franks told him, face grim as he listened to the frenzied voices over the communications network.

"Get back in here . . . Losing men . . . monster . . . Bloody massacre . . ."

Then a security guard stumbled around the corner, one hand clutching his side where blood flowed freely from a deep gash that bared the bones of his rib cage. His other arm barely propped up the pallid Professor.

First Carol Hines, then Dr. Cornelius pushed past Agent Franks and hurried to aid the injured men. Franks and two guards reluctantly followed. The rest stayed behind as the last line of defense.

The Professor groaned and stumbled, glasses askew, curled into a tight ball as he limped along, his stump tucked into his belly to slow the bleeding.

"Try to stay still, Professor. And stay calm," said the guard, laboring under his own wound.

"I'm bleeding to death," squawked the Professor, eyes bright with pain. Back inside the Professor's sanctum, the battle still raged with screams and shouts and shots fired.

"Command, we need a stretcher down here, fast!" said Franks.

Deavers's excited voice replied. "What the hell is going on down there? Someone shut me out of the net! How can I give commands if—"

"Sir, we need a stretcher," Franks interrupted.

"On the way," came the bitter response.

Agent Franks reached out to catch the Professor, allowing the man who'd brought him out to lean against the wall, then slump to the floor as his legs failed.

"A stretcher is coming, sir," Franks told the Professor.

But when he tried to help the man, the Professor pushed him away.

"I don't need a stretcher, you fool. It's my hand that's missing, not my leg."

"Oh, no . . . oh, goodness," Carol Hines whimpered when she saw the blood, the stump.

The Professor took a few lurching steps, then spied his colleagues. "Cornelius," he rasped. "Help me. Get me out of here."

Cornelius saw the gruesome limb, too. "Goddamn . . . we're gonna have to stop the bleeding."

"We need a tourniquet," said Ms. Hines, taking hold of the injured arm. "Dr. Cornelius, give me your tie."

Cornelius whipped the silk off his neck and Hines used it to bind the crimson stump. Franks hunched over the man who'd brought the Professor out, then stood, shaking his head. "He's dead."

Suddenly, more shots erupted in a blaze, followed by a frenzied call over the communications net. "We need backup! We're—" The voice was cut off in a choking scream.

"Who was that?" asked one of the guards.

Franks just shrugged. "Wasn't Cutler . . . maybe he's down, too."

"So what do we do, Franks?"

Franks looked at the dead guard on the floor. Then he raised his UMP and faced the others. "We have orders to stop Weapon X if the others don't, so let's go!"

"Hold tight, Professor," said Hines, indicating the knotted tie. "Try to keep your han—your arm raised. That should hold it for the time being."

"We must get you to the infirmary right away. Can you walk?" Cornelius asked.

"I can run, Cornelius," the Professor said in a voice that was surprisingly strong. "Just get me away from here. But not to the infirmary."

"Sir," Carol Hines protested, "you must be seen to."

"We must get to the adamantium reactor hold." The Professor pushed past them and hurried toward the elevator.

"What? Why, Professor?" Cornelius called.

"Because it's the only safe place from Weapon X."

"But security will take care of Logan, Professor."

"Don't be stupid, Cornelius. They don't stand a chance."

Major Deavers was a broken man. A bureaucrat without authority, an officer without a command.

From the security center, he'd watched the monitors helplessly as his men were butchered by Weapon X. He'd screamed into the microphone, knowing that his troops couldn't hear him—that the treasonous Cutler or maybe Erdman had deliberately blocked his transmissions. He'd pounded the console as his men died one by one, then en masse.

But for all the shouting and pounding, Deavers failed to do the one thing that might have helped. He could have gone down to the armory, put on a suit of armor, and joined his men on the front line. But he wouldn't.

A manager just doesn't do that sort of thing.

That's what Deavers told himself, anyway.

Now he wasn't sure who was alive—only that most of his men were dead. Some lay in the corridor, others near Lab Two. They were heaped to the ceiling in the Professor's own command center.

It's not my fault . . . it was a rebellion . . . a mutiny.

Deavers suspected his men had listened in on his conversation with Dr. Cornelius.

Maybe they thought I was indecisive . . . but I argued from the start that the heavy weapons should be issued. I can't help it if the bosses see things differently . . .

Deavers blamed circumstances for those first deaths—Anderson or Lynch violated protocol, got sloppy. But he also suspected his own men believed that Conran and Chase died because he—as their commander—was too slow to react. The major also suspected his troops were angry that he didn't issue the heavy weapons on his own authority.

Deavers thought that judgment unfair.

Men like Erdman, Franks, and especially Cutler . . . they don't understand there's a chain of command. That it's important for someone else to take the heat for the hard calls.

Deavers knew that Weapon X had cost someone big money. The way he saw the situation, it wasn't up to him to decide whether the experimental subject should be gunned down or not. That kind of decision had to come from the top, from someone above his pay grade.

One thing I learned in all my years—never stick your neck out. Not in combat, and not in management. Let men like Cutler and Erdman strap on the guns and go into the trenches.

Yeah, the peaceniks got it right. The best soldiers are the ones who never have to fight. I learned that lesson, all right, but Cutler never did. That's why Cutler never rose to the top.

Deavers's desperate rationalizing was interrupted when Specialist Rice burst into the command center.

"Rice, glad you're here," said Deavers. "I need someone to go down and reconnoiter Level Three. Most of—"

"Sorry, Deavers, I don't take orders from you anymore."

Rice reached out and snatched the command card off the clip on Deavers's overalls.

"Hey—"

"I need this card to access the main supercomputer for a critical download."

"Why?"

"Look around, Major. The crap's hit the fan. Too much critical data will be lost if the whole complex goes up in smoke. I'm going to retrieve it, copy it."

"You got orders? From who? The Professor?"

Rice snorted. "Orders. That's all you care about, isn't it, Deavers? Okay, let's say I got orders, from someone more important than you, more important than Cornelius, or even the Professor . . ."

"The . . . the Director?"

"I have orders, Deavers. That's all you need to know."

While Deavers watched, seemingly paralyzed, Rice opened the weapon case and drew out an automatic. Then he headed for the door.

"Rice!" cried Deavers. "Are you and the Director going to try and fix this mess?"

Rice shook his head. "There's no fixing this, Major."

Then Specialist Rice took off, leaving Deavers alone to ponder the ashes of his spiraling career.

"Security, Zone Three, respond," Franks called. He and eight other men waited outside the hatch to the command center, hoping for a response from inside.

"Security, Zone Three—"

A voice wracked with pain cut through Franks's transmission. "Sir . . . we're . . . we're . . ."

Then dead air.

Franks glanced over his shoulder at the others. "Lock

and load. No fancy stuff. No encirclement. Just shoot and scoot. And toughen up, too. Ignore everything you see in there except Logan . . . you shoot that bastard to pieces."

Franks slapped a 25-round magazine into his UMP. "On three . . ."

Three seconds later they burst into the command center, coming through the hatch firing, then fanning out to either side. Franks heard gasps and muffled groans over his headset. He had to stifle an exclamation of his own.

In the middle of the room, Weapon X spun to face them, arms flung wide, claws extended. The creature was bent low in a feral crouch, ready to pounce. Logan was covered with gore from head to toe—and this time it wasn't sheep's blood.

He stood on a mound of bodies piled two and three deep, packing the command center like a carpet of human remains. A few of the guards twitched or groaned, but most were dead and the rest dying. The walls were repainted in red, dripping darkly. Loose entrails, shredded organs, and severed limbs made the metal floor slippery.

Logan's eyes burned as he saw the guards enter. With a silent snarl, he took a step forward.

"Fire! Fire! Fire!"

One of the men cut loose. Computer panels exploded under the hail of bullets. The room filled with sparks and the deafening thunder of firearms discharging nonstop. A moment later, the fire control system activated, drenching the cloud of gun smoke with a fog of blasting halon.

"Can't see!" someone cried.

"He's moving past me, Logan's co—*ack!*" The call

ended when the agent's helmet microphone was severed along with his throat.

"Look out, I—"

A muscle-bound, two-hundred-fifty-pound guard flew out of the fog, slamming against the far wall with no more effort than it took an angry little boy to toss aside a toy soldier.

"Pull back! Pull back!" Franks cried as he fired blindly into the soup. He heard a scream and someone stumbled out of the mist—Agent Jenkins, his torso stitched with bullets. Eyes wide, hand reaching out for help, the man went down.

Behind him, Weapon X hurled forward. Franks fired, but the shot went wide. Then a cutting sideswipe knocked him to the ground and he landed hard, stunned.

As Logan swept past him, Franks tried to rise but found his legs oddly tangled. He wondered if his foot was caught. When he looked down, he saw his legs flopping on the ground a few feet away, both severed at the hip. He slumped uncontrollably to one side as a torrent of blood spilled out of stumps that were once thighs.

Dimly, Franks heard someone call his name. On the other side of the command center, propped against a shattered console, Cutler leaned, gasping. His chest gaped, lungs and a slowing heart visible behind dripping gore.

Cutler's mouth was moving, but his rasping voice barely registered over the communications net. Finally, as he fought for consciousness, Franks could make out Cutler's words, which he kept repeating until he died.

"I recognize him now . . . Logan. I know who he is . . ."

With his last breath, Franks keyed the microphone

and reported to Deavers, who'd been demanding to know their status for the last five minutes.

"Nothing left, sir," Franks wheezed. Then he sensed a movement nearby. With his last bit of strength, Franks lifted his head to see Weapon X looming over him. He closed his eyes and started to whisper his epitaph.

"Sir . . . he's coming . . . for me."

16

Apocalypse

"This is it, Cornelius. Break the seal. We will be safe here."

Cornelius shrugged. "Yes, if you don't count the radiation burns."

The Professor brought Cornelius and Carol Hines to a massive set of double, steel-plated, lead-lined blast doors. The elevator had carried them to the deepest level of the facility, where neither Hines nor Cornelius had ever been despite the many weeks they'd spent inside the secret complex.

The atmosphere was close and stale, the corridors warm from the ambient heat of the adamantium smelter on the level above. Recessed lighting in the steel-lined corridors seemed hardly adequate to dispel the gloom. Ozone and industrial smells suffused the subterraneous chamber, which constantly boomed and echoed as a result of thousands of automatic mechanisms still operating.

The doors themselves were branded with a black-and-yellow radiation symbol. Bold red letters spelled DAN-GER. Still clutching the blood-soaked tourniquet, the Professor gestured with his chin to a glass case embedded in the wall. "Ms. Hines, get that gun."

While Cornelius punched the Professor's code into the keypad and swung the huge doors open, Hines broke the glass and pulled the single M14 off the rack. Two fully loaded magazines were also inside the case. She grabbed them, too.

"Load it, please."

Carol Hines snapped the magazine in place and presented the weapon to the Professor.

"Not to me, you idiot. What can I do with a gun? Give it to Cornelius."

Hines thrust the weapon into the doctor's hands, happy to be rid of it. Cornelius held the weapon at arm's length, as if it were contaminated.

"What's going on here, Professor? Just what do you think I'm going to do with this rifle?"

"Fire it, Doctor. At the first opportunity . . ."

The Professor led them inside the reactor room and commanded Cornelius to seal the hatch. The place was fully automated, with banks of computers, terminals, and switching and rerouting stations lining the walls. Digital readouts continually flashed the core's internal temperature, pressure per cubic foot, and other critical information as the machines went about their preprogrammed tasks, oblivious to the apocalypse unfolding in the complex above.

As Hines approached the central terminal, built-in motion detectors activated the computer keyboard, the monitor, the communications equipment. She set to work, and in a few seconds views from the security monitors on the upper levels appeared on the screen.

Safe behind the sealed hatch, Cornelius turned to the Professor. "So you want me to fire this rifle, eh?"

"You may not be able to kill Logan, but if you could

shoot away the power packs on his belt harness. That should stop him."

Cornelius was no sharpshooter, hadn't fired a weapon since high school. And even if he had been, the entire premise of the Professor's theory was based on his fallacious assumption of control.

"This is ridiculous," Cornelius countered. "Even if Logan is still alive, the systems are down, he can't—"

"The system is not down," the Professor declared. "It is in the hands of another."

"Who?" Cornelius asked. *The bastard you were chatting up while the guards were being butchered?*

"It is not your place to know that, Cornelius."

"You've got a lot of gall, Professor. Asking me to shoot a man, but you won't tell me why—"

"Don't wave your morals in front of me, Cornelius. I would think that a man who murdered his wife and child would be a little more cold-blooded."

An audible gasp could be heard from Carol Hines. Cornelius faced her, but she'd already turned her attention back to the central terminal's keyboard, refusing to meet his gaze.

"And in case you've forgotten," the Professor continued, pressing his case, "not very long ago, you ordered the guards to kill Logan."

Cornelius nodded, face grim. "That's right, Professor. I wanted Logan dead, but I wasn't willing to get my hands dirty doing it myself. The fact is, I'm not a killer. I don't have murder in my heart."

"Well, you'd better find it somewhere or—" With a moan, the Professor dropped to one knee. Cornelius slung the weapon over his arm and helped the man into a chair.

"Look at you. You're bleeding buckets here. I have to bandage you up."

The Professor coughed. His face was milky from loss of blood, but his eyes were bright, their expression bitter. "I am considered deadwood, Cornelius. To be cleared away. Just deadwood . . ."

"Dead meat, more like it," said Cornelius as he removed the tourniquet. Blood trickled from the clotted stump, but Cornelius quickly covered the injury with cloth torn from his shirtsleeves. "You're delirious, Professor. All this stuff, your wound. You're going into shock."

"You are ever the fool, aren't you, Cornelius? If that door doesn't keep Logan back, you will soon discover what shock is . . ."

Cornelius refused to be baited by a dying man. "Yeah, well, I think the quicker we can get you to the—"

"Hines!" shouted the Professor. "Will you stop that infernal tapping! I can't think!"

She raised her hands from the keyboard. "Yes, sir. Sorry, sir. The computer shows Mr. Logan to be fully active—"

"I knew that, blast it!"

"His battery packs are more than eighty percent drained, soon they'll give out."

"Not soon enough, Ms. Hines . . ."

"No, sir. Actually, Logan is quite close. He's in Tunnel Two. Moving in this direction."

The Professor pushed Cornelius aside and stumbled to the terminal. "Get away, woman! Let me get in there."

The Professor stared at the screen. Cornelius didn't think it was possible after all the blood he'd lost, but the man managed to pale another shade whiter.

"Is this terminal connected to the main supercomputers?" the Professor asked.

"It is the main computer, sir."

The Professor realized they were standing directly above the buried computer mainframe. "Yes, of course," he said in sharp annoyance as he began to type.

Carol Hines tried to assist. "Pardon, sir . . . that's not the proper code—"

Cornelius called to her. "Hines? Let it go. It's out of our hands. I don't think we're a part of this game anymore."

Finally, a communicator chirped and the Professor spoke, his voice a rasp. "This is the Professor. Please answer . . . you must come in, please. Talk to me . . ."

Silence greeted his plea.

"Are you surprised that Logan didn't kill me? Why are you doing this to me? I am not part of the rabble. You must know that. Answer me, please . . . don't let me die here!"

"We don't have to die, Professor," argued Cornelius. "None of us. This gun. I can use it, to protect us—"

But the Professor ignored Cornelius, listening intently for a voice that never came.

"I can shoot off the power packs, like you said, Professor. Give you and Ms. Hines a chance to get away. I can—"

The shrill scrape of metal on metal interrupted them. Then a booming crash echoed off the chamber's walls as something heavy struck the floor.

"What's that noise?" cried Cornelius.

Ms. Hines covered her heart. "I think Mr. Logan has finally found us, sir."

The sound of footsteps followed, reverberating

through the massive chamber. Suddenly, the lights flick-ered, the consoles grew dim. Then everything went black for a seemingly endless moment, before the battery-pow-ered emergency lights automatically activated.

"The power's down!"

"Those sounds. Outside," hissed Cornelius. "Logan is in the walls. He's coming through."

"Help me! Help me, please!" screamed the Professor into the inactive communicator. He slammed the con-sole with his remaining fist. "Blast you . . . blast you for this!"

Cornelius looked at Carol Hines. "I don't know who he thinks he's talking to, and I don't care." Then he no-ticed she was trembling uncontrollably. "Are you scared?"

"Yes, sir. Very. Are you?"

Cornelius nodded. "Part of me, to death . . . But another part . . . I think I'm ready to see my wife again."

Hines stood close, looked up at him. "What . . . what the Professor said, about your wife—"

"It's not true. That's what the police think, and that's fine with me. The truth is more pathetic. I'm sure you don't want to know."

"No, I do . . . tell me."

"My child was born—defective. I searched and searched for a cure for the disease, but I failed—me, an immunologist, and I couldn't even save my son."

"He died?"

Cornelius looked away. "Paul was dying . . . slowly. A piece at a time. I worked every day and half the night in the medical laboratory searching for a cure while my wife lived daily with our boy's pain . . . saw it every hour, lis-tened to the cries. It finally broke her.

"One night, I came home from the lab, found them both dead. My wife had poisoned our son with some of my medical supplies and then killed herself."

"And the police blamed you?"

"I let them blame me. Madeline was a Roman Catholic. Her faith, her family were important to her . . . suicide is a mortal sin, so is murder. It was better all around if I got the blame. I had nothing to live for without her, anyway . . ."

A crash interrupted his recollections. From somewhere behind steel walls, machinery tumbled.

Cornelius's fingers tightened around the cold metal barrel of the automatic rifle. "Logan's inside now. He's got to be."

Carol Hines's slight body still trembled.

"Listen to me," Cornelius said. "When Logan comes through here, I'll deal with him. Finish him off, distract him—whatever I can do. You get out. Run as fast as you can. Forget about the Professor—he's gone already—and forget about me."

"But—"

"Listen. I've had enough of this life and I'm ready to die. Probably deserve to, for what I helped the Professor do . . . turn a man into a monster—"

Another crash, and the emergency lights flickered. They heard a long squeal as the turbines on the level above ground to a halt.

"The power's really gone now," said Carol Hines. "The turbines for the adamantium reactor have shut down."

"That's the last of our worries, Ms. Hines."

"The turbines maintain the adamantium coolant,

Doctor. Without power, it will reduce to the charged compound. We must purge the core or this whole complex could blow up within the hour."

The Professor, still hunched over the console, looked up when he heard her words. "All deadwood . . . all burned up . . . blow it all and we all die," he muttered. "Yes . . . that's what I should do. Blow it all up . . ."

From above, an oily substance dripped onto the Professor's bald head. Warm and wet, he thought it to be hydraulic fluid—until it trickled down his cheek and splashed onto the deactivated consoles. Even in the dim light, the Professor knew blood when he saw it.

He looked up just as Weapon X burst out of the ventilation shaft over their heads. A bellowing roar and Logan landed in a crouch, adamantium claws gleaming in the scarlet glow, to confront the astonished Professor. The man whimpered and stumbled back, transfixed by the sight of the thing he had toiled so long and hard to create and mold.

Chemically enhanced muscles ripping, mane wild, flanks quivering like those of a hunting lion about to launch, Logan bared gore-flecked teeth. The virtual-reality inputs had been ripped from his face and only loose, sparking wires remained. His eyes flowed scarlet tears. His naked hide ran with ribbons of blood. The battery packs still dangled from his waist. With every heavy step he left a crimson footprint.

"Shoot him! Shoot! Shoot!" shrieked the Professor. "Kill him while you still can!"

But when Cornelius looked into Logan's eyes, he saw pain, weakness, confusion—and humanity. Weapon X should have struck them all down, yet Logan appeared paralyzed, wavering, seemingly reluctant to lash out, as if his bloodlust had been spent.

Cornelius lowered the rifle. "Look, Professor. He's faltering. I think he's had it. He's too weak to attack, he's lost a lot of blood."

"That blood is what's left of our security guards, you fool! He's controlled and programmed to kill all of us. Use the gun now, while we still have a chance!"

Cornelius switched off the safety and raised the muzzle of the rifle, aiming from his hip. But Weapon X now seemed more human than monster, and he could not bring himself to pull the trigger.

"He isn't moving, Professor. He's finished."

"Do as I command, Cornelius!"

With his good hand, the Professor punched the doctor in the jaw. Cornelius flinched from the blow, his trigger finger twitched, and the M14 fired. With the weapon set to full automatic, a third of the magazine—eight shots— burst from the muzzle in less than two seconds, spraying the control room.

Some of the bullets bounced off the floor, some struck the computer banks behind Weapon X in an explosion of silicon, plastic, and glass. But three lucky shots struck Logan in the chest, stitching across his pectorals and making him dance like a marionette until he spun into the smoldering debris behind him.

Logan dropped. Cornelius blinked, the rifle held limply in his grip. "I . . . I got him. I got him. He's—"

With a low, throaty growl, Logan began to stir.

The Professor screamed. "The power packs, Cornelius! Get the power packs, shoot away the receivers. Shut down his brain!"

Still sprawled on the floor among the shattered computers, Logan lifted his chin, then shook his head to clear it. His bloody lips curled into an angry snarl when he saw the weapon in Cornelius's hand.

"He . . . he's still alive. Th-that's incredible," Cornelius stammered, his limbs paralyzed.

"Shoot, you fool. Shoot before it's too late."

Cornelius's eyes met Logan's. Hines screamed.

"You blasted idiot!" bellowed the Professor.

With a single thrust, Logan ran Cornelius through, the adamantium claws ripping into his belly, severing his spine, and bursting through the back of his shirt. With a wheeze, Cornelius folded around Logan's arm. His round glasses slipped from his nose, shattering on the floor, as his killer lifted him off his feet, then slammed his broken body onto the main computer console.

A moment of awareness was left in Cornelius, no more than a final, flickering breath. Enough time to see the demon's raging face blur into an angel's; enough time to watch a monster's wiry mane become a lustrous head of perfumed hair; enough time to hear his wife's delighted laughter for the rest of eternity.

"Idiot! Idiot!" the Professor screamed as he ran to the exit. Carol Hines followed, sobbing. At the double doors, she caught up with the Professor, tugged his good arm.

"Stop, sir. Stop. We must go back—"

The Professor pushed her aside. "Get away from me!"

"But we can't just leave him. We have to help Cornelius."

The Professor glanced back over his shoulder, half-expecting to be transmuted into a tall pillar of salt. Logan had pinned Cornelius to the computer terminal, and was slicing the doctor's tormented corpse the way he'd ripped into the she-wolf, piece by gory piece.

"There's no helping him, you stupid woman. Can't you see he's dead? I couldn't help him even if I wanted to. Neither could you."

The Professor stumbled through the now open hatch.

"Where are we going?" Hines cried.

"I must get to the reactor, so stop sniveling and pull yourself together. I need your help now."

Hines wiped away tears. After a final glance over her own shoulder, she raced to catch up to the Professor.

"Yes . . . yes, I'm with you, sir."

The two batteries failed almost simultaneously.

The larger power pack directed energy through the somatosensory cortex to the central fissure of Logan's brain, then along the top of the frontal cortex, which controls basic and skilled movements. As its reserves were spent, Logan collapsed like a balloon that had lost its air. All voluntary and most involuntary muscles were shut down at the same moment.

The transition was so abrupt, it was as if an on/off switch had been thrown. If it wasn't for the continued functions of the man's brain stem—thalamus, hypothalamus, midbrain and pituitary—Logan's lungs and heart would have stopped functioning, too, and he would have died instantly.

The second battery powered the microwave receiver wired into Logan's right and left frontal cortex via the direct inputs through his eye sockets. Drained of energy, the cortex-suppressing waves broadcast by the Reifying

Encephalographic Monitor were no longer being fed into the area of Logan's mind that contained his emotions, his memory, and his self-awareness.

Suddenly freed of the machine's hypnotic thrall, Logan's mind exploded in a psychedelic tsunami of wildly conflicting images; chaotic, divergent thoughts, and profound and intense emotions. He lay in a hallucinogenic fugue for mere seconds, but with his hyperactive brain, the passage of real time meant nothing. Bombarded by images, assaulted by sounds, he twitched and moaned, unable to absorb or comprehend the kaleidoscopic panorama. Soon the confused delusions coalesced into a piercing point of light, bright as burning magnesium, that expanded in his mind as his awareness grew.

Logan's consciousness reemerged from the dark depths of his unconscious on a glowing column of spiking brilliance that morphed into a spinning ladder—a pathway that spiraled down to the deepest core of his being. On each step of that ladder, a face, a name, an identity—yet all of them one and the same individual, the same soul that now inhabited the paralyzed, pain-wracked body that sprawled and spewed bile and blood on the reactor room floor.

As he lay, awaiting death—hungry for extinction as a release from the bone-searing agony of the past months—his mind was flooded with spectacular visions of violence, of pageantry, of martial glory, and of a gleaming figure at the very center. He knew that death would not come, for that was his burden.

He saw all the shapes he was and all the lives that he'd led, all the guises and masks which had been, which are, and which shall always be but corporeal manifestations of the "I" that was Logan. Mere physical forms shedded like snakeskin at the end of each existence, as the spirit moves on to occupy a new form, a new shape, a new individual. And for this brief moment, Logan knew and experienced them all.

So began the melding of his past with the world's history. . . .

I am . . .

Swathed in fur hides and uncured leather, flesh mottled with red clay and war paint. I beat back the onslaught of the Others—those who walk on two legs, who use clubs and spears, but are not men.

The rude stone ax heavy in my hairy hands, I smash skulls like eggs and, ravenous after the battle, I feast on my enemies' hearts and wash in their blood.

Called the Hand of God, I wield a sword made of bronze. My shield is leather and beaten lead. I fought and I died in the desert sands of Jerusalem, struck down by the demon Ba'al in a holy war long forgotten by mankind, though it echoes through eternity.

Here I die with my king, arrow-pierced Leonidas, as the Persian chariots burst through the Spartan defenses at the mountain pass called Thermopylae.

At Carrhae, I retreat with Cassius's legions, cut to pieces by the Parthians who tricked the Legionnaires into breaking formation, then massacred the Roman troops with cavalry.

In burnished steel armor, astride a stirrupless saddle, I beat back the Huns who seek to destroy Roman civilization and thrust the world into the ignorance and superstition of the Dark Ages.

I ride a Mongol pony into Samarkand with Genghis

Khan. We leave mounds of sun-bleached skulls and utter desolation in our wake. Harvesters of death.

My chain mail encrusted with rust and sweat-salt, I hack my way over prostrate Jerusalem's walls with the Knights Templars. I put the Infidel to the sword and liberate the Holy Lands in the name of my most holy Pontiff, Urban the Second.

At Bosworth, I wear a white rose and die in the marsh during Lord Stanley's bloody advance.

I am captain of the mercenaries, I besiege Magdeburg with the Roman Catholic armies of Gustavus Adolphus. No one could stop us. Overwhelm the Hessian defenders and butcher thirty thousand Protestant men, women, and children.

Both sides fight for the glory of God. I fight for plunder.

Wind chimes tinkle in the chill night air. The garden sparkles with crystalline ice. I wear a sky blue silk kimono; my skin is yellow. I dance in the falling flakes, silver blade flashing, dark ninja blood staining the virgin snow as black-clad forms fall dead at my feet.

Perfectly dealt, my strokes slash out a haiku of death, each cut a decapitation, each lunge a disembowelment.

I fight for the emperor and my shogun master.

I trek across the deserts of Egypt and the steppes of Russia with Napoleon. Our triumphs, our cruelty are legendary, our retreat through a freezing hell our penance.

At Veracruz, we remembered the Alamo by invading Mexico via the sea and defeating the Mexican Army in their own streets.

I die in a dusty ditch next to a wheat field in a place called Antietam, then spring to life.

On the walls of old Peking, I stand side by side with heroes, to beat back a horde of Chinese hatchet men who seek the deaths of all foreign devils.

For fifty-five days we hold, a hundred United States Marines who defeat a two-thousand-year-old empire.

I feel the wood and fabric of my SPAD shudder under the chattering machine guns. I watch a Fokker DVII crumple in the air, its wings burning as it plunges, spinning, to the Western Front far, far below.

I love a Blackfoot Indian girl named Silver Fox.

I meet Hemingway in Spain.

I fight in the trenches, breathe poison gas.

I parachute into Normandy on D-day.

I wage war in Malaysia, Vietnam, Korea, Laos, Cambodia, France, Belgium, Austria, Germany, Japan, Afghanistan, Algeria, Istanbul, and Peking.

In Jerusalem, in Actium, Rome, Paris, Fort Pitt, Yorktown, Moscow, Osaka, Cambrai, Flanders, Belleau Wood, Guernica, the Sahara, Caen, Berlin, Dien Bien Phu, and Hanoi.

All of them were me. Me. The Eternal Warrior. The Hand of God, the Master of War. An immortal spirit with no beginning and perhaps no end, only an eternity of suffering and strife and the tide of battle. No peace, no rest. No love, no family, no home. The sword my only mistress, the battle-rent banner my testament.

With stone and wood, with bronze and iron, with steel and adamantium as my tools, my weapons, I live the warrior's life, die the warrior's death a thousand times over. My lives line up behind me on parade, and I can see them all, like dim silhouettes marching over Golgotha.

I've suffered the spear's tip and the headsman's ax, the slashing sword, the arrow's pierce, the crossbow's bolt.

I've drowned. Been burned. Crucified. Blown asunder. Felt the hangman's noose.

And in the end, all that pain ever led to was a finality that is never truly a climax, only another beginning in the endless, eternal cycle of blood and conflict, as inevitable as the rising sun, the phases of the moon, the passing of stars, the falling rain.

Logan awoke as if from a long dream.

An endless parade of death . . . yet no release. Not for me . . .

Like smoke the wisps of memory scattered; the soul-shattering insights, the revelation of Logan's peculiar genesis and unique destiny forgotten, buried in his sub-conscious for a day, a century—or perhaps forever.

With blood-caked hands, Logan reached up to clutch the edge of the computer console. He opened his eyes, but even the dim emergency lights seemed too bright, too blinding, and he blinked against the glare. Pulling himself to his feet, Logan rose on unsteady legs and found himself standing over a corpse.

The man was middle-aged, with a reddish-brown beard, round glasses fallen from a ruined face, eyes closed as if in repose, lips frozen strangely in a half smile.

"I know this man. In a memory . . . from a dream . . . a dream of dying . . ." Logan's voice, hoarse from disuse, cracked into a wracking cough. Trembling on his unsta-ble legs, he reached up to find sparking wires dangling from his ruined cheeks. Without ceremony, he ripped them loose, wrenching the probes out of his brain in a gush of semiclotted gore.

He howled in anguish, and the pain served as a re-minder of more recent agonies. In a rush, memory re-turned. Faces and forms and familiar voices filled his

mind—inseparably these features were linked to his torment, their voices a barbed lash that stripped away his
soul and seared him bone-deep. They did things to him,
these people, things he still did not understand. They
kidnapped him, drugged him, ripped him to pieces, and
glued him back together again. And this series of unbear-
able events kept repeating itself in an endless loop.

And for that, they will all pay . . .

But, dominating his mind, there was one face above
all. A predatory face, lean and hungry, on a frame tall and
thin. Patrician features, hairless scalp, rectangular glasses
through which stared the eyes of a savage raptor.

A memory of pain . . .

Logan knew it was the face of his creator and his tormentor. His god and his devil. The creature who robbed
him of his humanity to forge him into a living weapon.

It was only fitting, then, that the Professor should become the next victim of Weapon X.

17

The Storm

Carol Hines punched in the Professor's code and opened the security door. The Professor led the way through a hot, narrow, winding maze of corridors and ventilation shafts to a steel access ramp. They climbed the incline to the adamantium smelting facility's control center. She soon realized their location. "Professor, if we could purge the core, we could at least save the complex."

"Of course, Ms. Hines. My plan exactly. After all, what could be more important than the data we've collected, the memory of Experiment X?"

Bypassing the enclosed control room, they exited the corridor on one of the open platforms above the reactor's fission gate—a circular, multileveled, bowl-like structure of gleaming metal more than a hundred meters across. In the center of the mammoth machine, the lead-lined, adamantium-encased exhaust pit descended fifty meters down and was covered by a steel grate. Walkways surrounded the entire configuration, and the Professor and Carol Hines now stood on one of the highest.

Fifty meters over their heads, the pipelined ceiling glowed amber in patches as flashes of fire and debris burst through straining metal seams, splattering metal magma through the grate to the exhaust pit below.

"The containment is cracking already, Professor. We must release the fission gate before the entire facility melts down."

"Yes, Ms. Hines, but it's a matter of getting Logan into the exhaust pit first."

"But sir, there's not much time left!"

The Professor's eyes were bright with feral cunning. "I need a lure of some kind, you see. Someone to trick Logan into the pit. Don't you understand? He would be incinerated in seconds."

Carol Hines looked at the Professor, trying to comprehend what he was saying. "I'm sorry, sir?"

The Professor loomed over her. "Yes, that is too true, Ms. Hines. I am sorry. Truly sorry. Let us take a moment to consider our options. It is clear what you must do . . ."

Carol Hines ducked as a shower of sparks burst through the metal plates above their heads. A loud crash followed as sections of melted pipes plunged into the exhaust port in a red-orange molten ball.

"Ms. Hines. I know you have worked long and hard for our Experiment X . . ."

"Yes, sir. Thank you, sir . . ."

"You have been a real boon to the good Dr. Cornelius, too."

"Oh, poor Dr. Cornelius." Tears pooled in the woman's eyes.

"Yes. He gave his life for the project . . . why, I dare say you would do the same, would you not, Ms. Hines?"

"Sir?"

"Give your life."

At last, Carol recognized the intentions burning behind the Professor's eyes and she understood what her role was to be in this, the final act. This time, however, she refused to be a tractable and compliant volunteer in her own destruction.

"No. No, sir. I would not want to die." Her voice, even to her own ears, was surprisingly strong.

The Professor fixed his gaze on her. It was hateful—an angry, disapproving, parental sneer. Though frightened, Carol Hines stood her ground, met his stare with her own.

"Bait, Ms. Hines. I need bait."

"Why . . . why would you want to hurt me, Professor?"

"Because, my dear lady—"

The Professor lunged, surprising her. Before she could regain her balance, Carol Hines tumbled over the rail.

"—there is no other way."

She screamed all the way down, until her body struck the hot metal grate mounted just above the exhaust port.

"Don't break your neck on the way down, Ms. Hines," the Professor called, "because I want you to scream and yell and draw that mindless beast into the pit."

While he ranted, the Professor climbed a staircase to the control booth. Before he entered the glass-enclosed, soundproof structure, he turned and shouted his farewell to the woman he'd consigned to the pit.

"Come on, Hines, scream, will you? Think of the horror of it all. Use your imagination."

At the bottom of the exhaust port, Carol Hines raised

herself onto her elbows and shook her head to clear it. She tried to rise, but her leg was bent at an odd angle and would not support her weight. When she looked up, she saw the Professor through the glass panels. His mouth moved, but she could not hear his words. Then Carol Hines lifted her eyes to the high ceiling, where molten metal was beginning to drip in glowing orange icicles. She screamed.

The Professor saw her mouth gape and laughed. "There you have it, Ms. Hines. Bravo!"

An electronic voice cut through the man's rants.

"Computer control operating."

"Computer, activate a satellite link to Director X . . . Code 324 Omega 99 plus."

"Activated."

"Now give me the current thermal breakdown."

"Two hundred thirty thousand at seventy thousand cubic meters."

"Advise on those numbers."

"Open fission gate immediately."

"Begin purge sequence and open manual control to me." As he spoke, the Professor reached out with his remaining hand and gripped the manual control lever overhead.

"Control open. Purge begin—"

The Professor turned to face the microphone. "I want you to listen to this," he said. "I want you to hear the end of your dreams, and mine."

On the level directly above the fission gate came an explosion as a door blew outward. In the center of the blast's corona stood Logan, framed by the glow. Seemingly untouched by the fire that swirled around him, Logan advanced through flames until he spied the cowering woman. With a throaty growl, he hopped onto a railing to stare down at her.

"Come, come, creature. Into the pit with you," yelled the Professor, his cries muted by the glass walls. "I'll crisp you like bacon, like the mutant meat you are."

Logan sniffed the air as if sensing a trap. Carol Hines whimpered and tried to rise, her movements drawing his attention. Grunting, he leaped off the rail to land in a crouch on the steel grate directly in front of her. Slowly, Logan paced forward, stalking her, all six claws extended.

Limping as she tried to back away, Carol Hines's voice broke, her words divided by sobs. "Mr. Logan . . . I don't know if you can understand me . . . I don't . . . don't want to die."

Logan's eyes were wide and alert, but there was no indication he comprehended her words.

"It's . . . it's the pain, Mr. Logan . . . I can't stand pain. I was burned once—chemicals—and I never forgot the pain . . ."

In the booth, the Professor sighed in disgust.

"Good God, Ms. Hines, don't beg. You are living the last few moments of your pointless existence. Don't waste them pleading to a mindless animal. How grotesque. How undignified."

Carol Hines stumbled and collapsed onto the grate. Instead of trying to rise, she averted her eyes and covered her head with her hands. "I know you want to kill me," she sobbed. "But please, kill me quickly . . . please, I beg you."

An animalistic rumble began in Logan's throat but emerged as rasping words. "I . . . I understand. I understand you . . ."

Hopefully, Carol Hines looked up.

"You don't matter . . . to me," muttered Logan.

His head slowly turned, until Logan faced the man inside the booth. "I want him—"

The Professor pulled the lever, and the blinking digital display switched from STANDBY to PURGE.

Over their heads, the glowing steel ceiling opened like a clamshell. Carol Hines looked up to see a dozen white-hot nozzles, like the exhaust port of a rocket. As one, the nozzles opened, too.

"Oh God!" she cried. "He did it. He opened the fission gate!"

She staggered to her feet, but her shattered leg prevented her from running. As molten metal and waves of invisible radiation poured down on them, Carol used her final seconds on earth not to cower, but to warn the man she'd willingly tortured to save himself.

"Run, Mr. Logan . . . Run!"

Then molten metal, seething, superheated chemicals, and waves of radiation washed over Carol Hines until she vanished in a writhing burst of fire.

From somewhere, the electronic voice of the computer boomed through the facility.

"Discharge: two hundred and forty thousand megatherms at seventy thousand cubic meters. Current rate: seven hundred FPS. Velocity: two thousand. Acknowledge."

In the booth, the Professor's pain-ravaged face was alight with savage glee. "Acknowledged," he told the computer.

Then he faced the microphone. "This is the Professor," he said into the satellite communicator. "Experiment X is destroyed, and I, I am his destroyer. Do you hear me? I beat you, you treacherous son of a—"

"Purge proceeding," said the computer, "six hundred FPS . . ."

"I served your every demand! Yet you turned against me . . ."

"System override . . . four hundred . . . three hundred . . . two hundred. Thermal rate noncritical. Purge sequence canceled."

"What?" the Professor roared. "You . . . you are controlling the fission gate, aren't you?"

"Purge shutdown complete . . . Fission gate clear of radiation. Temperature four hundred and seven degrees . . . Three-fifty . . . two hundred . . ."

"My God," the Professor moaned. "Is . . . Is there nothing you cannot do?"

As Carol Hines screamed her final warning, thousands of roentgens of ionized radiation washed over Logan, scorching his flesh, boiling his blood. Vaguely, as if from a great distance, Logan heard the woman's dying cries amid the clamor of the fission gate's exhaust ports, saw her faint silhouette disappear as wave after wave of unimaginably destructive energy was released, until his own eyeballs began to burn, his eardrums seared and turned to ash.

Then, with an agonized scream of his own, Logan dropped to his hands and knees as more radiation, along with splashes of molten metal and gouts of dripping adamantium, poured down from the leaking containment vat overhead. His cries ceased as his lungs singed and his vocal chords burned. His breath came in violent, choking gasps.

Logan was literally flayed alive by fire as layers of flesh, muscle, and tendon cooked away in a split second.

But as each cell, each nerve ending was incinerated, more nerve tissue, more cells were generated by his phenomenal biology to replace them. The phoenix-like process accelerated as more and more roentgens of raw radiation blasted him. Logan's flesh and muscle seemed to flicker in and out of existence and he became a walking metal skeleton, burned to ashes and restored, only to be incinerated once again.

Radiation has an affinity for bone tissue, and even a single dose of radiation as small as twenty-five roentgens produces a detectable drop of circulation lymphocytes—white blood cells. Continued exposure will quickly initiate cancer in even the most healthy individual, which meant that the elevated amount of radiation drenching Logan not only should have killed him ten times over but also caused acute, fatal radiation syndrome if he had by some miracle survived.

However, adamantium now sheathed his skeleton, effectively shielding Logan's blood-producing bone marrow from radiation damage, keeping enough cells alive and functioning inside of Logan's ravaged body to continue his extraordinary cycle of healing and renewal after each new wound, each new torment.

As raw agony coursed through every nerve ending in his body, Logan stumbled defiantly to his feet. With muscles stiff and scorched, with tendons crisped by fire, he shambled toward the distant control booth. Through eyes milky white and blurred by heat, Logan could see the Professor inside the glass-enclosed cage, pounding his remaining hand and ranting into a microphone. Though each step cost him enormous effort, though each movement was excruciating, a more powerful torture spurred Logan on.

As his fingers curled and shrank to bony knuckles under the stream of devastating energy, Logan used his adamantium claws to half-climb, half-drag himself up the metal staircase. At the window, he saw his own reflection—a glowing, living effigy smoldering with each vengeful step.

On the other side of the glass, the Professor felt Logan's eyes on his back. He turned to see Weapon X, still alive, still advancing on him like a relentless pit bull, wounded but determined to strike at the one who abused him.

"Good God in heaven," the Professor cried. "You are still transmitting to him. Controlling a corpse . . . a walking dead man."

With an awful crash, the pane exploded inward in a shower of crystalline shards. The Professor reared back, raising his bloody stump to ward off the razor-sharp splinters that rained upon him.

The Professor hit the floor as Logan landed, legs braced, to tower over him. Claws extended, Logan grabbed the man by the collar with black, blistered hands and lifted him until his ravaged, smoking face was mere inches from the Professor's own.

"Am I dead?" Logan gasped. "Is that what you . . . did to me?"

He stared into the Professor's eyes. He saw fear there, and madness, too.

"Dead!" Logan groaned like a tormented ghost. "A walking dead man, am I?"

The Professor's eyes widened as he stared with hatred at the furious, burning thing. He spit his defiance in Logan's face, then flailed his arms to break free. "I'll tell you what you are. You are an animal . . ."

The Professor's words detonated in Logan's mind. He screamed, "I am Logan. Logan! Do you hear me . . . I am a man—"

Logan jerked him over his head.

"—And you . . . you are an animal! You are my monster!"

With a crash and the crunch of splintered bone, the Professor slammed down, to sprawl across a console. Whimpering, he turned away from Logan to punch the intercom. "Security! Security! Help me," he cried. "For God's sake—"

Logan slashed down, parting the Professor's remaining hand from its wrist. As his claws retracted, a feeble gush of the Professor's blood spilled onto the console. The crimson gore made hardly a splash, as if there wasn't enough of it left in the man for a real spurt.

With the radioactivity fading, Logan's skin began to reform over pink, stringy muscle. His features began to reappear, though the flesh was pitted and blistered, his hair and ears gone. With both sinewy, fleshless fists he grabbed the Professor by the throat and yanked him to his feet again. The man moaned and tried to break away. The effort was a limp jerk in Logan's adamantium grip.

The Professor's eyes glazed over and he moaned again. Logan shook him back to reality. When the scientist looked into his monster's eyes, Logan's regenerated lips curled and he laughed.

"Now we both got our paddles bollixed, eh?" growled Logan. "But do you really think that makes us . . . even?"

The Professor turned away from Logan's stare, muttered an unintelligible reply.

"Well, I don't."

Three bright silver points sprang out of Logan's arm.

The Professor watched in horror as the claws slowly slid from their thick muscled sheaths. As Logan's grin morphed into a mask of rage and retribution, the Professor kicked and squirmed, helplessly, uselessly. Then the Professor began to howl, a long, mournful wail of dread, anguish, even regret.

Supporting the struggling man with his left hand, Logan plunged his claws into the Professor's groin. The man's eyes went wide and he bellowed like a gutted pig. Slowly, Logan slid his claws out of the man's body, then thrust again, this time piercing the Professor's quivering belly. The Professor's head lolled, his eyes rolled up in his head, he coughed crimson bile.

Logan thrust again, then again, and again—to pierce heart, lungs, throat. Finally, Logan raised his arm, touched the Professor's pallid forehead with the tips of his claws, and then—slowly and deliberately—he thrust the blades through the skull and into the brain. The Professor twitched once, and Logan lowered his corpse to the floor.

"Now we're square . . . got that, you bastard? Now we're even . . ."

Rage not yet spent, Logan bent low and lifted the limp body off the ground. With the Professor's dead arms flung wide, his glasses askew, Logan tossed him through the broken window and down into the seething pit far below. The Professor's carcass struck the superheated fission gate, and with a steaming sizzle, disintegrated.

Uttering a grotesque sound something between a snarl and a laugh, Logan turned his back to the shattered window and took a single step forward. Suddenly, the entire room seemed to shift on its axis. Hit by a wave of nausea and a jolt of lancing pain inside his skull, he clutched his head with both hands. Then, without a sound, Logan collapsed to the ground.

His first awareness was of pain. Cautiously, Logan opened his lids, to squint with tearing eyes against harsh white glare.

"Easy, mate. Take it easy," said a gruff voice close by. A rough hand touched his forehead. "It's me—"

"Langram?"

A silhouette loomed over him, its shadow blocking out the overhead light. "Didn't think you cared, Logan."

Logan tried to smile, but it hurt too much. "Actually, I was coming to rescue you—"

Langram put his finger to his mouth, gestured to the light fixture with his head. "They're very enlightened around here," he cautioned.

Obviously, the cell was bugged, maybe rigged with surveillance cameras, too, up in the light fixture.

"We're in jail?"

"We're prisoners, if that's what you mean."

"How have they been treating you?" Logan asked, still on his back.

"Better than you, from the look of ya. Here, let's get you up."

Logan propped himself on his elbows and blinked against the fluorescent glare. "Don't they believe in 'lights out' around here?"

Langram glanced upward at the bank of lights over their heads. "I think it's supposed to be psychological torture or something. Reminds me of my last desk job. Pretty scary stuff."

The spartan room consisted of bare concrete floor,

sickly yellow walls, high ceiling, one door, no bedding, a tin pot in the corner for a toilet.

Logan checked himself out, feeling his aching legs and bruised torso. No broken bones. Maybe a cracked rib or two. He felt woozy and nauseated, so he probably had a concussion. All in all, nothing to write home about.

His splinter camouflage suit was torn and bloody, his utility belt, knife, and wrist chronometer-compass were gone, and his pockets were empty.

Logan finally sat up and leaned back on his arms.

"Watch your right hand, there. I think it's fractured. The bones around your wrist seem out of whack."

"My arm feels okay, considering how the rest of me aches."

"Well, Logan, you're lucky we don't have any mirrors, or you'd feel even worse."

As he spoke, Langram casually brushed his bruised chin, then used his thumb to point left. Logan let his eyes drift as he spoke, and saw what Langram was pointing to. The cell was nothing more than a glorified steel closet. The door was metal, with a small wired window inset near the top.

"Comfy digs. How long have I been here?"

"A couple of hours ago, two Korean soldiers brought you in and threw you on the floor. I thought you were dead, but you seemed to have made a remarkable recovery."

As Langram spoke, he sent Logan a series of prearranged signals through seemingly innocent hand and body gestures, a trick known to most special forces troopers throughout the world. As he told Logan how he was tossed unconscious into the cell, Langram also walked his fingers backward along his own leg—signaling that, for the time being, they were stuck in that cell.

Next, Langram made a cutting gesture across his own throat, and Logan nearly grinned.

Mission accomplished . . . Langram had discovered exactly what the Koreans were up to.

Finally, Langram yawned and stretched, then flapped both of his arms once.

So the Koreans don't know our real escape plan, only the one that was in our mission profile. We're halfway home already—once we get out of this cell . . .

Logan wanted to tell his partner about Miko Katana of the SAT, about how she might already be somewhere inside the complex, working to free them. But trading that kind of information was impossible while the enemy was watching and recording their every word, every gesture.

Logan also wanted to ask Langram what he'd found—what the North Koreans were really doing in this facility.

Have to wait for the after-action report, I guess . . .

"Anybody else stuck in this dump?"

Langram flicked imaginary lint from his nose with his right index finger. "Nobody special."

One prisoner . . . and someone important to the Koreans. Must be that Japanese researcher Miko's looking for.

"When do they serve grub around here?"

"Here—" Langram tossed him a small wooden bucket. "I saved you some."

Logan reeled at the powerful smell of *kimchi*—aged, pickled cabbage—mingled with hot spices and the sickly sweet odor of rotting meat.

"Thanks," said Logan without a trace of irony. Ravenously, he shoveled the putrid mess into his mouth with both hands.

An hour later, they heard a sound on the other side of the door. Then the lock clicked.

"Uh-oh, visitors," whispered Langram.

He quickly sat up and slid across the bare floor, his back to the far wall. Logan followed his lead.

It seemed to take a long time for the metal door to swing open, but when it finally did, both men were taken by surprise.

Logan tensed. "Miko?"

"Huh?" grunted Langram.

Tac drawn, the Japanese agent stood in the doorway. Just as she opened her mouth to speak, alarms went off throughout the building.

"The surveillance team saw her," Logan cried. "Let's get the hell out of here."

"You know this chick?"

"No time for introductions now," Logan cried. "Let's move!"

Outside the cell was a hallway constructed of insulated concrete, with several doors on either side. Over the Klaxon blare, Logan heard pounding footsteps. A Korean officer rounded the corner and Miko shot him through the eye. His body jerked and slammed against the wall. Before the soldier sunk to the floor, Logan ripped the man's pistol from its holster.

"What happened?" Miko cried over the din.

"I think the North Koreans spotted you on the surveillance camera in our cell," Logan replied.

"Sorry, Logan-*san.*"

"Don't be. I was getting tired of that place any—"

He paused to fire the pistol. At the opposite end of the hall, a Korean private dropped his AK-47 and sunk to the floor. As the weapon clattered to the concrete, Langram dived, slid across the floor, and snatched it up. A spray of automatic weapon fire spattered the walls behind him.

Langram rolled on his back and fired around the corner. Logan and Miko heard a grunt, and another soldier dropped while two more scrambled backward. Logan's partner fired again and the siren abruptly ceased.

"Damn, I hate alarms," said Langram. Then he rolled to his feet and kicked the dead man's machine gun across the smooth floor to Logan. Langram joined them a moment later, and they moved swiftly along the narrow corridor, then around a bend.

"Look out!" Miko warned.

Logan turned as a man lunged at him from an open door, clutching a bayonet.

"Not again," growled Logan. He knocked the weapon aside, shoved the barrel of his own machine gun into the man's surprised face, and pulled the trigger. An explosion of bright red gore and gray brain matter decorated the wall, and the man flew backward.

"We must hurry," Miko called.

"Miko . . ."

The voice was faint, weak, but it stopped the woman in her tracks. She yelled something in Japanese, and the voice replied in the same language.

"What the hell is going on?" Langram asked Logan, his eyes riveted to the corridor behind them. "Why are we stopping?"

"Miko's an agent of the Japanese Special Assault Team. She's on a mission, too."

Langram's eyebrow went up. "Crowded around here, ain't it?"

"Miko . . ." The strange voice behind the cell door was louder.

"I'm here," the woman cried. She fished in her pocket and drew out a lock pick. Logan and Langram took posi-

tion on either side of her. In less than five seconds she
had unlocked the cell. When the door swung open, a
horrible stench clawed at their nostrils.

On the ground, a middle-aged Japanese man lay in a
pool of his own offal. The cell was similar to Langram's,
but filthy. Dried food and excrement encrusted the floor,
the smell of urine permeated the walls, and the smell of
decay clung to every remaining corner. Logan saw the
reason for the unwholesome conditions. The man's arms
and legs had been broken, and the bones still protruded
from his caves. His skin was purple and black around the
wounds, and gangrene was eating away at his vitals.

Despite the horrendous sight and smell, Miko hurried
into the room. "Father!" she sobbed as she rushed to the
man's side.

Logan watched the tragic reunion, his face grim. "You
know who he is?"

"Yeah," Langram replied. "His name is Inoshiro
Katana. Expert in chemical compression. I heard the officers discussing him when they thought I'd blacked out
during interrogation."

Logan nodded. "You might as well tell me what's
going on in this place, 'cause we're not getting out of
here alive."

As Langram spoke, he stared down the hall, where he
was sure the enemy was gathering to rush them. "The
North Koreans are making the nerve agent sarin. I've
seen tanks of trichloride, sodium fluoride, phenylace-
tonitrile—"

"What's the point of hiding it?" Logan asked. "Kang-
gye Chemical Factory churns out tons of the stuff for the
North Korean military. Everybody knows that."

"They're working on a binary delivery system here.

Two neutral agents stored in a small container. Both substances are harmless, but combine to form sarin at the moment of use. They're trying to pack enough poison into a dispenser the size of a can of soup—which is why Dr. Katana is so important to them."

Pounding footsteps thundered from the opposite end of the long corridor. The noise was followed by barking voices. The clatter of weapons and the click of thrown bolts echoed down to them.

"They're coming," Langram warned. "We've got to go if we want to at least make the effort to escape . . ."

Logan watched Miko stroke her father's hair. "What about him?"

Langram looked at the broken man inside the cell. "What do you think? We can't carry him, and we can't leave him here."

"Miko," Logan called. "They're coming."

"My father, I can't—"

"No, Miko. You must," rasped her father.

"But I can't leave you here."

Suddenly, the man's pain-etched face became stern. His words were a reprimand, as if he were addressing a truculent adolescent. "No, you cannot leave me here, Miko. You know what you must do."

"No, I—"

"You must. For my honor. For the family's honor."

"Here they come!" yelled Langram as he opened up. The booming chatter of the AK-47 was deafening in the tight quarters. At the end of the hall, several tan uniforms appeared, only to drop, stitched with bloody holes.

"Grenade!" Langram yelled.

The egg clattered to the ground at Logan's feet and he kicked the explosive back to its owner. Someone screamed, then the blast washed over them, filling the narrow corridor with choking smoke.

Ears ringing, Logan stuck his head around the corner. "They've retreated. This is our chance," he cried.

"To go where?" asked Langram.

Logan pointed to the corridor they'd just passed through. The explosion had blown one of the doors off its hinges. Instead of another cell, there was a flight of steps.

"Where's it go?"

"Who cares!" Logan kicked Langram's butt to start him off, and the man sprinted across the open corridor as bullets zinged off the walls, the floor. He dived through the doorway as Logan returned fire. Langram stuck his head out the door a moment later. "It's an exit!"

Logan faced the interior of the cell. "Miko, we've got to—"

The words stuck in his throat as Miko aimed her Tac at her father's head. The man looked into the muzzle of the weapon, eyes unwavering. Her hand trembled, just a little. Before she squeezed the trigger, the woman steadied her arm, then averted her eyes. The shot, though expected, made Logan wince. Dr. Katana twitched, then lay still.

Miko's sorrowful mission accomplished, she turned away from the corpse on the floor and squeezed past Logan into the corridor. Her face was grim, and she refused to meet his stare.

"Where are we going?" she asked.

"Through that door and up," Logan replied.

In a burst of covering fire, he and Miko darted across the corridor and up the stairs.

18

Breaking Point

"Got a problem here," yelled Langram.

Logan heard a steel door clang at the top of the stairs. With Miko guarding his back, Logan took the steps two at a time and charged through the hatch, to the outside. The night was cool and overcast, the lake's moisture heavy in the air. Logan had emerged from one of the circular "fuel storage" tanks in the middle of a field. Twenty or more identical tanks stood all around. None held fuel, however. Many were hollow shells, others hid smokestacks and ventilation shafts that fed air to the underground tunnels.

Intelligence was right for once, Logan realized. *The tank farm's just camouflage to hide the poison gas factory.*

Miko emerged from the stairwell, quietly closing the steel hatch behind her. "The soldiers ran right past me, down the corridor. I don't think they know we are outside."

"They'll know soon enough."

Logan heard a cry and spied Langram a few meters away, grappling in the shadows with a soldier. Both men had a grip on a single AK-47, each trying to yank the automatic rifle from the other. Another Korean lay limp on the ground. Before Logan could react, Langram kicked out, and bone snapped. The North Korean regular went down, knee shattered. Langram yanked the automatic rifle free and aimed.

Logan rushed forward. Soon the soldier tried to rise, but Logan smashed the man's larynx with his elbow. The Korean kicked booted feet as he slowly choked to death. His lips barely moved, but no sound beyond a gurgle dribbled out. Langram held the soldier down with his foot until the man died, silently and wide-eyed. It took a long ninety seconds.

"Glad you could make it," said Langram, winded.

"Did you shoot him?" Logan asked, gesturing to the second dead man on the ground.

"I was out of ammo. Shoved the barrel of my rifle into his eye."

Logan saw the AK-47 on the ground, its barrel bloody.

"Good," he whispered. "Nobody heard us yet . . ."

Miko stepped around the two men, Tac in hand. She carefully scanned the area with her night-vision binoculars. "Clear."

Langram and Logan tossed the corpses.

"An AK-47, two magazines."

"A 47 for me," said Langram. "One magazine. This is gonna go hand-to-hand real quick."

"I need a blade," grunted Logan.

Langram tossed him a web belt with a Korean-made bayonet and sheath. The blade was as long as Logan's forearm, thin and sharp. Logan strapped the belt around his hips, drew the knife, and twirled it in his hand. "It'll do."

"Logan, over there," Miko said softly.

Logan took her NVGs and immediately spied a Korean armored personnel carrier, large enough to carry ten men. The vehicle sat on an access road less than a hundred meters away, only partially obscured by a storage tank. The APC's rear hatch was open, the driver on the pavement, leaning against one of the six oversized tires, smoking a cigarette. In the glow of the interior lights, the cabin appeared to be unoccupied. Over the sounds of the night, Logan could hear the poorly tuned engine idling and smell its exhaust.

Between them and the road stood several storage tanks, each the size of a small house.

Best to get by them without too much noise.

"That's our ticket out," Logan said, showing Langram the vehicle. Then, to Miko, "Got the time?"

Miko checked her chronometer. "Oh-two-forty."

Langram and Logan synchronized the old-style windup watches they'd taken from the dead soldiers, then strapped them on.

"We've got one hour, nineteen minutes to get to our extraction point, four klicks away," Logan told Miko.

She seemed unconcerned. "Are we going to take that vehicle?"

"We'd better or we'll never make the rendezvous unless we run. There's a Pave Hawk coming for us, and if we're not at the extraction zone, we lose our ride."

She nodded, face neutral.

"Miko," said Logan, stepping closer to her. "I want you to know I'm sorry—"

She cut him off. "Do not speak of it again. I did what I must, and I will do as I must for the duration of this affair—"

"You're going to get out of here," Logan said. "With us. You're going to make it and so are we."

"Hai."

Miko would not meet his stare, but Logan saw death in her eyes. He'd seen it in the faces of other Japanese warriors he'd known, back when they were fighting each other, the Russians, the Koreans—pretty much everyone in sight.

Though there were modern Japanese making cars and video equipment, Logan knew that for nationalists like Miko, the samurai code of Bushido still lived, still exerted a powerful influence over their lives. *Miko believed in honor, duty—and she proved it by her risky actions, tonight.*

Langram lowered the NVGs and handed them back to the half-Japanese woman.

"That soldier is definitely alone out there," he said. "Maybe these stiffs are his pals and he's waiting for them to make their rounds. I say we flank him before he wakes up and notices his buddies are missing."

Logan nodded. "So what's your plan?"

"You two go left, I'll cut around that tank over there and circle him. We hit the driver in—" Langram glanced at his watch. "Four minutes. Unless I get there first."

"What if he drives away?" asked Miko.

"We wave bye-bye," said Langram. Then he took off.

Miko and Logan cautiously circled a "storage tank"— really just a wooden shell—and reached the armored personnel carrier on cue. Langram was there, waiting. He had already taken care of things.

"Where's the driver?" asked Logan.

"In a graveyard. Very dead." Langram replied. "I planted him over in the bushes."

Langram climbed into the personnel carrier and through to the driver's compartment while Logan went through the weapons bin, where he found the driver's machine gun, another on the rack, and a leather bag of ammunition dangling from a seat. In the cab, Langram threw a flashlight and a bag of rice cakes on the torn seat, then whipped a plastic-encased map out of a metal box and shook it open. "Better than Triple A, mate."

While the men studied the map, Miko quietly curled up in the corner, hugging her legs, her handgun dangling from one hand.

"We're less than four kilometers away," said Logan. "Get on this road, follow it along the river valley, past this fishing village to the hills beyond."

"That chopper better be waiting for us," said Langram as he jumped into the driver's seat. He shifted the vehicle into gear, and the APC lurched forward on its six massive wheels. Langram quickly made a U-turn and went in the opposite direction.

Logan climbed into the seat next to him and lay the machine gun across his lap. Miko had another AK-47 strapped to her back, the leather case of ammo on her shoulder. She rose up on her haunches, gazing placidly through the bulletproof glass at the road ahead.

"There's the highway, but there's no gate on this end of the complex," said Logan, rechecking the map. "You'll have to make one."

"Right through the fence," said Langram.

"You know that'll alert the Koreans."

"Don't look now, but I think they're already alert!" Langram yelled, grinding the gears and stepping on the gas.

From a false storage tank directly ahead of them, a dozen soldiers burst through a steel door. Leading them was an officer clutching a pistol and gesturing wildly at the oncoming vehicle.

"Maybe we can bluff them," said Langram.

A shot bounced off the armored car, then came a sustained crackling as all the soldiers opened fire at once. Bullets glanced off the thick-skinned personnel carrier like acorns bouncing off a car, filling the cramped compartment with noise.

"Guess that didn't work," cried Langram. "Hold on!"

He swerved enough to clip the first soldier who reached the roadway. The broken man flew backward into the arms of the men behind him. As his troopers were bowled over, the officer blew a whistle and fired a pistol at the APC. The bullet bounced harmlessly off the shatterproof glass next to Logan's head.

Then came a crash as the APC flattened a chain-link fence and rolled over the twisted debris. Another jolt, accompanied by blinding sparks and crackling volts, shook the vehicle as it ripped through the electrified fence. Langram jerked the steering wheel, and the six tires skidded along damp grass before lurching onto the tarred road with a bump. The heavy armored personnel carrier lumbered away, Langram put on the gas and got them moving at the vehicle's top speed of forty kilometers per hour. Logan watched the soldiers recede in the rearview mirror. From somewhere behind them, the angry wail of another alarm faded in the distance.

"We lost 'em," said Langram.

Logan gripped his machine gun. "The hell we did. They're gonna be up our ass in no time."

Langram looked at his partner, only half-surprised to see a grin on Logan's face.

"A bloody, broken heap on the cell floor a couple of hours ago, and now you're itching for action. I guess all the rumors I heard about you are true, Logan."

Logan ignored his partner. "Coming up on the village," he said. On the horizon, dark silhouettes were framed against the moonlight.

Minutes later, they rumbled through a ghost town. Headlights illuminated dark wooden shacks, every one abandoned. Doors hung from hinges, grass grew wildly around the ramshackle structures. The stone gate at the entrance to the village had tumbled to the ground. In the black water, boats were moored, some of them half sunk. Sundered fishing nets blew idle in the wind.

Farther along, a large cannery facility loomed in the night, completely desolate and tumbling into the river, piece by piece.

"The pollution from that poison gas factory upstream has been real bad for the local economy," said Logan.

Langram swerved to avoid a two-wheeled cart abandoned in the roadway. "At least there are no goddamn civilians to get in the way."

"No one lives in this place. It is a land of ghosts," said Miko, staring straight ahead. "Their leaders make poison while the people starve to death."

Logan frowned as he squinted into the horizon. Miko turned away from the window, lost in her own tortured thoughts.

The APC skidded around a corner, and Langram shifted gears as they began to climb up a low hill. They were still paralleling the river. To their right the forest had become dense once again, the land rising to low hills on either side of them.

"Almost home now," said Langram. "Less than a kilometer, then we can ditch this piece of junk and take to the woods."

As they crested the hill, the engine sputtered and Langram worked the clutch. "Don't die on me now you piece of—" A string of curses followed.

"I can't believe it's this easy," said Logan "Why haven't they chased u—"

His question was interrupted by a loud crack as the personnel carrier was rocked by a sonic boom from the antitank projectile that zoomed over their heads.

"Look out!" Miko cried.

Bridging the road fifty meters ahead was the boxy silhouette of a North Korean tank, surrounded by dozens of soldiers. Behind the tank, several large trucks were parked to the side of the road, disgorging troops.

"Hold on!" bellowed Langram.

With a lurch, they were thrown to one side as the APC left the road and bumped across rough, rocky ground to the dense forest ahead of them.

"We can lose that tank in the woods," Langram cried. His words were nearly drowned by the sounds of cracking tree limbs as their vehicle struck down a sapling and tore the branches off several low hanging pines.

Logan clutched the roof with one hand, his AK-47 with the other. As the APC rumbled up a steep slope, its wheels spinning through loose dirt, Logan saw fire burst from the muzzle of the tank still parked on the road. He heard the report of the cannon a split second later—just as the large shell ripped through the trunk of a tree in their path.

Wood splinters filled the air, and Langram hit the gas. Miko was thrown to the steel floor as the personnel carrier lurched forward. It hopped a ditch, skidding on wet, smooth rock. The APC leaned to one side. Langram fought the wheel, trying not to roll over.

"Got it," he cried as the vehicle stabilized.

Inside the cab, as Langram concentrated on driving, Logan and Miko hung on. None of them heard the tank's third shot or saw the muzzle's blast. But they only felt the spine-cracking impact as the sabot round tore through the carrier's steel armor like a rock through a plate glass window.

The personnel carrier shuddered, then blew into halves. Both ends tumbled down the hillside, spewing fuel, tires spinning.

Something lurched inside his brain. Logan found himself spinning through a void.

No, it's not me . . . I'm just lying here. It's the whole world that's rolling over.

He heard a mechanical *tick*. Then a *whir*, like the sound of a tape rewinding. The noise seemed somehow comforting and he lay, eyes closed, listening to the constant drone until it faded from his consciousness. Finally, another *click* snapped him awake. Logan heard a *beep*, and a woman's voice spoke his name.

"Mr. Logan . . . I don't know if you can understand me . . ."

He opened his eyes to stare at a metal ceiling, its recessed lighting dim. On the floor, bits of silicon and shards of glass sparkled around him. Looking up, he saw the observation window had been broken, spears of glass still in the frame, some spattered with black drops. Computers were smashed, their monitor screens shattered.

". . . Use your imagination, Ms. Hines," a voice boomed. "Think of the horror of it all . . ."

I can't think . . . must've been some party, and someone ruined it.

Logan rose, wobbling on unsteady legs. *My clothes are*

gone, he realized. *The soldiers . . . they must have taken them . . .*

Then his memory faded like vapor, and Logan wondered vaguely who "they" were. Woozy, he leaned against a computer console, staring at hands stained with clotted blood.

My own . . . or someone else's?

". . . He's lost a lot of blood . . ." said the voice.

"Yeah," growled Logan. "I'd like to see the other guy."

The voices came from all around him—the walls, the ceiling, the consoles. They spoke in a crazy loop. Logan heard snatches of busy conversations that did not seem to connect in any rational way.

". . . Deadwood . . . Please respond . . . Logan is alive . . ."

Despite his pain and bafflement, Logan smirked. "You bet I am . . ."

". . . But security took care of Logan, Professor . . . I'm bleeding to death . . . Bloody massacre . . ."

"There will be, pal, when I find you . . ." Logan wheezed. *Especially if you don't shut up and let me get my bearings . . .*

Logan slumped in a chair. Eyes closed, head drooped over a computer terminal, he tried to recall where he was, how he got here.

". . . Mr. Logan has shown uncanny tracking abilities . . ."

"Yeah, and I'm butt naked, too."

". . . Killing everyone in sight. Running amok, you might say . . ."

Logan opened his eyes—and saw a severed hand lying on the console in front of him. He jumped backward, out of the seat.

". . . Are you aware of what is happening at this time? I'm losing men in Zone Two . . ."

Logan warily scanned the room, slowly backing into a corner. "Who's pulling this stunt? Answer me!"

Near his ear, the voice boomed from a speaker—

". . . Deadwood. I'm deadwood, Cornelius . . ."

—and Logan knew.

It's a recording . . . Some kind of random playback. Nobody's controlling this. I'm alone here.

Panic gripped him. *Got to get out . . .*

". . . Weapon X has escaped . . . I am not in control . . ."

He bolted for the door. Took the metal staircase to a platform below. He looked down into a deep metal well, smoke curling up from the bottom. Logan soon turned away from the pit and found a hatch, blown open, its lock twisted on the floor. The yawning tunnel behind the door led to another corridor. At the end of that corridor, a long hall fanned out in either direction. Logan paused, wondering which way to turn.

Smoke . . . the smell of ozone . . . machinery humming. This place is industrial . . . maybe military . . . don't like the army and they don't like me. Better get out of here before I get drafted . . .

He crossed the threshold, past the broken hatch, and followed the long, blood-spattered corridor, then turned right.

Place is a maze—or a tomb.

He wandered through the dimly lit steel cave until he reached an elevator. There was no power and the doors refused to open, but Logan soon found the stairwell. He climbed the steps until he saw the radiation warnings.

Must be a reactor . . . gotta be people there. Nobody leaves a reactor running when they're not at home . . .

But the reactor's control room was deserted, the core running on automatic. The entranceway seemed undisturbed except for a section along the wall that was a shattered, smoldering wreckage. He detected a whiff of cordite.

Shooting . . . what went on in this place?

He saw a weapon lying on the ground, a Heckler & Koch UMP, barrel bent.

Why the gun? This can't be a military installation, too sharp. These computers are Buck Rogers . . . the army doesn't have state-of the-art facilities like this . . . could be SHIELD . . . maybe. But why would Fury's bunch mess with me?

Logan sniffed the air again, and this time he smelled blood. Finally, he spied the body of a portly, middle-aged man sprawled across the main console. Mesmerized, he approached the grim scene, gazed down at the dead man's features.

He wore a lab smock, stained crimson. His ribs protruded from a ruined chest. The man had been gutted, brutalized. Yet his face seemed composed . . . almost resigned, which made the violence done to him all the more horrendous to Logan.

He's been cut—real bad—three in the gut, then eviscerated. Brutal . . . senseless. Unless there's some kind of sick vendetta.

He stared down at the man's features, at the glasses shattered on the floor, and started to remember.

I . . . I know this man. In a memory, a dream. A dream of dying.

Logan reached into his mind for an identity, an emotion—some connection to this man. He came up with nothing. Whoever he was, Logan bore him no animosity. He left the reactor room, moved on.

He found a dead man several levels higher. The man lay face down near a cart of equipment that had been overturned. He'd also been slashed, his carotid artery laid bare by a bladed weapon.

Not the only victim, either. He knew there would be more.

Death. This place reeks of it. Hanging in the air like heat . . . but who did the killing?

Afraid of the answer, Logan held up his hands, stained by congealed blood.

All over me, but no wounds . . . my blood? Must be . . . or did I knife this guy? What'd he do to me? This corpse . . . the one in the reactor room. And that hand back there. That severed hand . . .

A memory flickered and died. Logan's limbs began to quiver and his back slammed against the wall.

Did I finally flip out? Lose my mind and kill everyone in here, and now I don't remember it?

He moaned and clutched his head.

Wouldn't be surprised . . . my old partner Langram warned me that this would happen, sooner or later. "In times of peace, a man of war sets upon himself." That's what he told me once. Said I was a man of war . . . or was it a born warrior? Anyway, why am I thinking of Langram? Is he here somewhere? Did I kill him, too? I need a fucking drink.

The recorded conversations, which sounded like technobabble for so long that they'd faded into the background, suddenly invaded Logan's consciousness when a frightened voice repeatedly cried out his name.

". . . Mr. Logan . . . Mr. Logan, sir." A woman.

". . . Come, creature. Into the pit . . ." a man's voice screamed, choked with emotion.

Suddenly, Logan's forearms ached. He rubbed them, felt muscles bulging under the skin. An uncontrollable spasm made them roil unnaturally. Pain permeated his arms.

". . . I don't know if you can understand me, sir." The woman again. Pleading.

A sharp pain lanced through his wrists, and he flexed his hands.

". . . I can't stand pain," the woman sobbed. She was barely comprehensible. "Physical pain. Burned with chemicals . . . Please, I beg you. Kill me quickly . . ."

Is it Miko? No. This doesn't make any sense.

Logan's fingers curled into a tight fist as agony gripped them. He stared down at hands frozen into clutching claws. Soon something warm and crimson. Three bloody wounds like stigmata on the tops of each hand. Then steel claws emerged from their sheaths, ripping through tortured flesh, extending their full length. He threw back his head and howled.

". . . Run, Mr. Logan, run!" the woman cried. A moment later, a scream, and Logan knew she was dead, too.

". . . Am I dead?"

This time, he recognized the voice. His own.

". . . Dead? Am I a walking dead man?"

". . . You are an animal!" screamed a voice tinged with insanity—and suddenly, a face to match that cry exploded into Logan's mind. Bald. Patrician. High cheekbones, rectangular glasses. Arrogance melting into an expression etched with fear.

My tormentor. He must die! Or is he already dead?

". . . I am Logan," his own voice boomed from hidden speakers. "Logan! I am a man . . ."

He stared down at the blood-dewed silver claws in disbelief. His mind broke as waves of memory drowned all reason. The violence continued to build in Logan's mind.

Animal? Yes, I am an animal, a beast and a machine. A thing they made me.

Logan held his arms extended, silver claws protruding from his wrists. He tried to rip one of the blades out, gashed his hand to the bone—and in the wound, under the gore, the silver adamantium steel gleamed.

They found me. Found me out. Learned my secret. Brought me here. Cut me. Got into my body.

". . . Animal! . . . You are the animal . . ."

Tortured me. Tore up my mind. Got to get away, away from here . . . now.

Logan ran. Blindly. His own recorded voice shouting in his ears, battering his brain with images of merciless and deliberate torment. Endless. Soul-searing.

I'm running. Running in a dream.

Moving full bore, he slammed into walls, burst through partitions, leaped over savaged corpses. The floor sprouted spikes that pierced his feet and still he ran. Time stretched and the atmosphere thickened. His legs and arms felt weighted, his progress slowed. Behind him came the sound of snapping fangs, like claws scraping on chalky tombstones.

Something on my heels, moving with me like a living shadow. Tracking me by the smell of my blood.

Logan ran faster, afraid that if he stopped or even slowed, the shadow thing would catch up, overwhelm him, suffocate him. Drag him down into the darkness forever.

And I won't be able to scream, or fight it off, because it'll be inside me . . . under my skin . . . inside my bones.

Using the abhorrent steel claws to slash through a bolted door, Logan raced up a flight of stairs—felt like hundreds. Each stair sprouted a ragged spike, each step became piercing agony.

Running like a truck. Barreling uphill with a full load . . . trying not to flip, to fall. Can't keep up this pace. I'm losing ground, and that thing . . . It's gaining . . .

He felt a force tugging on him, drawing him back even as he tried to surge forward.

It's grabbing at me. Snatching at me with veins like ropes, pulling me back. Tendons like chains, like wires—like strings and a puppet.

Then the field of spikes he'd been running through crawled along the floor, along his body. Suddenly, Logan was sprouting spikes, just like the floor, the walls. Long. Sharp. Gleaming metal. They burst, bloodless, from his shoulders, torso, hips, thighs.

Long, thin fingers curling around my ribs . . . Muscles stretching, spine bending back . . . It's tearing at me, dragging me back into its hungry darkness.

As he ran, Logan left a gory trail—crimson footprints.

It's on my trail . . . At my shoulder. Cutting me with spikes. Breaking into me. Hot breath, searing pain. Flesh burning, bones turned to magma. The putrid stench of death in my nose, my mouth.

The claws that reached into his body began to tear at his mind. Logan's senses dimmed. An electronic hum dominated his hearing. A blue pall fell over his eyes. He struggled against the almost hypnotic influence, but the blue fog turned ebony black, and the weight of the void fell heavy on his consciousness.

Can't get away . . . Must get away. Must run forever . . . fight forever. Never give in to the darkness. Never surrender to the beast. A man. Can't forget . . .

But out of the blackness, the shadow rose, suffocating him, dulling his mind, crushing his will. Logan moved his lips, but discovered he'd lost the ability to speak.

He felt an icy rage squeeze his brain. A rage that was not his own. A hatred for all men that he'd never felt before.

It's got me . . . and it wants revenge. It's turning me inside out. Darkness unending. Behind me, around me. It's everywhere. The shadow's everywhere.

I'm everywhere . . .

As the void washed over him and consciousness winked out like a thrown switch, Logan heard a tiny voice from somewhere deep inside of his abyss.

"Don't give up," it said.

Can't go on . . . bones dense like lead. Like iron. Knees giving in . . .

"Don't give up . . ."

Shot through like steel in the heart caving in—

"Don't give up."

—under the weight. The weight of the beast.

19

"It's extraordinary, is it not, Cornelius?"

The Professor stared up at the monitor, hands locked behind his back. "Amazing that Weapon X, a creature of such power, is shaken by his own shadow. Driven by fear of himself to something akin to a nervous breakdown."

Dr. Cornelius, at Carol Hines's shoulder, glanced at the readouts on the woman's REM terminal. Slowly, the device's waves were being reduced, releasing Logan's brain from its murderous dream thrall.

"It is impressive, Professor. More impressive still is the way he's pulling through. Fighting back. Despite it all, there's a core element to Logan's personality that battles on, even when the odds seem hopeless. Exterior camera, Ms. Hines."

"Switching . . ."

The image on the HDTV monitor morphed. The frozen picture of Logan's bleak dream-scape—a nightmare in purple and scarlet, with a desolate black void for sky and bony white spikes protruding from the virtual ground—was replaced by a chilly exterior shot of the complex.

Pale moonlight glistened off freshly fallen snow. A

frigid wind howled down from the nearby mountains, shaking diamond-dust ice crystals from the white-blanketed branches. The bitter-cold night unmarked by clouds. A spray of stars and a bright hunter's moon cut the sky's silky blackness.

"So you think he has pulled through, beaten back his fear and self-loathing, eh?" the Professor asked, his lips a challenging sneer. "We shall see what we shall see."

"Yes, I guess we will, Professor. Logan's still standing, isn't he?" Cornelius gestured to the image on the screen. Logan, silhouetted by the brilliant moon, legs braced in the snow, arms at his side, claws like icicles hanging from his wrists.

The Professor leaned toward the monitor, savoring the raw power of the thing he'd created and now controlled. On-screen, Logan's naked flesh gleamed palely in the moonlight, crowned by a shock of raven black hair. Slabs of bulky muscle, rigid as concrete, plastered his chest, and thick, corded bands crisscrossed his arms, loins, thighs. Legs spread, crouched—he was a juggernaut ready to explode, Logan's flanks quivered like an excited animal, his hot breath came in moist, steaming clouds.

The mutant faced a white-striped Siberian tiger— starved, of course, as per the Professor's instructions. Man and beast stood frozen in place, eyes locked. The cat curled its lips to bare merciless fangs.

"Logan didn't buckle," said Cornelius. "He didn't give in. He didn't even retract his claws when we gave him the power to do so."

The Professor placed his index finger in front of his lips. "Hush, Cornelius. He has found the snow leopard."

"Siberian tiger, sir."

"Yes, thank you, Ms. Hines."

Cornelius cleared his throat. "We could have set this up better, you know."

The Professor faced him. "How do you mean, Doctor?"

"If Logan actually had to hunt the cat down, confront it, to kill it of his own volition, instead of the tiger just being there, threatening him . . . this experiment would have been a little more telling if Logan's will were somehow engaged, I think."

"Yes," the Professor replied thoughtfully. "I suppose you're right. But still, this is an acceptable scenario for one possessing the subject's simplistic perceptions."

On the screen, the tiger opened its jaws. The snarling sound crackled through the speakers after a split-second delay. Its ferocity grew with each passing second.

"Please synchronize the sound system, Ms. Hines."

The snarl became a gurgling roar. Though the tiger was hungry—very hungry—it seemed cautious of its adversary. The tiger's flanks rippled, its tail flashed from side to side; the creature backed up and crouched, ears flat. Even then, it would not spring.

In the end, it was Logan who lunged first, attacking the big cat a split second before it leaped at him. The antagonists slammed into each other, Logan's arms rising and falling as he repeatedly stabbed the roaring feline.

"Look at that!" Cornelius cried. "Logan's right in there. He's just as wild and savage as before."

But the Professor shook his head. "He may seem so, Doctor, but in the past few days, Weapon X has been altered irrevocably. His savagery is now tempered by ego and ratiocination. It is not savagery we see, but cunning."

On-screen, Logan and the creature grappled in fury, neither gaining the upper hand.

"Look how he fights, Cornelius. Any hesitation, a moment of fear, trepidation, or merely caution—and he will be undone."

"Yes, literally," said Cornelius. On the monitor, Logan and the tiger rolled across the snowy expanse. The tiger's claws raked at the man's soft belly while he slashed at the creature's exposed throat. Blood drops decorated the combatants.

The Professor sighed. "It has, of course, been necessary that Logan not know of his indestructible skeleton . . ."

"Which won't help him if he gets disemboweled, anyway."

"No, Dr. Cornelius. In that case, he would learn the truth the hard way—and with much pain."

"Camera four, Ms. Hines."

"Yes, Doctor. Switching . . ."

The scene changed, and so did the contest. Now Logan was up, his knee thrust into the tiger's chest. The butchering began. Black blood stained the snow, and gore flew in great gouts at every blow from Logan's long claws.

"He's gaining the advantage, Professor."

"Yet not so long ago, Weapon X beheaded a grizzly bear without hesitation. Without so much as a tussle," the Professor said regretfully. "That is what I call gaining the advantage."

The tiger's quick movements were less frenzied. The beast was weakening from exhaustion and lack of blood. Logan continued to rip the creature, his own grunts of exertion mingled with the cat's growls of pain and rage.

"You have to have faith, Professor," Cornelius said. "Look, I'll lay you a hundred on Logan. What do you think of that?"

The Professor made a sour face. "This is not a game, Cornelius . . ."

"Give me a full close-up on camera number six, Ms. Hines!" cried Cornelius. "And wake up, or we'll miss half the action. I don't think I've seen Logan's reflexes faster than they are now."

"Switching . . ."

With renewed strength, the tiger reared up and lashed out with a vicious blow from one of its front paws. Logan pulled back just in time, the claw tearing a ragged canal across the muscles of his chest.

Cornelius faced the Professor. "You're telling me this is no game? If that blow would have connected, it could have gutted Logan and I'd be out a C-note."

The Professor chuckled. "You don't see it, do you, Cornelius? That was a feint. You are correct about his reflexes. They are more nimble. And so is the mind of our subject. Weapon X was drawing the creature out for the kill. Watch and learn."

"Pull in closer, Ms. Hines," said Cornelius.

The tiger drew back its front paw to strike again, leaving an opening for Logan to exploit. With a deadly lunge, he sunk his steel claws into the beast's soft throat until his fist met the animal's gore-streaked fur, and the tips of the blades protruded from the dead beast's wedge-shaped skull.

"A magnificent blow!" cried the Professor.

Over the speakers, the snarls ended abruptly. As Logan struck a second time, plunging his claws into the tiger's heart, his own raking breath could be heard over the loudspeakers.

"God! Another blow—straight to the heart. Son-of-a-bitch Logan is more brutal than ever." Cornelius faced the woman. "Give me readings, Ms. Hines . . . heart rate, respiration, adrenal levels."

Carol Hines checked her monitor, then blinked in surprise. "No readings, sir. Mr. Logan is off-line for this. He's performing without the influence of the REM device."

"Excellent," said the Professor. "Weapon X has executed his mission without benefit of our direct commands. Only our influence, his conditioning, and the reprogramming techniques we applied, are controlling him at this point."

"Fantastic!" said Cornelius, grinning. "Then I guess it's mission accomplished. Logan is functioning autonomously, per your original specifications, Professor. What do you say to that?"

"It is remarkable, indeed, Dr. Cornelius. His instincts and reflexes, though perhaps more pragmatic, more careful, seem quite undiminished. More important, his ferocity is still unparalleled."

Cornelius chuckled. "Pity I couldn't get you to take that bet, eh, Professor? It would have been easy money."

Peevishly, the Professor crossed his arms. "I will not sully the nature of our scientific endeavor with wagers, Doctor."

Cornelius refused to be cowed. After months inside this facility, after weeks of lockdown, he finally saw the end of this odious experiment just over the horizon, and his mood was high.

I have all the samples of Logan's blood and tissue that I will ever need for my immunology experiments to continue, long after I leave this place, mused Cornelius. *The Professor's right about one thing, though. The existence of Weapon X will alter the course of history. Not as a destroyer, however, as the Professor envisions, but as a healer and a boon to all mankind . . .*

On the HDTV monitor, Logan rose, bloodied but undefeated, the tiger broken and lifeless in snow turned crimson. The subject stared straight ahead into a fathomless distance.

Cornelius sank into a chair. "I believe you have underestimated your prize, Professor," he began. "In that little virtual-reality scenario of yours, Logan was set up. We gave him a chance to escape. Yet he didn't run. Instead, he turned around and savagely assassinated the lot of us. Then we jammed his psyche with his fear of his own mutant nature, and even that didn't faze him."

The Professor's eyebrow rose. "Meaning?"

"I'd say he came through your final test with an A, wouldn't you?" Cornelius replied.

"Yes, yes, he was aggressive enough," the Professor replied. "And yet he failed to kill Ms. Hines. An act of mercy that leaves doubt still lingering in my mind."

"We discussed this with Dr. MacKenzie in the postexperiment briefing," Cornelius replied. "He spared Hines because she was never a threat to him. It's as we conjectured—Logan will only kill if threatened with harm, or . . . well . . ."

"Out of hunger?" posited Carol Hines.

"Yes, or out of hunger. And why would he want to eat Ms. Hines, anyway?" Cornelius joked.

"Yes, all right, Cornelius," said the Professor. "I suppose we should consider this experiment a successful one—flawed though it may be."

Carol Hines looked up from her own terminal. "If I may say, Doctor, I think Mr. Logan only killed you in the VR scenario because of that accidental shooting. I don't think he would have attacked you if the circumstances were different."

Cornelius thought about it for a moment. "You may be right, Ms. Hines—"

"Hmph," grunted the Professor.

"In any case," Cornelius continued, "Weapon X . . . Logan . . . made a rational decision within the parameters of the situation he experienced, and relied on a modicum of rational judgment rather than reacting with naked aggression. Which makes him a smart weapon, indeed."

"I shall have to consider a new round of tests, turn Logan over to MacKenzie for the next phase of operations," muttered the Professor.

"Have the wranglers pick up Logan, Ms. Hines."

"Yes, Dr. Cornelius."

She tapped the intercom and a voice crackled in reply. "Cutler here . . ."

"Please bring the subject inside, Agent Cutler. Subject X should be taken to D-Block this time."

"Yes. D-Block. I know, Ms. Hines . . . over."

Cutler keyed off the intercom and rubbed his tired eyes. The hatch to the armory opened and Agent Anderson entered.

"What the hell are you doing here, Anderson? Franks is the name on this morning's duty roster."

Anderson paused, but would not face his boss. "I guess you just got out of bed, eh, Cut?"

"Yeah, ten minutes ago. You'd sleep for three whole hours, too, if the Professor didn't have you on duty for the nuttiest experiment on record. Logan was running around on the grounds outside, lost in some kind of delusion or something. I thought he'd run away, but the eggheads got him under their thumbs. Shut Logan down until a little while ago . . ."

Anderson would not meet the other soldier's gaze. Cutler noticed. "What the hell is wrong with you?"

"You . . . you didn't hear about Franks, then?"

Cutler stared. "What about Franks?"

"Two hours ago. The handlers were moving that Siberian from the cage to the compound. Tiger got him—"

"What?"

"Franks was prodding the thing out of its cage so Logan could hunt it down. The tiger turned, ripped Franks."

"How bad?"

"Took his arm off. Franks bled to death before Dr. Hendry could get to him. Lynch wanted to shoot the tiger as soon as he attacked Franks, but Major Deavers stopped him. Said the Professor would be pissed if Weapon X didn't have something to hunt . . ."

Cutler slumped onto a bench without knowing it. He stared at the far wall. "That bastard Deavers . . . that son-of-a-bitchin' suck-up."

"You can't blame it on the Major," Anderson replied. "Really, I saw the tape, Cut. There was nothing anyone could do for Franks."

Cutler nodded. Then he stood and quietly began to

suit up. As he donned his Kevlar armor, he began to speak—more to himself than to Anderson.

"Franks was okay," he said. "You could count on him. He took this job seriously, tried to do his best. Now he's just another goddamn ghost haunting this place."

"Come on, Cut, don't take it so hard."

"Don't take it so hard? That's a laugh. I'm not taking it at all. I feel nothing. Numb. Like I'm half-dead myself. Like I'm just a ghost, and so is everybody else in here. This . . . place. The desolation. This lockdown. This sick, twisted experiment . . ."

Anderson glanced at the overhead security monitor. "Hey, Cut . . . the walls have ears, y'know."

"I'm not the only one, either. MacKenzie told me people are freaking out, especially in the last week or so. The Professor's been on duty, like, twenty-four seven, running that damn dream machine they have down there." Cutler locked eyes with Anderson. "You been having dreams?"

"Huh?"

"Dreams, Anderson? Or nightmares?"

Anderson seemed guarded. "Who wouldn't . . . in a place like this?"

"Well, I've been dreaming. A lot. Different stuff. Last night, I dreamed about something that happened a long time ago. When I was active duty . . . a corporal in the Special Forces . . . in another country . . ."

"Jesus, Cut. Don't get spiritual on me, and don't wig out. I can't take it. You're security chief. The rock, man. If you crack up, what chance do the rest of us have?"

Cutler tried to shake off the ill mood, but found it completely impossible. He blamed it on the news about

Franks. The truth was that he woke up with a feeling of oppression, as if something bad were about to happen.

Or already had.

Maybe it was a premonition. Maybe he was thinking about Franks and didn't even know it.

Another ghost to haunt this place . . .

"Forget about it, Anderson," Cutler said at last. "I'm just pissed about what happened to Franks, that's all."

Cutler laughed—a bitter, mirthless sound—then lifted his helmet. "Suit up, and let's get this over with."

As they stepped out into the cold and tested their electroprods, Cutler remembered the night he'd caught up with Logan, outside the rundown gin mill in that crappy part of town. He'd wondered at the time who the guy really was, knowing only that Logan had some kind of connection to the military or military intelligence—as Cutler himself did, then and now.

At that time, Logan was considered an expendable "package"—a piece of discarded military hardware that was being recycled into something new with predictable military efficiency. But suddenly, things had changed. Now Logan was the valuable commodity and the people around him were the disposable ones—guys like Hill and Franks, Anderson and Lynch.

And me.

Cutler could not help thinking that maybe he deserved what was happening. Maybe the way he'd treated Logan was coming back to him. In spades.

As they moved across the snow to the scene of carnage, Cutler felt trapped, like he was stuck in an endless loop of twisted cruelty. The frozen black blood on the snow—glass-smooth; the slashed animal on the ground; the smell of spilled blood. All of it gave him a shiver of déjà vu, a sense that he'd been here before and would experience these things again, perhaps endlessly.

Just like one of the ghosts that haunts this place. . . .

Cornelius thrust his hands into his pockets and rocked on the balls of his feet. "So what have we got here, Professor? Logan thinks he's killed everyone inside this complex, all to get to you—the focus of his vengeance."

The Professor paced uncomfortably. "Yes, go on."

"Now, thanks to the REM machine's induced dreams, Logan knows he isn't human. Not only is he a mutant, but he now possesses a near-indestructible skeleton, a piece of technology that further alienates him—further separates him from his own humanity. And with all of that, he also knows it was you who harnessed his dark secret, who used that hated part of himself—the mutant part—and turned him into Weapon X."

"Indeed," replied the Professor, staring at the monitor. "So Logan had no choice but to destroy me, did he not? As we are compelled to destroy our old gods to make way for new ones. In the act of killing his creator, Logan's once inculpable savagery is transformed into the cunning of a ruthless killer—an inspired bit of 'psychological transference,' as Dr. MacKenzie called it." Finally, the Professor faced the doctor. "I savor these events, Cornelius."

Cornelius nodded before he twisted the knife. "Of course, you did hedge your bets a little, Professor."

"What? How do you mean?"

"Making up all that stuff about how you were actually working for somebody else . . . some great power or something . . . as if you were a stooge or a flunky instead of the genius behind Experiment X."

The Professor met Cornelius's gaze and knew the man was suspicious. "A mere psychological ruse . . ." murmured the Professor.

"It was a good one. Setting yourself up for your own murder, but then playing at being betrayed by the real creator of Weapon X at the climax. Were you trying for a little ambiguity—a way to cast a shadow of a doubt in Logan's mind? Or were you working for sympathy? Testing your subject to see if he'd reason that you weren't the real threat, that he'd spare you the way he spared Ms. Hines? Either way, it's clever. Really tricky."

The Professor offered an enigmatic half smile. "Indeed, Dr. Cornelius. All just a dramatic ploy that . . . proved a great deal about the nature of the beast, hmm?"

"Well, all in all, it's been a good day, right, Ms. Hines?"

But the woman did not reply. Lost in thought, she frowned up at the monitor. On the screen, the wranglers were approaching the motionless man crouched in the snow.

"Are you okay, Ms. Hines?" Cornelius asked. "You seem tense."

"Yes, Hines. You don't seem to be sharing the doctor's celebratory mood . . ."

"Something is bothering me, it's true," Carol Hines replied. "But I don't know if I'm free to speak of it, Professor. The information is classified. And I signed an agreement not to speak of the matter, even after I left NASA's employ."

"If your secret involves our work here, then surely you are compelled to speak," sputtered the Professor.

Carol Hines nodded. "Yes, sir. I suppose you are right . . ."

20

Redemption

Logan felt something touch his head, someone tug at his clothes. He opened his eyes and stared up at a seat swinging precipitously from a single bolt. His eardrums still reverberated from a terrible noise he could not recall from memory.

"Logan . . ."

He twisted his neck and spied Miko on the ground beside him. Her face was bruised, and a long piece of shrapnel—probably a chunk of the shattered APC—was lodged in her shoulder. The flesh around the metal was puckered and seeping blood.

He rolled over, checked her out. "Where's Langram?"

"Still in his seat."

Logan looked up and saw his partner dangling limply from the driver's seat. His leg hung on the steering wheel. Obviously, the cab had overturned, but Logan could not recall the exact circumstances of the accident.

He quickly rolled to his feet and checked his partner's pulse. "Langram's alive!"

Logan hauled his partner down, and saw blood oozing from a head wound. Langram's leg was also broken.

He's lucky. Clean break, not a compound fracture, but Lan-

gram isn't going to be jogging anytime soon. Guess I'll be hauling him up to the extraction point.

Miko crawled to Logan's side, struggling to stand up. "Take this," grunted Logan, yanking the AK-47 off his shoulder and handing it over to her. "Can you walk?"

"*Hai.*" She turned away; he stopped her. Before she could protest, Logan yanked the shrapnel out of her arm. She paled, bit her lip, but made no sound.

"You are samurai," he reminded her in Japanese, prompting Miko to smile despite her discomfort. Logan found the first-aid kit, dumped a tube of disinfectant into the bloody hole, then stuffed it with gauze, which he taped in place.

"Let's go."

Rising, Logan hefted his unconscious partner over his wide shoulders, then helped Miko off the ground. Outside the shattered armored personnel carrier, the dark forest was alive with sounds. Voices shouted from the woods below, mingling with the clank of tank treads. Searchlights pierced the night, shining between trees— but nowhere near Logan and company's actual position. They had lost the North Koreans for a little while at least.

"Which direction should we go?"

Logan scanned the area but could not see beyond a few dozen meters in any direction because of the dense foliage. *Is any part of this mission not a pain in the ass?*

"I need your compass."

Miko held the device under his nose.

"Northeast." Logan pointed. "Through that line of pine trees. There's supposed to be a flat plateau at the top of this ridge. We should be real close."

Logan glanced at his watch. The face was shattered,

but it was still ticking. *Almost twenty minutes before the chopper's ETA. Hope we're not too early, or the soldiers might catch up to us before the helicopter does.*

They heard voices, much closer. Then the sound of men moving through the forest floated to their position.

"Up here," whispered Logan. He stumbled along on a low rise, and caught a log to haul himself the rest of the way. Miko scrambled on the slope next to him, moving quickly despite her wound.

A searchlight beam stabbed through the trees, pinning them in its light as they crawled over the edge of the low cliff. Voices erupted, soon followed by the incongruous sound of a bugle.

"Here comes the cavalry," huffed Logan, sprinting between trees. Miko stumbled to the ground underneath a tall tree. Logan paused, waiting for her to catch up.

"I will hold them back, give you cover," she called.

"No! Come on."

"Do not worry. I will follow."

"There's too many of them. The soldiers will overwhelm you."

But Miko turned her back on Logan and aimed the AK-47 toward the distorted silhouettes dancing in the wavering glow of search beacons. Her weapon barked, sending tracers burning through the night-shrouded woods. Frenzied cries, then sporadic and ineffectual gunfire replied. Bullets whizzed through the trees and snapped against branches. Miko fired again and kept on firing. Logan heard screams and the slap of bullets against flesh.

Logan turned. Legs pumping, he continued the difficult ascent to higher ground. Behind him, he heard more shots—first rifles, then the steady chatter of Miko's machine gun. Muffled by the trees, the sounds of shattering glass and a dying man's cry made their way to his ears. Then a searchlight winked out of existence.

"Good girl," he grunted. Breath ragged, muscles weakening, Logan relentlessly pushed on. Over the sound of his breathing, he listened for noise of a firefight, but the forest was suddenly quiet. He risked peering over his shoulder, and saw the searchlights scanning the forest far below his vantage point.

Maybe Miko's on the way . . . maybe she'll catch up to me soon.

Struggling under his partner's weight, Logan placed his foot on a loose rock and it broke from the ground, pitching him forward. He landed on his face, Langram falling limply off his shoulders. When Logan looked up, spitting dirt, he found himself at the top of the slope, a small plateau spread out before him.

The landing zone . . . this is it!

Logan rolled onto his back, sucking in the cool night air. Heart racing, he lifted a shaky arm and glanced at the phosphorescent hands on the Korean watch.

Nine minutes to go . . . nine minutes to find Miko, get her back here . . . then we can all go home.

Logan moved away from Langram and got to his knees. But as he tried to rise, a shape loomed out of the darkness, and a booted foot smashed into his face.

Logan blinked back the explosion of light inside his head. Harsh voices barked at him. When Logan's eyes focused again, he saw khaki uniforms all around him. *North Korean regulars.*

Must've been waiting for us. Figures. This mission was FUBAR from zero hour . . .

More orders shouted in Korean. Warily, the soldiers

hemmed Logan in, though none seemed willing to get within reach of him.

"Know me by reputation, eh?" he muttered, aware that the bayonet was still in its sheath on his belt.

"Get up now, get up," the officer cried, no doubt exhausting his entire English vocabulary.

"Yeah, yeah, you got me." Logan staggered to his feet, hands above his head. A soldier moved within arms length to grab Langram, but Logan chased him back with a lunge and a sneer.

"No move, no move!" the officer screamed, waving his pistol.

Logan weighed his options, wondering if he should strike now or wait for a better chance—which might disappear altogether if the Koreans noticed he was still armed. Then excited voices emerged from the darkness beyond the circle of soldiers.

The ranks parted, and two soldiers tossed a beaten and bloody Miko to the ground next to Langram.

Logan wanted to go to her, but knew better. He noticed Miko stir, and her eyes fluttered, to focus finally on him. Weakly, she tried to smile, but gagged on blood instead. Logan saw that the woman's front teeth were missing.

"You dirty bastards." Logan's knuckles whitened as he tightened his fist, glared at the officer with a look that said he wanted to put his fingers into the screaming man's eye sockets.

The Korean officer seemed empowered by Logan's anger. Still out of reach, he displayed his pistol and aimed it at Miko's head.

"No." Logan's voice was a warning. Unemotional, stark. "You've got us. That's enough."

"Now she die!" the officer cried.

The shot cut through the night like a nuclear explosion. Miko's body jerked once as the top of her head was blown off. The sound of the single shot, and its terrible consequence, caused even the hardened North Korean soldiers to wince and avert their eyes.

Logan struck.

In a flash, the bayonet was out of its sheath and in his hand. Logan knocked the officer's pistol aside and the weapon discharged again, striking one of the surrounding soldiers in the groin.

Logan spun the blade and plunged it into the Korean's chin, up through the skull and into the brain. The officer went limp, cross-eyed. Logan yanked the blade free and threw the dead man into his soldiers' arms.

A half-dozen rifles crackled, splitting branches and chipping bark off trees. They missed Logan, who was already behind them, slashing one throat after another before the bayonet tip snapped in two, lodged in a Korean's thick skull. Weaponless now, Logan ran.

Fortunately for him, the Koreans had been using searchlights. To a man, they lacked night vision. Though Logan could see them clearly. Khaki uniforms standing out against the night.

Logan raced for the forest, bowling over a soldier and smashing his larynx with his boot. More shots whizzed around his head. Then a bullet caught Logan's shoulder and spun him around. He stumbled up a small rise and plunged into the bush.

Bleeding, Logan crawled behind a tree. He heard voices all around him. It sounded like a hundred men were searching the area. Logan knew it was only a matter of time before they hit the jackpot.

He thought of Langram helpless and Miko dead, and panic suffocated him. The bullet wound and the pumping adrenaline made his limbs quiver uncontrollably, especially his forearms, which were suddenly suffused with lancing agony. As he stumbled to his feet, the burning pain continued, more intense than the shoulder wound.

Logan traced his left wrist in the darkness. Under tortured flesh and muscle, something stirred.

The men who hunted him forgotten with the arrival of this strange new agony, Logan watched as the flesh on top of his wrists burst in a squirt of crimson. A moan escaped his lips as six claws made of pristine, ivory-colored bone emerged from sheaths hidden undetected under Logan's flesh. Curved, honed, the claws extended one foot from their base to their razor-sharp tips.

Nearby, a Korean soldier heard Logan's cries. He fired a shot into the trees. The shell struck the trunk next to Logan's head, sending wood chips and bullet fragments into his skull. Logan reeled as if punched, lights exploded in his mind. He stumbled and slid back down to the ground.

The soldier saw Logan's legs sticking out from behind the tree and alerted his sergeant. Cautiously, thirty infantrymen converged on the area, weapons aimed . . .

The Logan who emerged from behind that tree was not the same wounded, fearful man who cowered behind it moments before. That man was gone, smothered by a berserker rage that consumed him, scourged him, burned his personality away—transforming Logan into a vengeful killing machine, a raging bundle of superfast reflexes and instinctive fighting ability honed as sharp as his claws over centuries of constant strife. Logan was now a warrior born, connected by psychic strings to a range of martial skills gathered throughout a thousand lives lived in endless warfare.

Pale white claws gleaming in the moonlight, Logan dropped into a crouch and leaped from cover. The first to see him: the man who fired the shot. The North Korean saw the claws, too—before they plunged into his eyes.

Down without a whimper, the gun fell from the Korean's limp hand. Logan ignored the weapon. The feral savagery that possessed him now would not be sated without the satisfying feel of the blade ripping flesh and splintering bone.

A dozen soldiers turned as Logan burst from cover, their movements in slow motion to Logan's superaccelerated senses. He tore through their ranks, severing limbs, slashing throats, ducking and stabbing as the stunned soldiers vainly tried to defend themselves against the lethal living weapon that slaughtered them.

Rifles cracked. Machine guns chattered. Logan could sense, almost see the bullets' glow in the gloom, hear the wavering shock waves, and deftly avoided each shot. He stabbed and thrust, slashed and ripped his way through ten, twenty men as more soldiers emerged with a collective howl from the forest.

Logan waded into them, a murderous juggernaut. Grasping, desperate hands tried to drag him down. Logan shook them off like pygmies. Tenaciously, a three-hundred-pound giant in khaki locked his hands around Logan's neck. A double uppercut lifted the man—impaled—over Logan's head and his innards spilled to the blood-soaked ground.

One officer tried to rally the soldiers into an execution

squad. Logan discerned the tactic and charged the troops before they had a chance to assemble.

Another stepped forward and shoved a bayoneted rifle into Logan's belly. With a roar he decapitated the man, tore the rifle out of his guts and hurled it like a spear. The bayonet struck a different soldier in the chest, slamming him against a tree.

A demolition man tossed a satchel charge in Logan's direction. The high-explosives landed in a dead soldier's lap. Logan scooped up the package, shoved it into another man's arms, and tossed the howling trooper to his comrades. The explosion sent gouts of gore and bone-shrapnel ripping through the enemy ranks.

More soldiers began firing from the forest. Logan sneered, bared blood-flecked teeth, and dived once more into the bush. In the dark shadows of the forest, he circled the soldiers, stalked them, then butchered them, one by one.

The MH-60 Pave Hawk flew above the brown landscape, hovering only a few dozen meters over the ground—"nape of the earth," the military pilots called it, a most dangerous maneuver. Racing through the night, over the hilly North Korean terrain, at a constant, computer-controlled altitude of thirty-five meters off the ground, made for a bumpy ride. Each hill, each tall tree, had to be navigated. With the hatches open, and two of the eight soldiers aboard hanging by their safety lines out the door, the harrowing flight resembled the most sadistic roller-coaster ride ever invented.

The Pave Hawk, a Canadian variation of the United States Air Force Search and Rescue aircraft, was basically a Blackhawk helicopter filled with an array of specialized avionics that made a night flight over enemy territory at two hundred and fifty kilometers an hour possible. The low altitude was necessary to avoid North Korean radar, which was effective above a height of seventy-five meters. Avoiding radar was necessary when the aircraft in question was violating thirty-seven international laws and seven treaties by its very presence in North Korean airspace, never mind its mission.

Inside the soldiers' helmets, the pilot's voice announced their location. "LZ in thirty seconds . . ."

"Watch the night-vision scope," cautioned the copilot. "There are power lines strung all over these hills."

One of the soldiers hanging out the door activated night-vision goggles and scanned the river and the road that paralleled it.

"Colonel Breen, tank on the road."

The officer appeared at his shoulder.

"Over there, sir. Some trucks, too."

Breen stared at the tank, then saw the trucks, and more soldiers rushing into the woods at the base of the plateau.

"Colonel . . . the men down there are expendable. We're not supposed to land, not even to pick up the package, if the NKs are in sight," the pilot warned.

Breen frowned, and his eyes narrowed in concentration. Finally, the tall man spoke, "Lock and load. We're going down."

The Pave Hawk circled the plateau and came around for a second approach.

"I see firing down there, sir. And lots of bodies . . ." said the man in the doorway. As the chopper dipped, the observer dangled more than halfway out the door, one hand on his safety strap, the other on the NVGs attached to his helmet.

Breen squeezed his shoulder. "Keep your eyes open, Corporal Cutler. And be ready to take over that machine gun when we hit the ground . . ."

A graceful arc put the Pave low over the landing zone. Cutler let loose with a burst of automatic gunfire when the chopper made a first pass. To his surprise, the Koreans melted into the woods without returning fire.

"Descend, descend!" barked Colonel Breen, signaling the pilot to power down. Before the Pave Hawk settled on the ground, Corporal Cutler stepped out, into a field of death.

The plateau was carpeted with corpses. The pilot managed not to land on them only with deft maneuvering of his controls.

Through Cutler's night-vision goggles, the entire scene was a green-tinged nightmare of mass murder. Corpses were sprawled everywhere, and though they appeared to be the victims of a firefight, none had been shot. There was little evidence of explosives, either—no stench of cordite, no shattered ground or splintered trees, no bullet-riddled bodies. Yet virtually every dead soldier had been dismembered, disemboweled, beheaded, their insides and outsides ravaged beyond belief.

As the others fanned out around Cutler to secure the perimeter, Sergeant Mason cried out, "Got someone on the ground here! He's not Korean."

Breen raced to the sergeant and peered down at the man. Unconscious, he wore tattered splinter camouflage and had sandy hair in a buzz cut.

"That's one of them," said Breen.

The medic arrived a moment later, checked the man's pulse, shone a flashlight into his eyes. Suddenly, the man woke up, pushed away the light. "Who . . ."

"Easy soldier," said Breen. "We're getting you out—"

"Colonel!" another soldier cried. "Found a woman over here. Dead. Somebody blew her head off. Think she may be Korean."

"Leave her," said Sergeant Mason.

But Langram lifted his head. "She's Japanese," he cried, his voice hoarse. "Bring her out, too."

Breen looked into Langram's eyes. "Where is your partner? Where's—"

"Colonel. Found the package," Mason called.

Cutler turned at the cry. He was close and curious, so he crossed the corpse-littered ground to his sergeant's side.

Mason stood over a kneeling figure, long hair, splinter camo in shreds. The man's face was downcast, staring at the ground. Cutler couldn't tell if he was alive or dead.

"Need a medic over here," called Mason.

"Only got one doctor," said Cutler. "And he's still working on the other guy."

The sergeant looked around at the decimation. "What the hell happened here?" he whispered, face pale under war paint.

The kneeling man was covered in gore—his own and the blood of others. His arms were particularly ravaged, flesh seeping liquid crimson from deep gashes above the wrists. Mason reached out cautiously and touched the man, who did not react. Mason checked his pulse.

"He's fine. Calm . . . I don't get it. This guy's a mess, but he might as well be sleeping, based on his heart rate."

In the gloom, Mason used his flashlight to search for injuries. "Got it in the head. Look, wood splinters are still sticking out of the wound. Hold the flashlight . . ."

Mason thrust the flashlight into Cutler's hand, then felt the man's legs, then his arms. "His wrists feel weird, like they might be fractured. He's probably in shock. Stick with him, Cutler. I'll fetch the medic."

Cutler stood anxiously over the silent man, gazed at the dead laying in heaps around him. The stench of spilled blood was choking, and Cutler raised his kerchief to cover his nose and mouth.

The move seemed to startle the man on the ground. He winced, then slowly lifted his head.

"You okay?" Cutler asked softly. The kneeling man did not speak. When he opened his eyes and locked stares with the soldier looming over him, Cutler reeled back in horror.

Sergeant Mason arrived a moment later, the medic in tow.

"Cutler? What the hell's wrong with you?"

"That guy . . . the look in his eyes. Savage. Like he could kill me with just a stare. Like he wanted to."

Meanwhile, the medic had gotten the man off his knees and stumbling on his own power to the helicopter.

"Let's go, Cutler. We've overstayed our welcome. The Koreans are gonna come back any minute now."

But Cutler just stared at the man as the medic helped him into the helicopter.

"Jesus, Sarge. Who the hell is he?"

"Our package, son. He's on a classified mission and so are we. That's all you or I need to know."

That was answer enough for Cutler. Truth to tell, he didn't want to know the identity of the man. He would rather forget—forget this mission and the massacre. The look of soulless, bestial savagery reflected in that nameless man's eyes scarred Cutler. It would not fade from his mind.

21

Interlude and Escape

"Please, Ms. Hines, tell us your secret," said Dr. Cornelius, grinning.

The Professor frowned impatiently. "Yes, yes. Get on with it."

Carol Hines glanced up at the monitor, where a pair of wranglers in protective suits were about to collar Logan with their electroprods. Then she lowered her eyes and swung her chair around to face them both. "As I said, this happened when I was at NASA, working with the REM machine for several months—"

"Astronaut training simulations, as I recall," the Professor said.

Carol nodded. "That's how the work began. But after a few months of REM training, Dr. Powell of the Space Administration's psychology department devised a new experiment . . . one that would test the astronaut's reaction to fear."

"Indeed." The Professor listened more intently.

"The test was to be a routine simulation of a space shuttle reentry, but a specific set of circumstances would go wrong as the ship hit the atmosphere, building to the shuttle's destruction. There was nothing the astronauts could do to stop the accident from happening. That was the point of the exercise."

"And the subjects . . . they thought the experience was real?" Cornelius asked.

"Of course. From the moment of interface until the REM was switched off, the subjects believed what was happening was real.

"Dr. Reddy, the mission control chief, became furious when he found out the test had been conducted, angry that he was not informed. He also feared there would be adverse psychological effects, some of them lingering. But Dr. Powell brought him evidence to the contrary. According to Powell the astronauts seemed absolutely empowered, almost emboldened by their virtual near-death experience."

"Of course," said Cornelius. "They faced personal extinction but survived—the very same feeling we get after a particularly scary amusement park ride, but multiplied exponentially."

"Three astronauts experienced the simulation," Hines continued. "Two men, one woman, all of them experienced space shuttle pilots. In the weeks after the simulation, they each reported vivid, recurring dreams. A month later, one of the men died in a traffic accident—"

"I read about that," said Cornelius. "Head-on crash in Florida. A punk with a hot rod smashed into him or something."

"In truth, it was the astronaut who was flirting with death. He was playing chicken with a youth on a deserted stretch of highway. Neither of them swerved, so I suspect it was ruled a tie."

The Professor raised an eyebrow. "Humor, Ms. Hines? How uncharacteristic. Is this a tall tale?"

"Not at all, sir. As I said, the astronaut transformed into a thrill-seeker. NASA's public relations machine concealed the truth."

"And the others?"

"The other man was slated for the next shuttle mission—as its pilot, in fact. He was tested periodically in the ensuing weeks and deemed fit."

"And the woman?"

"Six weeks after the simulation, she disappeared without a trace. Left her husband and small child. The FBI suspected foul play, but NASA managed to hush it up, blaming her disappearance on marital woes. They found her, though, about three weeks later."

"And?"

"She was arrested in Nevada. The woman had joined a motorcycle gang. She started running drugs through Mexico, shooting heroin, working nights at a Reno brothel . . . in the end she got arrested by the local police for stabbing a young woman to death in a barroom brawl."

"Living on the edge . . . flirting with disaster," Cornelius said thoughtfully. "And the other pilot?"

"That's the strangest part," Carol replied. "It was Major Wylling—"

Cornelius sat up. "The pilot on the shuttle that crashed?"

"Yes. When the black box was recovered, the events that caused the disaster were re-created in simulation—and they precisely mirrored the false accident in Dr. Powell's psychological simulation. A leak in the coolant system led to a corrosive substance that came in contact with the superheating fuel cell, which then ruptured, causing the final, fatal explosion."

"A coincidence, surely," scoffed the Professor.

"A trillion-to-one coincidence, according to NASA's computers," Hines replied. "Dr. Reddy insisted the simulation was to blame, which the other scientists said was absurd on its face. At first, Dr. Reddy suggested Astronaut Wylling somehow sabotaged the system himself—a self-fulfilling prophecy. But Dr. Able, the chief engineer, objected to that theory. Said some of the key components involved in the crash were impossible to get to, and had been sealed for months before the fear experiment ever took place."

"Sounds like an academic food fight," said Cornelius.

"A bureaucratic war did break out between Dr. Powell's psych department and Dr. Reddy and his supporters in mission control."

"Who won?"

"To bolster his case, Dr. Reddy brought in other experts," Carol Hines replied. "Physicists. Theorists working in quantum mechanics. Dream psychologists. Brain specialists. Even a parapsychologist. They discussed the problem behind closed doors. I testified, because I ran the REM program during the experiment."

Cornelius rubbed his brown beard. "What did they conclude?"

"They spoke of Werner Heisenberg's Uncertainty Principle, Carl Jung's Collective Consciousness, and the simple power of suggestion. A psychiatrist lectured the panel on the potential of the subconscious mind and the possibility of a self-fulfilling prophecy without physical intervention. In the end, the majority concluded that the REM machine probably induced a prophetic trance in the participants of the fear experiment—a hypothesis, if you will. Some process similar to what the Oracle of Delphi or the Old Testament prophets experienced."

Cutler cautiously approached Weapon X, electroprod extended.

Something about this poor sap didn't feel quite right tonight. The way Logan stood over the dead tiger, maybe how his eyes were only half-closed, or how his head was cocked. It was as if he were listening. The fact that Logan had not yet retracted his claws troubled Cutler.

"Watch him, Anderson," Cutler warned as they approached.

The sound of Cutler's voice triggered something in Logan—a ghost of a memory, perhaps. Suddenly, he lifted his head, opened his eyes, and locked stares with Cutler, who reeled back in recognition.

All the other times he'd dealt with Subject X, the man was a zombie—eyes glazed, shuffling like a sleepwalker—but this time Logan was no limp victim, no trained animal to be "handled."

His eyes. Seen them before . . . I know who this man is.

Faster than Cutler or Anderson could react, faster than merely human reflexes could respond, Logan brought up his bloodstained claws and lashed out.

"My God, madam! What are you suggesting?" the Professor cried. "This is not science, it's magic, sorcery. Or perhaps divination."

"I am suggesting nothing, Professor," said Carol Hines. "I did not formulate the theory. I am only telling you what panel members—a group of highly esteemed scientists and researchers—concluded."

"What happened after that?" Cornelius asked.

"Of course, the truth was hidden from the public, even though Dr. Reddy insisted that the results of the simulation at least should be shared with other scientists. Reddy even gave the theory a name—the Nostradamus Effect, after the fifteenth-century prophet."

"Preposterous," the Professor snorted.

"You are not alone in thinking that, Professor. Dr. Powell and some of the others, including NASA's chief engineer, Dr. Able, used Reddy's intransigence in the matter against him. In the end, the blame for the shuttle disaster dropped squarely in Dr. Reddy's lap and he was forced out in disgrace."

"Understandably so, Ms. Hines," said the Professor. "What a ridiculous theorem. That man was a fool."

"And yet enough evidence exists to support the prophetic effect of the REM device, at least to one body of scientists," Hines replied. "Despite general skepticism about the Nostradamus Effect, NASA never again utilized the REM device, and its operation was phased out of training completely within a year."

Cornelius chuckled. "That's a great campfire story, Carol. Cute. Real cute. Next you'll be telling us that Logan will be coming for us in the dark of night."

The doctor glanced up at the HDTV monitor and blinked in surprise. "Where is Logan? And where are the wranglers?"

Hines spun in her chair. "Off camera, sir."

"I can see that, Ms. Hines. Put them back *on* camera, please."

"Switching, sir."

The next camera in sequence was positioned near the

elevator doors. It revealed nothing. And the security cam inside the car showed it to be empty, too.

Carol Hines keyed the intercom. "Security, where's Mr. Logan?"

"Wranglers have him, Ms. Hines."

"Wranglers, come in," she called. "Wranglers? Do you copy?" There was no reply.

"Switch to camera five, back in the field," Cornelius said.

Hines gasped when she saw the new image on screen. In the foreground, two wranglers lay dead, hacked to pieces, their body parts mingled with the slaughtered tiger's. In the background, Logan strode through a sundered chain link fence toward the elevator and the underground complex.

Suddenly, the Klaxon blare of the alarm echoed in the complex's steel corridors.

"Security!" the Professor cried. "What is wrong? What is the siren for?"

"Not sure," Major Deavers replied from the command center.

"This could be serious," said Cornelius. "Shut down Logan's transponder, Ms. Hines. That should send Logan into a mind loop and settle him down for good."

Carol Hines tapped her keyboard, then slammed her fist down. "No response," she said, her usual monotone shaded with panic. "The transponder is in override . . . from an outside source. There's nothing I can do."

"Security! I ask again: What is wrong?" the Professor screamed.

"Sorry, sir," a voice replied. "This is the guard outside of your lab. Someone is breaching the security perimeter, in the elevator, on his way down here. The level is in lockdown. We're armed an—"

His words died in a terrible scream. Over the loud-speakers, Cornelius, Carol Hines, and the Professor heard shots, shouts, screams . . . chaos.

The Professor was visibly trembling. "Don't worry," he whispered. "We're safe behind these walls. Logan doesn't know we're here, he—"

A grating sound interrupted him. Three diamond-sharp claws began tearing through solid steel. The door to the laboratory shook, then fell from its hinges.

Logan loomed in the doorway, snarling.

Desperately, Carol Hines tried to regain control of Weapon X through the REM device. As he burst into the lab, control of the subject eluded her, though she did manage to interface with Logan's brain sufficiently enough to project his thoughts.

On the HDTV monitor, Carol saw an image of herself in Logan's mind. Malignant and small—almost diminutive compared to the giant that he was. She watched in horror as her virtual doppelganger was beheaded with a backhand swipe of Logan's claws, only a split second before she felt the actual slash of death. Her own head leaped from its shoulders in a fountain of blood.

While her brain died from lack of oxygen, Carol Hines considered a final irony. *I was right . . . never should have stuck my neck out . . . sure to get it chopped off . . .*

Logan came at Cornelius next. As he lunged, the doctor saw his virtual twin on the monitor, in the guise of a grim, medieval torturer, with a surgical mask for a hood and angels of death—wearing the faces of MacKenzie, Hendry, Chang, and many others—hovering in the background.

"That's not right," moaned Cornelius in the moment of his long and brutal murder. "I'm a doctor . . . a healer . . . I help people . . ."

Finally, Logan turned on the Professor.

The scientist backed up. He begged, pleaded, whined, and finally howled as Logan severed one hand, then the other. Kneeling, then crawling, imploring Logan to spare his life, the Professor looked up at the monitor right before death cast its pall over him.

On the screen, he saw no genius. No architect of the flesh. Certainly not a god. Not even a man, really . . . just a frightened, sobbing little boy crying for his mother, pleading for mercy—utterly powerless in the face of a cruel, arbitrary, uncaring fate.

EPILOGUE

The slaughter continued all night. By morning, as the rising sun broke over the mountains, Logan had killed them all. Carol Hines. Dr. Abraham B. Cornelius. The Professor. Dr. Hendry and his cadre of physicians. Dr. MacKenzie and all of his psychiatric specialists. The guards. The wranglers. Even the technicians, maintenance workers, and kitchen staff.

At some point during the massacre, a communications specialist named Rice tried to download the Experiment X files and had triggered the recordings made during the experimental procedures. Those recordings continued to play over the loudspeakers in a random, disorganized loop for the rest of the night.

When the butchery ended, after the top secret experimental medical complex had been transformed into an abattoir, the recording of a long conversation continued to broadcast over the facility's audio network.

As Logan moved toward the exit of the underground facility, climbed the endless flights of stairs that led out of that hell to the bright morning and the snowy surface, the recording played on.

". . . Good morning, Ms. Hines . . ." Dr. Cornelius. Voice tinny.

". . . I was wondering, sir," Carol Hines. "May I speak with you? . . ."

". . . Sure . . ."

". . . I keep thinking about Mr. Logan . . ."

". . . Don't we all? . . ."

". . . and what we're doing . . . before I came here . . . was Mr. Logan here? . . ."

". . . I don't know what you mean, Ms. Hines . . ."

". . . Did Mr. Logan volunteer for this? . . ."

". . . Uh . . . No . . ."

". . . Was he abducted, then? . . ."

". . . I'm not too proud of this, but yes, I believe he was . . ."

". . . We're doing something bad, aren't we, Dr. Cornelius? . . . Mr. Logan was forced into this . . ."

". . . I don't know about forced, Ms. Hines . . . see, if you listen to the Professor, then this whole situation is all preordained. It's like Logan's destiny . . ."

". . . But how could the Professor know Mr. Logan's destiny, Doctor? . . ."

". . . To be honest, Ms. Hines, I don't know . . ."

". . . All I see is him suffering . . . the Professor seems to enjoy inflicting pain on Logan . . . it's like torture, sir, not science . . ."

". . . Well, you know, some men . . . they have the worst destinies . . . I should know . . ."

". . . Oh God . . ."

"Hey, don't cry, Ms. Hines . . . I'm sorry. That crack about destiny . . . it was a lousy thing to say . . ."

". . . I'm—I'm sorry about the tears . . . feel so silly . . ."

". . . Look . . . this poor slob doesn't have much of a life, anyway . . . he's a mutant . . . Logan isn't even human . . ."

". . . But he is human, Dr. Cornelius . . . you can't tell me that you don't see it . . . in his eyes . . . you can see . . .

he's a man . . . a man who's being turned into a monster . . ."

". . . I don't know what to tell you, Ms. Hines . . . I'm going on what the Professor said . . . Maybe anything other than that is out of my league . . ."

". . . I think the Professor is a liar, sir . . ."

". . . Maybe . . ."

". . . I wish I had never become involved in this experiment, Dr. Cornelius . . ."

". . . Yeah . . . me, too . . . now come on, cheer up, Ms. Hines . . . It'll be over soon . . ."

As Logan emerged into the daylight, he struck down his final victim, a communications specialist. Dying, the technician scattered computer discs into the snow. Logan left one bloody footprint, then trod on.

For Logan, this final killing was nothing more than an afterthought. His bloodlust was spent. Weary, he shuffled forward into the dawn. Within minutes, snow began to fall, and a massive blizzard surrounded him. Then, for a moment, through the white, windblown haze, Logan spied a figure standing on a rocky peak, framed by the rising sun.

Legs braced, strong and proud, the figure of a samurai, sword drawn, shimmered like a ghost—or a memory.

That vision is me, he realized.

Not the debased, fallen man he had been before he'd been abducted and dragged here. Not the mind-ravaged weapon he was intended to be. But the man he'd been long ago, during his never-ending lifetime, but in another century.

I fought for honor, found peace in the sound of wind chimes and the rustle of snow . . .

That snow covered him now, clinging to his blood-spattered form, icing his hair, swathing crimson flesh in virgin white. *Reborn* . . .

Logan searched his memory for more traces of his past, but so much was lost. He clung to that single pristine vision of a time when he had honor. Bushido.

A noise intruded. Beating blades. Rhythmic, mechanical. A helicopter approached the facility. Logan swiftly and instinctively moved away from it, into the woods, deeper into the winter storm.

He had lost his way a long time ago. Fought for so long. In the end, he misplaced the reason and battled only himself—

No. I will not be a tool . . . nobody's puppet . . . and never again a mindless weapon . . . I'm a warrior. A warrior born.

Throbbing overhead, the beating blades became louder, roaring unseen above, then fading until the sound lost its way in the wind.

They carried me into this hellish torture chamber, dead to the world . . . they carried me in, but I'm walking out . . . upright . . . on my own two feet.

The storm intensified, the frigid wind whipped his flesh, but Logan was impervious to the elements. The undefiled brutality of the wild called to him. In his mind, he answered . . .

I am Logan . . . I am a man . . . heading into the wilderness.

About the Author

MARC CERASINI lives in New York City and is the author of thirty books, including the *New York Times* nonfiction bestseller *O. J. Simpson: American Hero, American Tragedy; Heroes: U.S. Marine Corps Medal of Honor Winners; The Future of War: The Face of 21st-Century Warfare;* and *The Complete Idiot's Guide to U.S. Special Ops.*

He is the author of the *USA Today* bestseller *AVP: Alien vs. Predator,* based on the motion picture; and two original *24: Declassified* novels, based on the Emmy Award–winning television series *24—Operation Hell Gate* and *Trojan Horse.*

With Alice Alfonsi, Marc is the coauthor of the nationally bestselling mystery novels *On What Grounds, Through the Grinder, Latte Trouble, The Ghost and Mrs. McClure* and *The Ghost and the Dead Deb.* With Alice, he is also the coauthor of *24: The House Special Subcommittee Investigation of CTU,* a fictionalized guide to the show's first season.

He cocreated the *Tom Clancy's Power Plays* series and wrote an essay analyzing Mr. Clancy's fiction for *The Tom Clancy Companion.* Marc's techno-thrillers include *Tom Clancy's Net Force: The Ultimate Escape,* and five action/adventure novels based on Toho Studios' classic Godzilla, among them *Godzilla Returns, Godzilla 2000,* and *Godzilla at World's End.*

Marc is also the coauthor of a nonfiction look at the Godzilla film series, *The Official Godzilla Compendium*, with J. D. Lees. With Charles Hoffman, Marc is the coauthor of forthcoming *Robert E. Howard, A Critical Study*.

As many as 1 in 3 Americans
have HIV and don't know it.

TAKE CONTROL.
KNOW YOUR STATUS.
GET TESTED.

To learn more about HIV testing,
or get a free guide to HIV and
other sexually transmitted diseases.

**www.knowhivaids.org
1-866-344-KNOW**

09620